Stray City

Stray City

A Novel

Chelsey Johnson

An Imprint of HarperCollins*Publishers*

STRAY CITY. Copyright © 2018 by Chelsey Johnson. All rights reserved. Printed in the United States of America. No part of this book may be used or reproduced in any manner whatsoever without written permission except in the case of brief quotations embodied in critical articles and reviews. For information address HarperCollins Publishers, 195 Broadway, New York, NY 10007.

HarperCollins books may be purchased for educational, business, or sales promotional use. For information please e-mail the Special Markets Department at SPsales@harpercollins.com.

FIRST HARPERLUXE EDITION

ISBN: 978-0-06-279186-3

HarperLuxe™ is a trademark of HarperCollins Publishers.

Library of Congress Cataloging-in-Publication Data is available upon request.

18 19 20 21 22 ID/LSC 10 9 8 7 6 5 4 3 2 1

For K

I need the identity as a weapon, to match the weapon that society has against me.

—SUSAN SONTAG,
Reborn

Stray City

PART 1
1998–1999

My People

Portland in the nineties was a lot like me: broke, struggling with employment, mostly white, mostly hopeful even though there was no real change in sight. For all the drive-through espresso stands and downtown restoration, the new paint on aged bungalows and vintage glasses on young women, it was still an old industrial river town in a remote corner of the country. Hard to get to. Hard to leave.

The town matched something in me, the way a certain kind of guitar dissonance could strike an internal tuning fork that made my bones hum. I loved the slightly ruined quality of everything—the rusted joints, the mossy edges. The containers stacked in the weeds by the train tracks, the evergreen hills striped pale green with recovering clear-cuts. I'd go out to Kelley Point, where the Columbia and Willamette Rivers met, and the near-empty beach would be populated by enormous satiny driftwood trunks and rusting hunks of industrial debris, Latino families fishing and white dog owners throwing sticks and lonely men waiting for furtive sex in the woods while long low barges slid slowly by. All of us out at the end of the country, hoping for a quick small fix.

Tech money kept on puffing up Seattle and San Francisco like toxic blowfish but skipped over Portland. We just got the leftovers: the priced-out queers and artists, and the ongoing plague of gleeful professionals who couldn't believe how much Oregon house you could get on a California dollar. Seattle's grunge explosion had raised some hopes but left only a patter of shrapnel here. The Portland sound—there was no single such thing—couldn't be packaged and sold so easily. The major-label searchlights turned elsewhere and the music still flourished in the dark, mushrooming in basements and garages and warehouse practice spaces, in crammed clubs and beat-up ballrooms.

All of which is to say: there was no money in the place. No matter. All the better. Young people kept coming, seeking all the things you'd expect—music, work, drugs, adulthood, refuge from adulthood—but mostly, seeking each other. We came from dying logging towns and the rocky coast, from Salem and Ne-halem and Battle Ground and Boring, runaways from Boise, SoCal misfits, kids from the South and Midwest, the suburbs of anywhere. Some stayed a month, others a year or two, some stuck around. Me, I came at seventeen from rural western Nebraska, where adulthood came hard and fast and narrow, and queers kept quiet or met violence. Here I was no longer The Only but one of an ever-gathering crowd—young forever, queer forever, friends forever, or so we all thought then. My people.

Open relationship: It had sounded like a blue sky, a vast field, a sunny lake. It was more like the door kicked in on a basement. It had turned out the only person my former girlfriend of three years *didn't* want to have sex with—or *share* sex with, as she called it—was me. From a book called *The Ethical Slut* she had learned to articulate this in earnest detail. She called it Positive Communication. Too broken by it all to share sex with anyone, I'd moved out of our house and found myself in the shadow world of the dumped, sympathetic and untouchable, righteous yet damaged. Now, three months later, Flynn was still the last person who'd touched me, and at my worst moments, I was convinced she was The Last Person I Would Kiss, Ever.

The thought of rain was forming in the air as I locked up the letterpress studio that evening in early June, the night of the benefit show. I pulled my hood over my head and broke into a jog, my ink-smeared old Levi's slipping down my hips with every step so I had to keep tugging them up. Mist speckled my glasses. My look walked the line between Letterpress Punk and Totally Letting Herself Go. I hoped I could pull off the former.

It was Queer Night, I'd made the posters, my friends' band the Gold Stars was playing. Though I might have been going alone, everyone I knew would be there, I reassured myself—including Flynn, I deassured myself. But tonight I would reemerge.

Up Seventh Avenue, through the smash-and-grab warehouse district where you parked at your own risk, toward the rare beacon of La Luna: ballroom windows aglow, grand doors guarded by a moat of disheveled youth. And there at the door was my poster, hand-set with vintage wood type and cranked through the letterpress by my own arms. Someone had scrawled a careless TONIGHT! across my silky gold ink, a reminder that all my art was ephemera. I couldn't let it get to me.

"I'm on the Gold Stars list," I told the girl at the door, panting a little. She had a clipboard and a tongue piercing that she was clacking around her teeth. "Andrea Morales."

"Is your plus-one here?" The piercing gave her a slight lisp.

"It's just me. Plus zero."

I found my friends at the end of a narrow smelly hall in the smallest of the three backstage rooms. Meena leaped to her feet and socked me on the arm before clamping me in a butch side-hug. Lawrence waved apologetically from the couch. Others raised their bottles, went back to their conversations. No Flynn in sight.

"We were just planning an intervention to pry you out from under your rock," Meena said.

"Here I am," I said. "Fresh from the rock. Like a grub."

"You look good," Lawrence offered. Even when excited, Lawrence sounded, at best, optimistically woeful. She'd finished high school early and fled Salem for Portland at sixteen. Meena had found her at a show at the X-Ray Café and taken her under her wing, our androgynous teenage pet we smuggled into bars and clubs; we renamed her from Lauren Stanich to just Lawrence. Now she was twenty but still pale and scrawny, with elfin ears and dark blue eyes, the runt of our litter, a self-taught computer programmer who was allergic to the cat who was the love of her life. She played guitar with the focus of a surgeon.

"We've decided to set you up with someone," Meena said.

"Good luck," I said. "No one will get near me. What am I, Dumpster fruit?"

"People eat Dumpster fruit," Lawrence said.

"We're working on it," Meena said. "But I can't help you if you keep crawling off under a porch to lick your wounds." Everything about Meena Desai was strong—her arms, her eyebrows, her opinions. Meena believed she knew what was best for me, and for everyone. She fancied herself an unofficial life coach. She preferred to be right, and arranged her life and friendships for minimal disturbance of this worldview. Now she steered me to the snack table and handed me a beer from the tub of ice. "So stay close."

I promised I would and dropped onto the sofa, nestled between my friends with a cold bottle, ice-softened label ready to be peeled away.

Our shows were a kind of home. Out front, a dark room, everyone facing the same thing together, awash in sound. Backstage, scrappy girls in a borrowed room, old couches, graffiti on the walls, a pile of snacks to scavenge, trading information and gossip as the air thickened with smoke.

Every time the door opened, my chest tightened, but Flynn never entered. No one even said her name.

I relaxed. My people were with me. I was with them. Portland was still mine. And tonight, I was going to get some.

The drummer picked up her drumsticks and started tapping out warm-up fills on the edge of the couch, Lawrence began tuning her guitar, and the rest of us took our cue to exit to the floor.

Out in the ballroom the crowd had thickened. I scanned the room for new faces, for any possibility—I was back, and I was hungry. I dropped my empty bottle in a trash bin and when I looked up, to my surprise, my eyes lit upon Vivian.

Her chestnut bob was clipped back from her forehead with a barrette, and she wore a slightly-too-large thrift dress and knee-high boots. The sight of her triggered a surge of joy or relief—I could no longer tell them apart. Vivian was my Special Ex. We all had one, the one who's not so much an ex-girlfriend as a friend-plus, an old beloved song on the radio. She lived in Olympia, two hours away, which made her a peripheral and perpetual safe place. My ranger station. I didn't want all of Portland to know how Flynn had wrecked me, what a failure and fool I felt like, so I assumed an air of calm, efficacious regret at all times, but there had been moments late at night when I'd broken down and called Vivian. She had been extraordinarily patient and gracious about it. Nobody could talk me off a ledge like she could.

"Vivian!" I grabbed her jacket sleeve. "I didn't know you were coming down for this."

She started and then clasped her hands over her sternum. "Oh my god. You!" Vivian said. Then she smiled and hugged me. She smelled warm and faintly like Old Spice deodorant. I had found it off-putting when we dated, the sweet muskiness haunting the armpits of all her shirts and dresses, but now it just smelled *safe*. "I came for the show."

"Well yeah, obviously," I said. "Oh, Viv, I'm so glad to see you here. Thanks again for being there for me when I was really in the worst of it." I clung like a koala.

"Oh, honey! Breakups are tough. But so are you," Vivian said, gently releasing the hug. She gripped my arms and held me back a little, looking me seriously in the eye. "How are you doing now? Are you better?"

I joked that I missed the house more than Flynn. That wasn't entirely true. I didn't want the house without her, or to keep sleeping in that bedroom where she had opened her booming nonmonogamy practice.

"It's a good little house," Vivian said sympathetically. "But you found a great new place."

"Yes, great." An alarming neediness welled up in

me, threatening to slosh out in public. I sighed brightly. "It's wonderful. Sweet roommate. New space. Room to think. It's been good for me." I nodded for emphasis.

"Excellent. Breakup progress?" Vivian sounded like a doctor performing a checkup.

"I really think we should have broken up, like, a year ago." I laughed to convey my over-it-ness.

"Good," said Vivian. "It really seems like you're in a better place now."

"I am in a better place." I paused. "Isn't that what they say when people die?"

"You are too funny." She patted my bicep briskly. "And I need a drink."

I looked over at the bar. Flynn was standing there, wearing a worn gray T-shirt and a pair of black leather pants she must have procured since the breakup. The leather pants were tacky but fit her tall frame distressingly well. They made her look ludicrous yet hot. Like someone a good vegan would want to both scold and fuck. "I'll pass for now," I said.

Vivian followed my gaze. "Ah." Her eyes tightened like she was doing a math problem in her head.

"But you go ahead, of course," I said. "You know my stance on these things. No drama. I'll get mine later."

Vivian squeezed my arm. "I've always loved that about you. It's so good to see you, Andy. Be well."

She gave my cheek a quick, tart kiss, then turned and tucked a strand of hair behind her ear as she headed to the bar.

The Gold Stars took the stage and Meena said, "This is for Kat and Lucas. You're not victims, you're our heroes," and loosed a squall of feedback. I wove my way to the front, seeking obliteration by sound, and I got it. When I pressed a hand to my chest I could feel the drums and low throb of the bass beating there, a respite from my dogged heart.

When the Gold Stars bashed out their final racket, I wriggled loose from the crowd, my whole body ringing, and headed to the bar. I had just wedged myself between two stools and staked an elbow claim on the bar when a man's voice next to me said, "Hey." Pre-annoyed, I shot it a dark glance.

"Oh. Hey, Ryan." I knew Ryan Coates in the Portland way, one and a half degrees of separation. He played drums in a decent trio called the Cold Shoulder, a band that was always opening for other bands on the verge of fame; he also cut hair, including Flynn's, at a little punkish barbershop his friend ran. His own hair was tousled and artfully overgrown, an unwashed, winter-dim dark gold. He wore a tissue-thin Wipers T-shirt faded to dark gray and perched on his bar stool with an effortless lanky slouch betrayed by restless feet, one scuffed boot toe tapping the floor. "What are you doing here?"

"My friend Neil played in the first band," he said. "How's Flynn?"

"We broke up."

"Damn," he said.

"Months ago."

"Oh man. I'm sorry." He looked genuinely sorry.

"She didn't tell her barber?" I caught the bartender's eye and signaled for a pint. "Sometimes I wonder if she even experienced it."

"I guess she might have mentioned it," he said. "She doesn't really talk about that stuff with me, though."

"You can be grateful for that. I've heard a lot more than I ever wanted to know."

My beer appeared, tall and cool and serene, brimming. A stool opened up on the other side of Ryan and he invited me to take it.

"What's up with the Cold Shoulder?" I said, sliding onto the seat but keeping one foot on the ground. "Weren't you on that big tour opening for what's-their-name? I thought I read something in the *Willamette Week*."

"Yeah, that's done. We're leaving to play some California and Southwest shows next week."

"On your own?"

"Yeah, thank god. I'm ready to play for people who actually want to hear us."

"I know the feeling." I raised my glass. "To doing it on your own."

We clinked. And as I brought the glass back to my lips, I swung half a turn around on my bar stool and saw Flynn and Vivian standing at the edge of the crowd. Their legs overlapped. Vivian was holding her drink in Flynn's airspace, saying something so Flynn had to bend her head down to hear. Then Flynn gave a little kick against Vivian's knee-high boot, Vivian flashed her a smile, and I knew.

"Holy fuck," I said.

Ryan tried to follow my gaze. "What is it?"

A cold wave ran through me, skull to toes. I shook my head and couldn't look away. The bassist from the opening band and her girlfriend emerged from the backstage door, Flynn waved them over, and they all hugged each other. Everyone hugged Flynn. Everyone hugged Vivian.

How could I explain it to Ryan? It was irreducible to one line or a hollering monologue over a beer. And I didn't want to tell it to a straight guy. We all had a strong sense that lesbian drama was *our* drama, and maintained a protective shield from curious outsiders.

For men, *lesbian* was a porn category. I didn't need prurient sympathy. I needed the company of the only person in the room, it seemed, who was not involved.

"Internal politics." I smiled desperately, lifting my glass. "Let's drink."

The pint went down quickly. Ryan ordered the next round before I could get my money on the bar. It was hard for me to abide a drink bought by a man, so to even things out I downed it and bought us another. I had not been deeply drunk since the breakup, and had forgotten it could be fun and not tragic. Ryan's quick smile had an emphatic dimple, and his green-brown-blue eyes often widened when he spoke, so he looked both enthused and vulnerable. He was a good story-teller, and with little prompting spun a string of tour tales: about the big famous band's personal chef who traveled with them everywhere, the Cold Shoulder's aged van pulling up every night beside the two giant black tour buses and a semi full of gear and lighting, the fans who tried to get friendly with him in hopes he'd take them backstage. About how Geffen took them out to a fancy dinner in New York, later inciting an all-out indie-vs.-major band fight. They'd ended up not signing. Not "selling out." The guitarist was still bitter. Tell me more, I kept saying. I wanted to know about everything that wasn't this place.

The final band left the stage and the audience stomped and hollered for an encore. I saw Vivian raise her hands above her head to applaud triumphantly. "I'm out of here," I said.

"Me too." Ryan tipped back the last of his beer and set the glass down with a decisive thunk.

We pushed through the double doors and swooned into the damp drizzly night.

Stubble. I didn't know about stubble. I never knew a kiss could abrade—that a man's mouth scrapes and sands, rubs yours raw. I'd kissed plenty of girls, and even the ones who kissed rough, their mouths were soft and smooth as anything I'd ever known.

I jerked back.

"I'm sorry," Ryan said, so close the words went right into my mouth. "You're just—I thought . . ."

I was still holding my glasses in one hand and the corner of my T-shirt in the other. My myopia magnified his face while everything else dissolved into a haze of shadows and shifting shapes, streetlights as huge and soft and glimmery as wet moons, and a faint drone shimmered in my ears from standing too near the speakers at the show.

"The stubble," I said, wiping my glasses fiercely with my shirt, which was the original reason I had stopped by the shrubbery. I should have seen it coming, That Look he was giving me when I glanced up, but I had forgotten to expect it and in the moment it took me to process it, he read assent and moved in for the kiss. "I'm not used to that."

"I shaved this morning," he said.

"I guess this morning was a very long time ago."

His eyes crinkled, and he leaned in and touched his mouth to mine again. Alcohol on his breath, and mine: a comforting smell, tart and warm. I gave in for a moment, partly curious, partly titillated by how exotic and defiant it was to kiss a *man*.

There, I thought, *the person after Flynn has happened. The seal is broken.* I closed off the kiss and stepped back. "I shouldn't be doing this. Especially not out here." The wet rush of traffic on Burnside was only two blocks away.

"My apartment is right down the street." He slipped a finger into my belt loop.

"I'm not *that* drunk." I unlooped his finger. "Everyone's going to be leaving the show in a minute. I gotta move on."

"Wait, don't go yet." Ryan raised his head and periscoped around. "How about back there?" he said.

The doorway was on the back side of a low L-shaped office building, with a dim little parking lot behind it, ragged evergreen shrubs that had outgrown their last trim. It was dark and dry and filled with a deep shadow. I followed him and for a moment felt strange and shy. "This is messed up," I said. "I'm kind of messed up."

"But you want to, right?"

I thought about it. I didn't *not* want to. "Sure," I said, "what the fuck."

I couldn't remember the last time I had kissed a boy. Back in high school in Nebraska? My first few weeks at Reed? Maybe a gay friend at a party, or in a photo booth? I liked men fine, I did not hate them by default, as some of my separatist friends did; as long as they weren't catcalling or stalking me, I felt mostly neutral about them. They were other animals walking around with us, members of the same species, though outside of work I almost never interacted with them. I found it hard to understand the nature of the relationship between men and women—the millennia of baggage each carried seemed exhausting to me. Gay narratives were the ones that traditionally ended in death and tragedy, but for me, heterosexual love seemed far more doomed.

But this was neither love nor sex; it didn't even strike me as heterosexual, just sexual. It was the good kind of drunken make-out, laughing, loose but not sloppy, bumping up against the wall for support. At first I tried to dodge the stubble, angling to minimize contact, but then I thought, *Fuck it.* And the rasp of it felt good, like scratching an itch harder than you know you should. I wanted it to hurt, and it started to. Tears welled in my eyes. I kept them closed and sank my grip into the shoulders of this person, this *boy.* I didn't know if the ache down below was for him or simply for touch itself, but I bit down lightly on his lip and he bit back and for the first time in a year I knew I was wanted, and that was all I needed.

When his mouth moved to my neck I tipped my head back and opened my eyes. I took in the rough brick of the doorway, the blurry night beyond, the damp glinting surface of everything, the speakers' tunnel of hum in my ears, the hiss of cars on the wet street, the blue scent of rain, the smokiness and sweet human smell of his hair. He slid a hand up my inner thigh and I dropped my head abruptly and grabbed his arm. "Okay, that's enough for me."

"What? Come on." He was sleepy-eyed and ducked in for another kiss.

"I have to get home," I said. "Work tomorrow morning."

"Don't go home. You're so cute."

"You're so drunk."

"So are you."

"I'm so gay."

"Oh really?"

I slid out from between him and the wall. "Really."

"I'm sorry," he said. "I know, I know. I just got lucky."

"Lucky?" For some reason my throat tightened at that. I tried to clear it with a wry laugh. I rested my hand on his flat flanneled chest for a moment, then let it drop. "Right." I slipped my glasses on and the world came back into focus. "Let's go."

We emerged from the doorway as if we'd just woken up.

"Well, that was a surprise ending," I said, rubbing my eyes.

"Or a surprise beginning."

I looked at him askance. Was he kidding?

"What?" he said.

I shook my head. We both knew better. Surely. "Don't give me that crazy talk. Later."

I walked all the way home to Northeast. It took thirty minutes but I was charged up and drunk and the mist haloing the streetlights cleared my lungs and head. I pressed my fingers into my stubble-scraped chin and the sting's burn was a kind of warmth. I couldn't be-

lieve I'd done it. But for this one night, at least, someone new was into me. Someone felt *lucky.*

The house was a little sage-green two-bedroom
bungalow on Failing Street, with a roof that slouched
over the porch like a baseball cap pulled low, boxy col-
umns, and ragged wooden steps. The paint was peeling
on the trim. Moss grew on the foundation. The neighbor's orange cat was on the front porch again, sprawled
on the top step with a surly gaze. I half expected her to
demand a fee to pass. But she hopped up and tried to
slip inside behind me. "Sorry, girl." I nudged her back
with my foot. "Go on home."

The house was dark except for the light over the
stove. My roommate, Summer, was still at work at one
of the strip clubs.

Bullet sauntered into the kitchen, stretched in a deep
bow, and yawned loudly, a surprised creak. She was a
runty pit bull, big-headed and velvet-coated, slate gray
with a crooked white stripe down her nose. She was
Summer's dog, but more and more she turned to me for
love and food. I stroked her soft crumpled ears, gave
her rump a scratch and a pat. She watched me pour
myself a jar of water and followed me into my dark
bedroom.

I stripped off my smoky clothes and sat on my bed,
a futon I'd bought off a friend for twenty bucks. It had

been used as a couch for too long and retained a permanent taco fold down the middle, into which you inevitably slid. The platform I'd built for it with two-by-fours and a sheet of plywood squeaked whenever I moved. In a fit of superstition and pride, I had told Flynn to keep our store-bought adult bed, even though I was still paying off the queen mattress on my one maxed-out credit card. It was too haunted.

The back door opened with a creak and Bullet's ears went all bat. She whuffed, nosed the door open, and trotted into the light. Summer greeted her with a coo and said, "Andy? You home?"

Normally I'd come out, flick on the lamp on the kitchen table, and we'd share a snack. I'd sling myself into a chair and say, *You'll never guess what I did tonight. Seriously, never.* Summer would love it. What a transgression! What a deliciously vengeful move. Or was it? Men were easy, cheap, everywhere. They loved lesbians, or "lesbians." Some prize.

The person I most wanted to confess to was Vivian, the friend I had trusted most. But the telephone number where I could find her now used to be my own. So did the bed. I thought of both of their bodies in it—Vivian's soft stomach and slim neck, Flynn's broad rib cage and long hands. My grief burned with the nauseous heat of humiliation.

I lay carefully back on the futon and breathed slow and deep. Summer's bag hit the floor with a soft thump and a moment later the shower whooshed on. I'd tell her. Just not yet. I feigned sleep until I slept. Dissembling has always come easily to me.

Rules of the Lesbian Mafia

1. All lesbians are in the Lesbian Mafia

2. There is no boss of the Lesbian Mafia

3. Always unite against white supremacist hetero-patriarchy

4. Always have each other's backs

5. Power in numbers

Jesus Had a Twin

My chin was still raw the next morning, rosy and tender as if I'd come in from the bitter cold. At the bathroom mirror I wiped away the shower's blur and leaned in to close the vision gap. My black hair—naturally dark brown, but I dyed it black when I thought to—was toweled into floppy spikes, my brown eyes bleary, my skin winter-pale, and then here on my chin, this red badge of false courage. What had I been thinking? I hadn't been. Not-thinking had seemed like a good idea at the time. I sneaked into Summer's makeup and managed to powder over the scraped patch enough to mute the lurid glow, but it still stung to the touch.

The dog and I took a round through the neighborhood while Summer slept late. Bullet had started seeking me out first in the morning. I loved watching her ears bob, her broad muscled haunches ripple, as she trotted out in front of me. She was gentle as a kitten but people still crossed the street when they saw her anvil head coming. Queers and pit bulls have a certain species affinity: both feared and misunderstood, discarded by families, used for bait. Bullet was a rescue and she had her issues, but didn't we all.

Summer was still asleep when I mounted my bike to head to work. The June sky was gray with patches of blue hope. The Broadway Bridge took me up and over the river and coasted me into downtown, where gutter punks and junkies fringed the nineteenth-century buildings of Old Town. Outside Artifacts I locked my bike to a telephone pole studded with staples and wet layers of flyers. I was late, but the store was still dark. I unlocked the front door and flipped on the lights. Paintings hung all the way to the ceiling in a tall, boxy space full of vintage furniture. Living rooms and dining rooms and bedrooms with no walls. Former lives arranged to sell. I wound through the store, turning on every lamp.

"Hey, kid."

My surprise sent me fumbling into a gaunt Swedish vase that I barely caught in time. "Ted! You're here," I said stupidly.

My boss stood in the doorway to the back room,

tall and rumpled in his zip-up fleece and Levi's. He popped a tablet of nicotine gum out of its foil backing. "I had to get the van. Early estate sale." He tapped the top of his head. "Forget something?"

I peered at his close-cropped salt-and-pepper hair. "Did you get a haircut?"

"Jesus. Maybe you should keep that thing on for your own safety."

"Oh." I lifted off my bike helmet and ran a hand through my smashed hair. "Whoops. Not enough coffee. I was up late."

He raised a predatory eyebrow. "Oh, *really*." Ted loved vicarious thrills. Especially lesbian ones. I had learned to uphold a solid firewall and mete out just enough personal information to allow for both collegial bond and professional distance. "And what were you up to?" he asked hopefully.

"Can't tell you." My standard fallback: "Gay secret." *And how*, I thought.

He cackled. "Go get us coffee," he said, slapping two dollars down on the counter. "And watch the breakables on the way out."

At seven bucks an hour, I couldn't afford the stuff I helped sell, even with the employee discount. Even with the record-store job on weekdays and the letterpress gigs. But it was steady work, the part-time stability all of us sought or settled for. The Artifacts job paid for my house rent and my share of the letterpress studio. The record-store job covered utilities and first crack at the incoming used CDs—we all considered music a necessary expense then. The letterpress gigs varied month to month and determined the quality of my groceries and whether I could order PBR or well whiskey. One cracked plate on the job could wipe six hours out of my paycheck, as I knew all too well.

At the coffee shop around the corner, I ordered two coffees from the girl with the deer eyes and cropped hair and Joan of Arc tattoo. As usual, she paid me little notice. Meena had intel that the coffee girl was straight—one of those girls who affects andro queer chic and looks heartbreakingly good in it but actually only dates men. We resented this kind of girl. It was hard enough as it was without these decoys jacking up false hope, jamming the gaydar.

Back at work I moved slowly, tried not to break things. I busied myself dusting everything like a hungover housewife. A couple of customers came in, stroked the arms of Eames chairs, expressed desire without conviction, imagined their lives with this sofa or that table, and left. I couldn't fault them—I did it too. I would love a credenza, a painting, a lamp, and watch it for weeks and plan where it could go in my house, a luminous beautiful thing among the battered street finds and left-behind furniture, until a real person with real money came and took it home.

Summer shouldered through the door with a jingle at three that afternoon. Her cherry-red hair was pulled into a high knot and she wore a gray jacket with a huge fluffy faux-fur collar, like a giant squirrel tail pillowing her neck. She threw her sacklike purse down on a couch and curled up next to it. "What'd I miss?" Summer had grown up in Tennessee and Boston and her speech was curiously inflected by both accents—part drawl, part bark.

"No feet on the couch," I said. "It's a Knoll."

She moved her boots to the Conant Ball coffee table. I started to chide and she said, "Just kidding!" and put them on the floor.

"If Ted sees you he'll kill you," I said. "I take it back, he'll kill me. Actually, you're in a different kind of trouble if Ted sees you. I'm afraid you're his type."

She waved it away. "I dance for Ted every night."

I pictured the money Ted wasn't paying me landing at Summer's feet. "Seriously?"

"No. Maybe. I don't know. Close enough. How was the show? I am so mad I missed it."

"Loud," I said. "Good turnout." I felt my chin throb.

"You have a funny look on your face."

My pulse sped up. I couldn't tell her, not here. "I'm sort of breaking out on my chin?"

"I meant you've got this weird expression."

I picked up a spray bottle and started to wipe at an invisible spot on the counter, chin tilted as far into my neck as it could go. "Oh. Well. Flynn was there."

"Ah. Did you talk to her?"

"I only saw her from afar." I rolled my eyes. "Leather pants? Really?"

Summer laughed agreeably and studied my face, which I instantly lowered. "Seriously, are you okay?" she said. "You look kind of flushed."

"Hangover," I mumbled.

Summer excavated a vial of ibuprofen and half a bottle of Diet Coke from the depths of her bag and graciously set them before me. "Buck up before family dinner. You look like hell."

I froze. "Family dinner!"

"You forgot."

"I didn't forget. I just forgot it was tonight."

"Uh-huh. I'm headed to Nature's. Need anything?"

"No, I'm on it."

I was totally not.

Family dinner happened once a month and rotated from house to house. A half dozen of us pulled together a big meal and cleared a whole evening for it. Flynn used to come, but in the breakup, I got to keep family dinner. Clearly I needed it more. Or maybe Flynn had started a new family dinner crew. There was a lot I didn't know.

Like what, and how, I was going to pull together for tonight.

When Ted came back an hour before closing, I told him I wasn't feeling well. He looked at my face and believed me. "Get on home, kid," he said, and with guilty relief, I did.

On the way home, I stopped by the record store. I'd forgotten to sign my time sheet and I couldn't afford to delay my two-figure paycheck. It was a minor shop, a modest closet compared to Jackpot or Music Millennium or Crocodile, but it was a solid little neighborhood joint with an equal mix of vinyl and CDs, and where a clerk didn't have to be an encyclopedia, just an enthusiast.

The new guy in his black knit beanie was slitting open long boxes of new CDs and paid me no attention at all—off duty, I was a girl in a record store, the ignorable class—until I said hello. Still, I glanced over at him twice before I surreptitiously pulled the Cold Shoulder record out of the C section.

On the back cover was a snapshot of the band's practice space, some basement walled with a grid of mattresses, cluttered with gear. The singer-guitarist stood in the foreground, of course, looking directly at the lens even as he played; the bassist slouched behind him. Ryan sat at his drum kit, on whose bass head he had traced a two-headed calf, with one stick raised, the other a pale blur. His hair was shorter in this picture, falling forward over his eyes, and his head was turned slightly to the side. He had a good mouth. I drew the cover closer to peer at the grainy shadow of his jaw. The skin looked rougher there.

My fingers were sweating, slippery on the shrink-wrap. I rang myself up and slid the record into a flat brown paper bag, plain and anonymous as an envelope addressed to no one.

The house was quiet and dim, the last of the afternoon light slanting low across the dusty floor. I made myself a tahini and banana sandwich and took it to my bedroom, where the record player squatted atop a scratched teak dresser. The dog followed me in and sat down unprompted, tail wagging, ears perked. When I reached to pet her she ducked.

"You want my sandwich, not my love." I tore off a strip of crust and tossed it to her. "At least you're honest about it."

I pierced the sleeve's plastic membrane with my thumbnail and slit it along the edge, and the inky record slid smoothly out. I'd seen the Cold Shoulder play before, but I hadn't paid close attention. It was one of those times when Flynn was acting slightly askew; she had sent me out for a night With My Own Friends, because it would be Good For Me, and the effort of shoving my unease to the back of my mind had clouded my ability to focus on much else, including the bands I stood watching without hearing.

The needle announced itself with a staticky thump as I set it down on the circling record, cut into a jagged guitar riff, and then the whole trio kicked in, lean and artfully ragged around the edges. It wasn't the kind of music I usually listened to. I liked distortion, a girl holler or a voice with a rough edge, the blur and bleed of excess noise. Music that abraded in order to soothe. Music that wouldn't sound good as background music, music you would never hear played in a store. The Cold Shoulder was tight and melodic, almost . . . professional. I paid attention to the drums. Ryan hit hard but eschewed excess—no bombast or wild fills or ringing crash, but a taut, puncturing beat. I turned up the volume and lay on the hard wooden floor on my back.

This was my favorite way to listen to music, and the only way to meet a brand-new record. On your back on the floor, you don't just hear the music, you feel it. Your whole body listens.

The first time I experienced this it was accidental. It was back in central Nebraska, in the farmhouse where I grew up. My parents had left for a weekend tractor show in Lincoln with my brother, my older sister was at college, my little sister had gone to a friend's house, and they had let me stay home alone; I was seventeen and a Good Kid.

I invited my best friend, Sarah, to spend the night, and Sarah brought along her cousin Zoe, who was a year older and visiting from Minneapolis. Zoe had dyed her choppily bobbed hair black but still had white-blond roots, eyebrows, and eyelashes, plus pale golden freckles; it was an unearthly effect. The words GIRL BOMB were written on her knuckles in Sharpie. To Sarah and me, Zoe seemed very cosmopolitan, so sure of herself. We lived in a world of sugar beet fields and hog farms, a town with two bars and five churches and one restaurant, called Restaurant; our junior class had thirty-two people in it. A few kids would parrot their parents' grumbling about the new influx of migrant workers who came to work the fields and a nearby meatpacking plant, but if I protested they would assure me they didn't mean people like *my* family (our last name, Morales, came from my

Mexican-born grandfather, who'd died when my dad was twelve); occasionally someone would ask me how to say something in Spanish, which neither I nor my siblings knew after three generations of assimilation and a high school foreign-language curriculum that offered only beginning German. We all went to youth group on Wednesdays and church on Sundays, and the only thing to do on weekends was sit in our houses or stand around in the gas station parking lot or go get wasted at a gravel pit. Zoe, however, had a fake ID that got her into shows, she spent her free time in record stores and bookstores, she wrote a zine called *Catfight*. She wore boys' boxers and a translucent ribbed tank top to sleep in, and she had brought with her a crate of records. Sarah conked out around midnight, but Zoe and I were still wide awake, so we took the crate to the living room for a listening party.

We settled into the gap between the sofa and the stereo, a passage two feet wide where the hardwood floor was bare.

"Have you heard this before?" said Zoe, pulling out the album *Sister* by Sonic Youth.

"All I've heard by them is *Goo*," I said, feeling very young. I had not actually heard *Goo* either, just *of* it. I hoped that was enough. "Is that a new one?"

"Oh, no," said Zoe with a knowing laugh. "This is

from, like, five years ago. It's way better than their new stuff." She put it on and turned up the volume so that before the music even started the vinyl crackled like a distant storm. Then the drumbeat thundered in so loud and sure my breath caught, and Zoe smiled with approval. *Boom-boom-BOOM-boom-boom-boom-BOOM,* and then a knowing, insistent guitar stepped in, a nodding bass line followed it, and I closed my eyes. This music sounded dissonant and wrong but it sounded so *right* I could hardly believe it. Yet I did believe, totally, instantly.

I felt Zoe's mouth on mine and we toppled to the floor.

My back hit the boards and at once everything sounded and felt different. Through the wood that was once alive and whose internal structure remembered it, the waves of the sound traveled through my shoulder blades and torso and bare feet, through Zoe's knees straddling me and her palms flat on the floor beside my shoulders, and through, it seemed, Zoe's mouth moving in time with mine. I felt the sound with my whole body, discordant and delicate and harsh and beautiful, pulsing with a trapped urgency I recognized in myself—a sound like chasing and being chased, never catching nor being caught.

Jesus had a twin who knew nothing about sin, the

voice chant-sang. *She was laughing like crazy at the trouble I'm in.*

We kissed and kissed, and as the needle circled the fading feedback of side one, Zoe ran a finger along my drawstring waistband. I ached with want, but I worried that if I traversed that border I would never be able to cross back. "Not yet," I whispered.

"Are you sure?"

"Next time."

The player's arm lifted and swung back to rest. "Okay," Zoe said, "next time," and got up to flip the record. We made out until the second side ended, and then, dazed and high on each other, went to my bedroom. Zoe got into the bed with her cousin and I slid into the sleeping bag on the floor. She hung her arm over the side and we held hands until we fell asleep.

In the morning when we woke, my hand was resting on the floor and Zoe's was folded up near her chest.

We never told Sarah. Or anyone.

After Zoe and Sarah left the next day, I went back into the living room. The sunlight poured through the windows and I couldn't believe it was the same sunlight as before, the same home. The whole house looked different.

I carried the sweet ache of my secret for months. I would write letters to Zoe, but not *too* often, and managed to stop myself from spilling forth *Come back here, come over, please kiss me again;* I didn't want to sound desperate. I pored over each new issue of Zoe's zine, searching for clues about myself, or other girls, but it was mostly Riot Grrrl politics and show reviews and critiques of punk boys and pro-girl manifestos; Zoe wrote about girls in general, but not any girl in particular, no anecdote of listening to Sonic Youth with a girl she'd discovered stranded in a tiny nothing town three hours from Lincoln. How desperately I wanted to see that story written. *Next time* never came; I had blown it, forever, I worried, and now I was trapped on the wrong side of that border, all alone.

The more I fell in love with Zoe—or the idea of Zoe, Zoe in print—the more I realized that the feeling was not a new arrival but a part of me awakened, like sap stirring under bark. And that in all the miles and miles of green fields stretching toward the horizon as far as I could see from the end of our driveway, there was not a single place for that feeling to exist, except inside me.

So I kept it locked safely within, while on the outside I made myself so *good* it hurt. While my classmates fought with their parents and defied their curfews and drank and smoked and had sex, I dared not join them. The rebellion inside me was far worse. My friends would eventually get it out of their systems and settle down, maybe even here, but I would never do the one thing my parents unequivocally expected of me from the moment I was born: replicate them. No boyfriends brought home to dinner. No giddy phone call of *I've got good news.* No showers, no dance at the VFW, no headlines for the family Christmas letter. They would never give me away at the end of an aisle; I was not theirs for the giving.

Theirs was not the kind of God who was flexible about such things.

My strategy: to bide my time and stockpile as much favor as I could, to make up for or brace for the life to come. I attended youth group and Sunday school, scored straight A's, joined every plausible extracurricular, won scholarships to every school I applied to, babysat and saved the growing pile of cash in my underwear drawer, went to prom with a boy named Sam, cleaned my plate, fed the chickens and collected their eggs at dawn without complaint. My room was always spotless so my mother would never have cause to clean it and turn up something she might question. Behind my bedroom door, I read *Catfight* and other zines Zoe sent me. I mail-ordered the albums they wrote about, and then more from the photocopied catalogs that came tucked inside those records' sleeves, a world of ever-branching underground tunnels. In a decoy journal at my bedside

I sketched brief descriptions of my day, petty social squabbles and funny accidents and idle musings; but deep in my bookshelves I hid my real journal, which I nonetheless wrote in a coded diction, changing or avoiding pronouns, shifting into third person as if I were making up stories about someone else. I listened to my music on my Discman with headphones so the raucous noise was mine alone, and at night when I couldn't sleep I crept down behind the couch, plugged my headphones into the stereo system, and lay on my back on the floor.

My parents never heard a note.

On my last night in Nebraska, I stood at the end of the driveway, where the mailbox nodded toward the dark, dark country roads. The tall house stood alone in a cluster of trees, an island in an ocean of sugar beets, lit like a ship.

Good-bye, Nebraska. Good-bye, wide black sky. Good-bye, velvet humidity of the summer night air. Good-bye, pulsing cricket drone. Good-bye, fireflies.

Hello, moss, rain, towering firs, bridges, fickle skies, girls, life.

The Cold Shoulder song hit the bridge and it was a predictable but good one—it did exactly what a bridge can do, take a step sideways and shamelessly yank the listener's heart with it, and I let it yank mine for a moment. The feeling was familiar but I couldn't tell if it was the bridge or the song itself. Surely they had played it that night when I had half listened to them perform. I imagined if someone had tapped me on the shoulder and leaned in to whisper, *Guess who in this room you'll kiss in six months,* and pointed out . . . the drummer? of the Cold Shoulder? I would have guffawed or thrown a drink in that person's face, depending on their gender.

Actually, I would have said, *You have the wrong person. I'm with Flynn.*

And this prescient person might have looked around and said, *But is Flynn with you?*

Not at this moment she isn't.

Exactly.

At that point, I might have cut out and gone home; I might have found the house dark and locked, Flynn out for the night; I might have found the house lighted and locked, and Flynn tangling with someone in our bed. Vivian?

But I had stayed through the show, stubbornly clung to my illusion of a life partner, gotten thoroughly drunk, and come home with whiskey on my tongue and a lump in my throat to a girlfriend who was sound asleep, flat on her stomach on the far side of the bed, unrousable.

The third Cold Shoulder song was under way when

I lifted the needle and the record slowed to a stop. They were a fine band, solid, good, unlikely to become huge but who knew these days? Forgettable local bands had become national hits. You never know what other people will love.

I got up off the floor, a little wobbly still, and dusted off my back. Dinner was at Meena's in two hours and I hadn't even gone to the store yet. The last thing I wanted to do was let the family down.

Family Dinner

Because most of the time we lived on broccoli and tofu, beans and rice, grilled cheese and spaghetti, the point of family dinner was complex recipes, a luxurious if temporary abundance, and a what's-told-here-stays-here policy. There was also a no-lentils policy, unless we were cooking Indian. Call it a potluck and you would be banished to a purple bungalow on Hawthorne Boulevard for an infinite drum circle—we were *not* potluck wimmin.

Lawrence held up her offering: "This is a three-dollar bottle of wine but it tastes like a five-dollar bottle of wine." We cheered. Tonight there were six of us: Meena, Lawrence, Summer, and me, plus our friends Robin and Topher. Robin, an ex-girlfriend of Meena's who had long ago transitioned to inner-circle friend, wore her dark hair in a high pony atop her head and drew her eyebrows on with a black kohl pencil every morning. She regularly hit the Goodwill bins and re-constituted secondhand rejects into dresses that slunk over her lush fat curves like couture. Topher, our token gay male friend, was slight and fair and clever, with an easy rapid-fire laugh that made him terrific fun to watch movies with. He and Lawrence swapped thrifted sweaters and experimental novels.

We assembled at the Manor, Meena's house on Southeast Yamhill. With the settlement from a car accident in high school that left Meena's right temple flecked with glass scars, she'd bought a half-wrecked 1910 duplex and taught herself how to renovate it. We'd all spread grout or pried up carpet or patched drywall there at some point. She rented out the first side she finished and moved into the other side, where one room or another was always skeletal and piled with construc-tion materials. She had nearly finished the kitchen—all but the floor, which was still screwed-down plywood boards—and tonight was its close-enough christening.

I'd been assigned salad but remembered this only when I showed up with three apologetic pints of ice cream, my fingerprints denting their frosty sides.

"Where is your brain?" said Summer. "I thought I was the irresponsible one."

"Under the bar at La Luna," I said. My hand flew to my abraded chin.

"Nothing wrong with two desserts," Topher said, ladling a thin, pale batter into a pan. "My virgin dosa voyage might be a shipwreck." Meena stepped over to seize the ladle. Summer was sinking shards of lacy caramel brittle into the frosting of a layer cake. We were always telling her to just go be a chef, but the money and hours were so miserable that she always ended up back on the pole, where the cash was abundant and forthright. "Either way I'm dancing for someone," she once said. "Might as well get paid for it."

We crowded in elbow-cozy around Meena's candlelit table with our tattered but golden dosas. Topher bemoaned his ever-slim romantic luck, and we offered the usual sympathy and affirmations. Gay Portland was inexplicably and deeply gender-segregated and Topher's immersion in womankind didn't earn him any points at the Silverado. Summer was working on a new issue of her zine, *Boner Killer*, about egregious strip club patrons. Robin had started an apprenticeship at a tattoo studio and offered to practice on us. (Me: "Sharpie only." Summer: "Sure, I'll take another.") Lawrence was suffering a male colleague who wanted to go "cruising for chicks" together. Team Dresch was on the verge of breaking up and Meena was taking it hard. The Gold Stars were supposed to tour with them.

"Do you ever get the feeling you're a year too late?" Meena said.

"Homocore is over," Lawrence said.

"It is not," Meena said, and manufactured three reasons it was not, one of which was the Gold Stars themselves. She ought to have been a lawyer. But Lawrence was right—it was 1998 and the movement was aging out, the way Riot Grrrl had already been on the wane by the time I made it to Portland, only stragglers and a few half bottles left at the party. You wanted to be *part* of something, and we were—we just weren't sure what. Our own time had an end-of-the-decade, end-of-the-century melancholy. The electric feeling of being on the cusp—we wanted to know *that* again.

I aired my own problems with the Lesbian Mafia and the art show a committee of us were attempting to stage. Depending on which committee member you talked to, it was either *a lesbian art show* or *an art show of lesbian artists*. Or was it *a queer art show* or *an art show of queer artists*? The distinctions had caused hour-long arguments, tears and yelling, accusations of hegemony, and an e-mail chain hundreds deep.

We kept the conversation respectable through dinner, but with dessert came our favorite dish: gossip, that deceptively delicious idle viciousness that, like any intoxicant, you wake up ruing the next day. We were our own TV channel, our own weekly drama. We were a secret handshake, an extended family, a common enemy. The plots were thick.

Tonight, Summer offhandedly mentioned her concerns about our acquaintance M. Why? we asked, all friendly worry. Summer strongly self-identified as a Trusted Confidante, but she could not resist the call to tell a good story, whether it was her own or not. The story's benefit to our collective wisdom always won out over individual privacy. Her trademark gossip style was to bring up something she'd learned in confidence, minus a couple of identifying details, under the guise of important processing, a community problem to be solved, a case study that could enrich our collective self-knowledge.

"She just seems to be having sort of an intense time recently," Summer said, lingering on the N's. What did she know, what did she know? We each called up whatever meager intelligence we had about M, and Summer nodded knowingly, distantly. We had clearly failed to give her anything new. "Never mind," she said. "That's all." But we knew there was more. She was fat with it. We egged her on, she resisted obligingly, and then she set her elbows on the table and locked her fingers under her chin. "I can't really give any details," she began. But M had been on the left-behind end of a middle-of-the-night bed-hop with *someone* who was also sleeping with her own housemate's girlfriend. Instantly we set to guessing like jackals upon a fresh carcass, ripping away fur until we found the wound and gorged ourselves on thrilled outrage.

This mark would stay on the girl's record for years. The way we gossiped, there was no statute of limitations. The fucked-up thing you said at a Riot Grrrl meeting in 1992 could be revived as evidence in 1998. Our institutional memory was indelible—perhaps in the absence of any official institutional record of queer girl lives. We archived each other through an endless oral history, telling and retelling, anecdote into history into lore. And yet: you couldn't write anyone off, or out of the story, because our numbers were not all that huge. If no one ever slept with anyone's ex, if missteps and bad behavior disqualified people for life, we would all soon be single and sexless. So we condemned, censured, and kept on coupling in new and used configurations.

Given all I knew, Flynn and Vivian should not have surprised me, but still I couldn't believe it. These friends around the table, this family—I would have found them one way or another, but it was Vivian who first brought me in. Who made me, we used to joke.

I was a week shy of eighteen when I arrived at Reed College. Here, instead of being the queer girl invisible to the straights, I found myself the queer girl who was invisible to the queers, still so Midwestern, my dark hair pulled back in a ponytail, new sneakers, jeans from the department store. Most of my fellow freshmen arrived in band T-shirts and Doc Martens and haircuts I had never even considered a possibility, as if they'd already taken AP Cool I and II at their suburban magnet schools. They walked right past me.

I looked for the Riot Grrrls I'd read about in zines, but the local chapter had already closed up shop. A heart-pounding visit to the orientation-week meeting of the gay student group yielded a hangout and then a date with a junior named Siri, who showed up at the proposed coffee shop in a long skirt and hiking boots and a deadly little hat. Siri had sunny freckles and had already bought tickets to the Melissa Etheridge concert coming in December. She took me to a party off Division Street that was not only students but adult lesbians. I had still hardly met any lesbians my own age, much less an adult of the species, and the house was packed. These lesbians were pros, labrys-bearers with full libraries of everything woman-on-woman written since the seventies. I ran my finger over the spines of books named *Lesbian/Woman* and *Daughters of a Coral Dawn* and the complete works of Elana Dykewomon and miles of mystery paperbacks. Purple was everywhere: the front door, the blouses, the frames of eyeglasses, the collar of the cat inevitably named Luna. The place had a warm, herbal smell. It was a house where I would have liked to curl up in the afternoon and take a long nap.

But it was evening and lesbians were everywhere. Siri was utterly at home, stocked with knowing laughs, pausing to sing along to a favorite righteous line in the background music. I sat on a hard dining chair in the living room and tried to interact competently, my voice oddly strangled. All this *herstory*. I was so far behind. The magnitude of the studies I'd need to do loomed over me. I was in another kind of church. I missed, for the first time, Nebraska, where at least I knew the terrain and how to make my way through a conversation.

At the bus stop Siri turned to me and tilted her chin down coyly. A pit formed in my stomach. It was my second chance ever to kiss a girl, and I couldn't do it. I gave her a quick hug and said, "Thanks so much, see you at the next meeting." And scurried onto my bus. I glanced back as it pulled away. A breeze had picked up, and Siri stood there with one hand holding her hat to her head, the other hanging uncertainly at her side. I gave an apologetic wave, and her hand rose as if it were tied to a deflating balloon.

Maybe I'm not cut out to be lesbian after all, I thought. Maybe I had just loved Zoe, a fluke. Lonesomeness belted my heart. I went back to my dorm room and put on my headphones and lay on the floor, thin carpet over concrete, a surface that had never lived. The Discman rested on my chest, spinning inside.

Then in October, on the way back from a trip to Goodwill with my roommate, I was carrying a bag full of boy-sized T-shirts and acrylic cardigans and corduroys—an attempt to step away from my past by wearing someone else's—when I heard a girl screaming at the other end of the hall. We both stopped. The drums kicked in. It was a record. It sounded terrible and fantastic, raw, pissed. My roommate made a face.

"I'm going to go check on that," I said.

"Tell them to turn it down," said the roommate, a psych major from Wisconsin who res life had thought would be a good match. It wasn't really their fault. Sitting at my parents' kitchen table, I had accidentally filled out the form for their Andrea instead of the real one. Oops.

I followed the sound to an ajar door at the end of the hall, and knocked.

"Come in," said an alto voice, and the door opened to a girl kneeling on the floor with scissors and a long navy slip.

"This music—" I started.

"Oh, sorry, is it bothering you? I didn't realize the door was open. I can turn it down."

"No! No, it's not bothering me. I think it's great. I wanted to ask what it was."

The girl sat back on her heels and smiled. "That would be Blatz. I'm Vivian. Shut the door." She craned her chin forward. "What do you have in that bag?"

Vivian was nineteen and her world extended way beyond campus. School had defined my whole life thus far, but it didn't for the girls Vivian knew—some had graduated, some had left, some had never gone, and it didn't really matter. All of us were refugees of the nuclear family and its fallout, and some, like me, still embedded secret agents in our homes of origin but full citizens here. It was the world I'd glimpsed in Zoe's zines times one hundred, and real. Girls cut their own hair, built bikes, silkscreened T-shirts, taught each other self-defense, formed bands on the spot, and did not hesitate to turn up the volume. I had read some of their zines before and it made me shy, to know them but not to be known. One had a patch that said, NO APOLOGIES/NO ASSIMILATION/QUEER FOREVER, the bravest thing I had ever read; I repeated it again and again in my mind. I hung out at Vivian's side, doing my best to join a conversation I had been dying to have, and now I could hardly speak, I was so giddy and full of longing. People *knew* things: everyone's names and nicknames, bands of every -core, unlisted show venues, the encyclopedic subtleties of what was butch and what was femme, how to play the drums. They talked about sex accessories and practices I had never heard of, nouns I did not know could be verbs. I was a tabby among tigers.

"You don't have to be good at it, Andy," said Vivian as I groped stiffly at the neck of a borrowed bass. "Just do it. Expertise is a weapon of the patriarchy." Our band fell amicably apart after three songs and one show; I attempted a zine but could not write a word in first person (how did people confess themselves, construct themselves, so artfully?). But I could draw and letter, and people started asking me to do flyers and posters. I proved my mettle at Scrabble. I made myself brave and my new friends made me braver. After I cut off my ponytail and the sleeves of my T-shirts, I made out with two different girls in one week, dead-end make-outs but crucial evidence that I was one of them. Then Vivian got wind of it and pushed me up against a wall at a Bratmobile show, slid her leg between mine, and claimed me with a long, conspicuous kiss that would carry on for a year.

My grades slipped for the first time into B territory, but my life had surged into an all-encompassing present. I declared an art major and told my parents it was economics. I verbed some nouns. I crossed that border. I entered a whole world that no one in my hometown, least of all my family, had known existed, where I was not One of Them but One of Us. The split life I had been living—one for everyone else, one for me—merged into a single whole. My notebooks shifted back into first person.

Oh, Vivian. I put my head in my hands. My palms cupped my eyes with soothing darkness.

"Andy, you okay?" Lawrence said.

I dropped my hands. All five of them were watching me. Here we sat, grown-ish, around the table. The people who'd stuck around after the fallout. Low light warmed everyone's faces. The caramel lace glistened atop the remains of the cake. Since the breakup, I had avoided talking about Flynn if I could help it—she had once been a part of family dinner—and I tried to take the high road. I loathed the thought of my hardship being discussed. But why hide it? Maybe for once it was time to hold Flynn accountable. It was crucial to shape your own narrative. And it would pave the way for my coup de grace, the story of the night: my tragicomic man-kiss. I never got to drop the biggest bomb of the night, and here I had two right in my pocket.

"Okay." I folded my napkin and set it on the table. I cleared my throat. "I wasn't going to say anything, but. Something funny happened at the show last night."

"Do tell."

"You're not going to believe it. I wouldn't believe it if I hadn't seen it."

Everyone leaned in. Summer bounced in her seat.

"The first thing was, I saw Flynn. With her latest trophy. And who, of all people on earth, would that be?" I set both hands on the table and lowered my voice. "*Vivian.*"

I awaited the cry of outrage.

Summer and Meena exchanged a glance.

"Oh boy," Meena said. Lawrence pursed her lips. Topher and Robin looked down at their plates.

"Oh my god." I sat back. I needed the hard chair to hold me up. "You already knew."

"There were a couple clues, but . . ." said Robin.

"I heard a rumor from my Olympia sources," Meena conceded, "but I didn't want to believe it."

Summer widened her eyes and refilled her wine.

"*You* didn't tell me?" I said to Summer. "You tell everyone everything."

"I do not. Honestly, I didn't think you needed to know."

"Did you want to know?" Meena said.

"No! I wish I could un-know it right now. Forever."

"I rest my case," Summer said. "You were doing well. Or not so well. You didn't need it."

"I just can't believe you all knew," I said with a dismayed smile.

"This information," said Summer soberly, "it's not a gift."

"It certainly isn't. Can I exchange it?"

"So what's the rest?" Robin said. "You said 'the first thing.'"

They looked at me hungrily, and for once, I didn't want to feed them. To feed *myself* to them. "Oh, that's all," I said. "That was the beginning and end of the story. Turns out you guys know the rest." I choked out a sardonic laugh and reset my face.

They offered to help me process it all. They started to disparage Flynn and Vivian, but the more they said, the more they revealed. Each remark made me feel like I was being flayed with a tiny vegetable peeler. I stopped them after only a few. I reached for the knife to cut another slice of cake and said, "Please, let's move on. I'm done thinking about Flynn. Tell me something new."

We turned to another recycled plot. I knew that mine would be reserved for later, for my absence. It was how we bonded: shared concern for a friend.

Meena tipped a bottle of wine toward my glass. I wanted to undrink everything I had drunk, or drink so much I forgot everything I knew. I knew I shouldn't say yes. But knowing better, alas, has never stopped me from wanting. I said, "More, please."

The Lesbian Mafia Official Shitlist (Excerpt)

Straight men in lesbian bars

Straight women who make out for men

Chasing Amy

The fall of Anne Heche

"Lesbian" porn

President Clinton

Congress (excl. Barney Frank)

"I'm a lesbian trapped in a man's body"

~~Ani DiFranco~~

~~Folk music~~ *"All lesbians are in the Lesbian Mafia."*

"Ani DiFranco is no longer lesbian-identified."

"Well, a million other folkie lesbians still are."

"We don't need to hate Ani. We just no longer listen to her."

"I haven't listened to that shit since Puddle Dive—"

"We know."

"None of us have."

No Expectations

Barefaced and hoodied, Summer leaned back against the kitchen counter, eating a cold naked Tofu Pup. She dipped the rubbery thing directly into a jar of stone-ground mustard before every bite. A pink vinyl boot drooped out of her half-zipped backpack on the floor.

"Give me a minute and I'll make some real food," I said, collapsing into a chair. My back ached from bending over the type and cranking the letterpress's heavy inked cylinder over and over.

"Have to get to work. The Sandy Jug."

"But the manager is so evil to you."

"Awful. But . . ." Summer rubbed at her eyebrow ring. "Rent's due and I was out sick last week, so it's either that or the seven A.M. shift at the Acropolis."

"I'm amazed that people will go to a strip club at that hour."

"They do. And they order the steak."

"You deserve better, Summer."

"Don't we all?" She popped the last of the Tofu Pup into her mouth and licked the mustard off her fingers. She shrugged on her squirrelly coat. "By the way, someone called for you earlier. A dude."

"Who?"

"Aaron? Brian?" She stuffed the last of the boot into the backpack and zipped it shut.

"Ryan?"

"Maybe. Yeah. They all sound the same to me." I frowned, and Summer picked up on it. "What? Who is he?"

"A friend of Flynn's," I said.

Summer jangled the keys in her pocket, a sound like Christmas bells. "Do I sense a boundary issue?"

"No, no, he cuts hair," I said, to her visible disappointment. "Any message?"

"Just a number." On the counter was an envelope with her red Sharpie scrawl.

I waited until Summer's taillights had turned the corner, and even then still couldn't help taking the cordless phone down to the basement for good measure. I flipped on the switch and a string of Christmas lights illuminated a minor junkyard of boxes, bikes, and leftover furniture.

"You probably shouldn't call me here," I said when he answered.

"Well, hello," he said.

I sat down on the arm of a haggard easy chair. "Sorry. It's just, the walls here have ears. And mouths."

"What's to hide?"

"Nothing," I said. "But, you know, people get ideas."

"I have an idea. I just got out of practice and I'm starving. Come with me to the Old Nickel for some breakfast."

"It's nine thirty at night."

"It's been one of those days where nothing went right and I want to start over. Did you eat already?"

I admitted I hadn't, and that I was facing down some leftover couscous.

"But why?"

I laughed. "Yeah. That's about right." I scratched my neck. "I actually could go for something less wholesome."

"Oh really?"

"Like pancakes," I said.

"I'm leaving for tour in a couple of days, I just want to hang out." He stopped me before I could counter him: "Don't worry, I have no expectations."

"You have Scrabble in your *van?"* I was impressed, despite myself.

"Hang on." Ryan sprang to his feet, swerved out the front door, and jogged across the parking lot. I watched him through the rain-fogged window, a bright mirage.

The restaurant was old and divey, out on Southeast Powell by the train tracks. Smoke drifted over from the bar side. The booths were deep and red, the walls paneled in dark fake wood. The water came in amber-colored glasses with a pebbly texture.

Ryan slid back into the booth and unfolded the travel-sized board between us. "I feel kind of bad," he said as we plucked the tiny clicking letters from their drawstring bag.

"Why?"

"Because I'm going to beat you."

"That's funny, because I was feeling sorry for *you."* I reminded him I was a professional arranger of letters. Scrabble was blood sport.

"How about winner pays?" he said.

"Doesn't the loser usually pay?"

"Right. But if you really care about the game, you'll try to win even if you have to pay for it."

I narrowed my eyes. "I'm in."

A fluffy globe of butter the size of an ice-cream

scoop rested in a puddle atop the pancake stack. The pancakes were soft and mealy and tasted like cake, like childhood, like going out to breakfast with my family after church. In between Scrabble plays, Ryan tore bites away with the edge of his spoon, while I extracted tidy triangles from the stack with my knife and fork.

"I listened to your record," I said.

"Really? You have it?"

"I picked it up on the way home from work. It's good."

"I'd have given you one."

"It's okay, I didn't mind. I like to support friends' bands."

"We're friends?" he said, looking up from his tiles.

"Sure, we're friends."

The corners of his eyes crinkled; his brow eased. A sort of innuendo tightened the air. I didn't want to say, *What?*

Then he laid down HELIX on a double-word score, with the H on a triple-letter and nestled against an O for an exponential point burst.

"Still?" he said.

I fell back and made the requisite sounds of rage and dismay. He looked satisfied and said, almost apologetically, that his mother had brought him up playing Scrabble, with no maternal mercy. "That's what happens when you move around all the time. Just the two of us. Lots of evenings together."

"You guys must be close," I said.

He flicked his head a little. "When we had to be. She's doing her own thing now." He flipped the conversation back to me. "Let's talk about you. Where do you come from?"

"You think I'm not from here?"

"Nobody's from here."

"Flynn is."

"You know what I mean."

"Western Nebraska. Sugar beet land."

"*Nebraska*," he said approvingly. "My favorite Springsteen album."

"But it's all about New Jersey," I said.

"Good point."

"I came here for Reed," I said. "But I dropped out."

"Didn't like it?"

"I loved it. My parents stopped liking it when they found out I was gay."

"Oh." He carefully rearranged the letters on his rack. "Didn't take it so well, huh?"

"You could say that," I said.

We all have our coming-out story, or why-we-haven't-come-out story. More precisely, we have two. There's the official version, paragraph-sized for conversation, for when it comes up, usually on level-two get-to-know-you with friends and dates and curious coworkers. That one covers the basics: when, where, how, the end. You will tell it again and again over the course of your life, polishing it to a fine sheen, until it's as close to friction-less as you can get it. Then there's the real story, the full version, which you tell only a handful of people ever—even if you're one of the lucky ones with a good family, with loving parents who eventually accept you. Because, as Lawrence once said, when the only other time you've seen your dad cry is at a funeral, what does that mean about *you*?

Ryan got the short version: nineteen, home for Christmas, Mom overheard me on the phone, they blamed college, the end. "I couldn't afford it on my own, so." I cut my pancake triangle into smaller triangles. "I quit. How about you?"

"Me too. The quitting part. But I wanted to." He took a semester off at UW to tour and never went back. Later he went to barber school. Tired of grunge and Microsoft creep, he'd split Seattle for Portland. Three years later, he'd been here as long as he'd lived any-where.

For much of the game I'd been plagued with a vowel-heavy rack that spelled nothing but sounds of distress, and right then Ryan laid down two of his last tiles to make OF and IF, the F doing double duty on a double-word. He was now ahead by a solid thirty points and I still had five letters left.

He pulled out his wallet and set it on the table.

"Oh really."

"Whenever you're ready."

I laid down all my letters to spell STAKE, pluraling his IF, K on a triple-letter. I took him right out. "Ready," I said.

Ryan fell back in the booth, slumped to the side, and then slid out of view.

I peered under the table. He was stretched out on his back on the bench. I asked if he was okay.

"Reeling from my defeat."

"At least you got a free breakfast out of the deal."

"Aha. What if that was my strategy all along?"

"It was not!" I said.

"No, it really wasn't. I hate to lose."

"Me too." I lay down on my bench as well. Under the table it was dark and shadowy. I could see pale patches of gum stuck to the particleboard. Ryan's face was half shadowed from the table and half lit from behind.

"There's a problem," he said.

"That I beat you?"

"That too is a problem, and I plan to solve it. The other one I'm not so sure I can."

"What's that?"

"The problem is that I like you."

"I suppose that is a problem."

His eyes fixed upon mine. "But here's the thing. I think you like me too."

"You know what's a problem? Why do men always think that they can convert us? That we're not really what we say we are?" I said it with a smile, but my mouth felt hot.

"No, no, I'm not trying to convert you. I just have a hunch you'll like me more than you think."

"Oh really."

"Yeah."

I shook my head. "We'll see about that."

"We will? See, already it's looking good."

I laughed. "You're hopeless."

My arm was hanging over the edge of the booth, and I felt Ryan's hand bump against my fingers. I batted back at it. Then he slid his hand underneath mine. I let my hand rest there on his for a moment, on that warm plank of hand, a hand like a raft. There is no texture in the world quite like a human palm. The fingers sense it right away; a hand knows another hand the way a dog knows another dog, it responds to its kind.

I turned my head to look at him. He was looking

back at me. The table loomed above our heads like a low flat roof, protective, dim.

"You said you had no expectations," I said.

"I don't," he said. "Just a feeling. A little feeling."

"I'll be right back," I said, rising from the table.

In the restroom I washed my hands carefully, then leaned against the sink and lingered. The restroom's walls and ceiling were tiled in gold-veined mirror squares. There I was, repeated into infinity but fractured and increasingly hard to see. I returned to the table.

"Now I'm going," he said, and got up.

I slid into the booth and waited. I looked out the window and stared at the handle of my car door. Maybe when Ryan came back, I would get up and go again; I imagined we could trade off like that all night, infinitely patient. Go, wait, go, wait. I did not want to stay or leave.

The waiter brought the check. Ryan tried to pay after all and I battled him off: "Don't diminish my victory."

On the way to his van, Ryan's hand caught mine again. I pulled away deftly, as if we were just doing a high-five trick, and almost said, *Not here.* This wasn't our part of Portland.

But to the old people walking by, the families, the truckers, it didn't matter at all. Ryan and I could head to third base right there in the parking lot and the worst we'd hear would be, *Get a room.* I slid my hands into my pockets. Holding hands with this guy was not what I had signed up for. I just wanted the game. And pancakes.

Born Family

Okay, here's the real story.

My mother loved limits. They were a ten-foot fence guarding her and her family. Nothing could get in, nothing could get out. She was the most ardent kind of Catholic: a convert. As if to make up for her first twenty years of lax Lutheranism, she attended mass every day. She had converted to marry my father, who had been only casually faithful, a Mexican-American Catholicism relaxed by a couple generations of assimilation and intermarriage, but she took it all the way, one-upping him as if to prove something—perhaps to her own parents, who had disapproved of the relationship and worried her children would be "confused." Maybe it was living in rural Nebraska, a place where the weather is harsh and the landscape open, and she needed to buttress herself with the element-proof structures of the mind. Her convictions became her fortress.

My plan was not to crash the fortress but to build a small annex onto it. One brick at a time, a gradual reveal. I would go on with my underground life, my real life, but acquire the trappings of college degree, respectable work, even membership in the Catholic church downtown (whose progressive tendencies could be incrementally introduced into productive conversations)—a life that sounded good over the phone and at family gatherings. I would come home for every Christmas. And one day, I would ask to bring A Person, and they would be helpless in the face of her charm and kindness, and our love would radiate and encircle the whole family, and the annex would be complete. All of us within it.

Christmas was my first trip back home from college. I packed clothes I hadn't worn since the third week of school, washed my hair, and put on mascara, three things I did seldom to never. I shrugged on my old Andrea drag. It was part of my long game.

When I landed in Nebraska, the emerald fields I'd left in August were now wiped blank by winter. The white went on forever. Snowdrifts sculpted their way up the sides of the houses and outbuildings.

The man relatives: How are classes?

The lady relatives: Got a boyfriend out there?

My brother: "Yeah, right. She looks like a boy." He smirked at my short hair and my horn-rimmed glasses.

"It's a pixie cut, like she had when she was little," said an aunt helpfully. "I think she looks . . . French."

"A pixie cut," my father agreed.

"It's cool," declared Annabel, the youngest, and my mom gazed at her with fond relief, as if Annabel could see beauty the rest of us couldn't. She was the only one of us four who had blue eyes and my mother treated that recessive gene as if it had bravely fought its way to the top just for her.

For mass I changed into a skirt from high school and one of my mom's sweaters, and the symbolism killed me a little, all dressed up in a past that was long gone and a future that never would be. "Why don't you keep it," my mom said. The sweater was pale yellow with scalloped edges, like a decorative soap. "It's just darling on you."

"No thanks, Mom," I said. This became a ritual when I returned to Nebraska. She would call me to her room, make me try on her sweaters and blouses, and urge me to take them back with me. "I think it's more you."

"I think it's *very* you," she retorted.

I opened my mouth to ask just who she thought I was, then imagined that cellar door opening and swiftly closed it. I made myself smile. "Are you sure?" Of course she was. I accepted the sweater and thanked her, and she was pleased.

It was when I returned home my sophomore year, in 1993, that my plan broke down. I was in love with Vivian and Portland and my head was full of ideas from Reed, and my new confidence made me careless where my fear had always kept me in line. I wore a new Mom sweater and lipstick but couldn't hold my tongue when Alex said the Clinton health care plan would turn the country Communist.

The phone rang on Christmas Eve. Vivian. My mother answered upstairs and I took it in the laundry room.

"Hi. Save me," I said. I sat down in a basket of clean clothes. Vivian was at her parents' home in a Seattle suburb, still in reach of everything. We talked for half an hour and then she had to go; they were going out for Thai food. Her dad was a secular Jew and her mom just secular, and I envied this incomprehensibly simple Christmas of presents and a restaurant meal, as if everyone had a birthday on the same day. "I love you too," I said. "Can't wait to see you." Vivian said, "Hang in there. Be brave." I hung up the phone and opened the door and there was my mother.

She said, "Who were you talking to?"

"Vivian." My face grew hot. "My friend. From school."

"Everything okay?"

"Of course. Do you need any help? I'll do this load of whites."

For the next two days I could feel her watching me. I tried to snap back into high school Andrea, but my mother already knew too much, and for once she seemed to be contemplating action instead of denial. To be surveyed like this made my skin hot and my stomach heavy. Every sentence out of my mouth seemed constructed by a scribe in my brain who was always a second late in the transcription.

At school, the LGBT union wasn't the only student group I had tried to attend. I had also once ventured shyly into a Latino/a student group, where the leaders of the meeting peppered their rousing talk with Spanish phrases and cultural in-jokes that everyone else laughed at and bantered along with as I tried to follow, mentally taking notes on what to look up later. I had grandmas but no abuelas; I had grown up with John Denver and Amy Grant records, eating casseroles made with Campbell's soup. I enrolled in Spanish I, where the professor taught us Spain Spanish with the lisp and

European assumptions, and though I learned how to converse about pleasantries, order lunch, and take the bus to El Prado, I didn't return. Meena said, "It's just a group, don't worry about it. The South Asian student union does good things and I'm glad they're there, but it's a particular kind of person who loves an affinity group. I mean, how many of your actual queer friends are in the LGBT union?" None, I admitted.

Still, when I went back home I searched my father's face for what I thought was Mexican-ness, something still visible in him but diluted in me. I had his mouth, his brown eyes, but my skin was lighter. My hair was fine and dark brown, while his was thick and silvering at the temples. What was I looking for, though? Who knew how much of his ancestry, and thus mine, was indigenous and how much European? I realized I was seeking a trace of purity, as if such a thing existed— as if one's roots could be a single clean bright plunge like a carrot, instead of the complicated dirty tangle that most of us actually had. *Essentialist* was an accusation my friends and classmates had flung around liberally in arguments, yet secretly maybe we all wanted it for ourselves in some way or another—to have an essence. To *be* an identity.

"I wish we'd spoken Spanish at home," I blurted in the kitchen. It was now two days after Christmas. My father stood at the kitchen counter, flipping through the newspaper, while my mother prepared dinner and I made my own vegetarian spaghetti sauce. "I mean growing up."

"Where did that come from?" my mother said.

"It would have been nice to be fluent. To have that ability."

"Aren't you taking it now in college?"

"But it's not the same," I said. "It'll always be a second language. An add-on. You could have taught us, Dad."

"I couldn't have taught you much," my dad said. "No one really spoke Spanish in Westerly, Nebraska."

"*Then*," my mother added.

He folded up the front section and opened Sports. "My dad got held back in school three times for his English, so he made sure that's all we spoke. We had to fit in. It was hard to be different."

"People thought he was a Sioux Indian." This was a fact my mother disclosed often and with a certain delight.

"Lakota," I mumbled.

She rolled her eyes and asked why I hadn't gotten all fired up about Germany or Sweden, since I was at least as much those as I was Mexican. Why did I only want the Mexican part? She meant why didn't I want what she was.

"Germany's creepy," I said. "And there's no point in learning Swedish since there aren't many of them and they all speak perfect English." I turned back to my dad. "Do we still have family in Mexico?" My siblings and I had never met our grandfather; he died of a heart attack when my dad was twelve. "Have you ever wanted to visit them?"

"My dad's dad left home in Nayarit young and never went back. He didn't get along with his family. He had other ideas about how to live. Our family is here now."

"Your father is American and so are you," my mother said as she shut the oven door. "Don't let anyone tell you otherwise."

The day before I was to leave, they sat me down in the living room. I tucked my feet underneath me on the scratchy plaid couch. Behind me, the record player's lid was pinned shut by stacks of Christmas CDs. "We don't care how good an education it is," my father started.

My mother broke in, "I don't like what this place is doing to you. Honey, look at yourself."

"It's just a haircut," I said. "It'll grow back."

"It's not the haircut," said my father.

"It's your whole attitude," said my mother. "You didn't want to go to church, you won't eat the food your

grandmother made, you have a hole in your nose—"
She teared up at this. I didn't know she'd noticed—I
had removed the ring, slipping it in only to sleep. "We
don't know what kind of friends you have there, your
grades are slipping. You were never like this. We sent
away a beautiful, well-adjusted daughter and you've
come back—it's like we don't even know who you are."

"This is me," I said. "I'm more me than I have ever
been."

"Come back home. Stop acting like someone you're
not."

"What do you think I was doing here all those years?"

"I don't know what that means," my mother snapped.
"And who is this Vivian you're always talking about and
talking to on the phone?"

"My friend?" I hated the lie. I was so proud of the
word girlfriend. It was awful to neuter it.

"Promise me it is not what I think it is."

"What do you think it is?"

"I can't even say it." Her eyes were bright, her cheeks
red. How disconcerting to see a kind face grow cold—it
is such a subtle shift, the way the muscles switch into
place, harden. "Promise me. Promise."

"I don't know what to say."

"Promise your mother," said my dad.

I looked away from them, out the window. Wind

lifted a haze of snow off the surface of the fields. My parents had stopped farming and now leased them to a distant cousin. They were ours in name only. Like me, I thought.

I could have rented out that life for much longer, according to my plan. Later, I wondered if I could have told them the truth another way. *I promise you have nothing to worry about.* Or I could have said what they wanted to hear. But I thought of relating my lie to Vivian later. I thought of her hand stroking my arm and her sympathetic, disappointed eyes. I imagined how she would light up if I told her I'd come out. How, in doing so, I would become a real queer. I too would have a coming-out story. My long game looked to be shot anyway. *Be brave.*

"Do you want me to lie?" I said. "Isn't lying a sin?"

"God forgives us our sins," said my mother. "But not all sins."

I took a breath and said I was in love.

My father gripped the arms of his chair and closed his eyes, a pilot going down. My mom said my whole name, spoke it like a curse. The tacit, they could have lived with; it could have been my invisible cross to bear, its weight mine alone. After all, it was not a sin to *be* homosexual; it was a sin to *act* on it. And I—

Even in the long version, I keep the worst of it to myself.

All that is necessary to know is that my mother wept and my father's voice shook, but their certainty was ironclad. They had raised me Catholic and moral and with strong role models, and all my siblings were turning out right, so the culprit was obvious. I could come home and go to one of the state schools or they would find a way to pay for Creighton, but as a matter of conscience, they would not pay that institution another cent.

I shifted back into survival mode. I said okay, I would pack my things. I went limp and contrite just long enough to board my plane back to Oregon.

When my feet touched the carpet of the Portland airport, my knees trembled with relief. I didn't yet know that a few days earlier, on New Year's Eve, in another corner of Nebraska, Brandon Teena had been murdered. When the story emerged I felt sick for weeks. We all mourned this brave, sweet person we had never known but imagined we could. And I mourned the Nebraska that I once knew, also dead.

At Reed, I went straight to the financial aid office. Surely parental severance would qualify me for a generous package. But I learned that no matter how on my own I said I was, in the universe of financial aid I still belonged to my parents and their tax bracket until age twenty-four. That was five years away. The Reed staffer offered me loans and said she'd try to get me a better deal for the next year, but there was no way I could carry the debt of even one semester there on my own, much less five.

As my parents had expected, I packed my clothes and books and turned in my dorm key, leaving my roommate with a super-single for the rest of the year. But I mailed them back the one-way plane ticket they had booked for me.

Vivian and my friends took care of me, many with a knowing embrace. People shared their own stories, helped me find a place, hooked me up with extra jobs. I moved into a $150-a-month attic bedroom in a cozily dilapidated, haunted punk house.

"Come home," my parents pleaded, and then commanded. But I already was. I thought they would come around, but their pain was deep and real, and they transformed it into an instrument of force. Their immovability shook me. My sin was mortal. They needed to be certain of something and they stuck with the thing they'd known longer than they'd known me, the church. All my stockpiling of good behavior had been for nothing; my currency was no good with them, counterfeit from the start. They still wanted the other Andrea, the one I had made up for and with them.

For the first time I understood why queer people changed their names. It was about more than trying to be different or weird, though maybe it was a little bit that, to go by Tiger or Ace or Ponyboy or Dirtbag or whatever, my future girlfriend Flynn adding the F to her name. The name they gave you belongs to someone else, their invention of you; if you turn out not to be that person, you have to name yourself. But I stayed Andrea—I couldn't let go entirely of the person I'd always been. The tyranny of family love is that you can't help but love people who think God can't stand the sight of you.

The next Christmas I braved one last visit home, hoping a year would have taken the edge off. I missed the clear winter light and crisp air that made my eyes water and the smell of snow on wool mittens. I wanted my mom's Swedish pancakes and cheesy grated potatoes and the salsa my dad made in an old Sunbeam blender with canned stewed tomatoes and extra jalapeños. I wanted to go back to where I came from. In my vision, my parents would have missed me so much and be so relieved to see me that they would relent. How could they sacrifice their daughter? They would love me no matter what. They would reinstate me at Reed. My siblings would rally behind me.

Alissa was president of her sorority and spent half the time on the phone with her new, better sisters; Alex was all basketball and JROTC; Annabel gave me helplessly sympathetic looks. We all put on a play called *Just Like It Never Happened,* and I didn't know how to go off-script.

The day after I arrived, my mother invited me into town with her to do errands. Snow was piled along the curbs like a low mountain range and the pale sky promised more. After the grocery store, she pulled into the parking lot of the church.

"I'll wait here in the car," I said.

"Come in with me," she said. "Father Lane would be so happy to see you. Just say hi."

Nothing pleased my mother more than hauling her brood to church, and I needed points, so I swallowed and followed her inside. Father Lane's door was open, and he instantly rose to his feet when he saw us. He welcomed me with exceptional warmth and invited me to take a seat. I glanced at my mother but she wouldn't look at me, merely smiled brightly toward Father Lane and said, "You know what I'm going to do, I'm going to just run over to the butcher and pick up the roast while you two catch up. You wouldn't want to do that anyway, honey, the meat, right? I'll be back in two shakes." And she was out the door.

My mother, despite my vegetarianism, had attempted to put meat on my plate at every meal for the past two years. I looked at the door as it clicked shut behind her. I looked at the priest, whose wide, closed smile hid his teeth. From his frame on the wall, Pope John Paul II looked just past us with a benevolent smirk.

"Is this about what I think it's about?" I said.

"What?" Father Lane said like a bad actor. "Just wanted to talk about things that are goin' on in your life and ways that we can help. Any confusion you're goin' through." When he dropped his G's like that, super casual, you knew it was serious.

I said I was feeling clear about things. I crossed my legs and folded my hands over my knee. "But how are *you* doing?"

Father Lane sighed and his gaze came to rest upon the bookshelf across the room. "I've been thinking. Sometimes," he said carefully, as if reading the titles aloud from a distance, "sometimes you have to make a sacrifice to be your best self. You have a choice, you know, which road you want to go down."

"I know," I said, perhaps too certainly, because he started and sat back.

"How long have we known each other?" he said.

"Since I was five or something." He'd grown gray since then, and his neck had begun to sag, I now noticed.

"I know who you are, Andrea. You are a child of God. And you deserve to live in the light, not the darkness." In a conspiratorial tone, as if revealing a treasure map to a child, he told me that there was a place in Colorado that could help me, that could restore me to my best self and help me conquer same-sex attraction—a place that could end my suffering. I pictured euthanasia.

He slid a brochure across the desk toward me: COURAGE MINISTRIES. A plump, soft-faced man and what looked like a bulldagger in a wig and dress held the hands of two small children. A sentence below proclaimed a proven program for how to "come out" of homosexuality.

"That doesn't really work," I said.

"Oh, it can. It's hard," he said, "to transcend the body." He looked tired. "But the soul prevails."

I set my hands on the armrests, ready to push off. "May I ask you something?"

"Please do."

"Was it worth it? Giving up everything to become a priest?"

Father Lane paused for a moment. "Yes."

"Okay," I said. "Thank you."

I walked out and headed down Main Street. I found our unlocked car and got in.

My mother looked surprised to see me shivering in the passenger seat when she approached, a roast as big as a toddler in her arms. I reached over and popped the trunk for her. She shook her head and deposited it in the backseat.

"How was your talk?" she said warily. "That was quick."

"Helpful," I said. "Father Lane looks well." I turned up the radio, which was playing "The Little Drummer Boy." "Remember when Alex had to act this out for the Christmas pageant?" I said.

"Do I ever," she said, and sighed. "You kids were so sweet." *Pa-rum-pum-pum-pum* did its resigned descent.

We each kept an eye on the other the rest of the day. I knew she wasn't done.

I was twenty—they couldn't involuntarily commit me to something, right? Or could they? I was still listed as a dependent on their tax forms.

The next morning, December 23, my dad got ready for work early and my mom said, with a tight-lipped breeziness, that she'd ride into town with him to "tie up some loose ends." I knew in my gut that they were headed to the church—and this time, she was taking Dad. They were hatching something. That Bikini Kill line *Resist psychic death* ran through my mind. I had a narrow window.

My little sister, Annabel, who was fifteen and had gotten her farm license, drove me to the Greyhound station in Lincoln, tearful and worried. "I'm not supposed to go more than thirty miles from the house," she said. "And I don't know if the minivan counts as farm equipment."

"Please, if Mom gives you a hard time, you can blame it on me," I said. "Tell them I tricked you. Like, I said we were just going out shopping for presents. You don't deserve to get in trouble, and I can't possibly get any deeper."

"I wish we *were* just going shopping," Annabel said. "Do you have to go? Can't you just wait it out?"

I began to cry too. "I wish I could. I can't. I've been waiting it out all my life."

She nodded. "I won't blame you," she said.

I hugged her hard until I could form words again. Don't be silly, I told her, I was already a lost cause to them. "I love you so much. Take care of yourself. Blame me."

My parents had framed my transgression as a crime against God, but really I had committed a crime against them. I had blasphemed the family. I had wrecked the family's story, the story my parents had spent their entire adult lives writing. That was the unforgivable part. My mother had seized the chance for a redemption narrative when she sent me to the priest—my chance to play the prodigal!—and I'd blown it for all of them. They held strong. It was simpler—maybe not easier, but simpler—to write me out than to rewrite the whole thing. My sister Alissa got engaged; the Morales stock would soon be replenished. I would be dutifully invited to the wedding, but not to meet the baby born ten months later.

I did not go to that wedding, nor to Nebraska again—I stayed home, which now meant Portland. The next Christmas Eve, a group of us exiled by choice or by force pulled together a party. We called it, for the first time, family dinner. I shouldn't have been surprised by how many of us there were, but I was. Mountains of food, lights strung around the old piano in the living room, a stack of scratchy old soul records taking their turn on the stereo. I had a new girlfriend of six weeks, Flynn, with long hands and ripped jeans that hung low on her hips like a boy's, and we couldn't stop sneaking kisses. Our lust was so potent it would half wake us in the night. We would coo and slip our hands around and re-entwine our limbs and fall back asleep all blissed out. By week three we had said *I love you.*

Bolstered by this new love, the holiday camaraderie, and the spiked cider, I let the forces of habit and propriety override my better judgment, and during dinner I sneaked to the corner of the kitchen with the cordless and my calling card. I dialed home.

My mother wouldn't speak to me. "She and Alissa are busy working on the roast for tomorrow," my dad said. "We sure wish you were here."

A lump in my throat. His voice was gentler than I'd expected. "Me too," I said. "Tell everyone I say merry Christmas. Can I talk to Annabel?"

"We're praying for you, honey. We know you'll come through this."

"Come through what?"

"God can change anything," he said.

"Can I just talk to Annabel?"

He was quiet for a moment. "I don't know if that's a good idea."

"Good-bye, Dad," I said, and hung up.

Topher, whom I'd just met, came into the kitchen to grab a new bottle of whiskey and saw my face.

"Uh-oh," he said. He poured me a double while I

wiped my eyes and tried to breathe without shuddering. "To the orphans," Topher said. We clinked and I tossed back the bitter comfort. I loved him then.

Flynn appeared in the doorway and hurried to my side. "What did you *do*?" I leaned into her, fists curled against my chest. "Baby," she said sternly. "You didn't call your family, did you?"

"I couldn't help it," I said.

She shook her head, wrapped me in her long arms, and nuzzled her nose into my hair. My hand slipped inside her scratchy thrift cardigan and found the warm, soft T-shirt below. "Oh, Andy," she said. "You're my family, you know."

My heart sang. "I am?"

"Yes," she said.

"You're mine," I said, and relief rolled through me like a sob.

"Always," she said.

Always. The extravagance of that word! I sank into it. Always, always, always. And though it later turned false, for the first time I thought I could be okay, and that was enough.

Flynn walked me back into the living room, where Robin was now at the old piano banging out songs from a book of 1980s soft rock sheet music while others belted along. We traded the gifts we'd all brought, white-elephant style, and I ended up with a riding crop that made everyone whistle and hoot, and Flynn shot me a wicked look. It would never leave our closet, but we wouldn't have believed that if you'd told us then. The *always* I believed in could not fail.

In the end we all descended to the basement for a raucous, drunken, dozen-member jam session, and I played the same two barre chords on the guitar over and over, with little skill but with such force and speed my fingers became embers and my ears rang like bells.

Expectations

I couldn't stand it. The night after breakfast with Ryan, I dialed Vivian's phone number in Olympia. I expected to get her answering machine—with my luck, she'd be blocks away in Portland—but she picked up.

"What can I say? The heart wants what the heart wants," she said ruefully.

"Did you really just say that?"

"I'm sorry it turned out this way, Andy. I am. But it's really not about you at all."

"Well, it's obvious you weren't thinking of me," I said. "But what about Flynn? Didn't you know better?"

"What Flynn and I have is completely different," she said gently.

"Which you only know because I told you every-thing!"

I hung up and stomped around the house, burning in my bones. I tried to get Bullet to tug a rope with me but she let go after a few good-natured pulls and looked up at me, tail wagging. I took a few deep gulps from a bottle of astringent white wine that had been open in the fridge for a month. I called Meena. Not home. I called Lawrence. Not home. I called Ryan. He picked up.

"Rematch," I said. "Let's play Scrabble."

"Oh, you're ready to take me on again?"

"Oh yes," I said. "I feel like winning."

"You sound serious."

"Dead."

The streetlights flicked off as I pulled over in front of a grand, disheveled turn-of-the-century apartment house that filled its lot right up to the sidewalk. I was sunk in darkness, only a few lit windows brightening the street. I had not meant to feel furtive but now I did. At the bottom of the porch steps I stopped and looked behind me. I pulled my hood over my head.

The front door was unlocked. The banister was bald-ing, the wood smoothed by touch. Each stair creaked like a question. I answered by putting one foot on the next and then the next. *It's just a* game.

I was used to a maximalist punk-house aesthetic: a palimpsest of every current and previous tenant's taste, with furniture that had lived there longer than any resident. But Ryan's apartment had white walls and little furniture, only hundreds of records and CDs, neatly crated and stacked. In the corner, a guitar leaned against the wall. There was no other word to describe the guitar but *fucked*—the neck was broken and splintered, strings flailing. Ryan offered me a seat on the nubby sofa, a slim, lightly scratched-up Danish modern with great bones. He'd traded it with a friend for a television.

"How the hell did you convince him to do that?" I said, running my palm over a smooth teak arm.

Ryan shrugged. "People love to think they're getting a deal," he said. "To that guy, the television was worth more."

"And you didn't inform him otherwise."

The Scrabble tiles rattled in their bag like wooden coins. "How do you think that shop you work in fills up with all that great stuff?"

"You devil," I said. "I'm going to watch out for you."

"You've got nothing to worry about with me."

"We'll see."

Ryan took his seat across the coffee table and we got serious.

"This time, if you win," he said, "I'll give you a free haircut."

I considered this. I could use one. "What if *you* win?"

"But I won't, right?"

"Not if I can help it."

This time our game was neck and neck. The Scrabble board grew dense with entangled blocks of short words, every letter doing double duty, compacted to the point of unplayability. I sacrificed by stringing out a long cheap word to open things up, and Ryan regretfully yet decisively seized the opportunity to use all his letters. I clawed hard but never caught him again.

"I couldn't have won without your RILING," he said when we'd added up the final points.

"A benevolent move never did anyone any good in Scrabble."

"Your sacrifice is honored."

"No free haircut for me," I mourned, slumping back on the sofa.

"But you get a consolation prize."

"I do?"

"Let me see what I can do."

Ryan disappeared into the bathroom. Behind the door the faucet pulsed on and off. I resisted looking through his records—too obvious—and instead picked up a battered road atlas from the floor. I paged through it—most of the states had highlighter lines tracing routes from city to city—and paused at Nebraska. The town I came from was a tiny black dot. A dot like an atom, teeming inside. I touched my finger to it as Ryan emerged from the bathroom. He came over to me. I looked up from Nebraska, finger still on the dot, as he sat down beside me and pressed his lips to mine. Smooth.

"You shaved? Just now?"

"Out of courtesy. Just in case."

"Wait, are you my consolation prize?"

"If I can bring you consolation, I'm happy to do that."

I was curious, now that I was sober, what it would feel like, so I kissed him. Warm. I liked not wanting it but not *not*-wanting it—a safe feeling, like standing a few feet back from myself. "It's not wrong, is it? It kind of feels wrong."

"To whom?"

I thought about Flynn. I thought about her closing the door behind Vivian. I liked that Ryan had said *whom*.

"I guess I can do whatever I want," I said, and realized it was true. "This can be our secret, right?"

"You really overthink things," he said.

I closed the atlas and dropped it back on the floor.

It's not that I had never done anything with a guy. In middle school and high school, I'd had kisses, crossed a couple bases, though never all the way. In college I'd made out with a gay boy or two. And it's not that I'd never known cock: I had encountered them in many sizes and colors. They were silicone and lived in drawers and under beds. But when my hand grazed the one under Ryan's jeans, I could sense its neediness, its greed. I jerked my hand away.

"You okay?" said Ryan, pausing with his hand just under my shirt.

"Yeah," I said. "Just adjusting." Ryan pushed up my shirt and began to kiss my stomach.

I closed my eyes. His hair fell from behind his ears and brushed against my skin, like a girl's. *Human mouth touches human body.* Species solace. *This is what the species does.* Not mating, only pleasure. It was okay. It was all okay. With my glasses off, the bedroom and the person were blurred, nothing more than shifting forms, warmth on my skin. This was relief, to feel an objective sensation of affection. Not to be turned inside out and upside down, and yet still to feel good. No storming inside, just quiet seas, a clear sky.

"You are so beautiful," he said into my knee. And even though he was a man and I knew I'd never love him, to hear it felt like getting a whole report card of A's when you thought you'd failed out.

"Come on," I said. "I haven't shaved my legs in a decade."

"I like that," he insisted. "I like *you.*"

"I like you too," I said, and I did.

"See?" he said, and I laughed. Ryan was now kissing the inside of my knee, sneaking his way up my leg, even though I had ushered him away from my underwear twice.

The sex would have been easy; it seemed so uncomplicated in its mechanics. But I knew too well what it was like to be on his end with a girl, the power in it. I'd been there. I'd also given myself up with pleasure, many times, but I didn't want to for a man. It was too personal.

I drew my limbs in and said, "I can't. I can't."

Ryan looked up at me. His hair fell into his eyes. "You sure?" He bit my inner thigh above the knee and I felt a disarming surge but said, "Yes." I liked bumping up against my limit, feeling it firm and solid as a fence.

"Think about it," he said. "It's so fun."

"I bet it is."

"How would you know unless you try it?"

"I'm not bi-curious," I said.

"But maybe you're me-curious. Or why did you come over here?"

"Scrabble," I said. He batted my leg and I laughed. "I like a challenge!"

"So do I."

"Well then," I said. "Good luck."

Ryan sighed and crawled up next to me. We lay on our backs in our underwear and socks. I rested one hand on my bare stomach. He slid his hand into the other one and held it. My webbing stretched. His arm was much longer than mine. His whole body was much longer. Everything seemed of crazy proportions.

"I have to ask you something," I said. "What happened to that guitar out there?"

He sighed. "I got angry and smashed it. Sometimes I do that to things. Just objects."

"And you got angry with the guitar?"

"No. I loved that guitar. I'd had it forever." He put a hand over his eyes.

I felt a spike of concern—poor Ryan, his favorite guitar irreparably wrecked. Then the thought corrected: by *him*. Unnerving. I squeezed his hand and disentangled myself.

Rummaging around in the dark for my discarded clothes, I attempted a light tone. "We can never speak of this to anyone. Especially Flynn."

"She might come after me with her blowtorch," said Ryan. "So would my ex-girlfriend."

"Flynn of all people would have no right to," I said, pulling my T-shirt over my head, "but you might be right. Who's your ex? Recent?"

"Extremely," he said. "Let's not ruin a good night by discussing her."

"Was I wearing a bra?"

"I don't think so."

"I hope you're right," I said. "I only own one."

"You'll just have to come back and get it later." He sat up on the edge of the bed and handed me my glasses. I put them on and the room solidified into focus. There was Ryan, half-lit by streetlights through the window, smiling up at me.

"I think this has to be a one-time venture," I said. "I can't get into something complicated."

"But you *can* do something *un*complicated."

"Yes," I said. "Like go home now." I put a hand on his face for a moment—warm, still smooth, just the

faintest hint of sandpaper by his jaw—and felt an unexpected twinge. He could like me all he wanted and
it wouldn't make any difference. I knew what that felt
like. "Trust me, this isn't worth the trouble it would
cause."

"Come on," he said. "*You're* trouble. And you like it."

"Maybe I am." The thought pleased me.

"Maybe *I* am."

"I'm sure you are."

At the door he grabbed my sleeve. "Andrea," he
said. "I'm leaving tomorrow. What's your address?"

I fished a card for the studio out of my wallet, let-
terpressed brown cardstock.

The dark houses and quiet street were like a movie
set of a neighborhood, empty. The only sound was my
engine rumbling to life as I backed out and drove away,
back to the house where eagle-eyed Summer was mercifully still at work, where the dog would be the only
one who knew I'd ever been gone. Animals never tell.

My Type

The first time I saw actual type made of wood and lead, I fell in love. I picked up a plain, heavy Helvetica O and the weight of its curve, the purity of its shape, made me dreamy. I loved that letters were *things* you could hold in your hand. I went to the art department's basement letterpress room every day that semester, earned my own set of keys, and stayed late into the night setting type, plucking the letters like tiny statues from their compartments and lining them up in order. I slid the leading under their feet and over their heads and built the city of letters that became words that became real things. Computer text needed only eyeballs and fingertips. With the letterpress, you walked alongside it, turned the crank with your arms and hands, your shoulders flexing; your whole body brought it to life. I could fall into it for hours, forsaking all other schoolwork. Then I came back from that Christmas in Nebraska, and I had to turn in my keys.

But a few of us soon discovered that a lot of old letterpresses were hanging around in corners of the Northwest, and most people didn't think the hulking things were worth wanting or asking much money for. Lead ships. Dead stock. Dead ends, like us queers— and yet here we were, more of us than ever, multiplying by convergence and setting up shop in the business of reproduction. Obsolescence was our saving grace.

Four of us formed a small collective, scavenged buckets of heavy lead type, and went in on a space, cheap because it was mostly illegal, down in the industrial part of Southeast, close to the river. Bridges sloped overhead. Old train tracks cut through the asphalt, and cobblestones showed through the worn patches. We set up our print studio in a former warehouse with high windows, big jails of light that slid across the floor. Two Vandercook letterpresses and a few garage-saled table-top presses and a screen-printing station. The smell of ink, thick paper, sweet oil on old steel.

We all wanted to make art—prints, broadsides, show posters, record sleeves, chapbook covers—and swiftly learned that art paid few bills. But weddings did. Future brides and grooms were the reliable few who found letterpress timeless instead of time-consuming.

I turned out invitations and save-the-dates in scores, each one customized and as special as the bride and groom themselves, yet pretty much exactly the same. If these people put a year and as much effort into art as they did into their own weddings, they could have made feature films and finished novels.

But I needed the money and was glad for the work.

The one I was working on today would be held in a renovated barn in an orchard, fixed up and rented out for urban people who loved the idea of the country. I could hear my mother: "Married in a *barn*? Where's the reception, a feedlot?" But I could see it. In Nebraska I stepped into an octagonal barn once, empty and tall with light slanting in through high windows, and it was a kind of cathedral.

I had hand-drawn the barn for this invitation and had it digitally transferred to a plate, and while I was running proofs I imagined myself into my own tiny line drawing. I remembered the barns at my grandmother's house where my siblings and I used to play. The big corrugated metal one that housed the John Deeres and the combine and echoed your voice; the old wooden one where cows once lived but later only an extended family of skeptical cats. A pang of homesickness hit me. It didn't happen often but when it did it hit hard, dug deep. That smell of old decades. I even missed the ones I hadn't been alive for.

When I got home I went looking for the photos.

But my *Childhood Part I* album was nowhere to be found in my archives. In fact, the entire box of photo albums was neither shelved nor in the stack of things I had yet to unpack. The absence of it swelled. The box contained my whole childhood, the part where my grandparents were still alive and my parents still loved me and we were a family of six. I didn't want to look through it but I wanted to know I still had it. I pictured mice nibbling at the corners of the box.

"Fuck," I said, and called Flynn at home. Ex-home.

"It's in the attic," Flynn confirmed. "I'll be around until six."

Then where? I didn't ask.

The wisteria vines on the porch were shooting long green tendrils everywhere. "You should cut those back," I said when Flynn opened the door.

She shrugged. "I know. Hello."

"Hi." It was strange to get so basic, no nicknames or *baby*s. "Is anyone else here?"

"No."

I lowered my eyes and walked inside.

The tiny house had absorbed my absence and regenerated disappointingly fine. A vintage lamp there, an armchair moved here, the gaps in the bookshelves filled, a couple of unfamiliar objects on the mantel. I tried not to look for the evidence of another aesthetic at work. The place still smelled potently the same, like home.

"Do you want some coffee?" Flynn said. "I brought home some of this new single-origin we just got in from Guatemala. Really good stuff." Coffee was both science and religion to Flynn.

"I'm good. It's almost five. I don't want to be up all night."

"I can bag some up for you to have in the morning." What was with the charm? Guilt or reflex?

"It's okay, Flynn. I just want the photos."

I pulled down the attic trapdoor and unfolded the staircase. I paused halfway up, head and shoulders afloat in the dusty attic and the rest of me weighted below in the hallway. To my eyes, a floor; to my feet, a ceiling. The box was behind an unused ottoman toward the back. I crawled to it like a thief and extracted the last of my past from the house.

"Got it?" Flynn said, standing at the base of the steps. "That looks heavy."

"It's okay. I can handle it." On the day I moved out, I had made Flynn leave the premises. There was only so much assistance I could take.

"I found this of yours too. It was in the dishwasher." Flynn held out a mug that read ERRORS WILL BE MADE. OTHERS WILL BE BLAMED. I had taken it from a temp job at a financial office.

"You can keep it," I said, sidling past her into the living room. "I hate passive voice."

"Isn't that the whole joke?"

"It's not worth it."

Flynn dropped the hand holding the mug to her side. I felt like a jerk.

"You should contribute something to this group show we're putting together," I suggested, conciliatory.

"Already on it. Kate told me about it."

"Oh. *Kate.*" A light sting. I had known her first. "Good." *Please don't put in any photos of Vivian,* I thought, but I couldn't bear to say it—as if verbalizing it would give her the idea. Flynn was The Photographer among us. It got her into shows and it got her into beds. By now, at age thirty, she had an impressive body of work on both counts. Flynn had photographed me in the woods, on the street, at the coast, in fields, in bed, close up, far off, in black and white, in color—so prolifically that her record of me felt permanent. I had been in her shows. I was a whole series. I was one in a series.

"I'll let you know if I find anything else," she said.

"No," I said. Flynn looked quizzical. And the dreaded tears began to line my eyes. "I don't think I can come back here. Not just for five minutes."

"I want us to be friends," Flynn said. "I really do."

"I'm not clear on what that word means anymore." I thought, *If we were "friends" you would have sex with me.* "Maybe Vivian can tell me. She seems to have a new definition."

"Oh, Andy." Flynn tilted her head, brown eyes warm. Her hair was damp from the shower, peroxided forelock falling into her eyes. She reached a platonic hand toward me, my arms wrapped around the box of photos. "We didn't mean to—"

"Stop, I don't want to hear any more *we*." I shied away from the hand and wiped my teary eyes off on my own shoulder. "Sorry to be a baby. I should get going. I don't want to keep you." Flynn was dressed to go somewhere: jeans and boots and belt, a form-fitting T-shirt. Her chest looked muscular—no, flattened. I did a double take.

"Are you binding now?" I asked.

Flynn glanced down. "Uh, yeah. I'm trying it out." She looked up at me, a nervous certainty in her eyes, not far from the look that first time she paused by my table at the coffee shop and asked if she could call me sometime.

"It suits you," I said. It was true. Flynn was a beautiful boy—those big wrists, that saunter.

"It feels right."

Maybe Flynn at thirty was still becoming, I realized. Maybe the Flynn I loved was on the way out. Or maybe the Flynn I loved hadn't been around for some time now. It was easy to mistake proximity for closeness.

Pride

At the studio, a postcard hid beneath a pile of invoices and flyers in the mailbox. The image on the front was of a beach at night with a dubiously superimposed smear of greenish light hovering in the sky. I turned it over. The edges were yellowed and bent. The handwriting was fast but neat, sharp edges, no loops.

JUNE 8

Dear Andrea Morales,

Sipping a "moonshake" here in Florence, OR, a favorite flyover spot for UFOs, per our atomic waitress. Mateo insisted on a detour. He's a closet ufologist (← apparently a real word). I'm skeptical but holding my tongue. Who am I to say what's real? Maybe I've got my own version of lights on the horizon.

OK, back to the road—

—R. Coates

The caption on the postcard read, *JULY 1981—Five different people reported an unidentified object moving across the water near the dunes of Florence, OR.*

I read it twice. I turned it over and examined that smear of light. Along its curve was a suggestion of windows. I tried to imagine what those passengers saw, to look at the familiar coast with alien eyes. Would they find it beautiful or terrifying? Did they ever disembark, or merely cruise overhead, gazing down, like tourists on a double-decker bus? I supposed they risked death if they stepped outside. But otherwise they'd never know how cold the water was, how soft the sand, the long whiskers of dune grass brushing their legs.

The postcard was futuristic and already hopelessly past. I wanted to tell those people standing on the beach of Florence, The future isn't this. It's less alien and way weirder than you think.

I came home to a note from Summer: MEENA & I ARE AT HOLMAN'S W/ MARCY. COME!

I was intrigued. Marcy Barnes was our equivalent of a village elder or an ex-president; she'd played minor and major parts in several legendary Northwest bands, and she fixed amps out of her garage in Northeast, tucked under the bungalow she'd bought for, like, twenty grand in the eighties. She had a knack for dating girls before they went on to minor fame: the performance artist, the songwriter, the one who got a story published in the *New Yorker.*

Holman's was an ancient family-run bar with dark wooden booths and breaded mushrooms on the menu, the kind of old dive that young people took to—something about the sense of permanence, trendproofness, the scenic weathered elders at the bar for authenticity, a place that promised little but offered it reliably. The three of them had a booth in the corner and a pitcher of beer already under way. Summer was gazing raptly at Marcy as she told a story about Dead Moon. I slipped in beside Meena and listened. Marcy was old to us—thirty-nine—but she was a punk too, only the lines were deeper in her face and she had more stories. She wore her hair long the way a guy wore it long, and she wore men's jeans that rode low on her hips and motorcycle boots. Thirty-nine, I thought. When my mom was thirty-nine, I was sixteen. My mother and Marcy were two entirely different species. All the women of Westerly, Nebraska, were, by that age, of a gender unto itself. They wore their hair practical. Dressed medium. By choice or default, their lives cycled around the school day and the working week and the national holiday. They bought milk in plastic gallon jugs and baked bars. Television commercials for food and household products targeted them. They were consumers, savers, caretakers, voters. Marcy was a bass player, a smoker, a lover, no one's parent, no one's partner. She was a whole other possibility. She was a protagonist. She was wise and not wise. She had just kept on living, as herself.

When the waitress came over for me, Summer ordered deep-fried macaroni-and-cheese wedges.

"How's your veganism?" Meena said.

"Oops. I'm lapsing."

"That was quick."

"When these are gone I'll be vegan again."

"We'll pretend it never happened," I said, and splurged on a whiskey ginger. Beer was cheap but I was tired of cheap. I figured I'd get a two-buck grilled cheese so I could blow an extra couple of dollars on a whiskey ginger. This was how I was always thinking then, one dollar to the next. I would never entirely shake it.

We drank and talked. They tried to think of people for me to date. It reminded me of high school, scouring the rolls of the Technically Eligible, the surest way to kill any interest. I was not about to mention Ryan, especially not in front of Marcy, our elder statesman. *I'm lapsing?* No way. Not after all I'd gone through to get here.

Marcy's hand dropped to her lap, I saw her arm shift slightly, and Summer smiled. Summer's hair swished against Marcy's arm as she leaned over to grab the ketchup, and Marcy, though she was nodding at something Meena was saying, gave a little twitch of pleasure.

And I felt jealous. It wasn't that I wanted Marcy, although suddenly she seemed newly viable—why hadn't I thought of her before?—but that desire would have been brief, a cul-de-sac, and I knew it. I just wanted the feeling. I wanted the longing, the promise. That feeling of imminence. A very near future.

I could feel the postcard tucked in my jacket, flattening the pocket. The flying saucer, a glimpsed anomaly, like Ryan's bedroom. I ran my fingers along the lower edge of the card. Then I panicked and returned to earth.

They were talking about the Gold Stars. Marcy was releasing their new record on her label, Queue Up. Meena wanted us all to be in the photo shoot they'd conceived for the cover.

"Who's taking the pictures," I warned.

Meena put up her hands. "It wasn't me," she said. "Dana had already asked Flynn."

"Oh man." I slumped back. "There's no escape."

"You guys friends?" Marcy asked.

"That's the official line. Doesn't feel like it, though."

Meena squeezed my shoulder. "You will be."

"I don't know," I said. "Why does it always have to go like this, that the one who cheated or lied ends up fine, even a girl magnet, and the other, the one who did nothing wrong, is scrap?"

"Another whiskey ginger here," Meena called to the waitress. It materialized on the table with a cool soothing clunk. I grasped the plastic straw like a lifeline.

"Baby," Marcy said, "if no one ever slept with any of their friends' exes, we would all have to be nuns."

"So put me in a convent," I said.

"Those places are full of lesbians," Meena said.

"No escape," Summer said happily.

"Whee."

"In two days it's Pride, and there are seven zillion lesbians in Portland," Meena said.

"You'll be fine," Marcy said.

It sure would be easier if one of them would show up soon before I did another stupid thing with a man, I thought. This was what the brink looked like. "Of course I'll be fine." I straightened up. "I am fine."

My method had always been to put on a good face.

I had gone to house parties and queer nights the way I'd once gone to church, with neither faith nor hope. I'd shown my face, smiled, chatted a little, and escaped home.

"You can tell us how you really feel, Andy. We're your friends."

"I know," I said. "You're the best. I do tell you. I will." I looked down into my drink, the ice cubes softening, disappearing. Fine was the loneliest place a person could be.

Pride weekend arrived, metastasizing rainbows, as commercialized, tacky, and fraught as any holiday. The gay Christmas. We all claimed to hate it and we all went anyway. Clearly there were gays out there who had no ambivalence about Pride or it wouldn't exist, but we didn't know any. Pride was a reminder that our numbers were greater than we knew, and of the strength therein, etc.; also, that queer people could be as unoriginal and exasperating as any people. We fought for our humanity to be recognized, and indeed, there it was, unflattering shorts and all.

Saturday evening I biked downtown to the Dyke March with a posse of friends, a girl gang in fingerless gloves and cut-off jeans, shouting and laughing over our shoulders to each other as we pedaled. I still had not told any of them about my man-dalliance, but the attention and tension had charged me up like a battery and I felt a nervy glow. Holes of blue opened in the gray sky, and up ahead of us the South Park Blocks were teeming with hundreds of lesbians and all the satellite categories thereof.

The march itself was a jostling stroll to the waterfront. I was never a sign-waver, and chanting embarrassed me, but to be in an apparent, if illusory, majority, even for just ten blocks—every time I did it, I felt a concurrent hunger and sating of the hunger.

The chain-link fence, our end point, appeared before us. Behind it was the official Pride Zone: rainbow vinyl banners, tents, merchandise, a bad band, a cover charge. The gay cage. Our crew turned tail and headed to our bikes to cross back to the east side.

If anything felt like liberation, it was dancing all night together in a makeshift club all our own. Someone had taken over an old brick boathouse by the river and decked it out with Christmas lights and old couches, a plywood bar that served only beer and wobbly vegan Jell-O shots. No license, no name, illegal and perfect. We drank up, loosened up, and got down to the music, the more people the better—when everyone dances no one looks stupid. We shed our self-consciousness and our layers as the temperature rose. Summer tried to keep her work and her life separate but in the dance circle she broke into moves that impressed and alarmed me. I didn't know someone's legs could bend that way. As the crowd grew denser and even Lawrence wriggled into the dancing mass, I unhooked my sweat-soaked bra under my T-shirt and tugged it out my sleeve like a magic trick to the whoops of my friends. Our hair stuck to our cheeks, our lungs expanded, we made funny moves to entertain each other, the dance circle expanded and closed again, a pulse like a heart. Everyone gleamed, cinematically gorgeous to me under the strings of lights, and a lump rose in my throat. I had no safety net, no savings, no insurance, no future, but I did have this: this room, this feeling, these people. The world's best secret.

Summer threw her arm around my neck and shouted over the music about how she hadn't been so sure about me when I moved in, this friend of a friend laden with boxes and breakup shell shock, but now I was the best housemate she'd ever had. "I love you, Andy!"

"I love you too!" I shouted back. "We're in, like, an arranged marriage!"

"And it totally works!"

"I'm going to buy my wife a drink!" I yelled. "What do you want?" And I danced my way out of the teeming crowd.

At the bar stood a girl I vaguely knew in a T-shirt with the sleeves cut off, motorcycle boots, and a tattoo of her grandmother's face on her bicep. Her hair was cropped short but a soft dark comma curled into her nape. She offered me a sip from her flask, a smoky scotch that softened my mouth, and emboldened, I leaned into her and cupped my hand around her ear and said I thought we needed to make out now.

Up against the wall, my wrists bound with one strong hand behind my back while her other traced my waistband, I tasted the scotch in her mouth, felt her belt buckle press into me, and was giddy with relief. Here was the life I knew. The me I knew.

A second old postcard arrived at the studio mailbox that Monday. For once I was relieved that my studio-mates never bothered to sort the mail.

This one was a color photo from the late sixties or early seventies. On a road through deep dark redwoods, three bears stood upright with their paws resting on the hood of a plump baby-blue convertible. A handsome man in a sweater stood in the front seat, elbows resting on the windshield's rim, scratching his beard, while a young windblown woman perched on the rim of the trunk, leaning back, smiling uncertainly.

JUNE 11

Hello again,

Back in the state where I spent seven weird years of my youth. It was sort of like this picture: perilous or hilarious? Could never tell. Both and neither.

Hope these notes are OK. Tour is nothing but time. Endless transit with momentary touchdowns. (Like a UFO?) Our SF show was awesome—and now I feel lame for writing that. I'm not trying to impress you. Not that way. I would scrap this and start over but the picture's too good to let go. Just look at that side. Over & out,

—R.C.

I did miss getting mail like this: handwritten, real. The zines and pen pals that filled my box through the nineties had tapered off, and what arrived now was mostly bills and the occasional dutiful holiday missive from Nebraska. A birthday card with a twenty-dollar bill in it; a Christmas card about the real reason for the season and a folded form letter in which *Andrea continues to live and work in Portland, Oregon.*

The postcard went into my top desk drawer, next to the UFO one. They were tucked out of sight, but I liked knowing they were there.

Emboldened now, I grew determined to shake both the curse of Flynn and any lingering hetero residue from Ryan. I called the girl in the motorcycle boots.

She took me to the nickel arcade on Belmont. We shot down sea monsters and played air hockey and pinball, and though the talk between games was stilted, I secretly hoped people would spot us, and take note: Andrea's *back*.

After we'd converted an armful of Skee-Ball prize tickets into candy and matching skull key chains, we made out in the front seat of her pickup. She had cheekbones that could spread butter, and a lush chest subdued by two sports bras and a tight white undershirt. Her kissing was assertive and slow paced, like it knew where it was going and would get there when it felt like it, and I was feeling pretty optimistic about the whole thing, getting melty and hot, until she rested her hand on my jaw and said, "So. Here's my deal."

For the next forty minutes we had to talk about nonmonogamy. Nonmonogamists are like evangelicals, or new vegetarians, convinced they're onto a truth that everyone needs to know. I sighed. "Did you read *The Ethical Slut?*"

She said, "Isn't it great?"

I didn't care if I was her one and only, but I realized that if we kept going, it would always be like this, a 4:1 ratio of processing to action. I pocketed my skull key chain and left the candy in her truck.

Three days later I was printing proofs of the barn wedding invitation for the third time—miss Gemini bride wanted to try blue, no, silver, no, purple text—when the mail landed in the box with a promising muffled thunk. "I got it," I said quickly, wiping my hands on my apron.

And there was a third postcard, wedged between a font catalog and the utility bill.

One of my coworkers, Tiger, looked up from the studio's computer screen. "What are you laughing at over there?"

"Nothing."

"Come on, let me see."

"It's just this," I said. She came over to look. The picture presented a formal side view of a suited, mustachioed gentleman seated astride an ostrich. His back was upright, his legs stuck straight forward, and he clutched tightly at the feathers at the base of the bird's long neck. On the dusty ground nearby lay a melon-sized egg. A line of pink type slanted woozily across the top: *At the Cawston Ostrich Farm, Southern California.* The ostrich's pale, muscular thigh looked human.

"That's rad," Tiger said. "Who's it from?" She flipped it over.

I pulled it out of her fingers. "Just a friend. From out of town. Here." I handed her a catalog. "This has your name on it." I walked out of range and turned over the card. The handwriting shrank as it went, until it was so tiny it looked like embroidery.

6/14

Hello A.M.,

How are you? I wonder what you're printing over there. If you have ink on your fingers. In LA a B-list celebrity came to our show, a TV actor I never heard of and already forgot. That was called failed name-dropping. San Diego: moderate, in every way. I like CA but it makes me sad. It feels ruined. Like bad plastic surgery where you can still tell what used to look good. It's a state full of promises it can never keep, but it can't stop making them—a pathological liar that believes everything it says. All those backyard pools in the desert.

On a brighter note: picked lemons right off the tree. And we passed a street called Morales. It looked nice. —R

The next one, already the following day, had a photograph of a desert motel with a splendid atomic sign that read SKY RANCH MOTEL, replete with moon and stars.

6.15.98

&rea—

Hello and how are you? I wonder if you're getting these. Maybe you're shaking your head every time one arrives. I'm going with the principle that everyone likes to get a postcard. Now we're in Arizona. I lived here too as a kid. Our apt. was whatever but I loved the desert behind the complex. The lizards learned to run when they saw me coming. Once I saw javelinas. For some reason I want to tell you these things. I wonder what you had in Nebraska? Make me a list, I want to know it all. —Ry&

I thought of the sound of the chicken coop. I'd sit out there and listen to their cooing and burbling in the evening as I closed it up. No javelinas, but deer all over, and foxes and pheasants. Maybe ghost bison. I tacked this one up above my workspace—I wanted to pilfer that font—and waited for the next one to arrive.

But no more postcards came, only invoices and catalogs and paper samples. I found myself disappointed. Why had he stopped? Had he tired of sending one-way correspondence? Had he met someone on the road? I deflated a little. Then I grew annoyed—at Ryan for his doggedness, then for his disappearance, then at myself for caring at all.

Artifacts

On the first day of real summer, I did not even bother to detour to check the mail at the studio before pedaling over the river to Artifacts.

Ted found most of his stuff at estate sales and auctions, though his official statement—people always asked—was that the midcentury elves had left it at the door. Still, people came in all the time trying to sell us their stuff. They'd been watching *Antiques Roadshow.* They'd found something in the Dumpster or garage, in their mother's basement, or in someone's jewelry box. They needed cash and were certain, or hopeful, that what they held was worth something. Usually it wasn't. People, Ted said, always overvalue their own stuff. On gray days I was prone to a sense of doom that this was true of ninety-nine percent of the things in this world—in the end, nobody really wanted them.

The customer who jangled into the shop this afternoon was in her early forties, a little grizzled, testy. I was used to her type: they tried appealing to me woman to woman, but when I said it wasn't my call and they'd have to talk to the owner, I became just another female obstacle between them and a man who could do something.

I glanced into her box of marbles and milk glass and told her it wasn't the kind of thing we sold. When she feigned offense, I reminded her gently, "You didn't want them either."

"It's not that I didn't want them."

"Then why are you selling them?"

She said that she wanted them to find a good home. I suggested Goodwill.

The door jingled and in the corner of my eye I saw the customer stop to take in the space. In the moment before his eyes met mine and I realized who he was, I automatically indexed him: *Man, young, thinks he's cool, will drop knowledge but no cash. Brace self.* But then I saw it was Ryan. He paused with one hand in his jacket pocket and the other resting on the doorknob, a stance like his handwriting, upright yet at ease.

"Hi," I said, and broke into a grin I couldn't suppress. "You're real."

He pulled back his jacket sleeve and touched his wrist. "Apparently."

"Thanks for the postcards." The customer cleared her throat. "Hang on," I said to Ryan, "I'm almost done here."

"Is that so," said the woman.

I advised her that speaking to Ted was possible but likely futile. "Try Antique Row in Sellwood. One of those guys might be more into it." Her sour frown indicated that she had, and they weren't. She threatened to speak to my manager.

"Okay," I said. "He'll be here tomorrow."

Ryan stepped aside for her at the door.

"Charming lady," he said.

"Happens all the time," I said. "I'm due for a break." I taped the BACK IN 10 MINUTES sign to the door and grabbed the keys. "Want to step out with me? I mean, unless you came in looking for something."

"Just you."

I knew I shouldn't enjoy that, and this could only flag trouble, this guy showing up for me, but after a year of being the yearning one, it felt good to be sought. We pushed through into the sunny afternoon.

"So how are you?" he said.

"Good. How are you?"

"Good."

"Good," I said. It was like we were in an ESL class.

We walked down the alley and over to First Avenue, where tram tracks sliced through the cobblestones and the buildings were old and rococo with arched windows. Across a strip of trampled grass, the river sauntered along.

"So how was tour?" I nudged him with my elbow, went for the buddy approach. "Did you get any action on the road?" This was how many of my friendships had begun, with what my friend Molly called the Sexual Handshake. If there was sexual tension at the outset, you hooked up a couple times to release it, and once that was cleared out of the way you could get right to being straight-up friends. It might be a viable option here.

"What kind of a question is that?"

"You're in a band. And you're cute. I can say that objectively."

"Objectively, huh?"

"Sure. You have symmetrical features, and you're tall. Good smile."

"Is this a dog show? Are you going to measure my tail next?"

"Nice tail too."

"Yeah? You like?"

"Objectively," I said.

He tugged the back of his shirt down and I laughed. He said, "I wasn't really on the prowl."

"Not on my account, I hope."

"You're not going to make this easy for me, are you?"

"I'm not trying to make it anything for you." I knew I was being glib to the point of cutting, but I couldn't stop. My hand had shaken when I'd turned the key in the lock at Artifacts. I had to overcorrect.

Ryan sighed and slung himself down on a bench. "All right," he said. "Well, when I was in Tucson I found something for you." He reached into his jacket pocket. "It's not wrapped, so close your eyes."

I did, and held out my hand.

Smooth wood, warm from his pocket, touched my palm. I closed my fingers around a solid edge and opened my eyes.

It was a wood-type A for letterpress, the size of a small candy bar. I ran my fingers over it. The wood was nut-brown with age, and traces of red and black ink burrowed in its nooks. The A was raised and hard, clean, with a skateably smooth surface.

"Two of my nerdy favorite things in one," I said. "A piece of type and an A."

"Do you have an A already? You probably have a lot of A's. You probably have a whole alphabet."

"I have many alphabets. But I don't have one like this. I love it. Thank you." I sat down next to him. A small hard knot tied up my throat. I slipped the wood-block A into the pocket of my jacket and kept my hand on it, on the hard edges worn smooth.

"I'm sorry," I said. "I can be flippant."

"I know," he said.

"I just don't want to lead you on."

He laughed in disbelief. "Oh, is *that* what you think you're doing?"

"I hope not. Look, I don't want to mislead you or hurt you."

Ryan physically recoiled. The force in his voice surprised me. "*That* is not going to happen. I don't get hurt like that. I'm not a commitment guy."

"Good, because I'm not a commitment guy either," I said.

"Great." Our eyes were locked now, a game of chicken. We held our ground, radiating *I mean it,* each waiting for the other to look away, to acquiesce, *You mean it.* But the longer I looked the weirder it got. To look into someone's eyes, even in the spirit of combat, is to hold their gaze, an act of holding, beholding. I worked to keep my breath even, my face nonchalant. I would not relent.

Ryan narrowed his eyes and glanced ever so slightly to the side for a second, just a flicker, but I took that as a win for me. "Don't get me wrong," he said. "I'm glad to see your face."

"Okay," I said. "I'm glad to see yours too."

"Okay."

Our smiles both cracked and we looked away.

He asked me what I was up to that night. My pulse quickened uncomfortably and I invented a plan with Lawrence. I stood. My break was over. "Anyway, don't you need to unpack?" I said. We started walking.

No, he traveled light. He liked to come home with less than he'd left with. "By the end of a month you've worn those clothes so much you never want to see them again. I just leave them."

This astonished me. I had lain awake many nights cataloging everything I'd ever lost or failed to save. "Don't you miss any of it later?"

"No."

"I can't do that at all. I save everything."

"You're a pack rat."

"An *archivist*. I have a system. It's all filed and in order."

"Why do you keep all that?"

I said I liked having evidence. Evidence of what, he asked. "My life, I guess."

"Aren't you evidence enough? You've got a memory."

"But that's so ephemeral. The artifacts are proof."

"Who are you proving it to?"

I thought of the box of Nebraska photos, the volumes of albums of Portland, the library of zines, the drawers of band T-shirts from shows, the files of letters and ticket stubs and drafts of everything I had drawn or written over the last seven years. I wondered if my parents had kept anything of mine, if they'd boxed it up or tossed it. If they ever spoke of me, or if I had become that unfortunate event no one ever brings up, out of courtesy. "I don't know what I'm going to remember and what I'm going to forget. I don't know who will remember me and who will forget me," I said. "What if you died tomorrow and you left, like, no trace of your life? It would be like you never existed."

"Sounds good to me," he said. "Less trouble for whoever has to clean out my place."

"I want to make lots of trouble," I said. "I want them to be overwhelmed by it. Especially if it's my parents."

"Impressive," he said. "Hopefully you survive your parents."

"I have so far."

We arrived at the door. "Have a good time tonight," he said, and then sneaked a quick kiss to my cheek before I knew what was happening.

"Thank you for the A," I said, flustered. I let the glass door sigh shut behind me, and touched my cheek.

I rifled through the box of stuff on the counter. I couldn't tell what any of it was worth.

Biking home, I crossed the river with the setting sun at my back. The sky was streaked with pink and purple clouds behind me, and deepened to blue ahead. Yellow streetlights lit the leaves a luminous emerald.

I cycled up Sandy Boulevard, glanced furtively down the intersection toward Ryan's apartment only a few blocks away, lowered my head, and pushed up the hill, forward. But then I stopped and changed course. I turned off Sandy and glided down toward Ash, letting gravity carry me to his front door.

The buzzer, the wait, the wondering, and then footsteps coming downstairs, and Ryan turns the corner on the landing, leans forward to see the door, a quicker trot down the last few steps, a hand on the doorknob, in the entry I mount the first step and turn, take his rough face in both hands, and close my eyes.

Cutting Off

I woke just before seven. My heartbeat picked up at the sight of the dark sheets, the white walls, the thin unfamiliar light. Ryan slept soundly beside me, hair rumpled and dark gold on the pillow. When I touched his arm he made a contented *mm*, sprawled, and yawned, like a lion who'd gotten the whole antelope.

He barely moved when I slipped out of bed. "Bye," I whispered. He tried to wake. I said, "No, sleep. It's early. I'll talk to you later."

The contact lenses I'd slept in were foggy and sticky. I yawned and yawned to bring tears to my eyes, trying to clear them. I jammed the springy crest of my cowlick under my helmet and on the ride home recited my way through the whole situation. I told myself all about it so I wouldn't need to tell anyone else. I asked myself, *What was it like?* and I answered, *Like sex.* Some structural adjustments, textural differences. A brief stripe of unexpected pain and then I un-tensed and let it happen, my body and this other body slamming gently into one another. Have you done this before? he murmured, and I said, Shh. I closed my eyes and imagined a harness and a girl behind it, but this patch of fur around his navel kept rubbing against me, animal-like. I opened my eyes and turned into a person performing the act of being a woman having sex. A sense of observing even as I was doing. I did what women did in movies. I claimed pleasures and made moves as if I were deftly working my own control panel: try this, say this, good, it's working. And just as I was thinking, *This is so . . . simple,* unsure if that was a nice thing or a boring thing, it was over.

I asked myself, *Would you do it again?* And I answered, *No, definitely not, that was a one-time thing,* and I asked myself, *Really?* and answered, *I doubt it. I don't know. Who knows.* And I asked myself, *Do I have to call him later? Well, you'd have to be an asshole not to at least call. But,* I said, *isn't it this notorious thing about men that they don't call? That they just do it and forget it? So why can't I?* And I answered, *Since when did you get all essentialist?*

The more pressing question was, *What the hell are you going to tell Summer when she asks where you were?*

Extraordinary luck. There was no one home to answer to, except the dog, who was frantic with happiness and hunger. Summer too must have spent the night elsewhere and assumed I was home. I fed Bullet and trudged to my bedroom to strip off my Ryan-smelling clothes. My room was a mess. Yesterday in a fit of archival fever I had emptied the box of photos from Flynn's, along with another one of letters and end-of-move miscellany, but I had managed to organize and shelve only a fraction of it before I left for Artifacts. The bed, the floor, the stereo, the chair: every outside was covered with insides.

The volume overwhelmed me, in this bedroom now and the one I had left at dawn. I had no more answers for myself. What did he want with me? And why had I succumbed? Was I now a head he could mount on his wall? What a trophy, a Real Lesbian; what evidence of virility; what a terrible straight-male misconception come true. What I had done was a disservice to all lesbians.

I pulled off my clothes and took a good look at my body in the mirror behind the door: Did it look different? Could you tell? It didn't, from what I could see—it was its usual skinny-limbed, soft-bellied self. No new marks or scratches; the sex had been tame. My hair had gone wildly awry, though, sideways and up, plastered to one side and fleeing the other. Somewhere since my last haircut, whenever that was, it had crossed the line from artfully disheveled to shaggy bordering on mommish.

I pulled it back into a stubby ponytail at my nape. Several strands sprang immediately loose, and one insistently caught in my eyelashes. I snatched a pair of scissors from my desk and snipped the offending tip. The hair recoiled. I gave up and pulled out the ponytail.

Now my hair looked lopsided, so I snipped at the other side. Then the other. *This is when you should really wet your hair before proceeding,* I thought, but I couldn't resist making one more tiny cut, and then another. I neatened one side, then the other, then the bangs; then I took to the back and cut it close, sliding my fingers in and cutting it knuckle-short. The weight started to lift away, thick tufts falling to the floor.

Suddenly there was not much more hair to cut. The thrill abated. I set down the scissors.

This haircut was either bold and badass or plain bad. In the shower, I held out hope for a sort of andro/punk thing and the chance that once washed, it would assume its true shape.

Its true shape: the deforested landscape of a clear-cut, littered with stumps and brush. I did not look tough or cool. I did not look like a boy, or even a butch. I looked like a womyn who had earnestly forsaken hotness for political reasons. I looked like a brand-new baby dyke with no aesthetic resources. I looked like a cliché, poorly rendered.

The scissors went back into the desk—best to step away before I made things any worse. I flattened the miserable haircut under my bike helmet and headed down to the studio.

I was the only one there at that hour and the room felt cold and pale and serene. I set about dismantling a full page of lead type and returning the letters to their tray, a blessedly mindless and meticulous process. Thinking could be my worst enemy. I needed not to think, just to *do*.

Then again, I could hear the voice of the Lesbian Mafia in my head: *Doing without thinking is exactly your problem.*

I tied up the type of a show poster I'd been working on and brought it over to a Vandercook to run a proof. As I turned the quoin key and tightened the type into an impenetrable block on the press bed, the poster in reverse looked up at me, unreadable. In the mirror I too was always backward: the most familiar image of myself was an inverted one.

With the music turned up loud I didn't even hear

the mail arrive. But when I took a break to wash ink off my hands there it was, lying quiet in the box.

The postcard was vintage and printed on creamy linen-textured stock. *This is the way we swim in GREAT SALT LAKE,* it read in festive cursive and big cartoonish block type; around the letters, cheerful cartoon white people in modest bikinis and trunks lounged and reclined on the surface of the water.

JUNE 18/98

Dear Andrea,

I'm writing from the past to the future. I'll get home before this postcard does. I'm a little jealous of the me three days from now who just might have already seen your face. I'm also a little worried about this future me. The one thing postcard-me has that future-me might not is hope. I admit it! I have a little. Just a trace. Nonlethal amount. But there it is.

Why do I like you so much? I don't know. But really I do know. Maybe I'll tell you sometime. Your call. —R.

I sat down on a metal stool and read it one more time. Then another. I picked up the phone.

———

He didn't ask questions. He just said, "Of course," and arrived at my house an hour later with his neat black kit: scissors, combs, a glossy electric shaver. I sat in a chair in the backyard and Ryan draped a soft towel around my shoulders. I closed my eyes. No professional had cut my hair since I was a teenager. The tiny snips and tugs, the low hum of the razor at my nape, his fingers lifting and smoothing, my head in his hands—I wanted to trust him.

"There," he said after several minutes. "I think that'll do it."

"How does it look?"

"Sort of dark Jean Seberg." He lifted away the towel and with a soft brush dusted the last bits of hair from my nape. "Hot."

He set his hands lightly on my shoulders and kissed the top of my head for a long, still second.

That line by Isaac Babel sprang to mind: *No iron can pierce the heart like a period put exactly in the right place.* My shoulders dropped.

Ryan said, "Go take a look and tell me what you think."

In my room I closed the door and faced the mirror. Ryan had turned the shorn rug into a sleek, shapely cut, with the dark brown of my roots and the remains of black at the tips creating an unexpected depth. It looked intentional and brave. It looked like an Andrea I had not seen before. But who was still unmistakably me.

Before I went back outside to tell Ryan thank you, you've rescued me, I stood for a moment among all the artifacts of my self. The music. The clothes. The photos. The letters. The commas of black hair. All these things that came and went, or stayed, some forever and some for now, lay scattered at my feet. I got the broom.

The Good Part

Your *hair*! People liked it. I liked it too. I felt lighter, closer to myself. Wet, I was a seal. It stuck up in new and better forms of bedhead. I had new cowlicks.

"I have to get a picture of this one," Ryan said. It was morning. I had just sat up in bed, my tank top all stretched out from sleep.

I had never meant to sleep with him again. But there was the Scrabble rematch where we drank too many Moscow mules, and he tried to kiss me in the back of the bar but I said, *Not here,* and went upstairs with him intending to only make out a little, but once it started, the momentum picked up and it was as good as done. It was easier to do it than to push him away and have to discuss it. Then there was the Queer Night at La

Luna where I saw Flynn and Vivian entwined on the dance floor and immediately ducked out, and Ryan's place, right down the block, offered the nearest refuge, and I turned off every light and pushed him down onto the hard living room floor. There was also the Monday afternoon he called the letterpress studio and said into the phone, quietly but matter-of-factly, "I can't get anything done because there's only one thing I want to do, and it's to you," and a warm shock rose from the arches of my feet to my loins. It was flattering. It was that easy. I told no one else. I took what I wanted when I wanted it, and we both benefited.

"No fair," I said now, trying to conceal my alarm. "It's too early." Flynn had always taken pictures of me like this and I had never stopped her. I liked waking up to her gaze. But this photo would be evidence. I covered every track.

"But the formation is incredible," Ryan said. He had already picked up a disposable camera and was winding the film, a crickety sound.

I buried my face in my knees as he snapped the shutter. Before he could wind it again, I was up and out of the bed.

When the photos came back from the developer, two months and a tour later, they were grainy and brownish, backlit: one of me as a small mountain with a tangled crest on top; the next, the slant and tumble of my back and legs, blurred, as I escaped the sheets.

But that wouldn't be until he finished the camera. First the Cold Shoulder was touring Europe for a month, where they would be in tiny print on many festival posters.

Do you want to come along? he asked. Come to the New York shows before we fly out. It'll be fun.

I thought about it—I could go to New York for the first time, maybe take a bus to visit Annabel at Boston College. But I had no money. And I had no explanation to my people for why I'd suddenly go to New York. And even if I did, to be outed to his bandmates, to anyone who came to the shows—it might follow me back to Portland. I told him, and it was true, that I couldn't afford to take the time off work. You can sell merch, he said, we'll pay you. I've got to work on my own stuff, I said. I have so much going on here.

July in Portland. The rain had cleared town for the season, and the colors went from gray and evergreen and black to blue, bright green, gold, with long hot-pink sunsets. The studio was filled with warm daylight well into the evening; when I locked up Artifacts at six there still seemed to be endless hours ahead. The light was like food—I slept little and ate less.

I was also charged with the nervous energy of my secret affair. Ryan and I sneaked off on field trips: a taco joint in Hillsboro, a pawnshop in Scappoose, a diner in the tucked-away Lair Hill neighborhood, karaoke over the river in Vancouver. My adrenaline rose each time. For me it was the secrecy, not the sex, that radiated this contained heat. If you think it's no big deal for a lesbian to fool around with a guy on the sly, you're right, sort of, but you are also not living in Portland, Oregon, at the end of the twentieth century as a card-carrying member of the Lesbian Mafia. It was as good as treason.

It shouldn't have been so easy to get away with it. But no one was paying attention. There were a million things to do and people were caught up in their own lives, following more flagrant dramas, setting up tours, traveling. I'd been off the radar for a while and I stayed that way. I moved among them with my private knowledge like an illicit gold coin in my pocket.

Double life was my specialty, honed during my teen years, my formative mode. I picked it right back up. I remembered how alert a secret makes you, how the fear becomes sharpness and widens your eyes. When you're always watching out, you see more.

The thing is, I'd never known a person quite like Ryan. The guy was rootless without the ache, unlike everyone else I knew. He was hydroponic. He got everything he needed from the air, it seemed. You could put him anywhere with decent light and clean water and he'd be fine. He'd just grow there. That's what made him so amenable to touring. And touring was what made it possible for me to keep falling back into his company, carefree. He never stuck around long enough for anything to stick.

Ryan and I made a deal.

"I don't ever want this to outgrow the fun part," I said one evening as we drove along the river toward a bar in Linnton. He was leaving again in a week for the long East Coast and European tour and I was all revved up with liminal abandon.

"Sounds good to me," he said.

"Promise we never have to get to the processing part? The part with all the annoying habits and the noticing of them?"

"The part where we start saying how the other person does that thing just like their mother?"

"Exactly," I said. I thought of her then—imagined calling to tell her about Ryan. Her delight would kill me. Would erase me. I shuddered. "Thank god you'll never meet my mother," I said, too strongly. He shot me a glance. "I mean, it's not personal, no one does, since even I haven't seen her in, like, four years. Believe me, it's for the better. For all of us."

"Mine came to visit in January," Ryan said. "That was enough for a while."

"What's she like?"

"You think I'm going to tell you, now that I know you could use it against me?" He grabbed me at the ticklish spot above my knee, so I squeaked and swerved. "We're staying with the good part, right?"

"Right," I said. That's all I wanted to give him and get from him. The good part, the curated part, the part a person could fall for. Except without crossing over into the falling-for part. Just far enough to catch yourself in time. Good practice for the future true loves we would meet. I swatted his hand away from my leg. "Don't distract me. I need to steer."

And then he was gone. That was the thing: Ryan was always gone or about to be.

The evening of his red-eye flight to New York, I rode along to the airport with him and his bandmate Jesse in the Cold Shoulder van. The Econoline was tall and stiff, the inside spangled with scattered CDs and loose change. The last seat had been removed and the space walled off with an iron cage for gear storage. Jesse was the singer and guitarist. He had clearly perceived a need for The Cute One in the band and stepped up to fill the role. Where Ryan had a lurking, offhand grace, Jesse was all I'm-here-now assuredness. He was friendly the way celebrities are friendly in interviews, a flawlessly smooth niceness. The band was not famous but Jesse seemed to be prepping for it. You got the feeling that when he looked at you he was bestowing an honor.

They had offered me the passenger seat but I didn't want it. It seemed too much the girlfriend seat. The back was the friend-who's-parking-the-van seat. That was me. When we picked him up Jesse had eyed me and given Ryan a look, which Ryan ignored. I knew he was thinking, *So there's the girl Ryan's fucking,* and I wanted to say, *No I'm not, I'm not that*—but I was that. I didn't like it. I didn't want to be that girl in the eyes of men. I wanted to give off as neutral a scent as possible.

When we pulled up at PDX, Jesse got out first and headed to the back of the van to unload. Ryan reached for the door handle but I put a hand on his shoulder.

"I'm going to miss you," I said, low so Jesse wouldn't hear.

He glanced back at me, softening. "Are you?"

"But while you're gone," I said, "I don't want you to pass up any . . . opportunities."

One corner of his mouth tightened, a small twist. "Because *you* don't want to."

I shrugged.

He unclipped his seat belt and it zipped up with a whoosh. "Believe me, I won't either," he said. The door closed behind him with a neat, firm thud.

I felt a funny competitive twinge in my gut. I hauled open the side door and met him at the back of the van. "I meant opportunities to play Scrabble."

"I would never pass up the chance to beat someone at Scrabble."

Jesse wanted a hand with an amp flight case the size of an oven. Ryan grabbed a handle.

"I'm two games ahead," I said. "Just remember that. No one plays Scrabble as well as me."

"True." Ryan slung a duffel over his shoulder. "Maybe I need to practice more while I'm away."

"Maybe I do too."

He smiled and shut the back doors of the van.

When Jesse turned his back to head inside, Ryan wrapped his arms around me, quick but firm, and gave my neck a nip that sent a little vein of lightning down my spine.

Then the glass doors closed after him and his rolling suitcase stuffed with undeclared band merch.

I had to pull the seat forward a foot to reach the pedals, and the brakes needed a heavy foot. I tried not to whack another car with the van's unwieldy tail end as I pulled out from Departures. I needed to get back to my real life.

Once again I had split myself so neatly in two. One slender stem of my life was characterized by evasion, ducking, doors closed swiftly, a dark room with only me and Ryan inside, an escape hatch. But in the main life, I was an organizer in the Lesbian Mafia and printed art and commerce and went to shows full of girls who looked like boys and made my heart stop, and when I walked into any of these places someone knew me. Someone *knew* me. We knew each other. I've never known anything like it and won't again. To recognize someone anywhere you go. To recognize each other everywhere: the coffee shop, the sidewalk, the bicycle commute, the bookstore, the bar.

Even the woods. The Washougal River tumbled down forested slopes toward the Columbia, clear and cool and gouged with swimming holes along the way. On hot afternoons my friends and I would park along the road at mile marker 7 and work our way down a steep path to a deep pool canopied by trees. We congregated there, one carload after another, all kinds emerging from the trees to spread towels, blow up air mattresses, pull on river shoes to navigate the rocky banks. I loved all the bodies we revealed there, fat and thin, and how we uncovered or contained our bodies and their scars. Some wore bikinis or one-pieces, some pressed themselves into sports bras and boy trunks. All the hidden tattoos came to the light, beautiful and tacky, badges of courage and impulse and youthful poor choice. I had always meant to get a tattoo but my design perfectionism had interfered. There was too much pressure on the image. I still hadn't committed.

Bullet stood knee-deep in the water, sniffing the air, or flopped down in a sandy patch to sunbathe, graciously accepting the affections of friends and strangers.

One late-July afternoon, Meena and I floated in the middle of the swimming hole on inner tubes, me in a navy one-piece, Meena in a sodden tank top and trunks. "Don't look downriver," she said, so of course I did, and she promptly chastised me.

It was Flynn and a girl I didn't recognize. They walked along the shallow part, stepping from rock to rock. The girl's shiny black hair was piled on her head and her stomach was taut. A tote bag hung from her bare shoulder. Flynn, tanned and in long cutoffs, watched the girl's steps with unnecessary chivalrous attention.

"Wonder what became of Vivian," Meena muttered.

I slid all the way down through the center of the inner tube, let go, and swam underwater as far as I could, upriver, away. And while I swam I turned my thoughts instead to Ryan, how every time I touched him he responded, a simple power but it felt like magic, and the glances I'd sometimes catch him giving me. *What? Nothing.* I swam until my lungs couldn't take it. My feet touched down on pebbly sand and I straightened up.

I was at the other end of the swimming hole, not far from the rope swing. The water came to my chin. I was immersed but still breathing, eyes open.

This was what I liked about Ryan. I would always be able to touch bottom. My feet would always meet the floor.

This time, there were no postcards. No transatlantic calls. I was slicing huge sheets of paper into cards and posters, I was inking machines, I was sweeping the shop, I was swiping credit cards and pricing furniture, I helped Lawrence convert Meena's garage into a recording studio, my friends and I played Scrabble at kitchen tables with animals draped over our feet and laps, we were grilling in backyards, splitting three-dollar burritos at La Bonita, oiling bike chains, trading mixtapes, reading novels and zines, forming and dissolving bands, we were emerging into the dark of cleared living rooms and basements and clubs, stuffing sherbet-orange foam plugs into our ears or blowing out our hearing for a night. The Ryan affair was little more than a radio song in the background, a refrain that caught in my head every now and then.

There were a few girls I gave it a go with. I made eyes at a butch with a fox tattoo, and watched her go home with Robin. A painter who made mixtapes and cited contemporary fiction and queer theory seemed promising, even if she mispronounced Nabokov. We hung out twice, made out once; then I went to her art opening at a neighborhood coffee shop. Womyny nude paintings, self-serious and defensive. I imagined myself rendered poorly by her hand and ordered my coffee to go. There was a guitarist, a friend of Marcy's who had just moved from Chicago, who had a cool haircut and always wore gray T-shirts and yet when she moved in for a kiss, I had to fight an instinctive recoil—it was the scent of her skin, earthy and sweet in a faintly rancid way. There was the house party where I lured an enigmatic andro visiting from Seattle into a dark hallway make-out, then she suddenly confessed she had a girlfriend when she thought I was about to leave a hickey on her neck.

The only one who ever made it into my bed was Bullet, a dense sleek doughnut who stashed herself under the covers. As Summer stayed at Marcy's more and more, the dog came to depend on me. Together we would secretly eat meat. In a few years vegans would become butchers, but at this point everyone was still vegetarian, and I craved the forbidden despite myself. I'd pick up a few pieces of roast chicken from Nature's and we'd sit on the living room couch, watching the *Buffy* episode I'd taped on TV, and eat the evidence. Bullet rested her heavy head on my knee between bites, drooling on the cushions, and we'd fall asleep together.

Yet occasionally these nights would come where I would walk through the kitchen, opening and closing every drawer and cupboard, unable to find anything I wanted to eat. I would read the same page three times and then set the book down. I would change the record after only one side, or one song. It was then that I would sometimes fall back on the thought of Ryan, the uncomplicated warmth of his attention. I would close my eyes and imagine touching a hand to his chest and springing a trapdoor into which we could disappear. I could disappear. He became my fallback thought, a neural pathway I'd follow toward an idea of comfort. What was I to him? I wondered. A fallback in my own way? No strings. A girl who didn't require maintenance, processing, commitment. Easy. The person across the room with a little extra shine.

He was nine hours ahead, half a world away, waking up as I was falling asleep.

The Coast

There was his voice, in my phone. It was nearly September. I biked over to his place, chest all fluttery with what could have been anticipation or dread. He came to the door and at the sight of his face for the first time in two months, a little stubbly—"I haven't even had time to shave yet, come in"—and his hair still wet from the shower, his eyes tired but brighter for the shadows beneath them, I felt shy with pleasure and recognition: There you are. Hi, face.

"Hello, friend," I said.

Ryan leaned in to kiss me right on his front step. "I'm not even going to say sorry," he said. "I'm just happy to see you."

He looked good to me, the careless jeans hanging

low, the holey T-shirt, and I longed to press up against something that warm again. I followed him upstairs.

He poured me a glass of water and said, "Let's go away for a few days."

"You just got home."

Ryan gave the apartment a look like it had been lying around watching TV. Useless. "I can't get used to sitting still yet," he said. He was flush with cash and wanted to enjoy it before they did the actual accounting for the cost of the tour. "Someplace we don't know anyone. Like the other side of Mount Hood. Or the Painted Desert."

I hadn't meant to pick things up again but here I had all this fondness, and that fever had kicked up again at the base of my spine, a sweet low burn. I wanted to see something that went on forever. Something that would put me in my place. I suggested the coast.

"The coast it is," he said.

"Except I can't afford it," I said. "I wish I could."

"It's on me. Really. Let me do this for you. Early birthday present."

We drove to Manzanita on a Tuesday. The town was quiet. Our cottage was on a narrow street with no sidewalks, where gnarled salty trees crowded around the homes. The locals had started to emerge again, post–

Labor Day. We took Bullet with us—I'd left a note on the table for Summer saying that a letterpress client had offered two nights at a beach cottage in trade, and that I'd taken the dog with me for company—and she galloped in gleeful laps on the beach, scattering seagulls. Ryan threw her tennis ball over and over, while I let the cold, cold waves lick my shins for as long as I could stand it before running back up to the warm sand, where Ryan and Bullet and I chased each other around until we were all panting. Riding the tandem bike we rented along the quiet streets and dunes, salt water drying on my legs where I'd run into the icy ocean, I felt so good. Sunblown, my muscles working hard, Ryan behind me to help propel us forward. *I'm steering,* I thought. I had never been the one in front, the one who called the direction. I was used to always looking to the other person for guidance.

When we disembarked, I impulsively slid my hand into his. My fingers were cold and his palm was warm and callused. They locked into place.

So this is what it's like, I thought as we walked down the main street. *To hold hands and not garner a single glance. How strange.* It reminded me of one time at a show when, bored, Summer let me try on her six-inch platforms and suddenly the whole space was different. I inhabit a small body, five feet two. The world of shoulders is one I know well. But now I could see clearly, my head level with all the others, an unobstructed view. Behind me the regular-sized girls were patiently, miserably tiptoeing and peering through the gaps between necks and heads. *This is what it's like to be tall?* I had said in wonder and indignation and envy. *They just walk around able to see everything. And they take it for granted.*

This too was like being tall. I opened my mouth to explain this to Ryan but when I glanced over at him I saw a look on his face that I hadn't seen before. Contentment. No slyness, no skepticism, no wry guard. He looked completely *himself.*

He caught my glance. "What?" he said. A vulnerable smile.

I was walking in his country now. This was what it was like for him to be Ryan. This was his nature. I suddenly did not know what to say. I just wanted to look at him. And I did.

"Are you hungry?" I said.

He slid a sly look down my body—there was the one I knew, there was our default, the shield of the easygoing tease—and said, "Always."

It was easy to walk into that café with him, easy to slide into a table by the window, easy to drink a whole bottle of wine with him, easy to laugh, easy to be with him, not because or despite that he was a man but because he was my friend Ryan, my friend I was having an affair with. It was easy when we stepped out into the cooling night, drunk, to wrap my arms around his neck and impulsively kiss him in the open air for the first time. And when he started to say, "I love . . ." and I tensed, he took the easy way out and finished with "this." Easier for everyone.

Those few days in Manzanita I was another person. I was exactly myself, in one way: impetuous, unafraid to be seen, for once not skulking and periscoping; but in another way, I was an alternate Andrea Morales, inhabiting a character that someone else had intended me to be—my parents, biology, God, et al. Me, flipped. A mirror side. It looked like me but it wasn't.

The night before we left, he said, "Tell me about girls."

I was in a T-shirt and underwear, knees straddling his sides.

"What do you mean?" I said, unbuttoning his jeans. "You've been with girls."

"What is it you like about them?"

I studied his eyes. "No," I said. I leaned forward and kissed his lips: a quick, firm, closed-mouthed kiss.

"What's it like?" he persisted.

I said, "It's not like in porn. And it's not like this. And it's not for you to know."

I kissed him again, purposefully, planting a seal, and he wisely let it go.

Back in Portland I said good night and drove home with the passenger seat empty. I unlocked my front door, let Bullet run in ahead of me, and dropped my backpack on the couch. "Summer?" I said, switching on a lamp.

No answer. I could hear the dog lustily drinking in the kitchen. She sauntered to her bed, flopped flat, and descended down a long sigh directly into sleep.

I stood alone in the quiet dim house, one lamp lit. I inhaled the smell of home. I wondered if this was the scent of my T-shirts, of my hair, if this was what another person smelled on me when we hugged. You don't notice it until you leave for a while.

I looked at the telephone. I could ask Ryan. But there was a problem. *I love,* he'd started. The Fun Part was over.

So I didn't call. And the next day I cut a postcard from a letterpress test run—layers of type on the front, crisscrossed dates and words and images—and wrote *Thanks for coasting. What a trip it's been. I'm headed underground for the next few weeks to get this art show up. Consider me on an extended tour. See you on the other side.* I signed it with only an X—a kiss, a rating, an illiterate signature, an unknown—and dropped it in the mail.

When I turned twenty-four a week later, Summer and I hosted a massive family dinner at our house, replete with a cake shaped like the state of Oregon. Folds of frosting mountains, blue veins of rivers, a candy heart marking Portland. I took the slice of coast where Manzanita lay unmarked. I ate it all, every crumb, and scraped my plate clean.

Our Art

The problem with the lesbian art show was that exclusion was oppressive, and who were we to judge, replicating systems of value that had excluded, et cetera—so said some of the steering committee, which operated on consensus. We would be *inclusive.* Unable to bear it, or the hours-long meetings that had stretched weeks into months and pushed the show back to October, I quit the forever-stalled steering committee. It was the manual labor that made me happy: printing, postering, building up the space. We'd masked the windows of our makeshift gallery on Northwest Everett with sheets of butcher paper, and to unlock that door, or to knock and be let inside, was to enter the good kind of secret— one I couldn't wait to share.

For the weeks leading up to the show, I would let

myself into the space for hours before and after I put in full days at Artifacts or shorter shifts at the record store. A couple of the Mafia organizers had rented the warehouse on Northwest Everett on the cheap. The yeasty, roasted smell from the brewery blocks drifted in through the creaky iron-framed windows. Behind us, a crane dangled. The developers were trying to name it "the Pearl District," starting to buy up auto shops and warehouses, ready to erase the open sky with condos that didn't seem plausible yet. When I could, I brought Bullet to the space to hang out with me. At night, we liked the company, and it felt safer to have a pit bull with us, even if she was as vicious as a lamb. I loved being in the big raw room, with drywall dust on my hands and knees, the sweet pine smell of cut two-by-fours and the slick tang of new white paint, the decisive hammers and whining drills, the advance copy of the Gold Stars CD echoing from a boom box on a folding chair.

On opening night, First Thursday, the clouds burned off into a bright fall afternoon. At Artifacts, I paced all day. There had still been so much to do when I left the warehouse that morning and I hated missing out.

Meena picked me up with Robin and Topher's new housemate, Marisol. Fresh out of Southern California with a BA in women's studies, Marisol was new in town and had answered their roommate ad in the *Willamette*

Week. Tonight she wore burgundy lipstick and wedge boots and her soft young cheeks still held a coppery glow. You could tell she hadn't lived in Oregon long— she hadn't paled and moldered and gone woolly. No job yet, but she was sunny with optimism. I envied her. "Welcome," I said. "Good luck. Let's hurry."

Outside the warehouse, the blue hour turned the windows' glow gold. The space was huge, with concrete floors. We'd erected low walls throughout and repainted everything white. The art was all hung and installed. We had actually pulled this thing off. If you stood back and took in the whole space, it looked like a real show. Legitimate. Three bartenders served wine in plastic cups and everything.

Ted showed up with a fellow antique dealer, a tall silver-haired guy with wire-rimmed glasses and a skulk. On my way to the bar I found them, standing in the center of the first room, doing a slow scan. I looked at them looking at us and got a weird feeling. "Stop it," I said.

"What?" he said. "Congratulations, by the way."

"You're judging."

"Of course we are," said the other dealer. "Aren't you?"

"Just . . . stop male-gazing," I said, and Ted laughed gleefully.

"Excuse me," he said, "I have to go delve into the world of lesbians, uncensored. I can't wait."

I hit him on the arm. "*Ted.*" I launched into the burden of representation, but he cut me off at the word *society* and said, "Good work here, Andrea. Give me the lecture tomorrow at the shop."

"Ignore the shitty stuff," I called to his back. Two nearby women shot me an offended look. "You too," I told them.

You couldn't avoid it entirely, though a few of us had conspired to group the weaker pieces together and hang them toward the back so they wouldn't contaminate the stronger work. Summer stopped in front of a watercolor of two women entwined, surrounded by runic symbols. "Is this by that woman you sort of went out with?"

"I don't want to talk about it."

"How did that make it in?" Lawrence said.

"All lesbians are in the Lesbian Mafia. Therefore all self-declared lesbian artists are in the Lesbian Mafia art show."

Meena said, "The downfall of Portland art is that it's too fucking democratic."

"Everyone's got an opening," Lawrence said.

"Come on," I said, "let me show you Ginger's rabbit prints. They're amazing. Unspeakable things done with carrots."

"Oh god, I can't even look at that wall," Meena said, turning her head away. "I actually can't." It was a display of feathers and bones and paintings on leather arranged in a quasi–Native American aesthetic. The artist was, naturally, a white woman, the girlfriend of an organizer.

Summer rested a hand on my arm and asked me confidentially if I had seen Flynn's contribution yet.

"It wasn't up yet when I left for work," I said.

"Do you want to avoid it?"

"Of course not," I said defiantly. "Let's go look."

The photos were medium format, square, hung in a four-by-four grid. But they were not, as I had feared, full of Vivian or any of her other lovers. They were full of me.

There I was, tiny in a field, back to the camera. Me at the coast, lying in dune grass. Me waist-deep in a river, bare back. Me surrounded by tall, dark, wet trees. A shot of the back seat of my hatchback with a tossed-aside harness and a rumpled Pendleton blanket.

Flynn called the series *Queer Nature*. Her description said, *I wanted to take the queer subject out of the urban environment, where we always suppose they* are. *I wanted to represent queer as part of nature, as natural.*

In the photos I was always alone, but the gaze of the camera was so careful and intimate that you felt the presence of two. *Take a few steps back, Andy. Look down.* My face looked so young, cheeks still full with youth, no circles under my eyes. I had been more photogenic then. So willing. I had looked at the camera with no self-consciousness. Looked at Flynn. *Just look at me. Not the lens, my eyes. Good. That makes me want to fuck you.* My eyes had smoldered a little, and *click.*

I felt him before I saw him—a touch at the dip of my back.

I flinched. I hurried to compose my face. "I didn't know you were here!"

"I've been here twenty minutes," Ryan said. I'd figured he might show, but the sight of him there among every lesbian I knew was like seeing a cat in an airport: two worlds that ought never intersect.

Summer, now a few paintings down, gave us a glance. I stood a little straighter.

"That's you?" Ryan nodded toward the photos.

"That's me." We stood and stared at the me of a year ago, two years ago.

It was jarring to look at my own face, to know now

what I didn't then. This was the me who had been loved so much. Had loved so much. The edge in my throat now was not regret, but knowing what the younger me didn't: that one day I would look at photos of this time, of this hopeful, love-lulled me, and it would exist only behind glass.

I could feel Ryan next to me. I did not know how to look at him.

"Come by tonight," he said in a low voice. "You still have the key, right?"

"Do you need it back? I can drop it in the box." My eyes darted to Meena, only a few feet away. She leaned into something Marisol said, laughed, and adjusted her tie.

Ryan's eyebrows tightened. "Ah," he said. "Are you still on tour?"

"This is my real life," I said. "Actually, it's more like *you* were my tour."

The look on his face.

"I didn't mean for it to sound like that," I said.

"No, I get it," he said. "Now you're home."

What could I say but yes?

Ryan turned and left and the only thing I could do was let him go.

Meena came over and rammed me with her shoulder. "Hey, sad-eyes. Why are you still looking at those?"

"I'm not." All I saw now were the frames.

She sighed, misunderstanding, and slung an arm around my neck. "Let's move on."

"Oh, I *have* moved on." I caught sight of Flynn across the room, dressed sharp in a tie and man's blazer. A voluptuous brunette with baby bangs slunk alongside her in a bright vintage dress and an army surplus jacket I recognized as Flynn's. Meena and I looked at each other. "Let's turn this corner," I said, and we veered around the wall.

In the corner was a narrow, black-curtained booth. I hadn't seen it yet—someone else had installed it. Meena went in first. She came out a minute later with a stricken look and motioned for me to go next. "I need a smoke. Find me outside."

I stepped into the dark little space. Headphones hung on the wall above a placard with the title (*Im*)*possible Future: For Brandon and Lana*. I slipped the headphones over my ears and peered through a tiny window into a lit-up diorama of a miniature bedroom.

"Nebraska" by Bruce Springsteen played low through the headphones. The wallpaper was a photocopied map of the southeast corner of the state, with all the routes out of Falls City, Nebraska, highlighted in red pen. I followed the highway off the left edge toward where I knew it would eventually lead to my own hometown. I felt a flare of territorial indignance. What Portlander was making this art about Nebraska? Nebraska was *mine*.

The sheets were rumpled. On the bed a toy suitcase was open, packed with clothes. A tiny first aid kit rested atop them. On the floor, a stuffed duffel with a jacket thrown over it. On the dresser, a little handmade desk calendar was flipped to December 30, 1993—the day before Brandon Teena died, I realized. Outside the frost-edged window, a toy enameled pickup truck waited, packed, a tarp pulled down over the back.

The room looked as if he'd just stepped out—had gone into the kitchen for a glass of water, maybe, or out to warm up the truck—but would return any minute to click the suitcase shut, load it up, and go.

The weight of it sank into my chest and filled my eyes. They'd come so close to making it out alive. I didn't even know yet about Matthew Shepard, who only yesterday had been discovered tied to the fence post in Wyoming where he'd been left to die, and who at that moment lay in a hospital bed, still living, barely. All I knew was that for all our art, for all our writing, for all our self-defense workshops, for all our banding together in our cities and oases, queer survival was still not guaranteed.

When I came out of the booth, the room teemed wall to wall but Ryan was gone.

I found Meena outside and she offered me a smoke. My fingers trembled as she lit the cigarette for me. "That hit a little too close to home," I said.

"I'm so glad you got out of Nebraska," she said.

"Me fucking too." I inhaled too sharply and coughed out a ragged cloud of smoke. "But I also feel guilty that I bailed. Maybe I should have stayed to fight for the queers who are still there. Maybe I could do more good there than here."

"You can't do much good if you're dead," Meena said. "Or totally fucking miserable. You should have seen yourself when you came back from there."

"It's been almost four years," I said. "Can you believe it?"

"Best four years of your life, I bet."

"Yeah," I said. "I'm in no hurry to go back."

She waved her hand at the bright windows of the warehouse and the loose crowd filling the sidewalk and spilling into the street. "I mean, could you have done *this* in Nebraska?"

I shook my head and couldn't speak for a moment. It was the first time I'd had a chance to step back and take in the whole scene.

"You have plenty of work to do right here," Meena said. "We all do."

Of course, she was right. I had left Nebraska and it didn't miss me. Nebraska wasn't mine just because I was born there. Nor did Brandon Teena own or belong to the place that claimed his life. He wasn't Lana's, he wasn't his mother's, he wasn't Nebraska's. He was all of ours now. Because he was killed for being one of us, he became ours. We claimed him. Maybe he would love that, if he could know. Or maybe all he needed was to belong to himself.

I woke the next morning with a white-wine hangover like some suburban divorcee. From my bed I thought I had hallucinated the smell of coffee, but there was Summer in the kitchen, in the morning(!), stirring the French press with a chopstick. The layer of grounds was thick as chocolate cake.

I sat down on a chair and laid my cheek on the smooth Formica table.

"Morning, lamb chop." Summer poured me a deep cup of coffee and ruffled my hair. I sat up and leaned toward her hand—I loved to be petted—but she was already reaching for her cup.

"I thought you'd be at Marcy's," I said, trying to

sound neither relieved nor petulant. I had thought I would love living mostly alone, but now that it was fall I would get these night-blooming orphan fears. Evening would slide in earlier and earlier and the house would grow too dark; I'd turn on the lights, and then it was too bright and empty, a still life. The indifferent murmur of the radio was no comfort.

Some touring band was camped out all over Marcy's house, Summer explained, so Marcy had popped a Benadryl and spent the night here. Summer leaned against the counter and settled back with her mug in both hands. She took a long languid sip, looking at me over the rim. My legs tensed: Summer walked fast, talked fast, and drank her coffee fast. Something was up. "So," she said offhandedly, "what on earth did you say to that guy at the show?"

"What guy?" I said through a shallow yawn.

"The one you were talking to over by Flynn's photos."

I studiously rubbed the sleep from my eyes. "I don't remember."

She took another slow sip. "Huh."

Heat in my cheeks. "What?"

"You should've seen the look on his face when he walked away."

"What do you mean?"

"He looked—stunned. He kind of blinked, like this." Trouble must have flickered across my face, because Summer straightened up. "Did he say something to you? Did you tell him off? What's the story?"

I said there was no story. "That's Ryan. He and Flynn used to work together. He's the guy who cuts my hair."

"Oh," she said, disappointed. She looked for a bright side: "Gay? Topher would think he's cute."

With a strategic note of uncertainty, I said, "I don't *think* so?"

Marcy sauntered into the kitchen, braless under her loose black T-shirt, her graying hair rumpled. Summer leaned into her as she poured the rest of the pot into Marcy's mug, and Marcy kissed her temple. Oh, to wake up with a person you like and have coffee, still pajamaed, in your own kitchen. It was a luxury you could not buy.

I claimed a need for fresh air and zipped my down vest over my pajamas, pulled on a wool hat. Out on the front porch, I sat on the top step with my black coffee. The sky was pale and soft, fog dulled the edges of the dark pines, the porch lights across the street still burned uselessly. The orange cat from next door skulked up from under our porch and wound around my feet. I pulled her into my lap and she melted into me, dense and warm and vibrating. The cat had gotten skinny, her fur a little ragged.

The beauty of a new affair, I thought, is the illusion it affords you that everything you do is great. You each get to invent the other as the person you most want them to be, and yourself as the person they most want.

But the invention had broken. I didn't get to be that person anymore. The disappointment surprised me, a knife edge in my throat.

A screen door banged as the neighbor emerged to grab the Sunday paper. I called out, "Hey, I think I have your cat over here."

"Not my cat," he said.

"I thought she came from your house."

He waved the paper toward the front door. "She belonged to the downstairs tenants. But they moved out last month."

I rubbed her collarless neck. Under the fur, it was so thin. "Did they leave any forwarding address? They must be worried about her."

"Well," he said, "they had a baby."

"Oh." We knew what that meant. You saw it any time you went to the Humane Society under *Reason for surrender.* "Assholes."

"Tell me about it. The baby's bedroom was right

below mine. I had to sleep in the living room to escape the crying."

The last thing I could afford right now was another mouth to feed. I rubbed the cat's downy cheeks and she rammed her head into my hand with pleasure. She gave my palm a delicate, rough lick. Her mouth was, I reasoned, a small one.

I would just feed her until I could find her a home. Maybe this good deed would make up for my bad behavior. Hail, cat, full of grace, please accept this can of by-products, blessed is your ignorance, forgive us humans for the things you do not know we have done.

Secondhand News

Portland had only one lesbian bar, the Egyptian Club, which everyone called the E-Room. A scowly woman called Mom took your five bucks at the door, which I think was half to filter out the curious or unserious straights and half to keep the place alive since it was empty much of the time. It wanted to be a lesbian pleasureplex but usually felt more like a tomb. The first room had pool tables and a bar slumped with haggard old dykes, possibly trolls who'd turned to stone a decade ago when someone accidentally switched on the lights. The dance room was painted matte black on all surfaces. It had hard little plywood booths and ultraviolet lights that lit up the thousand cat hairs clinging to our T-shirts, and the deafening music echoed off the half-empty floor, attempting to fill the space bodies had failed to. The third room was for karaoke, a long narrow rectangle with a small, harshly lit stage near the entrance, a bar that occupied most of one side, and tables crammed deep into the dim recesses of the back, where a fire exit was the only way out.

It was Meena's twenty-sixth birthday and she had got it in her head to celebrate with karaoke at the E-Room. We always went with equal measures of irony and hope, every six months or so—just long enough to forget that after the last time we'd sworn never to return.

Only now that we can never return, now that the E-Room is razed and gone, a LEED-certified New Portland condo built over its ruins, do I know that those lesbians I had always mocked or turned away from, those bulldaggers and diesel dykes, those denim vests and feathered bangs, those mullets and dated glasses, eyes roaming the room, were not worst-case scenarios—they were me in another life. Where did they *come* from? we always asked each other, imagining there was some other Portland lesbian universe we didn't know about. We didn't get that they weren't from Portland. They came from the gritty Tonya Harding suburbs and the tough little mountain towns and the foggy farm-strewn valley to the only designated lesbian space in hundreds of miles. I claimed my rural Nebraska–ness as my badge of authenticity but couldn't have recognized it if it hoisted itself onto a bar stool right next to me. I just picked up my pitcher of Pabst and hurried back to my friends to pore over the songbooks. We'd scored a table right up front by the stage.

"Since when do you like karaoke?" Summer said as I filled out my slips. I claimed that I always had, I was just getting braver. Meena wanted to do Scaryoke—where you let other people choose your song, title revealed only when you're called to the mic—but in the face of desperate opposition, she leveled a benevolent compromise: "Okay, you can only sing songs you've never done before." We submitted. It was her birthday. Authority was the greatest gift we could give her.

I wrote down a few options and handed them to Meena. Technically, I cheated—Ryan and I had sung "Rocket Man" at the Vancouver bar, but none of my friends had ever heard me do it, so I decided it was fair game. Meena gathered all our slips and brought them to the KJ. I poured myself a beer, sat back, and looked up.

He was fiddling with the microphone stand, adjusting it to his considerable height. He wore the beat-up Alaska T-shirt I always liked. Only a month had passed since the lesbian art show and the pathetic unanswered e-mail I'd sent afterward, yet he looked different—

maybe it was how the stage light gilded the hair that now fell over his eyebrows and shadowed his cheeks so they appeared sculpted and the stubble almost gleamed. When he looked up to find the screen, his eyes grazed mine and froze.

Summer elbowed me. "Hey, it's that guy, isn't it?"

"Sure looks like it." My face flushed hot and I was grateful for the darkness.

She crossed her legs. "He must really like lesbians." She took a deep sip from her straw.

"Don't they all," said Lawrence, flipping to the next page of the songbook. "There's two more at the bar."

Ryan shook his head and cracked a helpless half smile as the screen flashed "HEARTBREAKER" IN THE STYLE OF DIONNE WARWICK. And the opening riff began its downward tumble, into a song whose breeziness belies that it offers not a moment of emotional, or respiratory, respite.

"*Why do you have to be a heartbreaker, when I was being what you want me to be?*" Ryan sang it with a tuneful nonchalance, no showboating, no eyes-fixed-to-the-screen timidity. The lyrics were getting to me, and maybe him too, but he pulled the classic karaoke strategy of faint skeptical detachment, replete with tongue-in-cheek hops into a sweet creaky falsetto.

"He's good," Summer said.

I agreed, feigning surprise. But I already knew what he could do. Karaoke shines a harsh light on a pop song—by spelling out every lyric and whoop and separating song from star power, it drags vapidity and lazy repetition out into unflattering view. Ryan knew how to pick a song: how to find a semiforgotten hit that showed its good bones, how to pull out an underdog that made you want to find the original, how to nail the feel-good hit that was a pleasure to hear again.

"What are you doing here?" I said through a smile as he neared my table to vigorous lesbian applause. I stood and stepped away as if heading to the restroom. "Field studies?"

"What are *you* doing here?" he said. "You called this place a shame vortex."

"But it's *our* shame vortex." I peered toward the back of the room, where his table had to be lurking in the shadows.

"I'm with Jesse and his girlfriend," he said. "We just wanted to try a new place. Should we leave?"

"Of course not," I said, and then silently cursed myself for missing the chance to tell a straight man to leave a lesbian bar. Once again, I had failed my people. "I'm going to the restroom now."

Five minutes of graffiti-reading later, I returned to the karaoke room just in time to hear my name.

Back in that Vancouver bar, I had scoffed at Elton John (arena pop, mom music, that transitional claim he was *bisexual,* which with his baby bangs and silly glasses seemed as much a mean joke as a cop-out)—but with a wise shake of his head Ryan had tamped down my petty complaints and we'd sung "Rocket Man," trading off lines in the verses, singing the chorus together. Revelation. It was the saddest song I'd heard in years. Afterward I went out and bought the record for fifty cents and listened to that song over and over when I was home alone.

Then, it had been the two of us among the locals, loose with our anonymity, our private familiarity. Disco light dappling our faces. Now it was only me. Ryan way back in the dark. My friends between us, watching. I sang, "*I'm not the man they think I am at home, oh no, no, no.*"

My irony failed me, and I wasn't that much of a performer anyway; all I could do was sing like I meant it. Summer and Topher held up lighters and waved them back and forth in time. I squinted toward the shadowy depths of the room but the stage lights blazed out my view. I fixed my eyes to the screen, kept singing. I wouldn't look again. *Burning out his fuse up here alone.*

There, we're even, I thought as I walked back to my seat. Our unintentional sad songs. Truce.

But we weren't: the next one he did was "Different Drum," a kiss-off, back-off song. Those lyrics should have been mine, and he knew it; I could tell he was singing the song *as me*. It was in the twist of mock sympathy, the slight cock of his head on the verse, and the little cowlick-twirl he did at the start of the chorus—my thinking-during-Scrabble habit. *It's just that I am not in the market for a boy who wants to lo-ove only meeee.*

He slid a glance right at me on the final line, *We'll both live a lot longer if you live without me.*

I couldn't believe it. Was it coy or was it war? I hadn't been planning to sing again but I immediately put in a slip for the Johnny Cash version of "It Ain't Me Babe."

By now the place was filling up. The air thickened with cigarette smoke, and the KJ—by this point, toasted—turned on a fog machine. The evening's first group rendition of "Love Shack" marked the point of no return.

An hour had passed since any of us had sung. Summer was at the bar waiting to close her tab when the KJ called out my name. "We can just go," I said. I was over it. My response was too late. But the crew wouldn't have it; they whooped me on, and I wove through the now-full and raucous tables to get to the microphone.

At least the Cash song was short, I thought, though now I felt sheepish and petty.

But the song was not "It Ain't Me Babe." It was one Meena had brought up for me at the beginning of the night: "Second Hand News" by Fleetwood Mac. I'd never sung it before, but I stored the tape permanently in my hatchback and it had backgrounded my travel for so long now the whole album was in my bones. With only a measure of intro, the words popped up on the screen and I plunged in after them.

An easy song, easy key, no weird notes, room to breathe—this would be fine.

Halfway into the song, a pack of lesbians we all knew emerged like crime fighters through the powdery smoke of the machine and the blue cigarette haze. They wore surplus jackets and denim and black hoodies, boots and thrifted wing tips. The Brotherhood, they called themselves. They had taken to visiting strip clubs together, affecting a playboy attitude, and talking a rueful, boastful, had-to-let-her-go talk, even though they were as young and vulnerable as any of us. They were handsome, but alone none of them was anything special; their power was in numbers, their benign gang. I received a thumbs-up as they swaggered by. I smiled as I sang, "*Won't you lay me down in the tall grass and let me do my stu-uh-uff.*"

Then Flynn came into the light, at the back of the pack, and instantly I knew I was headed for Karaoke

Shame. Karaoke Shame is a remorse hangover you can sum up as One Song Too Many. That last song of the night that you somehow thought was a good idea and you wake up regretting. But knowing when to leave has never been my strong suit. See also: Flynn.

The song launched into its final section, which I'd forgotten about in my smug familiarity. It turned out Lindsey Buckingham sings "*Now now now now now*" for thirty-three endless seconds. The real song sounded more like *bow*, but the karaoke cast it as *now*. Seventy-two in a row. *Ryan would have known better*, I thought ruefully as the blue screen filled with *now* like a test pattern.

The pack stopped at our table. I could see Meena's and Summer's mouths moving, nods exchanged. Flynn, hanging back, surveyed the room. Her eyes lit on her old buddy Ryan, who stood at the bar, and they waved at each other. She peeled away and walked toward him.

"*Now now now now now*," I kept singing. Panic as I saw Flynn high-five Ryan, and I watched each new *now* turn from unsung white to sung yellow, counted them off until the screen was all yellows, thank god, I was done—

And the screen refreshed with a whole new block of *now*.

Buckingham had sung it with an entire band behind him, but I stood alone with a preprogrammed soundtrack, stammering along, pinned to the wall, lit up. The KJ released a merry poof of dry-ice smoke. The burnt-sweet smell swirled around me. I kicked my toe against the ground in time. My solo turn had gone off the rails. *Now* went on forever.

Ryan caught my eye and gave me a sympathetic thumbs-up. I mimed a gun to my temple, eye-rolled, and he smiled for real. *It's all okay,* I thought in the moment before Flynn looked at him, then at me, then back. She leaned in to his ear, and I pivoted back to the screen just as the *nows* emptied and released me into a few final helpless wails of "*I'm just second hand neeeews.*" The song collapsed into a merciful fade of guitar noodling. I bolted.

"Good one," everyone said politely, already wearing their coats. The Brotherhood lurked around our table, waiting to replace us.

"Cross that song out of the playbook," I said with a game grin. Come on, it was great, they said, but sympathy leaked out around the edges of their reassurance. Lawrence handed me my jacket. As we said our good-nights and see-you-at-that-things, Flynn walked back to us from the bar, whiskey in hand.

There was a moment when I could have pretended not to see her, turned away and led the charge to the front door, but I hesitated; I had to steal a fraction of a second to try to read her face, and she caught me—her mouth turned up in some kind of smile and it was too late. In the haze and darkness all I saw were the cheekbone shadows and an illegible glint of the eyes beneath her forelock.

"Hey," she said, and I said, "Hey," and the brothers watched and my friends watched and Ryan in his corner probably watched too; they held their pencils poised above their song slips, squinted at the lyrics unfolding on the screen with unusual interest, took great care to button their coats. In that moment I would rather have been up at the microphone singing *now now now* alone. Instead, Second Hand News and her ex one-arm-hugged, arching toward each other carefully, strangely. My sense of space felt all askew. It amazed me how familiar she still was, how I still didn't know her body as anything other than one that moved close to mine.

"Good song," she said.

"It really wasn't, but thanks," I said. "We're just on our way out. Enjoy the table."

"Hey, I didn't know you and Ryan were friends now."

"He cuts my hair," I said quickly.

"Oh. He said he'd given you drum lessons?"

"He told you that?" I shifted on my hip. Meena, in my peripheral vision, looked surprised.

"What, was it a secret?"

"No, no, it's true." I very carefully wiggled my jacket's zipper into its slide. "I just didn't want to tell anyone yet because, well, to tell you the truth—because I'm still so bad at it."

Flynn made a that's-so-cute face. "Hand-eye coordination never was your strong suit." She gave me a fond smile.

I wanted to kick her. But I said, "Oh, just wait. You'd be surprised." I shot a *help* look back at my friends, and Topher saved me with a faux-exasperated round-up motion.

I stewed in the back seat on the ride home. The problem was, Flynn was right. Oh, the curse of the ex who actually knows you. But why did she have to be right? She didn't get to be right about me anymore.

At home I took the cordless phone into my room and called Ryan. His answering machine picked up. "It's me," I said. "About these so-called drum lessons? I don't know why you said that. But maybe I can take you up on the lie. I really want to hit something. Hard."

Lessons

In wool gloves and a down vest, I biked over on a cool gray Tuesday to the practice space, a rented chunk of warehouse in North Portland—old brick and big black iron windows, a view of the train tracks and glimpses of the river between silos, a dusty space heater whirring in the corner. Ryan sat me behind a stripped-down practice set: a snare, a tom, a kick drum, and a high-hat. True to our old rule, we did not process.

Flynn was right. I had no skill. My foot moved and my arms jerked into action a half second later. "Why did you tell her drum lessons?" I moaned.

"It was the first thing that came to mind." He was trying not to laugh at me but soon gave up.

I pointed to my head with a drumstick. "Haircut!"

"I don't know, I cut Flynn's hair, I didn't think to

cross the wires. But look, here you are. Stop kicking for a minute."

I had been thumping on the kick drum. Ryan made me take my foot off the pedal and focus on my hands first. He broke it down: tap, tap, tap, tap with one hand, then tap-tap, tap-tap, tap-tap with the other. "Just go steady until it feels like a part of you. Then bring in the kick."

I obeyed. The beat smoothed out. It stuttered some-times when I added the kick, but Ryan sat down at his full kit and hit the snare rim like a metronome. I caught on, kept up. He threw in some fills. I kept going with my basic tap-tap, tap-tap, tap-tap, he let me lay down the beat, and he started to embellish it.

We sounded all right, the two of us playing. The good parts were all him, but I was at the base of it too. Each hit traveled through the sticks and up my arms. My whole body was doing this work. The sound filled me, for once a sound I was making.

"I never knew I could do this," I shouted over the beat, and immediately lost it. "I mean, I can't yet, but."

"You can. Now you just need a band."

Meena always said a band is only as good as its drum-mer, and I told Ryan I didn't have the heart to bring anyone down like that with my anti-skills. "What if we were just a band like this?" I said.

"Two drummers?"

"Yeah." I sneaked in a crash of the cymbal and lost my footing for a second. "You're going to have to sing."

Ryan waited until I found the beat again and then skipped into a familiar galloping rhythm I couldn't quite place until he started to sing the first verse.

"Stop it!" I cried.

"*When times go bad, and you can't get enough—*"

I gave in and hollered along, "*Won't you lay me down in the tall grass and let me do my stuff,*" and then I tried to knock the stick out of his hand with my own.

"Torture!" I said. "No fair!"

He was still laughing and I was too.

I remembered that I liked hanging out with him, how it could feel easy like that. He didn't try anything with me, and this—being friends, teacher and apprentice, playing together—seemed to neutralize the disturbance of our affair. I'd defeated the aberrant sexual thing that had briefly threatened to destabilize my life. We had normalized: the lesbian and the straight guy, just friends, as God and nature intended. What a relief.

He sent me home with a set of drum pads and I practiced in my room, tapping along to records. I put on "Schizophrenia" by Sonic Youth and there it was, that boom-boom-BOOM-boom-boom-boom-BOOM. And I was not only listening but playing along. The song filled me to all corners all over again. The simplest beat can get you just like that. The simplest beats of all keep you going every day—your footsteps down the sidewalk, the pulse of your blood through your heart.

The Cold Shoulder van pulled up in front of my house after two weeks of lessons. Ryan got out and started unloading a set of drums, a root-beer Gretsch kit.

"Got room for these in the basement?"

"Yes. But wait, no, I can't take those."

"Sure," he said. "I like to live light. You need to practice. It all works out."

I was too delighted to feign protest. "Promise you'll come get them if you ever need them back."

He promised.

Those drums! I was smitten. I wanted to play all the time. My improvement was negligible, but I loved hitting them. When I played, I could think of nothing else, as every part of my body and my mind jostled together in the effort of making a steady beat. My palm skin thickened. I ran my fingers over the calluses while I sat behind the counter at the record store or Artifacts. I was turning into one of those people who's always tapping on things.

"He *gave* you his drums?" Meena said, and frowned. "What does he expect in return?"

"Nothing," I said.

"I wouldn't be so sure."

She had a point. I did not want to owe him. That's when I got the idea for the guitar.

It lay in its case, now a coffin, under the living room couch. Ryan had left me a spare key when he toured last summer and it still jostled on my overstuffed key chain. I thought I could arrange a trade with a guy I knew at The 12th Fret, either for printing jobs for his band or use of my employee discount at Artifacts.

Late December. Ryan's thirtieth birthday approached. My chance. I took it.

He came down to the basement for my lesson that day. The small high windows were dim with grime and the gray afternoon, but I'd hung a paper shade over the ceiling bulb and stapled a string of Christmas lights along the bare beams, and the soft light transformed the junk around us into homey clutter. I sat him down on the drum stool. "I have something for you," I said. I handed him a Polaroid I'd taken of the broken guitar before I had turned it over to the luthier. It leaned against the backdrop of a black-painted wall at the shop, the splintered neck gleaming like bone at the break.

"What's this?" He turned over the Polaroid as if the black back would explain something.

"You'll see."

"It might have to be the cover of the next Cold Shoulder record," Ryan said. "Can we use it?"

"Of course. It's yours. But that's just part one. Wait here."

I ran up to my room and came back down with my angular sheet-wrapped bundle. "Close your eyes," I called from the steps. He obeyed. I set it on his lap. "Open."

Ryan unwrapped the sheet and there was his beautiful blue Telecaster, restored, back from the dead, all the well-earned old scratches and scuffs still visible but the neck sleek and glossy and intact. "Holy fuck." He ran his fingers down the length of it, turned it over. "What have you done?"

"Is it okay?" I said.

He looked like a kid whose lost dog had been found. "Yeah, it's okay. How'd you do this?"

I told him I'd sneaked in while he was at practice and stolen it out of the case.

"You criminal." He grabbed my shoulders.

"That's right." *Criminal:* it flushed me hot. We locked eyes. I shrugged out of his grip and pushed him down to the floor. The guitar slid onto the carpet remnant. He flipped me onto my back and held my wrists above my head, pinned them there against the cool concrete with one hand, and with a single swift twist of the other my jeans opened.

"You went into my house," he said.

"Yeah, I did."

"You still want in?"

"Only if I need to." I tried to steady my breath.

"Anything you need right now?"

"Maybe."

"It's always maybe with you."

I pulled one hand free and pushed his head down to my zipper.

The Christmas lights blurred.

End Times

The year flipped into 1999: the last year of time as we knew it. We all joked about Y2K and the bunker-hoarder people, but even we skeptics couldn't help but think it might be a good idea to spend the next New Year's Eve in a remote cabin with a well-stocked woodpile. It was the end of the century and time no longer seemed the reliable forever it used to. It had taken on a finite quality. A twilight fever set in.

Ryan time had always been liminal time. Now, when all time was liminal, how easy it was to slip into his again. Everything was temporary.

The Cold Shoulder played a word-of-mouth show at Satyricon before they headed down to Austin to record their second album. They had to crowd-test the new songs before they rendered them permanent. Ryan put me on the list and I brought Lawrence for company.

Lawrence and I huddled outside under an awning with droopy, steaming slices of pizza from Dante's. On one side of us, Old Town slunk low, all seedy and bejunkied. On the other, the construction cranes stood sleeping above the warehouses.

"What's the strangest thing you've ever done?" I asked.

Lawrence chewed on a piece of crust. "Strange how?"

"In bed. Like, something I wouldn't have guessed."

She looked at me askance. "That's between me and—I'm not telling."

"And *who*?" I rammed her shoulder with mine, but I was relieved. "Never mind, you can keep your dirty secret."

"Why, what about you? What's the strangest thing you've ever done?"

I flushed. "Not telling."

"Well, you brought it up."

"And I realized there are some things no one really needs to know."

"Was it with Flynn?"

"Sex with Flynn happened so long ago I barely remember it." It wasn't true. There had been a self-harming regret period when I'd made myself an expert in conjuring the voracious thrill of our early days. Now that I'd rather forget it, I couldn't—I'd made it a historic event. Sex with Ryan had never measured up.

"I think you really need to get laid," Lawrence said with concern that verged on alarm.

She had no idea, I remembered. I said, "I think you're right."

Satyricon was packed. The club's layout was frustrating, narrow and pillared, and the air was cottony with smoke, but I loved it. The sour-warm smell of old beer and cigarettes was always a strange comfort to me. The walls were thick with show flyers and staples, the palimpsest of a life lived at night, the place's history ineradicably attached to it in traces and staples and the stubborn tissuey residue of skinned posters. Years accumulated—and stayed. I moved so frequently that I'd started keeping things crated, learned to file and live out of the boxes. Would I ever be able to just *live* in a place? To stay, indefinitely?

An ache in my chest was interrupted by the thud of a kick drum. The opening band was a quartet of early-twenties boys who vamped and windmilled to songs that were the equivalent of clip art, as if the crowd were studded with A & R reps. Which it may have been— you couldn't tell anymore because the major labels hired people who looked like us. Or who *were* us, our peers who were half apologetic, half desperately optimistic they could do good within the system. Thrilled to get a paycheck, and trying not to think too hard about where it came from.

When the Cold Shoulder finally came out, Lawrence and I worked our way to the side of the stage, where the sound mix would be off but the sightline was good.

I'd imagined I was getting somewhere on the drums but to see Ryan really play, freed from the elementary school of our practice sessions, exposed how little I knew. How patient he was with me. Jesse and Mateo were showmen; they held their guitars in that low-slung effortless born-with-it way that boys so often did, like *Oh, this thing?,* and knew how to unleash with immaculate control. This was my third time watching the band and you could see the professionalism wearing down their interesting edges. Something a little calculated about the new choruses and bridges, a self-consciousness to a hook, certain stage moves I'd seen them do in exactly the same spot before. To my relief, Ryan drummed with dignity—focused, sharp, no drummer face.

"Your friend's good," Lawrence hollered over the clamor.

A thrilled horror rose in my chest that I could just say it, right now, like running down a diving board and leaping without pause; before I changed my mind, with my eyes still fixed on the stage, I said, "What if I told you I'd been sleeping with him?"

Lawrence leaned in, cupped her ear. "Huh? You're leaving when?"

"What? No." I clutched her arm. Her mishearing suddenly seemed prophetic. "I'm not *leaving*."

"They just started," she hollered. Only twenty and her hearing was already half-wrecked from years of loud shows and improvised toilet-paper earplugs.

"Never mind." I shook my head. "Later."

But when the band stopped and the sound system came on and the crowd began to shuffle out I couldn't bring it up, not without the noise to cushion it, and Lawrence had forgotten anyway; it was just another throwaway shout. We waited for the room to clear and then made our way backstage to say hello.

A different kind of energy filled the air, the energy of a room full of men. Because I was used to a backstage of girls—that's how skewed my world was, how fortunate I was—the aberration was my norm. I seldom even thought of myself as *woman* or *girl*, just person. Just human. I only became *girl* or *woman* when men walked into the room or I walked into theirs, when that gaze hit me like a hot breath. As a woman you walked in and were assessed, ignored, or both. These guys—

decent guys, cool guys, not even fratty dudes—filled more space, physically; the room felt smaller, the air thicker. The smell of damp jackets and band sweat and smoke. Making my way through them was like weaving through trees.

An arrowhead of sweat darkened Ryan's gray T-shirt. We kissed cheeks, like friends or Europeans. I felt the eye-flick of assessment from two girls perched on the end of a couch. *Don't worry, citizens,* I wanted to say, *I'm just a tourist.*

"I want to introduce you to Lawrence," I said. I turned to pull her in, but she was nowhere to be seen. I had lost her on the way. "Except she seems to have vanished."

"Really! How convenient."

I knocked his arm. "It's not like that."

"Whatever." He looked genuinely irritated.

"Give me a call?" I said.

"Maybe."

"Hey, that's my line."

"I'm borrowing it for a while."

Impulsively, I leaned in and whispered something in his ear. His eyes went heavy.

"What was that?" he said.

"An idea."

"Fuck you."

"I'm going now."

"Get out of here," he said, but he was smiling.

What are you doing, Andrea? I asked myself all down the hallway back to the main room. But I knew what I was doing. I knew he would succumb to me. This must be what it felt like to be Flynn.

The club was nearly empty, the house lights on. My sneakers stuck to the floor with every step. A man pushed a wide dry mop, sweeping empty cups into a clattering herd.

Lawrence stood outside. "I couldn't take the sausage party," she apologized. "There was a competitive conversation about Pavement bootlegs."

I could have told her then, as we walked down Northwest Fifth toward the car. Or on the ride home. But what was the point? There were things even your closest friends didn't need or want to know.

This time around, Ryan was different with me. Underneath his movements was a new tautness. His hand tracing my ribs and side was not the new lover's hand, discovering the landscape of the body, but the hand that has returned and is defining the limits—the surveyor's hand. He knew what I liked and he was ruthlessly determined to give it to me. When I slipped into performance mode, the mannered pleasure I found hard to shake during heterosexual sex, he placed a hand over my mouth and looked me in the eye, slowed way down. "No. Tell me when you really like it," he said, voice low. And he doggedly worked his way there, generous with his mouth. Until I did something that I'd never done before: I faked coming. This wasn't as easy as I thought it would be. The sounds and the moves were no problem, a common script, but the pretense of bliss was exhausting. I was all too present in my head, my body a mere attachment. After my last simulated whimper, I flipped over to my stomach so I could turn my face away and offered myself to him, eager to be done with it all; he took me up on it and came mercifully quickly inside me. I slid away from him, got up, and took a cigarette from his jacket pocket, overcompensating with a cliché.

"A cigarette! Really?" he said, skeptical but satisfied. I smiled, shrugged, and lit up. The only part I enjoyed of smoking was lighting the cigarette and taking the first drag, when the burning paper smells briefly sweet. I sat on the bed and handed it to him.

"Did you ever end up telling anyone about us?" he said.

"Not a soul," I said. "It's all ours."

"Not even your best friends?"

"Especially not my best friends."

He took a careful drag. "Why not? What would happen if you did?"

"A gossip bloodbath. Not fun."

He raised an eyebrow but kept his gaze on the ceiling. "Right."

"I mean it. I'm protecting you," I said.

"You're lying." The voice that came out of him was low, dark, extruded through his teeth. His whole body had become tight and still. I tasted the bitter root where I'd thought there was only sweet. I *had* lied, but not in the way he thought.

"I'm not lying," I said. "I guess I should go home now."

He looked at me and his eyes went soft again. "No. I wish you wouldn't."

For his sake, I wished I could say, *Me too.* I wished I could say he was good enough to bend my nature toward his. But he couldn't. And for my sake, for reality's sake, I wouldn't fake anything again.

I slid my legs off the side of the bed and stood. "You're a good one," I said, and I leaned over to kiss him apologetically.

He sat up and stamped the rest of the cigarette out in an empty mug. "I'm not sure I like the sound of that."

"I meant it."

"As you pull on your sweater."

———

There were no more drum lessons after that, no more anything with Ryan; the Cold Shoulder was practicing their new songs for the studio, and then it was February and they loaded up and drove to Austin to record. The long-anticipated Gold Stars record finally came out, my face among the crowd of lesbians on the back cover, and Meena and Lawrence headed down the West Coast to tour. It was a dim, rainy time of year and we all bunkered down, hiding from the gloom, wallowing in our own. Summer was always at Marcy's. Family dinner had been postponed two months running, and still no one knew what I'd done. Including me.

My Ailment

Ted suggested I had mono. For a week I'd been dragging my feet around the shop, slumping at the counter, yawning through the customer small talk. I'd never been so tired in my life, even though I was sleeping nine, ten hours a night. "Who've you been kissing?" he said.

"Shut up," I said. "No one."

"Get it checked out," he warned. "Don't go wiping out my customer base."

I was too tired to bike, so I drove to work and back clutching the wheel like a senior citizen. The insurance had run out on my poor Dodge Colt, and for the last few months the car had sounded like it was dragging a metal ladder from the undercarriage.

At home, a cloudy bubbling pot of rice was threatening to spill over on the stove while Summer stirred another steaming pan. The scent of garlic and chilies was nearly unbearable. "I made you dinner," she said. "Extra spicy."

I slung myself into a chair and said I wasn't feeling well.

"Even better. A little heat clears out the system."

"Seriously, Summer." I covered my face with my hands. "Don't get too close. I might have mono."

"Oh my god, who could have given it to you?"

"No one. I just . . . got it." I wondered if I should try to call Ryan in Austin. I was ready to be pissed if he'd given it to me.

"Does your throat hurt?"

"No."

"It will. Here, eat while you can."

While we ate, she said there was something she needed to tell me before she told everyone else at family dinner. "You should hear it from me first."

"I won't tell anyone." I leaned in. "I'm so good with secrets."

"I'm moving in with Marcy."

I slumped back. "Seriously?"

Marcy had a notorious pattern: instantly in love, and instantly out, on a precise one-year cycle. Always the girlfriend moved in with her too soon, and always it ended in explosion or collapse.

"Yes." Summer was crestfallen. "Aren't you happy for me? I'm in love."

"Of course," I said, and apologized. "It's wonderful." What else could I say? I thought of how I'd felt when I first moved in with Flynn, the thrill of certainty sweeping away all pessimism, only the supremest optimism. Lucky Summer. That feeling was worth the pain of losing it. And there was no warning a person away from someone they wanted, even if they knew better. See also: self.

"But she's allergic to dogs," I remembered. "What about Bullet?"

Summer was ruefully, stubbornly in love; she looked at Bullet as if the dog were a favorite Goodwill sweater she had outgrown. "I have to find her a new home. A really good one."

"Can I stay in the house?"

"I'm sure you can."

"Then I'll keep Bullet." I was already feeding the neighbor's abandoned orange cat. I'd started calling her Edith Head, after the gown designer in old movies, and she had moved more or less permanently to our front porch, sneaking inside through a tear in the screen door on warm days. I wasn't sure how to afford feeding the dog on top of it, but I couldn't let a pit bull loose into the wilderness of noncommittal punks whose housing situations changed quarterly. Especially not Bullet.

"Really? You would be the best parent." Summer stroked Bullet's big hard head and tears filled her eyes, but they were fond tears of life change, not remorse. She had already moved on as if the dog were just another roommate. "You be a good girl for Andy."

"You're not gone yet," I said.

"Right," she said. "But I have to go to work now."

Before she headed out, strapping on her bike gloves, Summer said, "Go to the doctor."

"Okay."

"Tomorrow."

I handed her the helmet hanging by the door. "Be safe," I said, as I always did.

"Be good," she croaked, E.T.-style, and held out her index finger. I pressed mine to it.

"Always am."

Her blinking red bike light weaved down the block and around a dark corner.

I had come to love this stupid little bungalow with its narrow kitchen and the walls we'd painted peacock blue and pumpkin orange and pool-table green, the overstuffed bookshelves, the fig and pear trees in the yard, the slanting porch, my Christmas-lit basement with its carpet-scrap corner and drum kit. I loved Summer, even with her unorthodox hours and her long red hairs trailing across the bathroom floor. That feeling of being left behind crept darkly into my peripheral vision, and I tried to blink it away. After all, I got to keep the house. I could stay. I just had to find someone to live with me.

Outside In, the free youth clinic, was quiet and clean. Gray carpet and gray late-morning light. Two teenagers cloaked in green army jackets and a taupe odor sprawled across three chairs, making out, facial piercings clicking against each other. A blond girl with no makeup and a band T-shirt sat in a corner, legs crossed, ankle jiggling. A sick, skinny kid who was maybe thirteen, young enough to be gender-indeterminate without even trying, slouched on the carpet, hood up, knees up, and glowered wearily as if still on the sidewalk warning off predators.

I'd been luckier than they were, and I didn't forget it. I'd had half a great education, enough work to keep myself afloat, good health so far, and good friends abundant with love and favors and job tips and housing connections. I'd had the foundations, at least, of a family who schooled me and taught me how to work within the system, and when that net tore, my chosen family stepped up to catch me. But in this room we all shared something: broke, uninsured, and under twenty-seven.

"Andrea Morales?"

I followed the nurse back to a clean, quiet room.

The nurse had her graying hair pulled back in an easy low ponytail and the corners of her eyes turned downward in a forgiving curve. "I think I have mono," I said. She asked me about my symptoms as she measured and weighed me and looked at my throat. Then she handed me a urine cup and sent me down the hall.

Back in the exam room, I was only a few pages into the foreign mainstream universe of *People* before the nurse returned and delicately closed the door behind her. "You don't have mono," she said.

"Thank god."

"You're pregnant."

It's always obvious in retrospect. But my periods had often been erratic and light, and I never paid attention to them. Why would I? Stress had rendered my cycle unpredictable—it was not unusual for it to disappear for a month or two. I'd suffered a few waves of nausea, but it was flu season, and I'd never had a great immune system. In one very slim folder of my mind, the one labeled RYAN, I had remembered that condoms were important, because god forbid I carry an STD back over the lesbian border; but in my main operating system,

I was simply gay, always had been, always would be. Pregnancy was not a possibility you even considered.

"But I'm a lesbian," I said.

Kindly, she asked, "Did you have sex with a man?"

"Just a little."

"It can happen on just one go."

"But I used condoms."

"Oh, honey," she said. "I have to ask you some questions now as a matter of procedure."

Yes, I knew who had gotten me pregnant. Yes, it was consensual. No, I was not afraid of him. No, I had not told him yet.

"Let's get a blood draw," she said. "Do you have an idea of how far along you might be?"

I thought back to when the drum lessons started. There'd been the time we tangled on the basement floor, but that hadn't led to sex in the straight sense; I was too cautious about the possibility Summer would come home. The only time it could have happened was the night I'd faked it, a month ago. I started to explain and found I could not stop. For once, confession felt like a true unburdening. The seal on my secret split, and I told the nurse everything. I talked while she pumped the armband tight around my bicep and I paused while she checked my breathing with the cool stethoscope, because she asked me to be quiet for a moment and breathe, and then I picked up again as she drew my blood.

The nurse sat on her swiveling stool and rested her clasped hands on her knees. She asked what I wanted to do. "You do have options."

I looked down at my abdomen, the opening in my gown where a tender stripe of my skin peeked out. Options? It was a cluster of new cells versus me, my whole life. I'd barely even had a chance to start living it.

"There's only one option," I said. "I can't have a baby."

She nodded calmly and wrote down the names of three clinics.

"Are you sure I'm pregnant?" I said.

"We'll have the blood test results tomorrow. We could try an ultrasound today."

"Would I see it? The . . . thing?"

"It's possible."

"God no."

I couldn't believe it was real, even as I dialed Planned Parenthood from a pay phone three blocks from Outside In. The voice on the line was kind, matter-of-fact. They called me "dear." They said they could see me next Tuesday. I said Tuesday sounded good. That was five days from now. How much could the cells multiply in five days? Not much, I figured. And I didn't want to know.

The receptionist suggested I bring a friend or partner for support. I said, "I'll be fine." I wanted it out, quick. The sooner it was gone, the more *over* this would all be. I was done with affairs. I was done with faking it. I was done with secrets. It was time to clean up my mess, all by myself. In five days I would expel this last trace of Ryan from my life. He didn't even need to know. No one did. I would box up the whole weird affair and store it in the farthest corner of the attic. Better yet, recycle it.

If it was even true. I bought a three-pack of pregnancy tests in a downtown drugstore and stowed them deep in my backpack. It wasn't until nearly midnight, alone in the house, that I had the nerve to try them.

Positive, positive, positive.

I went to the kitchen and poured myself a glass of water. When I tried to drink from it, my hands shook so much I had to set the glass on the counter and brace myself. I walked out the front door and stood on the porch in the cool damp night. I slid my hand under my shirt and touched my flat abdomen. All I could feel was my own warm skin. Whatever was inside me was tiny and deep, secreted away.

I started walking. My eyes were so wide they ate everything. Everything I saw, I thought, *This is what I saw on the night I found out.* The neighborhood was tucked into itself. Small bungalows, cracked sidewalk, lopsided fences. Green grass and bare trees. Who was born here? What did it mean to grow up here? Where were the secret places the neighborhood kids knew? The Portland horizon was close and dark with trees, a basin packed with houses, the sky plum and cloudy with city light. My eyes filled with windows and rooftops and cars and chain-link. I wanted prairie and field and a black sky with translucent cloud-streaks gauzing the moon. I wanted a single house like an answer at the end of a long dark driveway, a window glowing beacon-yellow. I wanted my mother. I nearly choked on such a want.

The next morning I wrapped the used tests in a plastic bag and threw them into a Dumpster on MLK while walking Bullet.

I borrowed Summer's dog-eared purple copy of *Our Bodies, Ourselves.* The embryo was probably the size of a lentil or maybe a pea. That was nothing! A mere legume. It hardly even existed. Five days couldn't go quickly enough. I was seized by the urge to eradicate, eradicate.

I opened my closet and dresser and pulled out all

the clothes I hadn't worn in more than a year. Jackets from high school, wrecked jeans from college, oversize T-shirts for bands I didn't even like anymore, socks cross-pollinated with Flynn's: I was like a bird who'd stashed every feather it molted. I had nested in old selves for too long, afraid I'd need them again.

The Sexual Minority Youth Resource Center was housed in a cinder-block building on Belmont Avenue. I unloaded four bags of clothes into the free box in a soft cascade, and three street kids dove right in and started pawing around like puppies. I thought, *You're all babies.* One immediately wriggled into an old acrylic ski sweater. "Looks good," I said, and the kid gave me a thumbs-up. A surprising wave of love caught me off guard. I wanted to defend them all with knives and fists. *Fuck everyone who let you go*, I thought. *I would never. Ever.*

I ran my fingers over the lead type on the press bed. The sweet plasticky smell of the sticky ink filled my head and throat, as if I were drinking it; it smelled strangely delicious and I wanted to suck it in, then worried that I shouldn't even breathe it, then thought, *Oh, what does it matter.*

I spread glossy gold ink over the drum of the Vandercook and cranked through a test run of Save the

Date cards. By the time these people's wedding arrived in September, this whole fiasco would be seven months behind me and still receding. Eventually it would shrink to the vanishing point and disappear.

I looked down at my torso. Nothing looked different. My body was still entirely my own. It still looked like the body I knew. At this point, what was inside me was only a cell cluster. It was just *knowledge,* really.

But how could I ever un-know it? You can burn the book but not the story. I did not like this thought.

Just to scare myself, I imagined another September. *Big as a house.* Me, as a house. I adjusted the leading in the bed and thought of what it would be like to hold a brand-new human in my hands. What would it be like to be raised by me and my friends? To grow up here, in this rainy lush place where it almost never snowed and everyone could be in a band? To become one of those Portland kids who had always seen piercings and tattoos, who knew what a heroin addict looked like, what a gay person looked like, what a protest looked like? Who carried a bus pass and hung out on the steps at Pioneer Square, who knew how to compost and the safest way home by bike, who never carried an umbrella and never knew parental rejection? I would have liked to be such a kid.

Get real, Andrea.

The Breakup

In the morning, the phone rang with the results of my blood test: I was seven weeks along. I said, "That's truly impossible," with a wave of relief—clearly they had the wrong results!—until the person explained that they count the two weeks before conception. I said, "So really it's only five weeks," and she said, "In a way, but officially, you're seven weeks pregnant." I said, "None of this makes any fucking sense," and hung up. That evening, the phone rang and at the sound of Ryan's voice my skin seemed to turn inside out. I pictured him on a sagging couch in the studio's break room. Or at a corner pay phone in the mild dry Austin evening, his arms bare in a T-shirt.

"What's up?" I said. My voice curdled; I cleared my throat.

"I'm back."

"What?" The receiver grew slippery in my hand. I glanced at the kitchen. Summer had paused the hand mixer and was carefully scraping down a mixing bowl, ear turned toward the living room. He wasn't due back for five more days. "Did you finish early?"

"You could say that. Let's get a drink."

My mouth had gone dry. "I can't. I have family dinner at Robin and Topher's, and then there's some house show by Division. Is everything all right?"

"You sound weird."

"No I don't."

"Yes you do."

"I don't want to talk about it," I said. "I have to go. Why are you back early?"

"I don't want to talk about it."

"Fine," I said. "Good-bye."

He hung up.

A minute later the phone rang again. "Just come over," he said. It was unlike him to plead. "Have a drink with me. One round of Scrabble."

"I told you, I have to go to family dinner."

"Oh." He sighed. "Never mind."

"Are you okay?"

"Don't worry about it."

We hung up. I called him back.

"Hey. I'll come by for a minute. But I can't stay long."

As I pulled on my coat Summer leaned out of the kitchen and asked whom I'd been talking to and I said it was Ted. I said I'd broken something at the shop—which was in fact true, I'd knocked over a sixty-dollar Blenko vase, there went the day's wages—and I'd meet her at dinner after I'd taken care of it.

Every parking space on Ryan's block was taken. I circled until I found one across the street from that shadowy doorway where we'd first kissed. If only I'd gone straight home from La Luna that night. If only I had grabbed an extra beer from backstage and not bothered heading over to the bar. If only someone had already taken that bar stool beside him, or I'd left a minute later and worked my way through some other opening in the crowd. If only I'd not seen Flynn and Vivian and could have coasted along in cozy ignorance for just another night. If only I hadn't gone to the show at all, and had lingered in my den of crowd-shy sorrow a day or two longer. I rewound, replayed, rechose my own adventure. To think that if I had made one minor different move on the night it all started—that a mere minute could have sealed off this long, unfathomable tunnel I had fallen into—I never would have even known it could exist. There were a hundred ways to delete one minute of that night so that now I would be headed guilelessly to family dinner with no secrets and no in utero guest and no idea what it was like to fuck a man, an entirely other Andrea, the Andrea I wanted to believe I was, and the Andrea everyone still thought I had been all along. To undo the months that followed was far more complicated. At a certain point, you can't blame chance. Only yourself.

I walked slowly enough that my hair was soaked by the time I reached his front door. I let myself in.

The apartment was warm and the familiarity of the scent jolted me. It smelled like a period in my life, already taking on retrospect. Ryan had lived there two years and still it looked temporary, with its white walls, that plain little Danish sofa, the lone shelf of records and CDs, the stereo stacked on a side table, one rug at the entryway, a thrift-store painting of a horse above the sofa.

Ryan slouched on the couch with his repaired guitar, plucking out a countermelody to the record playing on the stereo. A suitcase lay open on the floor, half-emptied. He had showered and shaved—his hair was still damp—and dark circles shadowed his eyes. "Hello, you," he said, and started to lift off the guitar.

"Don't get up, it's okay," I said, shrugging off my

jacket and kicking off my wet shoes. "What are you playing?"

He strummed a terse flourish. "A little song called 'We Broke Up.'"

I wasn't sure how to take that. "Is that what we did?"

"It's not about *you*." Ryan hit a low sour chord and set the guitar aside. "The fucking band."

"You broke up?" I stopped. "The Cold Shoulder broke up?"

Ryan rubbed his hand across his face. "I'm so tired," he said, pushing himself to his feet. I couldn't help it, I hugged him, and he hugged back. His gray sweater was soft and worn thin. I could see the black T-shirt underneath. His head dropped to rest on mine for a moment.

"I'm so sorry," I said.

"Want a drink?" he said.

I did, desperately. But I could not bring myself to do it. *Tuesday*, I told myself. *I'll drink Tuesday. A lot.* I pulled away. "Water's fine. What about the new record?"

"The record." He opened the fridge and peered inside as if it contained a distant view. "The record. Is four songs long."

They had fought in the studio: with each other, with the engineer, with the songs. Ryan cut short my dismay.

"It's okay," he said curtly, setting two glasses down on the counter with a thunk. "It always happens. Bands have life spans. They don't last forever. There will be others."

"But you loved the Cold Shoulder."

"Jesse wanted out. He wants his own deal. I think he thinks he can be the next Elliott." Ryan gave the ice tray a sharp twist and the cubes popped loose, a sound like joints cracking.

"What about the songs you recorded?"

"Either we'll make a posthumous EP out of it or they'll just be the Great Lost Recordings. The record label's going under too. Mercury bled them dry." It was happening more and more these days: the vampiric deals the majors had struck with the small indies were collapsing. It was bad enough to see your home-grown culture stolen and sold back to you in facsimile at the mall. Even worse when the original pillars of it then started to crack. Story of the decade. The nineties could break your heart.

He allowed my sympathy but it seemed not to touch him. He handled it all like a journalist, detached, merely reporting, and focused on pouring the water into my glass as if measuring it precisely. He said, "At least the band went out on a high note. We never stuck around long enough to get bad."

"You got to have only the good part," I said.

"Yeah. Story of my life, right?" His laugh was light and bitter as beer. "Speaking of. Here you are."

"I'm definitely not the good part." My voice caught in my throat.

He asked what I meant. I said, "You don't want to know," but then of course he did, and I wasn't prepared to talk my way out of it.

My hands slid deep into the pocket of my sweatshirt and met over my abdomen. I took a deep breath.

Ryan's face when I said those two words: realization, then narrowed eyes, then fear, and then he turned away and walked to the stereo, where the record had spun out and the needle circled, *thk . . . thk . . . thk . . .*

He knelt. "Fuck," he said with each precise move— "fuck," resting the player arm in its cradle; "fuck," a gentle snap of the wrist to settle the record in its sleeve; "fuck," easing it into the cover; "fuck," done. He shelved the record and sat back on his heels, his back turned to me. "What next?"

"The obvious," I said.

"I'll pay for it."

"They have a sliding scale," I said. "I can do it."

"No, let me help. Fuck. You probably hate me now."

"Why would I hate you? It's not like it's your fault. Unless there's something I don't know. Should I?"

"No! I was careful. We were both careful. Weren't we?"

"Well, I slept with someone who could get me pregnant, so that's on me. That was optional, and I did it."

"That's me. I'm always optional, aren't I?"

I said I didn't mean it to sound like that and he said well it did. I said, "Wasn't I just as optional to you?"

"Clearly *you* think so," he said.

I raised my hands. "I can't fight about this right now. I have to go to dinner."

"Just tell me when your appointment is," he said, "and I'll be there."

"Thanks, but I can do this on my own. I'll be fine."

"That's what you think," he said. "You shouldn't go there alone."

I pulled my hands deep into my sleeves. What did I know about Ryan after all? I knew his body, I could name all the places he'd lived and all the bands he had played in, I knew selected stories; I knew from his guitar that he could, on impulse, destroy something he loved. I knew he liked to have space. It was one of the reasons we had worked: I gave him infinite space, and he gave me easy doses of affection. So it seemed. But I had never wanted to talk about the girls I'd been with—I had to hold in reserve *some* queer part of myself—so I had never asked him about his. Now I wanted to ask, *You've been there?*, but held back. If he had, it wasn't my business. And if he had, wasn't I just another one—an ordinary girl, and biologically stuck with it?

I tried to suppress a shiver as I zipped up my damp jacket.

"You're leaving now? After that?"

"I'm sorry," I said. "I'm so sorry about your band, and I'm so sorry I messed up your life, and I'm sorry I got . . . pregnant, and now I have to go pick up a giant bottle of bourbon to bring to dinner."

"Of course. The *family.* I suppose they all know already?"

"Hell no. You're the only one I've told."

"Are you going to tell them now?"

"It's not my plan."

"You'll never tell them, will you," he said. "As if all this never happened."

"It's not like that, Ryan."

"It did happen," he said. "You can try to forget it if you want, but in real life, all of this happened. I was real."

I couldn't bear the look in his eyes. "I know," I said.

"Were you even going to tell *me*?"

One last lie. "Yes."

I left.

Robin and Topher and Marisol lived in a house known as the Spawn, a lightly haunted, peeling pink Victorian on Southeast Salmon Street, not quite far enough away for me to fully compose myself en route. I opened the door agitated and shivering, whiskey in hand, and Topher caught me in the entry with his Polaroid camera and a bright flash.

He greeted everyone like this, laying out the Polaroids on the coffee table to cure. Our faces emerged from ghostly to glowing. Summer's cherry-red hair betrayed half an inch of dim roots but she was an expert at assuming a pose; when the lens turned to her she snapped right into a coy vamp, finger on glossy lip, until the click of the shutter released her immediately back into whatever she'd been doing. Marcy allowed a resigned smirk—*You kids,* her face said, even as she kept hanging out with us. Squinting Lawrence wore a Boy Scout shirt with too-short sleeves rolled above the elbow. Robin tilted forward in her pleather jacket, a long wavy strand of hair trickling over her shoulder, the glint of her labret piercing a hot little star in the flash. The flash gleamed off the pink dining room wall and Meena's narrow glasses. Marisol was twenty-two but looked sixteen, with her plush cheeks and knee socks. In my picture, I was saying *No!* and reaching for the camera, eyes wide, lips round, hand a blown-out blur in the foreground, a moment too late. This would be me that night—both reaching out and begging *no.*

Family dinner was Southern-themed, and they'd turned the heat up to the seventies, "for authenticity." The tangy musk of barbecue sauce and humid sweetness of hot corn bread overrode the usual whiff of cat litter.

When no one was looking I fixed myself a whiskey ginger that was secretly all ginger and prowled the kitchen, tasting everything until we could finally eat. My hunger astonished me. I loaded up biscuits with barbecued seitan and sweet pickles. My mouth watered, pooled. I couldn't keep my eyes off the serving dishes, a jolt of hoarder's panic every time someone forked off another slice of seitan. The greens, on the other hand, tasted bitter and sick to me. All I wanted was to drench everything in sight in that barbecue sauce. I offered to take the used dishes into the kitchen, just so I could devour everyone else's last abandoned bites. Meena came in and caught me licking my plate.

"Girl, your nose," she said, and I reached up and swiped off a smear of sauce. "What's up with you?"

"Well," I said, "I don't even know how to answer that."

Then Robin came into the kitchen and told us to clear out. "No cleanup yet! There's pie."

"Pie!" I set down the plate. "We can help with that."

"Wait, what did you mean by that?" Meena said as we headed back to the dining room with dessert plates.

"Pie? We'll eat the hell out of it."

"No, what's going on with you," she said, but by then we were back in the dining room and I waved it off.

"Nothing."

As inconspicuously as I could, I polished off two wedges of peach ginger pie, buttery and rich, oozing with orange flesh and thick syrup, and finished Lawrence's half-abandoned slice of chess pie, a sticky, sickly thing I'd never heard of before and found visually repulsive but couldn't stop eating anyway. I looked around the table at my friends, my family, to see if they noticed, and realized I knew the details of their faces so well I could draw any one of them without looking. I imagined being brought up among these people, what a weird good world that would be.

"Smoke?" Topher extended a pack toward me.

While I'd faked my way through my whiskey-less ginger, everyone else had hit the booze generously, and now they pulled out cigarettes and started to light up.

I said, "I thought you guys didn't smoke inside."

He said, "It's okay, it's family dinner. And it's pouring out there. Light on up."

Summer set her elbows on the table, blew two perfect smoke rings, and raised her glass. "You guys, I have good news."

What would smoke do? I tried to summon the information from eighth-grade health. Drinking was bad, smoking was bad, what about secondhand smoke? Something about birth weight? How much did it take? Why did I care? "Can we open a window?" I said.

Summer gave me an annoyed glance.

Robin raised the dining room window an inch. "Is that enough? It's chilly out there."

I said, "Maybe I can switch seats with Lawrence." She sat closest to the window.

"Okay." Lawrence got up.

"What's up?" Meena said. "Andy's acting bizarre."

"Nothing's up." I slid into Lawrence's seat. "Go ahead, Summer."

"Look at her face!" Meena said.

I pretended to wipe my mouth as I took a deep filtered breath through my napkin.

Summer looked from Meena's bemused smirk to my half-masked face. "Is this about your mono situation?"

"You have *mono*?"

"No, no, no," I said. "I don't have mono. I'm fine. Come on, Summer has news."

"What was it then?" Summer said. "Did you go to the doctor yet? Are you contagious?"

"The doctor?"

"Spill it, Andy."

Everyone looked at me. I couldn't speak.

Six faces on me. I had to come up with something. *Think, think,* I thought.

Over the course of the Ryan affair I had trained myself to practice having a thought—I would come up with an acceptable thought to be having, and then set it aside in reserve while I delved into my real, inappropriate thoughts about my secret. Then if someone asked what I was daydreaming about I could grab the stored thought and present it. *This cringey poster I'm supposed to make. That review of our art show in the Willamette Week. This one thing I read about hyenas. How when I was twelve a wood thrush hit the living room window and I stored its body in the laundry room freezer for a week.*

But they'd caught me now with nothing—only the truth came to mind. My heart began to beat so hard I felt it in my ears and eyes. "I can't talk about it," I said. "Another time."

Now concern set in. Was I sick? No, I said, not really. Had something happened to me? I looked traumatized. What the fuck happened?

To my dismay, tears came to my eyes. I hid my crumpling mouth behind my hand and begged my body to stop betraying me. I knew one rip could take out a whole net, and all the fish would swim out just like that.

"What the fuck? Oh my god, Andy, were you hurt?" Meena's eyes brightened with fear.

"No, it's not that at all. It's okay, it's okay, it's okay," I said as tears streamed down my cheeks. They had backed me into a cul-de-sac of concern. I had no way out.

I said, "I'm pregnant."

A moment as they all silently translated the word. Meena looked like she'd been shot.

"You're fucking with us," said Marcy.

"I wish."

"How the fuck—"

"Were you assaulted?" said Robin.

"No, I wasn't assaulted," I said. I silently struggled to formulate a plausible case for immaculate conception.

But Meena was already white-knuckling her fork, eyes narrowed. "If you're about to say what I think you're going to say—frankly, I would almost rather hear that you'd been roofied."

"Meena!" spat Robin.

"Whoa," Lawrence said.

"Oh my god," I said, "can we appreciate the fact that I'm unmolested, even if it means I did the unthinkable?"

"Hold on now." Summer swept her hands above the table as if spreading a tablecloth, and brought them down with a hard smack. "You fucked a *man*?" she said with an incredulous smile. "Super-lesbian Andrea?"

Topher mimed falling out of his chair, then took it all the way and puddled at Robin's feet. Robin reached down and petted his forehead. Marisol watched us all like we were a movie, eyes wide.

"Not only did you fuck a man, you got *pregnant*?" Robin said.

"How did you even *do* that?" marveled Marcy, a mix of disgust and awe in her voice.

"I can't even *believe* you would do that," Meena said. "And look where it got you."

"Forgive me, Father, I have sinned," I muttered.

"It's not funny. Who the hell is this cock-toter? Why didn't you tell me?"

"Hey now," Topher grunted from the floor.

"Why didn't you tell *any of us*?"

"Especially me, your housemate, who this would especially affect. I mean, you were the first person I told *my* news. Which I guess we've all completely forgotten about now."

"Please tell your news," I said. "I beg you."

"What is it?"

"Wait, we'll get to it. We have to deal with this."

"I didn't tell you because I was going to just take care of it," I said. "And because of *this*. Because this is what happens. Now everyone's upset, and I feel even more fucked up about it, which I didn't think was possible."

"I'm upset because I *care*," Meena said.

"Yeah, that was my parents' line too."

Topher's face emerged above the table. "Back up, back up, back up." He pulled himself into his seat. "Who is the dude? How did we get here?"

I told them the barest skeleton of the truth, but it was clear the lie stretched back months. I could see them all rewinding, pausing, replaying. *Even while we . . .* As clearly as if subtitles scrolled across their foreheads, I saw them thinking, *Who are you?*

If someone would just say it, I would answer, *You know who I am. You are who I am.* But what if they no longer believed me? I felt gelatinized with panic.

"This guy Ryan," I said, and Summer said, "The

one who gives you 'drum lessons'? The one who 'cuts your hair'?"

"For the record, those were not actually euphemisms."

"That guy? Is your *inseminator*?" Meena said.

"We're not in a hog unit."

"You *mated*."

"Oh my god, please, stop. Look, it was just an affair. It wasn't supposed to happen like this. He was just, like, a friend with benefits. I was on the rebound."

"That's a hell of a rebound." Marcy was leaning back in her seat, swigging from a bottle she held loosely around the neck.

"Well, I hope it never happens again, because I'm really not comfortable with dudes around," said Meena.

"You work with dudes," I said. "You play shows with bands with dudes in them."

"That's work. This is life."

"What about Topher?" said Lawrence.

"*I'm* more masculine than Topher," Meena said.

Topher looked wounded and I hit Meena's arm. She said, "Did you just hit me?" but Robin overrode her with, "It's not about masculinity. Topher is othered too, and he's conscious of his male privilege."

They looked at me pointedly. "Okay," I said, "so is Ryan."

"Really. He's white and straight. Like, how in touch with his male privilege is this guy?"

"He's vegetarian," I fumbled. Groans all around. "He speaks Spanish better than I do." Admittedly a sore spot for me.

"I speak Spanish better than you do," Meena muttered.

Marisol swatted her shoulder. "Cállate. That's not fair."

"I don't know, he's really pretty good, I've never heard him say sexist shit. He was raised by a single mom?"

"Oh, Andy. Are you out of your mind?" Robin said. "Have you been away from straight men for so long that you've forgotten what they're really like?"

Summer returned to the table with what appeared to be a pint glass full of bourbon. "No, this is exactly the problem—she *has* been with one. She's been acclimated."

"A, I'm done with him," I said. "And B, Summer, what about all the men *you* get up on every day? Is that a problem too?"

Summer snapped, "It is not the same, and you know it. I do it for *money*. I do it to make a living. And I don't fuck them."

"Andy, what about those girls you went out with? Did they know?" Meena asked.

"Men spread disease," said Robin.

Topher looked offended. "Excuse me?"

"Lesbians get STDs too," young Marisol, well trained, countered earnestly.

"Not from each other!" Meena said, recoiling. "And if they do, it's because one of them was either with a guy or slept with someone else who was. There's always a penis at the root."

Summer made a gagging face. "Please never say that phrase again."

"Gold star until I die," Meena said, and Marcy raised her bottle.

"Andy is clearly insane, but also, fuck all y'all and your gold stars," Summer said. "We don't always choose." Apologies rose around the table but she shook Marcy's hand off her forearm and said, "No. Enough."

"I did have the choice," I said. "I don't know why I did it. Maybe I just wanted to mess around with someone who definitely, for once, had no chance of fucking any of my friends. And maybe I didn't tell because I didn't want to be judged by the Lesbian Mafia."

"You *are* the Lesbian Mafia."

"Not for long, I bet," I said.

"You're still a lesbian," Lawrence said. "Aren't you?"

"Maybe you're *bisexual*," Meena hissed. We all winced. *Bisexual* was a word we seldom spoke outside of our initial coming-out phases. It was a beginner concept, for newbies and outsiders. *You think it's going to ease the shock,* Vivian had warned me in college, *but no. It just means that your mother will forever hold on to hope that you will one day come around and end up with a man.* My mother. Stomach clench.

"I am not"—I funneled my voice into a vicious whisper—"*that.*" I couldn't even say the word. It sounded so mechanical. Or like something under a microscope, squirming on a glass slide. It made me think of nematodes. We knew girls who were bisexual. Or whatever. Girls who we thought were one of us who then went for a roll in the hay with a boy. Which was fine. We just didn't necessarily want to know about it. Sometimes one would come to a lesbian party with her new . . . boyfriend, and you felt awkward for the guy standing there, being a good sport, and for the girl, knowing she must feel a little alienated among her own people, and you kind of hoped it would work out and kind of hoped it wouldn't, and you just weren't quite sure what to say.

Because to us *bisexual* was the earnest white girl in your women's studies class who had a nice boyfriend and wanted to clock in a little more oppression. The Riot Grrrls who hated that they wanted boys and sometimes professed their girl-love physically, an extension of their politics more than their desire. Bisexual was the way celebrities avoided it, or faked it. Or couples in the bar or the classifieds who wanted a third. Or women who remained happily married or boyfriended to a guy who was okay with their getting with another woman, or who just felt emotionally open to the possibility, who thought they could get into it if they gave it a shot, like hot yoga.

"I'm a lesbian who experimented," I said forcefully. "That's all."

"Maybe we should get back to Summer's news," Lawrence said timidly.

"It's going to be hard to top this," Topher said.

"Fine. I'm moving out," Summer said, stamping her cigarette butt down hard on her pie plate.

"Because of the baby?"

"No! I didn't even fucking know about a baby! I'm moving in with Marcy"—Summer flung a hand toward Marcy, who braced her with a hand on her back and a worried smile—"which was what I was about to tell you all. But we've been a little *upstaged*."

"Well, I rather doubt there's going to be a *baby*," said Meena. "Andrea may be crazy but she's not *crazy*."

I was so tired of Meena knowing me into submission. "Oh, you think?" I said, purely to mess with her. "What if I did have it?"

"You can't *have* it!" Meena said. "How would you even do that?"

"Of course she can have it," said Marisol. "It's her body."

"You have no idea what I'm capable of," I said.

"God, if you wanted to have a baby you should have just used Topher's sperm," Robin said. "You could have had a nice little gayby."

Topher crossed his legs. "Don't pimp me."

"We could all name it," Lawrence said. "And raise it without a gender."

"Hell no," Meena said. "It is ethically wrong to procreate. The planet is horribly overpopulated and human reproduction is destroying everything."

"One baby's not gonna ruin the earth," said Marcy, who didn't yet recognize the glassy fervid glint Meena would get in her eye when you bumped against one of her deeply held convictions.

"I'm dead serious. This is a moral and ethical imperative—"

"Meena has an interview at Nike."

Everyone turned to Lawrence, who had been sitting on her hands, a frown deepening on her face. Then we all looked at Meena, who gave Lawrence a death glare. Lawrence cringed but shrugged.

"What?"

"Advertising?"

"Marketing?"

"Beaverton?"

"What the fuck is wrong with you?"

Meena said, "I need health insurance! I need a real job!"

"But *Nike*," Robin said. "The worst sweatshops of all."

Meena said, "I'm not going to give them any good ideas. I'm still going to do my own art on the side. I'm still going to do the band. I just, I need a real job."

"What happened to 'selling out'?"

Unnerved, Meena tried to redirect the searchlight back to me. "Oh, *I'm* selling out?" she said. "At least I didn't secretly fuck a man."

"Yeah, but you're basically fucking *the* Man," said Robin.

Meena and I both stood at the same time and said, "Fuck this."

"This is rich," Marcy said appreciatively. Finally she was getting her money's worth.

Robin folded her napkin and said, "Well, then," at the same time Topher pushed back his chair and said, wincing, "There's more pie?"

No one wanted pie. Well, I did, rather desperately,

but I didn't want any commentary about eating for two. I offered to do the dishes, hoping to linger in order to defer the furious talk that would erupt behind my back if I left first, but Robin and Topher and Marisol refused to let any of us help. They wanted to leave for the house show; two bands from Oakland were playing, and Marisol knew one.

I hated to peel away from the group, leaving them to discuss me, but I couldn't face a party. While they gathered the remaining alcohol and figured out who'd drive, I said good-bye, passed the coffee table strewn with Polaroids, and stepped outside.

The night had turned cold, clouds parted to reveal a sharp full moon, and I drew that first breath so deeply into my lungs it hurt. My secrets were gone. The Andrea I'd been was over. But instead of feeling that she'd died, I somehow felt wildly, recklessly alive. The wet sidewalk before me gleamed under the streetlights and I lengthened my strides down the block toward my car, charged with an inexplicable idea that I couldn't quite believe I was having. Could I?

My headlights were on, dim and dying.

I stopped in my tracks. "Oh fuck," I said. "Please. Please." But sure enough, the car could not start. A whine, a click, silence.

Lawrence found me trudging up Southeast Twentieth, near the cemetery. She pulled up beside me in her blue Corolla wagon and waved me in.

I wished I could lone-wolf it and say, *I'll take the bus,* or even tougher, *I'll walk.* But my adrenaline had ebbed and fatigue had hit me full force. I got in. Cool air still blew from the vents. "Thanks," I said. "Aren't you going to the party?"

"Meena is trying to get with Marisol and I don't really want to be around to watch."

"Oh." I blew on my cold fingers. "Are you into Marisol?"

Lawrence sighed. "She's not really my type. I was just excited there was someone new in town."

"Well, she got to see Meena at her most Meena tonight, so there's the true test."

"Oh my god, that dinner was so intense," Lawrence said.

"Do you think she'll forgive me? God, will anyone?"

"It was a shock, but honestly? I don't think it's *that* big a deal." Lawrence lowered her voice. "You know, I gave a blow job once in high school." She looked scandalized and amused by her own admission.

"We all know about your famous blow job, Lawrence. But it didn't knock you up." I looked at her.

"Kind of nasty, aren't they? I'd rather never do one again."

Lawrence shuddered. "I am so glad I'm a lesbian."

"Me too," I said. "Mostly."

"Mostly glad or mostly lesbian?"

I started to laugh and Lawrence did too. "Neither. Both. Oh my god, Lawrence, I'm fucking pregnant. That's what I am. I think I'm a whole other gender now."

"We can work with that."

The car had warmed up by the time we turned up Twelfth Avenue. "Lawrence. What if—" The toasty aroma of baking bread wafted through the vents. I looked out the window. Above the Franz Bakery, a giant loaf of premium enriched white rotated lazily. How could something so mass-produced and processed smell so real and good? "What if I just went for it? I mean, this is never going to happen again. It's like, here's my chance."

"How would you afford it?"

"I have no idea," I said. "Food stamps. Something. Maybe Summer can get me a dancing gig."

"Let's be honest, Andy, you can hardly touch your toes."

"When you're naked, you can get away with a lot. Or maybe Meena can get me a Nike job."

Lawrence cringed. "She's going to kill me."

"She'll get over it. Once she gets her first paycheck."

We pulled up in front of my house. "Whatever you do," Lawrence said, "I'm here for you. I mean it."

I leaned across the stick shift and hugged her tight. She tolerated it for a moment and then writhed gently away. Before I shut the door, she said sternly, "But there's one thing that's not negotiable." She looked troubled.

A shiver of dread. "What's that?"

"That child had better respect cats."

I solemnly swore.

That night in bed, I lay on my back and rested my hands on my abdomen. Of course it was far too early to feel anything. But I knew it was in there.

"You and me," I whispered in the dark. Two selves. "Do you think we could do this?"

Reasons Not (But What If)

REASONS NOT	(BUT WHAT IF)
▪ I have no money	
▪ will landlord even let me (is it like a pet clause)	
▪ roommate—no one wants to live w/a baby (Ryan?! doubt even he would) (plus complicated)	
▪ I HAVE NO MONEY	
▪ diapers terrible for environment	

- never want to live
  w/plastic toys on floor
- what if it's a boy

- raise a feminist boy
- chance baby will be
  queer too—genetic
  factor?

- how would I work and/or
  how much does day care
  cost
  DAY CARE
- this is not the life I
  planned

- then again technically
  nothing so far is a life I
  "planned" and still,
  amazing

- I'm too young

- when else are you
  going to do it
  not exactly a teen
  pregnancy and besides
  all those girls in high
  school managed it
  sort of

- pain of birth
  AAAAAAGH

- there are drugs

STRAY CITY · 251

- no sex ever again?
  lesbian untouchable?

- don't know any queers
  with babies
  besides, like, Adrienne
  Rich
  2nd wavers who came
  out late in life after
  husband etc. I mean
  people my age.
  would I have to hang out
  only w/straight moms at
  playground

- don't like word
  "mommy"

- what if baby calls me
  "mommy" and won't
  stop

- what would I do about
  Ryan
  child = child support? =
  bound for life?
  yikes

- big change
  haha

- could help out some, at
  least

- HAVE TO TELL PARENTS?! ☠
- entire life as I know it OVER?
- will lose friends

- will find out who real friends are
- what if it's cute
- what if it's smart
- what if it's an amazing person who fixes things no one else could
  like the world
- what if I end up loving it more than anything I've ever loved
- what if I already maybe almost do

- no idea how to raise a kid

- kid raised by us would be different
  ULTIMATE DIY PROJECT

- NO MONEY

- have lived w/o money
  since age 19
  money isn't love
  have mountains of love
  uncontrollable love
  feeling is already
  kicking in & I'm not
  sure I want to stop it

Out

The curtains were drawn on Topher and Robin and Marisol's house when I biked there the next morning to rescue my car. I was lucky: the battery had recalibrated enough to nudge the engine to sputtering life, so I wrangled my bike into the hatchback and drove to the studio, where I worked most of the day in eerie solitude. Summer stopped by our place that evening to swap out clothes, and the Gold Stars had band practice. I drowsily watched *High Art* on the couch with Bullet, growing more and more depressed in the process, and reminded myself it was just a movie, just one of those Saturday nights when everyone was busy. Tomorrow I'd be back in the thick of things. The Unrest Auxiliary of the Lesbian Mafia had a meeting to plan some direct action—since the art show had closed, we'd been working on pranks to mess with the downtown stronghold of the Church of Scientology.

When I arrived at the house at noon sharp, Jade, the lead organizer, was the only one waiting for me in the red-painted living room. A housemate was cooking something with cumin back in the kitchen.

"Is it true?"

I stopped unbuttoning my coat. "Is what true?"

Family dinner, it turned out, was not the verbal sanctuary we alleged it was.

"Who told you?"

"It doesn't matter." Jade looked at my stomach and asked what the plan was. I said that wasn't her problem to worry about. What was my relationship to the biological father? We're friendly, I said.

"Is he straight?"

"Yes."

"And you had . . . a relationship with him?"

"I don't know if I'd call it that."

"You slept with him? Multiple times?"

"It sounds weird when you put it like that."

"It does, doesn't it," she said pointedly. Then she adopted the self-care voice, a tone of firm, mannered earnestness. "Look. Andy, why don't you go on home. Rest up and do"—she gestured toward my abdomen—"whatever it is you need to do."

"But I'm here to work."

Jade gritted her teeth. Clearly I was being uncooperative. She said, "We have plenty of actual lesbians to carry on the Lesbian Mafia's work."

"I'm still a lesbian," I said. "And every lesbian is in the Lesbian Mafia."

Jade pressed her nail-bitten fingers into her temples and said if the Lesbian Mafia weren't clearly lesbians, then who could you count on to be one? Words had to *mean* something. And I said, Well, I'm definitely *queer*, and she said, Come on, "queer" can be anything, married suburbanites with a leash and a pair of nipple clamps claim they're queer. I said, Can't someone be *culturally* lesbian?, and she said it was a matter of *practice*, and I said, What about all those young girls stuck at home who know they're lesbians but haven't met any others yet, do they not count?, and she said, They get a pass, and I said, Like babies in purgatory?, and she said, I don't know that Catholic shit, don't confuse the issue: you're with a dude. I said, I'm not *with* him, I just did things with him, and she said, So you're totally done with him? and I said, Yeah. She said, Never again? I said, Who cares?

She gave me a look.

"I'm a card-carrying member," I said. "I literally *printed the cards.*"

She threw up her palms. "Thank you for your service?"

"Fine," I said. "I'm out. Good luck."

Jade sighed with relief. "Thank you, Andy. Good luck to you too. I really mean it."

"I'm sure you do," I said. She gave me a stiff, sympathetic hug at the door.

I realized I had traded one small town for another.

I thought about some of the most dogmatic anarchist punks I'd known, whose parents turned out to be bankers and oilmen. I thought of the class-discussion radicalism police who leaped to call out everyone else on their shit, desperate to cover their own. How even I had thrown myself deeper into the Lesbian Mafia as soon as I started sleeping with Ryan. It seemed in our urgency to redefine ourselves against the norm, we'd formed a church of our own, as doctrinaire as any, and we too abhorred a heretic.

By the time I got home my whole body felt like it was aflame with anger and shame—a cold fire, a numbing burn. The only place I could bear to be was outside. I summoned Bullet and grabbed some treats and her leash. Ryan called while I was pulling on my rain boots. I said I was going to the river and he could come along if he wanted. I didn't think he would, but he said sure.

Bullet paced in the back seat. When Ryan got in, she licked his face.

"How are you?" he said gently as I ramped onto Highway 84.

"I honestly don't know," I said.

"Let me come with you to the clinic on Tuesday. Please."

I checked my blind spot and accelerated to merge. When I was settled into the flow of traffic, I said, "I'm not going."

"Not going Tuesday or not going at all?"

I shook my head. "At all. I think."

"That would mean . . ."

I nodded.

"Andrea, that's crazy."

"Totally."

"I mean it's really fucking crazy."

"I know," I said.

"Aren't you a *lesbian*?"

I shot him a look. "What does that mean?"

"Seems like this would really mess with your whole identity." He said *identity* with dental precision.

"Do you want to get out right here?" I said, swerving toward the shoulder. Bullet stumbled across the back seat.

"Jesus," he said. "I'm sorry."

I wanted to tell him about getting kicked out of the Lesbian Mafia, but to do so would disclose the existence of the Lesbian Mafia. I couldn't break the code like that. I said, "I've had a bad fucking day."

We parked in the muddy potholed clearing that was the lot and Bullet scrambled over Ryan to get out. A dirt trail led through dead corrals to a vast winter field, brown and gold, a gray path curving through it, power lines overhead. Bullet opened up and ran for no reason other than to run, legs like pistons, ears streaming backward. She galloped in huge elliptical laps as if she were pursued by happy demons. It was impossible not to laugh.

"Joy," I said with relief. "There it is."

"Hers or yours?"

"Both." I realized Bullet was my dog now, my animal family. I'd protect her. She'd protect us.

The path turned sandy and wound through scrubby willows toward the half-flooded river. Bullet thundered past us as if she were on a racetrack.

The river was swollen and slow, dark blue in the afternoon light, with only a small high strip of beach to stand on. Bullet rooted around in the willows and came up with an abandoned flip-flop. Ryan took it from her and hung it on a high branch.

"I'm trying to get my head around this." He pulled

out a pack of cigarettes and paused to light one. I shielded the flame for him, felt its brief warmth on my palms. "I never wanted kids. Never."

"Why not?"

"I don't know. The same reason I don't want a horse?"

I had always wanted a horse, but I held that back. "It's not really the same," I said.

"Yeah, you can sell a horse," he said. "I wouldn't have thought *you* wanted a kid either."

When I was growing up I'd always thought I'd have kids, because everyone had kids, and I preferred making blanket forts and playing Legos with my younger siblings and cousins to sitting in the living room with the tedious adults, but when I moved to Portland and grew older and smarter I wrote off that feeling as gender conditioning and compulsory hetero et cetera, and besides, I didn't want kids then, I didn't want to be pinned into a *Good Housekeeping* life like my older sister and my high school friends, I wanted to stay up all night working in the studio and to sleep around and to go to shows with my friends. Queers got to live young for as long as they wanted, forever even.

"I didn't," I said. "I don't. Except maybe this one."

"I should have guessed," he said. "You keep everything. One more for the archive."

"Fuck off."

"You think you can really do this?" he said.

"You don't think I can?"

"I'm not saying you can't. I just know that I'm not cut out to be a parent. I'm not very patient."

"You've been patient with me," I said.

"That's what you think."

I wished I had one of his cigarettes. I jammed my hands into my pockets. "I know I wasn't easy." I kicked at the ground, sending sharp little pebbles scattering. "I thought I would be, but I wasn't. I'll try to be now. I'm not asking you to be a parent, Ryan. I don't need money or a custody deal or whatever. You're off the hook. You can have your life."

"I don't know how that's really possible."

I asked what he meant and he said, "I don't know how to go about my ordinary life while you're having my baby."

"*Your* baby? I'm just a warehouse?"

He raised his hands in surrender. "Sorry, sorry, I mean a baby, that I contributed to."

"My baby," I said. "If you don't want it."

"Our baby. To be honest."

"Fine." I picked up a twisted stick, a severed root really, and flung it out into the water. Bullet bounded in after it. "You want this to be an *our* thing?"

"It's not what I'd hoped for us, honestly."

I looked up at the gray sky. It was the color of dirty sheets. "What happened to 'no expectations'?"

"What's no expectations?"

"That first night. At the Old Nickel. You said you had no expectations."

He looked confused. "I don't even remember that."

"I guess that was, like, ten months ago," I conceded.

"My god, the things you hold on to."

Bullet dropped the stick at my feet and shook, spraying cold river water across our legs.

I threw the stick again, but Bullet abandoned it to the river and disappeared into the willows, nose to the ground. "I'm just saying. I fully expect you to walk away. And you can. You probably should."

"This kills me about you."

"What?"

"You refuse to need me for anything, even the thing that you would most obviously need me for."

"But you hate needy. You like space. I thought that's what you liked about me."

"That's the problem. You're always just beyond me. And for some reason I keep going toward you. Because at a certain point I became determined to win you over to . . . I don't know—"

"To win?"

"Just to prove I *could*. But I can't. Andy, you realize that if you keep this thing, you're connected to me for a really long time, right?"

Ryan looked as vulnerable as I'd ever seen him. Maybe I didn't have to fight so much. Maybe I didn't have to be so alone. Maybe another parent wouldn't be the worst thing to have on my team. Maybe we could evolve into some kind of collaboration that could work, whatever that would look like.

"Do you want in?" I asked.

"Do you want me in?"

"If you want in."

"Don't shut me out."

Ryan's voice was plaintive, and I glimpsed the boy he had once been, previously incomprehensible to me. I rested a hand on my abdomen and felt unsettling gratitude for the embryo stealthily growing there, and for the mistake of its conception, and for Ryan, my inadvertent but crucial cocreator. I already loved this thing. I didn't know you could love something that barely even existed, something you'd never seen or felt, undetectable yet unmistakably present—this must be a feeling like faith. With that hand on my abdomen I looked at his face, the face of a person who stared at me so directly now, and I wondered if the genetic blueprint of the mysterious being inside me would build eyes like those eyes, a face like this face, if worry would etch itself like this into the corners of his or her mouth.

"Hey," I said, "come here," and I reached out and pulled him to me, or myself to him. I rose up on my toes and met his rough mouth with mine. An image of field stubble, corn and wheat fields, flashed in my mind. A barn at the far end of it. When I pulled away, he looked at me with pleased disbelief.

I said, "You're in. Me too."

Bullet emerged from the willows with a wide triumphant grin, her head and shoulders slicked with some reeking gray-green death.

Meena showed up at the house Friday afternoon with a brown paper bag from Reading Frenzy. "If you're seriously going to do this," she said, "you need to be prepared. The straight world will try to eat your kid's soul."

"You would know, I guess," I said. "Since you're working for them now."

"Shut up," she said. "Wait until you need health insurance. Oh guess what, now you totally do."

I emptied the bag onto the table. A couple of zines, *Mother/Fucker* #4 and *This Baby Is a Pipe Bomb* #1 (the author never made it to issue #2); a book called

The Anarchist Baby: Strategies for Resisting Corporate Childhood; and *The Lesbian Parenting Book.*

"Thanks," I said. This, I understood, was her olive branch.

"I'm here to help," she warned. I suspected by "help" she meant supervise.

I flipped through the books, all of them brand-new, and worried aloud that they must have cost a lot.

"I have a real job now," Meena said. "Which also means, I need pants."

"Obviously."

"What I'm trying to say is, will you go to the mall with me?"

"So *that's* why you came over."

"Just get your coat, nerd."

It was our shameful secret pleasure: Meena and I loved going to Lloyd Center. To Meena, it evoked the Houston suburbs of her youth. To me, living within ten minutes of a mall never ceased to feel exotic. Where I grew up, the mall was a two-hour drive, a special trip planned weeks in advance, while here in Portland it just *was*, whenever you wanted. In college we'd sneak away to it, circle the ice rink where Tonya Harding used to practice, settle into the rickety seats of the brown-carpeted, gold-foil-trimmed movie theater, meander through the hushed, low-lit department stores and try on clothes we'd never buy. It was our basest place, a site of no righteousness, where we both were humbled, guilty, pleased, American.

The salesman in the Nordstrom men's department shot us a look of faint disappointment as we sauntered in: one shortish, stocky butch whom little would fit, and an even shorter one in thrift-store pants with the hems hand-scissored off. Commission unlikely.

"I think I got kicked out of the Lesbian Mafia," I said with a dark, defensive laugh to Meena in the dressing room.

"The Lesbian Mafia? Please. They're not everyone."

I sat on the padded stool next to the mirror. "Maybe the lesbians, period."

"It's not like there's an official membership."

I snorted. "Get real. Of course there is."

The salesman rapped on the dressing room door. "Can I get you ladies anything?"

"We're good, *sister*." Meena hated being called "lady." She dropped her Dickies and stood there in her boys' tighty-whities that bagged at the crotch. "People are going to freak out. But they'll get over it. If I can get over it—which I haven't yet, but I will—they can too. And if they don't, fuck them."

"You're still not over it?"

"I'm not over that you didn't trust me."

"I do trust you," I said.

"You don't. We used to tell each other everything. And I still tell *you* stuff, but whenever I try to go deep with you, you close up so quickly. Even after Flynn. You're just like, 'I'm okay. Not much to report.' Even though I'm supposedly your best friend."

She was right. And I'd rather break a lover's heart twenty times than a good friend's once. But I hadn't seen any other way. For months after Flynn and I broke up, I couldn't even wear short sleeves—I had felt too exposed in them. "I'm sorry, Meena. I just needed to hole up inside myself for a while. Trust issues."

Meena jammed her shirt into the waistband and turned to a new angle in the mirror. "I mean, in our six years of friendship you never ever indicated you would even *consider* a *man*. I can't even imagine it."

"I never did consider it! It was a total fluke."

"So it's over?"

"Those need a belt."

She straightened up and glanced at herself in the pants, then me, in the mirror. "It's over, right?"

"It's changed."

"Oh god, is he your *boyfriend*? Please say no."

"He's in it to help. That's all."

"People are going to ask you. And me. We need to know what to tell them."

"Does it matter? I'm still me." I pointed at my belly. "Me plus one."

"Girl, no one's going to buy that," Meena said.

"I don't care if they buy anything. I'm not selling."

The attendant's shadow darkened the slats. "How's it going in there, ladies?"

Meena looked down at the excess fabric crumpling around her ankles. "Well, Mary, nothing quite fits." We took them anyway.

When Meena dropped me off, I found Summer and Marcy sorting through the dishes while the Slits blasted from the boom box. The kitchen and living room were scattered with half-packed boxes.

I took the cordless phone to my room and called Annabel in Boston.

"*What?*" she shrieked. "How far along are you?"

I said about two months. "Andrea, you can't tell people yet," she said, alarmed. "You could still miscarry." My little sister turned out to know an extraordinary amount about pregnancy. Several of her friends who had graduated last spring were married and cooking up firstborns already. And, she told me, our sister, Alissa, had a fourth on the way.

"*Four?*"

"Yep. There's finally going to be a boy now. All under age six," Annabel said. "I don't think there's much else for her to do in Sioux City."

"Sewer City," I said. "Bet she's glad now she took up with *Jeb.*"

"He's a meatball."

"What are the kids like?" Technically, they were my nieces. But they were abstractions to me. Names in a Christmas letter.

"Little meatballs," Annabel said. "Cute but kind of nuts. Alissa dresses them in matching outfits and presents them at holidays as if they're the stars of a Broadway show. They all start with *A* too."

I said I wished I knew them now. What if one of them turned out to be gay? "They need to know about their lesbian aunt."

"We need to talk about that part," Annabel said. "What does this mean exactly?"

In some ways it was harder to come out as gay-with-one-exception than it was to come out as gay. I prepared to do a lot of explaining. But Annabel had different questions than my friends. Such as: "Are you in love with him?"

"No way," I said. "But I like him. I feel . . . affection."

Annabel made a dark *hmm.* "Is he in love with you?"

"I think he knows better," I said.

She said she didn't get it, but she wanted to come visit me when the baby was born. "When are you going to tell Mom and Dad?"

"Oh god, are you kidding? I *can't.*" I wrapped my arms around myself.

"But they'll be so happy you're with a guy."

"But I'm not *with a guy.* I'm still a lesbian."

"Oh. Are you seeing someone else?"

"No."

"And he's the father of your kid?"

"Well, technically."

"And he's going to help you raise the baby?"

"That's the plan so far."

"Then you're pretty much with him. At least in Mom's eyes."

I begged her not to tell our parents. "She'll be so fucking *happy,*" I said. "I can't take it."

Annabel laughed. "She'll just tell you to get married. And start sending you baby crap."

I got serious. "It's way more complicated than that," I said.

Annabel still didn't understand how the last five

years of my life would be swiftly, tidily edited out of my mother's story, negated—but never from mine. They *were* my life. They had made my life. And I loved my life. I said, "Please promise me you won't tell. Promise, promise, promise."

She promised.

"You told your *family?"* Summer said. She was sorting through a soft mountain of dresses on the table.

"Just my little sister. And she promised not to tell my parents."

"You have to be careful with that," Marcy said, wrapping plates in pages of the *Willamette Week.* "You know about Sharon Bottoms?"

"No," I said. I picked up a mug with a little ceramic beaver sitting at the bottom that you didn't know was there until your coffee level dropped and the face emerged. "Hey, this one's mine."

"She was that lesbian in Virginia? Her mom sued for custody of her kids and won. They took them away. *Solely because* she was gay." Marcy shook her head. "That was only a few years ago."

"Jesus. Would your parents do something like that?" Summer said.

The thought of my mother reaching out to pick up my baby stirred panic in me. I thought of the brochure on the priest's table. I crinkled newspaper carefully around a wineglass that said *We've Got Tonight: Prom 1986*. I said, "I wouldn't put it past them."

"By the way," Summer said, "have you found a room-mate yet?"

Credit in the Straight World

Who else would move in with me?

He had so few things. Two trips with the Cold Shoulder van and his apartment was empty. Crates of LPs, a couple of boxes of leftover band merch and records, the slim Danish couch. The guitar. A real mattress. Ryan took up hardly any space, outnumbered by my sprawling archives.

We dropped the boxes in Summer's empty room. On the floor was a scattering of dust bunnies and bobby pins; in the closet, wire hangers. She'd left in a hurry, impatient to get to her new life with Marcy.

"What's with that cat?" he asked. Edith Head, who was nowhere to be seen while we carried in the boxes, had now emerged onto the porch and was mashing her head against his shin.

"She mostly lives under the porch. Summer's allergic. Was."

"Well, let her on in."

"I guess we can."

I held open the door and Edith swanned past, stopped in the entry, and took a look around the place, tail flicking back and forth in a slow question mark. Then she dove under the couch.

Finished, we sat on the top step of the porch. It was newly April. Pink and white cherry blossoms soft as kitten ears carpeted the gutters, smelling like fleshy candy, sweet decay. The afternoon and evening lay ahead of us with nothing planned. I hadn't thought we'd be done so early. What were we going to do?

Edith emerged from the house, rolled onto her back, and stretched her paws over her head. I reached out and rubbed her downy belly. According to the neighborhood, she'd had a litter of kittens before she shacked up with us. What was it like to have so many? I tried to picture ten babies squirming in her belly, packed in like sticky gummy bears, a tangle of umbilical cords like the cables behind the television. How extravagant that humans have only one, with all that space to itself. No wonder we turned out so entitled.

Ryan opened a beer and tipped the bottle my way.

I hesitated with the rim at my lips. "I don't think I should," I said.

"Not even a sip?"

I handed it back to him. "From here on out, I want to fuck up as little as possible."

He sighed. "Good policy."

Ryan stayed up late. I woke early. We shared the same bed for a few overlapping hours in between. How strange now to wake up beside him, with no sense of alarm, nor any devious thrill. Back when every minute with Ryan felt forbidden, stolen, my senses had stayed keen. Now the urgency was gone, and with it, my desire. We had sex a few times—lights off, I tried to project a fantasy—but neither darkness nor surging pregnancy hormones could summon my lust. Our bodies slammed methodically, a rehearsal of mating. He sensed it and asked me if it was the pregnancy. I said yes. We stopped. We went with that, for now.

Ryan rehearsed or went out in the evenings and I worked days at Artifacts and as long as I could at the studio, trying to earn as much money as I could while I was still mobile and responsible only for myself. Sometimes we wouldn't see each other until ten or eleven at night. Sometimes, if I could stay awake for more than ten minutes after I got home, we made big late-night snacks, a mountain of nachos or popcorn or spaghetti, and I sat on the counter eating as he drank a beer and we talked. Sometimes one of us would eat leftovers while the other read on the couch, or I would get ready for bed while he showered to go out. Sometimes we would pass each other in the short hallway between the bedrooms and smile awkwardly like strangers in a supermarket aisle. A certain companionable rhythm set in, our lives like two instruments playing at different speeds, falling in sync for brief regular overlaps.

With Flynn I had merged. We yoked together our routines, shared our friendships; even our cycles synced. The intensity gave the illusion of a life impossibly full. Living with Ryan was like living with open space. There were times when I'd come home and hear him drumming in the basement, and I wouldn't announce my arrival. I'd go about my routine, walking carefully so as not to alert him. The steady beats beneath the floor were like a sense of purpose, spare but persistent. I would catch myself moving or breathing in time with it. This incomplete music.

"I'm a scab," Ryan said. This was a few weeks into our cohabitation and he was lying on his couch—now our couch—with a pillow over his face, already ten minutes late for practice. As if to prove something, he had joined another band almost immediately. But it turned out the megalomaniac singer, a trust-funder who preferred things tailored to his liking, had fired his entire original band and then thrown together a new session lineup, instructing them to play exactly like his former band members.

"So quit."

"We just got booked to play the Craig Kilborn show in May."

"So quit after that."

"If I can make it to North by Northwest that should be enough money to hold me for a while."

"The singer's an asshole to you."

His hands fluttered up and his voice rose to a womanly pitch. "I just have to let it flow around me. I have to be the pebble in the water," he said, as if quoting someone. His hands and pitch dropped again. "Whatever." He sat up and rolled his shoulders and I saw once again how he could slip detachment over himself like a loose shirt. He sent this ripple through his body and then turned to look at me with a calm sweetness. Those creek-colored eyes.

Yet evidence started to surface that Ryan was no quasi-Buddhist pebble. I found a smashed plate in the bottom of the trash can. A split drumstick in the basement. I remembered that boot-level dent I'd noticed in the wall of his emptied apartment. And the guitar, a thing he had loved.

He was always gentle to the living. So I let these things go.

I began to see billboards and advertisements in a new way. A family frolicked on an afternoon-gilded lawn, a woman threw her arms around a man's shoulders and they gazed at a screen together, everyone grinning and buying, grinning and selling. Insurance, restaurants, real estate, cleaning products. It played out everywhere, this smiling and selling—selling to *us*. To what we were supposed to be.

It's the gays who say, *We are everywhere,* but straightness really *was* everywhere. The world was sodden with it. Versions of the relationship I was now in played out in everything ever written, acted, sung, sold, declared. The abundance of representation dizzied me. There was so much written and sold about the love and trouble between men and women that if you lined it all up end to end the whole world would be wrapped as thickly and totally as a rubber-band ball.

The unsolicited validation was stunning, and it kindled a new rage in me—rage that I could find almost no evidence of what I'd had with Flynn, or Vivian, or even living with Summer. Our worlds hardly even existed on record, while this one played publicly in endless permutations.

The billboards beamed down at me, *Yes, you.* The magazine covers flaunted answers to questions I'd never thought to have. What does he *mean*? How to excite him? How to placate her? Who wants to talk? Who doesn't? Who drives better? Who cares?

The traffic roared by, oblivious.

To think that doing it with a man had once felt illicit or subversive, when it was just . . . normal. It was a straight world after all. We all lived in it, but I had tuned it out for years, and now I could not.

But how do you tell this to the person you sleep beside each night when they ask why you're being so quiet, is something wrong? You don't. You say, "I'm just so tired all the time now."

When Ryan was around, Lawrence liked to talk music gear with him, and her conversation would even become animated; Meena widened her stance and narrowed her eyes, either half ignored him or listened intently to everything he said, scanning for an offense. She preferred to come by while he was out, and I was okay with that. Summer never came back—unlike me, she was in love jail, all Marcy all the time, and besides, she felt guilty about Bullet. When my turn came to host family dinner, Robin offered to hold it at the Spawn instead, due to my condition. Whether my condition was pregnancy or Ryan I didn't ask, but I let them have it. I invited Ryan but he said he had rehearsal, and we all let it rest at that. And what a relief it was to join my friends for dinner, even to dive into full gossip, with no need to moderate or explain. When I came home that night, he asked, determinedly casual, "They say anything about me? Was it a bloodbath?" I said, "No bloodbath. They asked how you were and that was that." True, but I wondered if their restraint was less decorum than avoidance or bewilderment. The family stayed in our comfort zone this time. We needed it.

I met some of Ryan's people too. He took me to a barbecue on an unseasonably warm May Day. Men drank PBR from cans. Girls in sundresses and little vintage cardigans clustered by the back door and perched like herons on the deck and the arms of chairs. They fingered each other's hems and sleeves with murmured admiration and gazed at me with a curious, distant serenity. I didn't know what to say to them. My jeans were partly unbuttoned, which I tried to mask with a belt, and my untucked thrift-store T-shirt was a little too snug on my soft, barely swollen gut. I smiled and kept walking as if I had a purpose.

Out in the yard by the grill I found a couple of women

who were rugged and funny and crass, who had tattoos and played in bands or did photography or wrote. They were in their late twenties and early thirties, a little older than me. They pried open bottles with their lighters and smoked while I sipped my ginger ale. I wanted to say something that would make me real to them, more than a background girl, but couldn't find the words. One of them had a black shepherd mix who leaned into my legs and gave me something to do with my hands. And there were a couple of gay men, one long and bald, one bearded and inked—

All these little signifiers seemed to mean so much at the time, when I was twenty-four and everything meant everything. Any space I entered, I looked for people I could feel safe with.

I liked some of these people. They weren't the billboard heteros. We overlapped in music and clothing choices, in art and vintage furniture taste, in electoral politics. We'd read the same books. But I never stopped being aware of my hands or the sound of my own voice. I missed my friends and the relief of being unexplained and understood.

The afternoon dimmed to evening and drunkenness settled in. Everyone but me got looser, louder. Ryan moved among them effortlessly. He paused and joked, he introduced me, he had a comment for everyone. I couldn't tell whom he was closest to, or if there were any he didn't already know. At parties, I always clung to familiar social rafts, jumped from one and latched on to the next as quickly as I could. But Ryan sauntered through, equally close to everyone. Or to no one at all.

Coming Soon

I had sworn to my friends that pregnancy wouldn't change me, but my body didn't listen. Nausea never set in—I must have inherited my mother's gift for gestation—but I had never been so hungry in my life. I worked harder than ever, begged to pick up shifts again at the record store, asked Ted for a dollar raise and settled for fifty cents. I needed to start saving money but I was eating it all. And falling asleep behind the counter.

The pregnancy mystified Ryan, tangible to him only in the form of my newly B-cup breasts, which were too tender to touch. I'd stopped talking about my symptoms after he said, with an unhappy glance at my still-ambiguous belly, "I don't like that it's doing that to you." But I liked that it was drawing on my strength; I thought I had plenty of strength to give. Even though

I was tired and hungry, I felt superpowered with my increased blood flow and lion-sized metabolism.

But pregnancy was a lonely place sometimes. No more late, long, confessional conversations in dark bars. No more shows in clubs. No more queer dance nights. No more house parties, where bands played in dank magical basements that felt like a true underground in every sense, or where friends DJed while we crammed into emptied living and dining rooms to dance in the haze, loosened and drunk on cheap booze, escaping to porches and stairwells to make out. No more of certain coffee shops, even, where ashtrays brimmed on tables. The air of queer space was blue with smoke, and I couldn't breathe it anymore.

Up until this point, my lesbian universe had steadily expanded. The more people who moved to Portland, the more people I met, the larger and fuller my world became. Once word got out about me—and it spread fast—that universe seemed to contract. There were no more Lesbian Mafia official emails. I learned about parties second- or thirdhand, or after the fact. When I did run into people I knew, out at a reading or a barbecue or an all-ages early show or coffee shop, I often sensed a transparent membrane between us, a certain remove in their smiles and *hey.* Maybe it was all in my head, but I imagined they were ready to turn away to talk to someone else, someone real, someone with prospects.

This stung, but not in the same way it would have a month ago. The real separation I sensed opening between them and me had little to do with Ryan and everything to do with pregnancy. I had another life to manage. My survival instincts had shifted focus.

"How are things?" Meena said when she picked me up for my first actual ultrasound appointment at eighteen weeks. She had insisted. I had told Ryan it wasn't anything big, just a routine checkup, he shouldn't change his work schedule, and he'd looked relieved. He said okay and headed to the barbershop. But Meena was keeping an eye on me, always ready to take charge of my situation.

"Good enough," I said. "Busy."

"How are things *really*."

"Good enough. Busy."

"Where's your boyfriend?"

I didn't rise to the bait. "Ryan's at work," I said.

"A little weird he didn't come for this."

"I didn't ask him," I said. "It's too . . . coupley."

A man-faced, mom-haired nurse named Donna settled onto a stool next to me and rubbed the ultrasound wand back and forth over my belly like a giant eraser. The screen was dim and vague, the snowy static of my interior, and then a black cave opened and a silvery humanoid shape swam into view with a single kick. Meena and I both gasped. She grabbed my hand. I'd seen other people's grainy ultrasound pictures before, but this was *live*, moving, inside *me*. With its oversize head and limbs curled up like that, it reminded me of Bullet nestling in to sleep, a large-headed pup. My eyes started to fill, but I could hardly bear to blink. I squeezed Meena's hand tight.

The nurse measured and clicked around. "Everything looks good." She held a Doppler wand to my belly and I heard a fast buzzy thump, 164 beats per minute.

I looked up at Meena. Tears streamed down her cheeks. "Don't tell," she said. I promised her I wouldn't.

She composed herself in the parking lot. "That just got real," she said. "I can't believe there's a baby inside you."

"It's a fetus. Not a baby yet."

Meena gave me a look and I said, "I'm trying to fight eighteen years of Catholic indoctrination. It's not easy."

Meena turned the key. "Whatever it is, you have two hearts now. Holy fuck."

Annabel's voice was slightly breathless on the line. The phone had rung at seven on a rare morning when

Ryan and I were both still in bed. "They're coming to see you."

I yawned and Ryan pulled a pillow over his head. I said, "Who?"

"Mom and Dad. I'm so sorry."

I couldn't breathe. "What?" I choked.

It had slipped. Annabel couldn't lie, never could. After I fled Nebraska that final Christmas, my parents barred me from talking to her for this reason. They'd said it wasn't fair for me to put my little sister in that position, asking her to keep my confidence. I'd had to agree, for her sake, and—although Annabel and I broke that barrier as soon as she escaped to college— that concession confirmed that the family's fracture was all my fault. My choices, not theirs, had broken us. That old cruel thought struck me again now in a deep tender place I'd forgotten.

I had to put my anger in reserve. I sat up and shoved my glasses on my face. "When are they leaving?"

We calculated that it would take them two and a half days, even with their road stamina. "I'll call them and find out," she said.

But there was no answer at the house in Nebraska. "Oh god," Annabel said when she called me back. "I think they're on their way."

I ran around the house, straightening cushions, pulling books like *Stone Butch Blues* and *The New Fuck You* and *Odd Girls and Twilight Lovers* off the shelves.

"And you said I'd never meet your mother," Ryan said.

"I was pretty sure of it at the time."

"Will they still be here when I get back?"

I dropped the questionable books in a box. I had forgotten the new band had been invited to play Craig Kilborn. The taping was in two days. They were leaving for L.A. tomorrow.

"Oh god, I'll be alone with them." I wrapped my arms around my waist. "Ryan, what if they're planning to take the baby?"

"They can't take the baby. It's not born yet."

"I'm serious. They could try."

"On what grounds?"

I paused. I had been about to say, *That I'm a lesbian.* But there stood Ryan. "I don't know," I said. "I'm unfit?"

"I'll cancel. I'll cancel right now if you want," he said.

I pictured my mother looking him up and down, appraising the father of her future grandchild. Her satisfaction would kill me. I told him to go, or he'd get kicked out of the band.

He said he'd love to get kicked out, and it wasn't like he was getting paid for it.

"But my parents don't know that, and they'll like that you're doing something that looks like a money-maker—" I recoiled at the sentence, sat down hard. "That is the most capitalist, heteronormative thing I've ever said." Was pregnancy ruining me? Meena would feel so righteously vindicated by this. My inner Lesbian Mafia shook their heads knowingly.

A bandmate pulled up in front of the house at nine A.M. and honked. I was in the middle of my second breakfast, carrying around a bowl of oatmeal while I picked up stray shoes and magazines. I set down the bowl and followed Ryan to the doorway. His hair was wet from the shower. I was still in the T-shirt and boxers I'd slept in, uncombed and bespectacled, teeth unbrushed, and when I hugged him I apologized for sullying his cleanliness.

"No," he said, "you smell like sleep. You smell like our bed."

"Do I smell like fear?"

He inhaled my bedhead. "You smell like a sweet little animal who's just emerged from the den."

I grabbed his jacket with both hands. "I want to turn off all the lights and lock the doors until they give up and turn back."

He wrapped his arms around me and held me unusually tight. "You'll be okay."

"I don't know if I will." I burrowed my head into his chest and closed my eyes. I hadn't wanted him to stay but suddenly I was afraid to be alone.

"You will. You're the toughest person I know," he said. "It's one of the reasons I love you."

My eyes flew open. All I could see was T-shirt black as night. "You what?"

"Sorry. I guess that breaks the rules."

"The rules? I think they're suspended at this point." My body flushed with warmth, the kind where you can't tell if it's longing or sickness. I inhaled, I exhaled, I burned. There was only one response I could give. I said, "I love you too." It came out flat and plain as a recited fact.

"You do?"

"Yes."

"Are you sure?"

You should never ask someone if they're sure— you're looking for reassurance but you only introduce doubt. A knot formed in my gut and I made myself look him in the eyes. "Yes."

His hands slid over my shoulder blades. My muscles tensed, and to lessen the pressure, I leaned into him. A smile sweetly distorted his good-bye kiss, and then the bandmate honked again and Ryan cursed and left.

I stood in the middle of my living room and looked around at the mess I still had to clean up. What did I know about love? I had loved Zoe, a fledgling love, love of the idea of love. I'd loved Vivian, a love that was a passage to the more lasting love of friendship. I'd loved Flynn, a huge love that filled and then gutted me. I loved this fetal creature with a disorienting new kind of love, inexplicably self-sacrificing and self-oriented at the same time. My feeling for Ryan wasn't like any of those kinds of love. There was no wilderness in it, no desperation. But there was undeniable affection. There was a person who still turned toward instead of away from my touch. There was a person who, however he defined it, however improbable it seemed to me, loved me. I thought I could call what I felt for him love. Love was what I wanted more than anything to surround and scaffold this kid. I couldn't afford to take such a thing for granted.

If you have to convince yourself it's truth, it's a lie.

Parents

The phone rang. They were at the corner of Fremont and MLK, at the convenience store where Summer and I used to walk to buy orange juice and corn chips when we were hungover. My dad: "Andrea, we're in town." A huff of desperate joviality in his tone.

"So I hear," I said. "I'll meet you."

"No, no, we'll come there," he said, as if this were a concession to me.

I brought Bullet out to the porch and shut the door behind us. We sat on the top step and waited. The sun was warm and the kids across the street were drawing with pink and yellow chalk on the cracked sidewalk. Edith Head slunk out from under the steps, spotted Bullet, bristled, and bolted. Bullet, fearfully monitoring a fly circling overhead, didn't even notice. I stroked the dog's velvety back to dry my palms. My thumping pulse filled my ears.

A beige Honda Accord with Nebraska plates pulled up across the street.

They got out, stood, looked around.

I raised a hand. Here I am.

There they were, coming up the walk. Their jaw-lines had softened. My father's eyes seemed to have changed shape, the lids heavier. My mother's light hair was thinner and silkier. Still familiar was her glance of concern as she noted my scruffy hair and unmade-up face, but it converted to delight at the subtle swell of my abdomen. "Oh, Andrea," she said, reaching forward to touch my stomach. Bullet saved me by thrusting her muzzle between us to sniff. My mother jerked her hands back.

"Is that a pit bull?"

"Yes," I said, without the usual disclaimer of how harmless she was. "Welcome to Portland. I can't quite believe you're here."

My mother looked around. I saw her register the pit bull, the mossy roof, the weedy front yard next door, the neighbor kids, the nice house on one side of us and the less-nice house on the other. *We should hug,* I thought. But I couldn't yet. Instead we all acted as if they were just stopping by.

My mother asked about Ryan and I told them he was in Los Angeles taping a TV show with his band.

"Television," my mother said, impressed.

"Is this the kind of man who's always going to be on the road?" my dad said.

My mom elbowed him and smiled. "When will he be back?"

I said I wasn't sure, he was recording while they were down there—a lie—and it depended on how many tracks they'd need him for. "The upside is that the longer he works, the more he gets paid." I thought they'd like to hear that. I hated myself for saying it, for saying all of it.

They wanted me to show them the house but I suggested we go out for dinner first. My mother said she needed the restroom and excused herself. "Don't worry, I'll find it," she sang out as she disappeared into the entry. "Take a left from the living room," I called after her. My father took a look at the orange velour easy chair genially deteriorating on the porch and sat down on the top step. I asked how the grocery store was doing. He said fine, but a Wal-Mart was coming to the town half an hour away and he was a little worried. I asked about Alex and Alissa. He said they were great, named the children and their boilerplate developmental accomplishments. I wondered how he would report back about me. My mother had been inside for several minutes. I said, "Let me go check on Mom."

The restroom was empty. I walked into the bedroom and found the closet door open. My mother stood inside it, leafing through Ryan's shirts that hung there. She lifted a flannel sleeve to her face and sniffed it deeply, eyes closed.

"Hi," I said.

She jumped. "Is this all the clothing he has? He needs some new shirts."

"Please, let's go eat," I said.

I got into the back seat, a kid in the car again. I buckled my seat belt. My dad asked, "Which way?" I met his eyes in the hazy rearview mirror and was swept by a huge sorrow over how much I'd missed. I closed my eyes and piled my brother and sisters into the minivan beside me, all four of us jockeying for the two captain seats. How well we'd thought we knew each other then. How we took for granted that we all knew Alex got carsick but would try to read anyway, Alissa sang the best and gave the hardest slugbugs whenever you spotted a VW Beetle, and Annabel wouldn't eat anything cheese flavored and could burst into tears on the spot if you looked at her wrong. How when we stopped for gas we knew exactly what everyone would get: square sugary Chuckles for Mom, a packet of sunflower seeds for Dad, peanut butter cups for Alissa, crackers sandwiched with foamy orange cheese for Alex, a tube of bright pellet-like Sixlets for Annabel, waxy sweet Nibs for me. We wore each other's old clothes. We knew exactly how to make each other cry, and where each was most ticklish, and how to piss off whoever was having a friend sleep over. A pile of Morales kids, heading grumpily, sleepily into mass, slotted into the pew with my mother's head held high as she sang the major-key hymns she'd grown up with now in somber Catholic keys. And we waited afterward, milled around the church basement while our parents talked forever and poured coffee from an aluminum tank into small Styrofoam cups. We lined up on the bleachers for Alex's basketball games. A rare vacation to the Black Hills, to the Flintstone campground, in a borrowed pop-up trailer. Four stockings on the fireplace, made of felt and sequins from kits. For almost two decades, we were this. And then what? Now my parents lived alone in that big house and waited for us to come home once or twice a year, or never.

Parenthood seemed like it could turn into the saddest thing in the world. I had to try to be good with them now.

"You're not still a vegetarian, are you?" my mother asked when I ordered a veggie burger. "You have to eat meat, honey. It's not fair to the baby."

I was going to push back, and then remembered those nights last summer when the dog and I would secretly eat chicken together, back when I thought I could get away with everything. None of my friends were watching now. I gave in and changed my order to a grilled chicken sandwich. *Sorry, chicken,* I silently apologized. My mom crossed her arms, satisfied.

"I'm surprised your doctor hasn't talked to you about that." She shook her head as if the doctors in Portland were clearly out to lunch, inferior to the good sensible Nebraska doctors. "It's not just about you anymore."

"I don't really have a doctor," I said.

Her jaw dropped.

"I don't have health insurance," I explained.

"Get some!" she said.

"Have you ever tried to get insurance when you're already pregnant? Does not happen." I told her I was eating lots and sleeping well. I told her I never felt sick.

She and my father exchanged a look when I mentioned the free clinic.

"This guy should marry you," my father said.

"He doesn't have insurance either," I said drily.

"You must give this child a chance to be born into grace. It's a gift from God," my mother said. Her eyes teared up. "Oh, Andrea. You have a chance now to have a normal life. To turn your life around. Don't let it go."

"What's a *normal life?*" The words felt heavy and sludgy in my mouth.

"You have to ask that?" my father said with terrible sympathy.

"I can't marry him," I said.

"Why on earth not?"

I don't love him enough. I couldn't say that to them. Or to him. But I knew it was true. I swallowed hard. I thought of the Sharon Bottoms case. I said, "We can't afford it right now. We'd need to save up a lot more."

"Well, for heaven's sake, we'll help," said my mother. "I love weddings."

My father put a hand on her arm. "Just make sure you do it before the baby is born."

"Oh, right," I said. "Purgatory." I took a deep gulp from my water glass and filled my mouth with ice.

Mercifully, the server brought our food. I took a jaw-unhinging bite of my sandwich, hoping to temporarily disqualify myself from conversation. My mother stabbed a french fry with a fork and gave it a thoughtful nibble. "Will you be able to quit your job?" she asked. "What *is* your job?"

They called the next morning from the Days Inn downtown. They wanted to take me to Target and Babies"R"Us and buy me things. I said I couldn't, I had to work. Then I called Ted at home and asked if I could come to the shop early.

They visited me at Artifacts—"I can't believe this old stuff is so expensive now! This is what my *mother* had"—and showed up at my house that evening with plastic bags full of objects I had never imagined would be part of my life: plastic bottles ("with bonus nipple"), pacifiers, a towel with a hood, a pillow shaped like a broken doughnut. My mom asked if my friends were throwing me a shower. "I can't imagine," I said, then worried *she* would return to do so, and added, "that they wouldn't."

She said I had better register, then, so they wouldn't accidentally double up on the things she'd just gotten me.

It was the night of the television show. We all sat in the living room. I had called in Lawrence and Meena for reinforcements, and they showed up with a six-pack I hastily hid on the back step and two pints of ice cream.

I made a huge bowl of stovetop popcorn and soaked it with unsalted butter, the way my grandmother used to make it. Even though my mother would be confused by their haircuts, Meena, when called upon, broke out impeccable manners—she had actually gone to finishing school as a teen—and Lawrence was so elfin and wounded-eyed that no one could find her a threat.

On the show, an actor made unfunny jokes about his childhood and talked about what an honor it was to work with this director. A hundred ads ensued, full of straight people wanting each other or doing right by their children and pets or recovering from disgusting ailments. Then the host announced the musical guests.

I ran to hit Record on the blank tape in the VCR.

The band stood arranged in their spots, faces brightly lit, the lead singer's megalomania all agleam in his discernibly made-up face, and launched into a song.

"There he is," I said. "In the back." The camera only caught glimpses of him: a couple of shots of his hands rolling out fills, a shot of him tossing back the hair that always swung into his eyes while he drummed. Mostly he kept his head down and played like a pro. Lawrence remarked that she'd always appreciated that he didn't do drummer face. My parents leaned forward and stared.

It's strange to watch on television someone you know

intimately in life. They become a figuration of themselves, a reduction, a play character on a set. I had only ever seen Ryan moving through the space in front of me. Now a blue backdrop and bright spotlights saturated all the colors, and the music sounded tinny, the instruments more separate, without the amplification of a club and the crowd's absorption. The song fell just short of catchy, with a distantly familiar guitar riff and a hook that repeated but never quite stuck, all while the singer struck aerobic poses and soared his grit-in-honey tenor as if he were playing Madison Square Garden.

My mom kept leaning to the side as if she could somehow see around the singer and bassist, who blocked her view of Ryan. "That's him," she kept saying. My dad ate his popcorn one kernel at a time. "What kind of music would you call this?" he said.

Meena snorted. "It wants to be glam rock."

"Huh."

"What do you think of it?" Lawrence asked.

"Different."

"That singer is goofy," my mother said.

I couldn't help but laugh. "That's exactly what he is," I said. "He doesn't know it, though." She was so pleased by my laugh she flushed and laughed too. Our eyes met and for a moment she was my mom again: my first harbor and home, one of the first faces I had ever seen. She had built me with her body the way I was building this one. She had been twenty-three then, even younger than I was now, a kid herself with baby Alissa on her hip. She had known what she was getting into. Or she had thought she did.

I get it now, I wanted to say to her, *I get it.*

But then I didn't: how could she have let me go? To heal now, over *this*, would send the message that their freeze-out had worked. The Christmas letter: *In the end, Andrea met a man. We are blessed.*

That night I sprawled across the whole bed. I called Bullet up and she settled in on Ryan's pillow. I finally had no secrets, so why did I feel like I was lying?

My parents checked out of the Days Inn the next morning—they had to get back to the store and the dog. Before they left, they came by the house. I brewed a full pot of coffee and baked oatmeal muffins from one of the handful of recipes I had kept from home. It broke my heart a little. All these years we could have had a normal relationship, the kind of life where parents come to visit and you make them breakfast, the hospitality in your hands now, your own adult kitchen.

"Have you met Ryan's family yet?" my mom asked, neatly slicing off the top of a muffin.

"Not yet." She raised her eyebrows. I said, "He doesn't have much. Just a mom. Soon."

"Well, family is the most important thing. You'll see," she said. My father agreed.

My throat tightened bitterly. Was I not family? Had I not been the most important thing? I swallowed and said stiffly, "I know. It's a good thing family can take many forms." My heart raced as I said it, as if it were so radical, so defiant. But it didn't even register with them.

"Once you have that baby, all your selfishness just goes out the window. You are not the same person you were." My mother smiled and her eyes filled with tears. She grabbed my hand across the table. "Oh, honey. Do you know how many years we have prayed for you?"

"All in God's time," my dad said, patting her back.

I withdrew my hand and stood up from the table. I pleaded morning sickness. When I returned from some hands-on-the-sink deep breathing, my father slid an envelope across the table.

Inside was a cashier's check for $10,142.

"What the fuck?"

"Andrea Jean," my mother said.

"When your grandmother died, she deeded the farmland to you four kids." For several years my parents had leased the land; when Annabel turned eighteen, they'd decided to sell it and divide the proceeds "for when each of you got married and started families of your own."

"So Alissa and Alex already got theirs?"

"Yep."

"And Annabel?"

"We put hers and yours into CDs. And now . . . here you go."

All these years I'd been on my own, the stress and the hunger, my only safety net what I could stitch together myself with my friends, and here was one that had been waiting for me the whole time—or had it? If not for the baby, would I ever have received it? Would I not have known until my parents died and someone went through their affairs in a safety deposit box at Citizens' National Bank?

I wanted to ask. But I didn't want to know.

"We'll be back for the baptism," my dad said as we hugged good-bye on the front porch.

"Or bring the baby back to St. Peter's for the baptism," said my mother. "And your husband."

"He's not my husband."

"He will be." She patted my arm. "Oh, why don't you come have the wedding in Westerly?"

"There's not going to be a wedding, Mom."

"Fine, go to the courthouse, whatever." She assumed a look of exhausted benevolence to transmit that she was being Open-Minded. "But bring that Ryan home."

They waved into the rearview mirror as they pulled away.

I closed the front door behind me. "That's not home," I said—to no one, to everyone, to myself, to the baby. "This is home."

I lay flat on the floor and wept. Here was my chance to regain citizenship in my family of origin by having this baby in their nation: the land of man plus woman equals baby as God intended it. All I had to do was continue doing what I was doing now: live with Ryan, let him love me, find some way to try to love him, let the baby arrive, and convert our remaining ambivalence into love for *it* with the alchemic force of its need. There it was. There was the way back in. Sheer inertia—mere inertia—would carry me there. Assimilate and convert, like my parents had. The child could have grandparents, cousins, biological aunts and uncles, like I had. The child could meet Nebraska; I pictured it playing on the parked combine in the pole barn, running across the huge lawn with a cousin in August, my dad settling the kid onto the tractor seat in front of him to ride down the long driveway to the mailbox. I could show the kid my secret places in the barns and the attic.

For that matter, I could show it where I had hidden my real journals. But could I explain how I split into two selves then? Why I disappeared for years? What happened in those six, seven years in Portland when I came to queer life, when every light came on inside me? And why I let it go? I would mourn it for the rest of my life.

I felt like I was losing my parents all over again. They had left me, and I had left them. I couldn't follow them, didn't want to. As my ears, hair, neck, turned damp, I hoped my grief wouldn't wash into the baby. I laid my hands atop my belly. *You will never have to know this kind of sorrow. Not if I can help it.*

Feel This

They had been gone only hours when the band manager dropped off Ryan. Bullet huffed at the sound
of the van and ran to the front door to meet him. She
full-body-wagged at his entry, her hips and shoulders
samba-ing back and forth. He walked right past her and
asked, "Are your parents still here?"

"You just missed them. Say hi to Bullet, she's excited to see you."

"At least someone is," he said. "Hi, Bullet. Hi, Andy."

"I'm glad you're back," I reassured him. I closed my
eyes and kissed him. "Welcome home." As if on script.

The evening was warm and mild and we opened the
bedroom windows to let in the clean new air. I sat on
the bed while Ryan unpacked his three items of clothing
and shaving kit from his backpack. I still couldn't un-

derstand how he lived with so little. He said he was disappointed to miss my parents. I said, "No, you dodged a real bullet."

He asked me what happened, how it went, how I was feeling.

"It would take me multiple notebooks to process what happened on that visit," I said. "I don't even know where to start. I'll tell you when I figure it out." I braced myself with my arms behind me. My soft belly was starting to firm up, especially when I slouched. "Look at this," I said. "Pretty soon it won't just look like a beer gut."

Ryan glanced at it incuriously. I realized that he never touched my belly anymore. "Do you want to feel it?" I said.

"Is it doing something?"

"Just growing."

He kicked his empty backpack under the bed. "I have to go shower off the travel," he said. Most of us then reveled in grubbiness, letting our natural funk accumulate and radiate a kind of pheromone aura, punk perfume; our jeans and jackets developed a patina so thick it felt like suede; but not Ryan. He preferred to be clean.

"Tell me one thing about the visit," he said when he returned, damp and relieved. He dropped his towel and I averted my eyes. The naked man body still embarrassed me. You get used to seeing naked women all your life, but a man's floppy cluster looks so exposed and hapless. I concentrated on smoothing the sheets.

"We watched you on TV," I said. "My dad thought it was 'different.' My mom called the singer goofy."

Ryan laughed and pulled on his boxers and I looked up at him again. I did like his chest, firm and flat, and the trail of fine gold fur down his belly that brushed against my hand, like an animal, when I reached down to try to get myself off during sex. I couldn't coax myself to do even that anymore. I wondered when I would ever have sex again—as in *real* sex, to me, not this mammal act that no matter where it started always seemed to turn down the same street and end at the same place. I was only twenty-four, how could I already be *done*? Meena had a theory that whatever you do to someone in a past relationship will happen to you in the next one, and vice versa. So maybe I'd become Flynn. Poor Ryan. I'd inflicted lesbian bed death on him.

"Your parents nailed it," he said. "But now I'm worried what they said about me."

"You? You're fine. You're the best news they've ever heard."

"Hell yeah," he said, zipping up his jeans. "They want me to marry you?"

"How'd you know?"

"Don't look so shocked. Catholic parents. Pregnant daughter. Safe guess."

"Right." I pressed my hand to my chest and exhaled. He studied my face.

"Maybe I should."

"Should what?"

"Marry you," he said.

"Very funny."

"Is it? Why's it funny?"

My stomach flipped. Did he know me at all? "You don't even mean that." I forced a conspiratorial laugh.

But his face was unreadable. Eyes intent, an elusive smile. "How do you know?"

"Because you're Ryan. You would never get married. It's totally not your style."

"Like how fucking a guy was totally not your style." He bumped his knee against mine.

"I can't marry. It's too—heterosexual privilege." I grasped at the nearest impersonal reason.

"Would it kill you to have a little extra privilege for once?"

"It might," I said. I stared down at our feet, which faced each other on the floor, his long and bare and clean, mine small in black ankle socks flecked with dog hair. I started in about how I already had all kinds of privilege others didn't—

"Oh my god. Stop. I'm just teasing you," Ryan said.

"Really?"

"You're way too easy to wind up. I couldn't resist."

"You didn't mean any of it?" I said.

"Just testing."

I kicked him, harder than I should have. "You scared me."

"That didn't take much," he said, rubbing his sore shin, and though his tone was dry I detected a little sadness in the downturn of his mouth.

That evening Ryan wanted to go out for dinner, but he shook his head at every one of the usual spots I named. Nothing sounded right. Finally he said, "Let's split town. Just get in the car and go somewhere."

"Where? Like for dinner?"

"I don't care, let's just take off for a while. Portland is driving me out of my mind."

"How? You just got back."

"Back to all the same people, the same four bars, the same scene, the same weather, the same mediocre burritos, the same local politics and liberals fighting each other about shit they all agree on—nothing ever *changes* here. I didn't notice as much when I toured all the time, but now, fuck, doesn't the monotony kill you? Let's get away from all this while we still can. Just you and me. Like we used to be. The good part."

But I had work. The dog. The cat. And I didn't want to leave. I wanted to tether myself to this house, this block, this town. I wanted to lock all the doors and windows and burrow in. I wanted it all to be irrevocably mine, mine, mine. I wanted to deepen my roots until they could not be ripped out.

"The good part's here," I said.

Every night now it happened when I switched off the light and Ryan put his arm around me. In the darkness, I backed into this warm body, this firm arm, and I could not shake a disembodied sense of disbelief: *Is this really my life? Is this really what I am doing?* I imagined I was in a neighboring dimension. My real life was in the next room, or just down the street, or just the other day.

Did Ryan feel my pulse pick up, my muscles tense when they should have relaxed? Could he sense how far away I could go inside my body? If only we could find that place at the edge of each of us, where we overlapped just enough to live this together.

Inside me, the quickening. First a feeling like carbonation, then the baby started to flick, twitch, thud. No one else could feel it yet, my skin was smooth and still. But underneath, restlessness churned. I was doubly alive. And kicking.

The first warm night in June, sheets tangled around our feet, a solid real punch woke me up. My eyes opened. I rested a hand on my belly and felt it again, from the outside as well as within. I reached under the sheets for Ryan's hand.

"Ry. Feel this."

"What is it?" He rolled onto his side and allowed me to set his hand on my belly.

Again: thud.

"Do you feel it?" I said.

"Is that—it?"

"It's aliiiiive."

"You've been feeling that all this time?"

"Yeah. A lot more than just that."

From under his palm, under my skin, two more nudges.

"Knock knock," he said.

"Who's there?"

"The end."

"You can't stop there," I said with a laugh. "The end who?"

He thought for a moment. "The end of life as we know it."

"Apocalypse now," I said. He took his hand off my belly and covered his eyes with it. I was about to laugh until I realized he was serious. "Come on," I said. He didn't reply.

I went to the bathroom, peed all of six urgent drops, and collapsed back into bed with pillows wedged between my knees and under my belly, the soft fortress I now required for sleep. I was drifting out of consciousness again when I heard him whisper, barely audible, "I do love you."

I didn't know if he meant for me to hear, or was waiting for me to answer. The words hung there like a fog until it was too late for me to say anything; the silence had accrued too much portent. So I let it melt into my own shame. I couldn't say it back. I slowed my breath and pretended to sleep.

Ryan let go of me and turned onto his back.

I heard him ease out of bed. The hush of a dresser drawer opening and closing. Then the dog's stretch and creaky yawn before she followed him out of the room.

It was quiet for a few minutes, as I lay there in the dark, half-conscious, half-listening. A drawer in the kitchen slid shut. Front door hinges creaked. A jingle like change in a pocket—Bullet's tags. The screen door banged. A hiss, a curse.

I heard Bullet's claws tapping on the hardwood floor again, and the front door latch click shut so softly I could barely detect it.

"Ryan?"

No answer. Out on the street, an engine rumbled to life.

I sprawled out in the bed then and slept without pretense.

PART 2
1999

[Note on Kitchen Table]

June 10, 1999, 5:45 A.M.

A—
Trouble sleeping. Going out for a bit.
I'm OK.

R.

[Answering Machine Message]

June 10, 9:20 A.M.

Hey, it's me. I'm in Toppenish, Washington. Had to stop for gas on the reservation because I almost ran out. But, uh, anyway, I'm out for a drive. I needed some air. So . . . I might go check out the gorge as long as I'm out here. Catch you later.

[Answering Machine Messages]

June 10, 6:45 P.M.

Hey. You still at work? I'll try there.

June 10, 6:48 P.M.

Okay, so no one answered at Artifacts, and I can't remember the studio number, so I'll try again later. Do you miss me yet?

[Answering Machine Message]

June 10, 9:35 P.M.

Andy. I know you should be home now. Are you . . . just . . . not picking up? This old calling card is about to run out of minutes. Please don't make me resort to quarters.

I'm okay, in case you're wondering.

Come on, pick up.

Andy?

[Postcard]

6/~~10~~ 11/99

Because otherwise you'd never believe where
I've been. NORTH DAKOTA. Most human-less
landscape ever. Hardly any houses for miles &
miles and the rare ones you see are almost always
abandoned. A post-extinction state. You could die
out here and no one would know unless they found
you before the animals picked your bones clean.

(I'm still alive. In case you care.)

I haven't stopped driving yet and you haven't
picked up the phone yet. But by the time this
reaches you neither of these will be true. xR

[Answering Machine Message]

June 11, 9:15 A.M.

Hey, Andy. Are you okay? I can't help but worry. I'd call Lawrence or Summer or someone to check, but I don't know their last names. I don't even know if those are their first names. Uhhh . . . it's like . . . seven there, I guess? I'm going to have some more coffee and call again at eight thirty. Eight thirty your time. I have to figure out the time zone, I'm not really sure where it changes again . . . or where I am exactly. Doesn't matter. Just please be okay. I love you.

[Answering Machine Message]

June 11, 10:40 A.M.

Crickets?

Crickets.

All right. Okay. I don't know where you found that recording, but I get it.

Here I thought we were just having, like, comically bad timing.

Did you get my postcaaahhh oh, no, it's too soon. Time. I have no fucking idea of time right now.

I drove so many hours and the speedometer is busted. Where are we? Where are you? Where am I? I don't know what the fuck to do. I'm just gonna . . . Okay. The phone card is almost out. Oh, before I forget, you'll never guess who's with me. Goddamn Edith Head. I don't know how she got in the van, must've been when Bullet got out and I went to put her back inside, but here she is. Popped out from under a seat near Spokane and wanted to spend the drive under the brake pedal. I had to hold her in my lap the whole time, and it—

[Postcard]

["Lobo," Giant and Cunning killer wolf who for
more than 12 years roamed the Itasca and Red
Lake areas in northern Minnesota killing more
than 1,000 deer before a persistent farmer-
trapper finally outsmarted trapped and shot
him. On display at MORELL'S CHIPPEWA TRADING POST,
Bemidji, Minn.]

6-11-99

*A—This is me after driving 30 hrs and not-really-
sleeping in the van. Fur a mess. Glassy eyes. Stiff
as rigor mortis. But Lobo feels no pain. I keep
telling myself I don't either. (The first time I
had Thai food, my mom ordered me a dish that*

smelled like peanut butter and tasted like fire. Thought I was going to die—eyes streaming, everything burning. My mom said not to think of it as pain, but just another kind of sensation. "It's just a new feeling." Ok, I thought, not pain. Not pain not pain not pain.) (I'm telling my legs that now. And my back. And myself.) I don't think I can drive anymore. I miss your voice.

—R.

[Postcard]

[Paul Bunyan and Babe the Blue Ox,
Bemidji, MN]

6/12/99

Dear A,

*Camped out here last night in the van, at the foot
of Paul & Babe. There's a big lake and a tiny
carnival. Two teenagers working the concession
stand took a shine to me—stoked to see an adult
in a Buzzcocks shirt. To them, I'm basically a yeti.
They gave me free food and a ride ticket and held
the cat while I took them up on it. I'll never take
the Tilt-A-Whirl again. I'd like to say that's the*

last mistake I'll make on this trip, but I'm trying
not to make any more promises I can't keep. —R

P.S. For the record, Edith loves hot dogs
P.P.S. Montana is beautiful, let's go there

[Postcard]

[Beaver building its dam]

6/13/99

*Beaver is the mascot of the local college. Saw an
actual hair salon today called the Beaver Look.
Also found a great dive bar here, HARD TIMES,
decked out in old signage and shabby taxidermy
and Xmas lights, you'd love it. It's late so after
this drink I'm going to sleep early so tomorrow
a.m. I can start back home. Meanwhile Leah from
the ticket shack lent me her old Snoopy sleeping
bag. One thing I've learned: lone man in van = a
suspicious figure, but lone man w/ cat = someone*

people want to help. No one fears a man with a cat.

I'm starting to wonder what happens when these postcards arrive. Starting to wonder what will happen when I arrive. X R

[E-Mail]

TO: hellbox@teleport.com
FROM: jrc2000@lycos.com
SUBJ: [no subject]
DATE: June 14, 1999, 10:05 a.m.

Dear Andy,

Greetings from SURF'S UP! Internet Café. I'd
have emailed yesterday but the place was closed.
Sunday. Small town—almost everything closed.
The day unfathomably long. Not sure how to
explain it but time feels different here, now. All
this unencumbered time, so large and formless
I can't figure out how in my usual life I not only
filled time but RAN OUT of it. I mean there was

work, of course. And time with you. Time w/ friends, time alone, time reading on the couch, going out for food. So much time spent taking things out, using, putting back, cleaning, fixing, ugh. Practice time, writing songs, rehearsing. And then TOUR time. Hours of useless time in transit or waiting. Waiting to arrive, waiting for sound check, waiting for dinner to come, waiting for the audience to show up, waiting to start the show, waiting for the opener or the headliner to finish, waiting forever at the end of the night to get paid, to leave at 2 a.m. with an envelope of cash—time slashed up so no piece of it was actually usable.

But now, it's just me and time. A totally different time. Like that Tilt-A-Whirl shook me like a cocktail and poured me out into a different place AND another time. You and Portland and home are on the other end of this long highway, but you're also on the other side of time. A time. So far away.

The only time not going slowly is the clock at the internet café. Have to sign off or they're gonna charge me for the next 15 minutes and I'm low on $. But I'll check again this afternoon or tomorrow

a.m. If you're not going to take my calls at least
WRITE ME.

Love, me

PS: Might not be able to actually leave today—
I have to take care of one thing before I head
back—will explain later

[Poster]

[ballpoint pen on blank back of community ed. flyer, adhered with duct tape to side of pay phone near Paul Bunyan and Babe]

**LOST CAT
ORANGE W/ WHITE BELLY & FEET
GREEN EYES
BLUE COLLAR
FEMALE**

**ANSWERS TO EDITH HEAD (MAYBE)
LAST SEEN SUNDAY 6/13
@ PAUL BUNYAN PARK
ESCAPED FROM OPEN VAN WINDOW
¡¡¡¡¡REWARD!!!!**

[Answering Machine Message]

June 14, 8:40 P.M.

Hey, Andy. Today I waded out into the lake and was thinking about that time we went to the coast. It was so fucking good to get out of town and just have some space to ourselves, you know? As much as it sucked being your secret, some of those times together were also like—I don't know, like capsules. This space where just the two of us existed. I miss that feeling. I wonder if you do too.

[long sigh]

I don't know why I'm still calling.

[Note in Glove Compartment]

My name is RYAN COATES
If something bad should happen to me
please contact ANDREA MORALES of
Portland, OR
503-275-8355

[E-Mail]

TO: jrc2000@lycos.com
FROM: fendermgmt@spiritone.com
SUBJ: where are you????
DATE: June 14, 1999, 10:56 p.m.

Ryan, what's up?!? You bailed on rehearsal yesterday AND today and no one can get ahold of you. CALL ME!!!!

BIG NEWS: I got you guys on the bill with Everclear at the Roseland. July 4. You're welcome. Now get your punk ass in line before Donovan fires you!

Sean

[E-Mail]

TO: fendermgmt@spiritone.com
FROM: jrc2000@lycos.com
SUBJ: RE: where are you????
DATE: June 15, 1999, 9:07 a.m.

Sean,

Everclear? Is that a joke? If so, HA HA HA HA
HA HA.

If not, I'm out.

Actually—I AM out. Tell Donovan I'm firing him
from my services. For a drummer more suited for
this band, tell him to look in Beaverton.

Ryan

[E-Mail]

TO: hellbox@teleport.com
FROM: jrc2000@lycos.com
SUBJ: hi
DATE: June 15, 1999, 9:11 a.m.

Andrea,

I'm back at Surf's Up! to see if you wrote. But you didn't.

Also checked the news to make sure Portland hadn't been nuked or something. Still standing. Guess you are too.

Ryan

P.S. I quit the bad band. It felt like a victory. Now neither of us has to be embarrassed when someone asks you what I do.

P.P.S. The other day the junior punks asked me about the Cold Shoulder—they'd never heard of us but they saw the sticker on the van. I thought about telling them some stories, dropping some names for them. They'd have loved it. But man. That person, that edition of Ryan, is like a character in a story I'm done reading. I thought, if I bring that guy into the van now, I'll never be rid of him. That'll be my identity.

I said we were nothing, we just played for fun.

Then I had to go be by myself for a while.

[Postcard Never Sent]

[BLACK BEAR, BROWN PHASE]

6-15-99, Hard Times

(not self-pity, the name of the actual bar I'm at)

OK, A, I'll give up on getting an answer. I think maybe this postcard is you: a black bear I caught in a brown phase. My mistake. First of ma—

Forget it. Fucking metaphors.

[Letter Never Sent]

Tuesday, June 15

Dear Andrea,
When I was a kid, I used to practice Not Needing.
Like, I wouldn't eat for 24 hours, just to prove I
could. Or I would not sleep, staying up two nights
in a row. School would feel very strange. The floor
tiles shimmered like a mirage, I was always a step
ahead or behind, out of sync with the plan in a way
that revealed how inconsequential it all was. Or I
would not talk for a day, practice no eye contact,
make myself invisible. When we lived in Tucson
I turned off the A/C window unit in my room, in
August, and let the full heat of the day fill the room
and swell, brutally honest. First the sweat just, like,

gleamed its way out of me, and then it rolled down my shirtless boy body. All I'm saying is, I was good at it. I've been good at it.

I never wanted someone to need me until I met you, who doesn't. Maybe I want it <u>because</u> you don't. There have been times when I think you do. But they're rare. More often, you're deep inside yourself. Always opening your notebooks to draw or write, or to look at things you already drew or wrote, endlessly researching yourself as if there were a mystery to solve. I can't solve it.

~~All I can hope is that now that I've been gone five days, six, you've realized you do need~~

Christ, I can never send this to you.

[Letter Never Sent]

6/15/99

Diamond Point Park/Bemidji, MN

Dear kid:

Let the record show that I'm not what it might seem. A guy who just drives away one day, never looks back. Who loses a cat. I did do all of that, of course, but . . . I sense the record could be wrested from my hands. So I better write my own. I plead my case to you because you still don't know I'm gone. You might never know.

I could spend the rest of my life trying to right this ship.

Or I could let it sink, and swim to shore.

Baby, I hope you learn to swim early. I never learned and it's a bit late for me. That's not even a metaphor. I'm being literal now.

Aren't I wise.

Neck deep,

Ryan

[Telephone Call]

**Pay phone on Paul Bunyan Drive at
Fourth Street,
June 16, 1999, 1:15 P.M.**

MAN: Uh . . . hello?

ANDREA: Hi. I'm looking for Ryan. Is he there?

MAN: Um . . . Ryan who?

ANDREA: Ryan Coates.

MAN: I guess I'll check.

Ryan? Is Ryan Copes here?

[muffled conversation, shuffling of receiver]

BOY: Hello?

ANDREA: Where *are* you, Ryan? What the fuck are
you doing?

BOY: Um . . . *(clears throat, sighs)*

ANDREA: You know, it's one thing for you to pull
your own vanishing act, but did you really have to
take the fucking *cat*?

BOY: Edith Head?

ANDREA: Ry?

BOY: *(drops voice)* Mmm-hmm?

ANDREA: Hold on. I'm not in the mood to fuck
around. Who is this?

BOY: Joey. I'm a friend of Ryan.

ANDREA: Oh really. Are you in a band too or
something?

JOEY: Yes?

ANDREA: Of course. What band?

[pause]

JOEY: The Buzzcocks.

ANDREA: Please don't fuck with me.

JOEY: I'm sorry. It was the first thing I could
think of.

ANDREA: Who are you really?

JOEY: Joey. I'm in high school. I work at Dairy
Queen.

ANDREA: But you know Edith Head.

JOEY: Yeah, I love Edith Head. We're homies. Leah and Everett and I feed her hot dogs.

ANDREA: Oh. Do you have her now?

JOEY: No, she stays in Ryan's van. Except when he walks her.

ANDREA: He walks her.

JOEY: Yeah. At first when he put the harness on, she walked backward to try to get out of it.

ANDREA: *(unable to suppress laugh)* Oh my god.

JOEY: Now she walks like an alligator.

ANDREA: What the—never mind. Is Ryan there? Can I talk to him?

JOEY: Mmm . . . I don't see his van right now.

ANDREA: Will you see him soon?

JOEY: I hope so. It's been a couple days.

ANDREA: Just tell him to call Andrea, will you?

JOEY: What number?

ANDREA: He knows the number.

JOEY: Who are *you*?

[pause]

ANDREA: He hasn't said?

JOEY: No.

ANDREA: You better ask him.

[Newspaper Clipping]

[Bemidji Pioneer, *Thursday, June 17, 1999]*

INCIDENT REPORT, JUNE 14

Miscellaneous: Two callers reported houses being egged; A "for sale" sign was used to smash out a front window; Dumping of dead fish was reported in Little Bass Lake; Possible domestic on Beltrami Ave.; A vehicle was weaving in and out of its lane on Lake Ave.; Loud music was reported on 14th St.; A Nymore caller reported an intoxicated man causing a ruckus in the road, "will not listen to his wife and just go to bed"; Minors were reported consuming in Greenwood Cemetery; A Bemidji caller complained that the waterfront carnival draws "unsavory characters," says a man has been living in a van parked by Paul Bunyan for four days.

[Telephone Call]

Late dusk, the sky still deep dusty blue. At the small waterfront carnival, the concession shack is locked, and workers are walking around turning off lights, shutting down rides. Lake Bemidji is dark and flat, with flecks of light along the rim. Footlights beam up at the statues of Paul Bunyan and Babe.

How many pay phones have I called you from? Gas stations, hotel rooms, the street corner outside the venue. Truck-stop diners, the smell of frying food, cold wind whipping past the pumps. Heavy black receivers, beige plastic handsets, calling cards, the ten-note song of your number.

Back when I was secret, you would race to receive my call before Summer could pick up the phone. The answer was quick and a little breathless—*Hello?*—a nervous question to which I was the answer. When at last you came out about me, I was relieved to be made visible, but I've always missed that early excited urgency, that tight hush. Now I'd kill for the ordinary *Hey* it became.

I feed quarters into the slot and punch the numbers. I clutch the heavy black receiver with both hands.

A ring and a half, then: "Ryan?"

"There you are!" I say, brilliantly.

"There *you* are. Wherever you are."

"It's so good to hear your voice." I close my eyes.

I hear a door close behind you. You're on the cordless.

"I guess your friend Joey found you?"

"Yeah. I'd been lying low for a couple of days. Long story."

"I bet."

"God, I've missed you, Andy. I'm so ready to come home. Fuck it, I'll leave tonight. I'll leave now."

"Without Edith Head?"

"What?"

"You'd just drive off and abandon her?"

"I—"

"Because I've got the number here of one Jim Musburger who found her curled up under his car."

Babe the Blue Ox is staring at me with that weird painted smile. Paul gazes above it all. "I didn't mean to lose her," I say. I explain how I left the window partly rolled down for air. I didn't think she could fit through a three-inch opening. I didn't mean to take her with me at all. "If I'd known she was in the van in the first place, I would have—Edith was not part of the plan. I mean, there *was* no plan. I didn't mean to do any of this."

"You just accidentally drove to—where is this 218, *Minnesota?* Where are you staying? Whose number is this anyway? Is this where Joey lives?"

"No, it's a pay phone." I feel my hackles rising, though I know I need to be apologetic. "It's been a weird week."

"I'll say it has. And you lost Edith? Fuck, Ryan!"

"I didn't lose her, she escaped. It was an accident."

"Kind of like how you accidentally left me."

"I didn't leave you. I didn't want to leave you. I just went for a drive."

"Oh, you left me."

"I left you messages. You never answered."

"I'm not going to dignify that with a response. Where the fuck are you?"

"This town called Bemidji. It's where Paul Bunyan is from?"

"Paul Bunyan is a mythical creature, Ryan."

"Where are *you*?" I ask.

"Uh, Portland. *Home.*"

"No, I mean where are you right now?"

"Where do you think I am?"

I think a moment. Then I see it. "Out on the porch, in that teak chair the dog chewed."

"I am, actually."

"See, I know you."

"Yeah? What am I wearing?"

"I bet you're wearing . . . a T-shirt with the sleeves cut off."

"Which one."

"The Oregon Zoo one."

"Wrong."

"The green one with the horse on it."

"I can't fit in either of those anymore." Your tone is both accusatory and pleased.

"Oh, I know. That old Alaska shirt. The one you stole from me."

"That shirt is mine," you say. "You gave it to me."

"I had to. You homesteaded it. You wore it forty days straight."

You laugh, a sound I'm relieved to hear. "I did not!"

"Practically."

"You never wore it."

"But I loved it."

"You left it." A sting in your voice.

"It's yours," I say. "I'm glad you're making use of it."

"Thank you."

I can't resist: "I bet you're wearing my jeans too. The cutoffs."

"They're the only thing that fit."

"And your neck is tan. And your arms are tan. And your hair is growing out a little."

"It's only been a week."

"See, it's not so long."

"It feels pretty fucking long."

I breathe deep, exhale. "Confession. I'm pretty much out of money. I have to figure out how to get back now. The whole thing's a mess I never meant to get into, I swear. I miss you, Andy. I miss you so much."

You're quiet for a moment. "Let me give you this guy's number, okay? So you can get Edith."

I tell you to hang on while I go get a pen.

I lay the handset down on its side and run to the van. This could all be okay. You're waiting for me while I get this pen, and you'll still be there when I return. This is how it will work out.

"I'm back," I announce, but the operator's automated voice is warning me to add more coins. I drop in my last quarter. "I'm back?" I try again, and you give me Jim Musburger's number and ask if there is an address where you can send my credit card.

I flip through the mauled phone book leashed to the booth, take a deep breath, and hope for the best.

"Care of *Hard Times*," you repeat. "For real?"

"I have a lot to tell you when I get home," I say.

You're silent.

"Andy."

"Yes."

"Do you miss me?"

"I did."

"What do you mean?"

"I missed knowing you would be there when I got home, or when I woke up, or eventually. That was the thing I was hanging on to. That even though we're kind of an unexpected pair, we'd have each other at least. I thought that—I thought you were someone who wouldn't leave me. But that wasn't fair to you. It's not who you *are*. You're someone who doesn't stay still."

There are few things I hate more than being told who I am, the pin fixing me to the corkboard. A stab of anger. I say, "Let's talk about who *you* really are, huh?"

"Haven't we done that enough? I'm over it."

"Yet you think you know me? That *this* is who I am, the person who fucks up for *one week*? What about me as the person who's been on your leash for a *year*, all lovesick and foolish, waiting for you to get over yourself and your fucking identity crisis?"

"Hey," you say, but the burn is rising, traveling up my spine like a hot wire, and it feels good and I don't stop, or can't: "The one who against all better judgment said okay when you wanted to keep the baby?"

"What? You wanted the baby too."

"No, *you* wanted the baby. I wanted *you*. All I wanted was you."

You make a sound like an exclamation point. "You *had* me."

"I never did. Did I? You knew that, even though you tried to make it otherwise. You knew it, deep down."

The creak of the chair shifting, the jingle of the dog's tags as she bumps up against your knee—maybe I just imagine these things. When you speak again, your voice is kinder, which I hate. "Maybe you're right," you say.

"I don't want to be right." It's true, maybe for the first time in my life.

"Look, you were never meant for this. Neither of us were."

"What's *this*?"

"All settled down like good normal Americans. You know, the nuclear family. What was it you said that one time—it sounds like something to detonate."

"That's what I thought when I was a *kid*."

"I know, I loved that."

"I've changed a little since then," I say.

"Ryan, do you really want to come back?"

"Why wouldn't I want to come back?"

"Well, why did you leave?"

"I didn't," I say. "I didn't mean to. I just went for a drive. And then I just kept going. It just felt good."

"Good how?"

"I don't know." I think back to that morning—the sun coming up over the Columbia River, the Bridge of the Gods, how eastern Washington kept unfurling so much open space. "It was like leaving for tour, but without the itinerary and the people and all the *stuff*, just the feeling of *setting out*. Like your regular life goes on hold and into its place slides this new temporary life where everything is yet to come. That feeling."

"That does sound like a good feeling."

"But also as I drove I started to think that maybe if I weren't around all the time, you'd start to miss me, like you used to when I was on tour. You always liked me best when I was leaving or coming home."

"That's not true."

"Really? I think it was."

"I don't—I guess—I don't know. Doesn't everyone kind of feel that way?"

"Is that how you felt with Flynn?"

"Well . . . that was such a different thing."

"Andy. Just tell me what you want from me."

"Ryan," you say, and it sounds like a plea. "I don't want anything from you. And I think that's the problem with me. Do you know what I'm saying?"

I get that woozy suspended sensation like the moment before an elevator settles to a stop. "Oh," I say.

"I'm so sorry," you say.

"Is it because I left?"

"It's because I'm me."

I can't feel anything. I look out the telephone booth at the empty intersection, where the stoplights keep changing for traffic that isn't there. "But what about . . . the kid?"

"I can't hold you to anything, Ry. I told you from the start, I never held you responsible."

"So if I come home? Then what do we do?"

"What people do, I guess. Figure out a deal."

"Like some every-other-weekend type of thing?"

"Is that what you'd want?"

I picture myself back alone in my sparse apartment on Ash Street—which I'll never get back, it's already been rented out, the only place I can think of as home is there—but with a tiny folding bed in one corner. And a milk crate of toys. I picture a trip to the zoo to gaze at the misplaced animals in their fake environments, with their own boxes of toys to distract them from the fact their home is just a simulation. Trying to buy some kid's love with an ice-cream cone or a whale-watching trip.

"I can't do that," I say.

"Okay," you say. "It's up to you. For now, just get Edith back as soon as you can. You'll go get her, right? Tonight?"

"Of course I'll fucking get Edith," I snap. "I love that cat."

"I've missed her so much." Now your voice clogs with tears, the first I've heard.

"So that's who you miss? The cat?"

"She depends on me."

That's it. "Edith stays with me."

"What? No! Edith is *mine*. I knew her before I ever met you! I *named* her!"

"She didn't move in until I did," I say. "She's the one who followed me here. She got in the van on her own volition. And if I'm the one feeding her and taking care of her, I'd say that makes her mine."

"Okay, then by that logic the *baby* is mine," you say.

Of course. "Brilliant," I say. "It was always yours. And when it's old enough to start asking questions about its father, what are you going to tell it?"

"Her."

I press the receiver closer to my ear. "What?"

"Not *it, her.* She's a girl."

"How do you know?" I lean heavily against the glass wall of the phone booth.

"I freaked out because I wasn't feeling any movement, so Lawrence took me to the clinic and the ultrasound gave it up. I didn't ask, but the tech slipped and told me."

"So much for your freedom-from-gender philosophy," I say.

You don't even get annoyed with me. "I know. I didn't want to know. But I'm so relieved it's a girl. I mean, no offense, a girl is just—I wanted a girl."

"Why would I take offense?"

"Well, you sound kind of mad."

"I have no reason to be mad." But I am. How lucky she must feel, unburdened of yet another inconvenient male to try to work into her life. I hate when I think like this; I wish I could spit out the bitter taste but instead I swallow it. "Have you told anyone else? Does Lawrence know?"

"I swore Lawrence to secrecy."

"That's going to work out great."

"I really think it will. She gets it. I don't want the baby to be burdened by this before it's even born."

"She," I say.

"She. Anyway, I'm not telling another soul. Maybe I shouldn't have told you? Would you rather not have known?"

"Of course you should tell me. If anyone—I didn't— I don't—Fuck, Andrea. I don't even know what to say."

"Makes two of us."

I close my eyes. The two of us: I try to find my way back into that space, in the dark. "So have you already picked out a name for her?"

"No."

I can tell you have. "I don't believe you."

"Maybe."

"Come on, just tell me. I need to know who I'm up against here."

"Ryan, it's not a competition."

But it kind of is. "I'm kidding," I say. "Just tell me. Trust me a little."

"Okay. Don't make fun though. It's Lucia."

"Lucia." I hadn't expected something so not-gender-neutral.

You say, "I like the light in it."

"Listen to all that love in your voice," I say, and my own voice alarms me, sour and dark. It's the voice I heard in every bad boyfriend my mother ever had. Is this what I could come to? Despair.

I slam down the receiver as if it's the enemy. The jolt in my forearm is like a live spark. I slam it three more times. Each slam feels better than the last, the hard impact, the surprised clang, the cradle's arrest. On the final slam, I lift the receiver back out and yank, hard. There's a pleasing *pop* inside the creaking silver cable, then another. I pull and pull, barely feel the receiver banging into my chest with each tug, although tomorrow sore little bruises will attest to it. The handset breaks loose and the cord falls and swings against the metal shelf with a scratching-swishing sound. I stumble backward into the wall of the booth, clutching the black receiver, which is suddenly light and small and silent.

[Letter]

~~Dear Andrea,~~

[Note on Unfolded Bar Napkin, Notarized with Ring of Beer]

LEASE!!!

<u>RYAN COATES</u>⋆ will live at 901 America Ave for the rent of

$1/month for up to 3 mos. in exchange for honest labor to fix the shithole up.

<u>BUD HENDERSON</u> will provide supplies.

If either party fails to hold up his end of the deal, Donita will whip his ass behind the bar.

Signed this day June the 20, 1999

<u>Bud Henderson</u>—LANDLORD

<u>J. Ryan Coates</u>—TENANT

<u>Donita Nyland</u>—WITNESS AND ENFORCER

★ CAT ALLOWED if guarantee of no piss smell

[Letter (Sealed, Never Sent)]

June 24

901 America Ave.
Bemidji, MN 56601

Dear Lucia,

I found a place. When was the last time I could say that? Feels good. I remember now. Doubt I'll be here long, but still.

I'm sitting on the floor of the living room. Under the greasy carpet I found oak in decent shape. The house is tiny, the kitchen is basically a lean-to cobbled onto it. It's pretty wrecked. But it has solid bones and better yet a working shower. So this is the part where I teach myself how to fix up *a busted house—a claim I'm not sure why I made, but I intend to make good on it. This guy Bud, I've known him a week and he's handed me the keys to a house. It seems this is a town where people just trust each other. How novel.*

You're not quite real yet but you will be soon. I'm real now but there's a chance I won't be, to you. Still, there's something of me in you—I hope it's the good part. I wish I could give you more than biology, but what do I have to offer? I had plenty of men in my life, in my mom's life, and some of them were good and some of them weren't. I liked the ones who talked to me like a person instead of a kid, who didn't try to win me over. The stoner carpenter in Albuquerque, the newspaperman in Jacksonville. But they all lost their shine or my mom detected the shifty ground beneath them, and away we'd go. "Onward, Ry-ry," she'd say. "There's no future here." The future was always falling away from people. She lived stubbornly on the island of the present, always being here now. What was right was whatever felt right in the moment. It wasn't until I left home that she found the Colonel, this retired military guy who bought her a condo in Norfolk, Virginia, and sleeps in his old bed from the family plantation (*don't get me started*), and she settled in for good.

It occurs to me only now that all the moving around might have been for me. Maybe she thought none of the men were good enough for me. Maybe she didn't trust their influence. Or maybe she wanted the influence to be hers alone.

Whatever. That's over. I am who I am.

I'll tell you this one thing I've figured out in my life: things recede so quickly if you let go even a little. For better or worse. Family members, friendships, old wounds, old futures. You can fight this and hang on to everything & let the drag accumulate until you can hardly move forward, like Andrea. Or you can open your fists and let go. Shed. Keep what you need for now & trust that what you need later will show up then. Keep your eyes on the road & you'll be safe. Safer.

Me, I'm going to sit tight and pull myself together. For a month, or the summer. I figure by the time you're born, I'll know what to do.

Later, little stranger—

J. Ryan Coates

PART 3

2009

Borrowed and Blue

The wedding was in an hour and Andrea was still sitting in her kitchen in an old black hoodie and battered jeans, empty glass in hand. She eyed the bottle of vodka on the counter—oh, for just *one more* Moscow mule—but she'd already had two, and Lucia had just appeared in the kitchen doorway. Instead, she climbed up on the counter and shoved the vodka, a precious leftover from her thirty-fifth-birthday dinner, back into its high cupboard. On her way back down, one knee of her jeans tore open.

"Mom," Lucia said, "you need to put on your dress." Lucia had been wearing her flower-girl dress since breakfast: a thrifted white frock her aunt Robin had altered to fit and modernized with vintage ribbons and jewelry and a raw scissored hem. In the reinvented dress, Lucia looked like a smaller, lighter replica of Andrea as a kid—full cheeks, paler skin, hazel eyes, light brown bob. Reclaimed. But strangely cute and girly. Normally Lucia preferred T-shirts and jeans and mismatched brightly colored Converse sneakers.

"Hello, fashion police," Andrea said. "I had to unload and set up like a hundred chairs at Topher's earlier and I haven't even had a chance to walk Bullet. Poor girl." A warm breeze came in through the open window, and Andrea inhaled deeply. "I hate weddings."

"Why? I think they're fun," said Sydney, Lucia's friend and bandmate. Her wire-rimmed glasses and little overbite made her look so serious.

"You would, Syd." Andrea gave Sydney's lapels a gentle tug. Syd was all lit up because she got to wear a suit for the occasion. Her pants were slightly too short for her skinny foal legs and her blue-and-yellow-striped socks flashed with every step. At ten, Sydney was still a string bean and fit perfectly in boys' clothes; Andrea dreaded, on Sydney's baby-andro behalf, the day when her straight body would begin to curve. Lucia turned ten in a month and was already four and a half feet tall. They had no idea how swiftly they grew. To them, it had taken forever to get to ten. They were already nostalgic for eight and nine, epic years. Five was archaeological. But hadn't that been just months ago? Andrea was still wearing underwear she'd bought then.

"But you still want to do this, right?" Lucia said.

Andrea wrapped an arm around her daughter and rested her chin atop her head. "Of course I do, baby."

Lucia leaned back from her embrace. "Where's Beatriz?"

"She's already over at Topher's."

Sydney pouted. "I wanted her to fix my tie."

"I can fix your tie," Andrea said. Syd glumly submitted to Andrea's deft but clearly less exciting retying. When Beatriz fixed your tie, it made you cooler, like a secret agent on her squad; when Andrea did it, she was just a mom straightening you up. Andrea had accepted this. "There you go. You look sharp, kid."

"Mom, Syd says we need something old, something new—" Lucia looked to Sydney, who finished out the phrase: "Something borrowed, something blue. Do you have anything?"

"Really, Syd?"

"Uh, *yeah*," Sydney said.

"Where do you pick up these things?" Andrea marveled. Sydney's parents were straight yet happily unmarried, with a faint but detectable whiff of polyamory. When they had their first kid, they changed all their last names to Juniper. They lived in a big royal-blue house two blocks off Alberta and grew all their own vegetables and volunteered at the rock camp.

"Everyone knows that one, Andrea," Sydney said.

"Of course," she muttered. The culture was waterlogged with this stuff. Anything having to do with marriage, babies, gender, it was like weather. You could board up the windows and bar the door for only so long—eventually you had to go out in it. And no matter how you tried to shield your kid, it seeped through every seam and shingle. "Don't you guys want to run through your song a couple more times before the ceremony?"

Lucia and Sydney were in a band called the Tiny Spiny Hedgehogs, on guitar and keyboards (which also supplied the beats), respectively. Originally they had been called the Now, until Syd discovered it was un-Googleable. They had formed at the girls' rock camp last June; their drummer dropped out on day three and Sydney and Lucia rolled with it as a two-piece. Sydney had recently decided she wanted to be a rapper, and they were struggling to integrate this into Lucia's earnest guitar songs. But they'd managed to write one for the wedding. Andrea hadn't heard it yet—they usually practiced at the Girls Rock Institute after-school

program or at the Junipers' house, thank god for the
Junipers, while she finished up her teaching day.

"We practiced all *week*," Sydney complained.

"We'll sing through it while we look," Lucia pleaded.

"Fine, go plunder the basement. I'll get dressed."

They begged to go search the attic instead, and Andrea gave in and dropped the trapdoor stairs for them.
Up they scurried. "Don't get too dusty," she called
after them.

"We won't," they said, scrambling into the pleasant
gloom.

The attic was Lucia and Sydney's favorite place to go,
when they could, and now, on a warm afternoon in September, the air up there was temperate, even cozy. Lucia's two-bedroom house was tiny, but the attic crowned
its entirety, a vast low realm. It smelled like a habitat,
or another dimension of time, a place where mysterious things could materialize. Sunlight filtered in from a
small square window at each end, and a single overhead
bulb in the middle lit up the wooden floorboards and
the brown paper backing of the pink insulation stapled
to the sloping ceiling. Here they had survived long seasons as orphans on dry pretzels and orange juice, had
determined the fates of kingdoms with epic games of

gin rummy, had plotted the first world tour of the Tiny Spiny Hedgehogs with an atlas and a red notebook, and had attempted to summon the new ghost of Michael Jackson with a Magic 8 Ball and a flashlight until they frightened themselves so badly they scrambled down the drop-stairs screaming in gleeful terror, causing Lucia's mother to leap up from the table and send school papers scattering across the floor.

These days, at ages ten and almost-ten, Sydney had to duck and Lucia could just barely stand up straight without grazing her head. They fell to their knees and headed into the shadow city of boxes and bins jammed into the depths. They opened a plastic bin full of baby clothes and blankets, three cartons of photo albums and boxes of negatives ("Your mom looked like a boy," Sydney said with admiration, holding up a snapshot of Andrea with short hair and horn-rimmed glasses), a box of college papers and folders, and a bin full of shoe boxes containing laminated expired bus passes, tiny gumball-machine plastic figurines, broken necklaces, scraps of paper with a sentence or phone number jotted on them, lanyards from long-ago music festivals.

Sydney said, suspiciously casual, "I think we should get a drummer."

"I like the beats you make on your keyboard. You're better than a drummer." After Lucia's first summer at rock camp—where she ended up in a five-member band that had meltdowns every afternoon, and whose deeply angry eight-year-old singer had hit one of the bassists in the face with a microphone for trying to sing backing vocals—she loved playing in a band of just two. Sydney had more than enough opinions for them to deal with. Then again, maybe if they got a drummer, Lucia could gang up with her to outvote some of Sydney's more dubious ideas.

"Yeah, but I want to free up my hands so I can move around the stage," Sydney said. "I've been watching YouTube to get new moves." She swung her hands in front of her chest in an aspirational hip-hop gesture.

"So you'd be like the *lead singer* then?"

"No, only on the songs where I rap. And you could do the backing vocals."

"I don't want to be a backup singer," Lucia said. She and Sydney always traded off verses, and shouted or sang choruses in unison or harmony. Why would they change what worked so well? "Anyway, who would we get to drum for us? Or"—her stomach turned, she blinked hard—"do you already have someone in mind?" For example, a new best friend. The thought was devastating, to be demoted to Sydney's second best while Sydney would always be her first best. Lucia had plenty of acquaintances but she preferred one true and total friend.

"We could ask Nsayi," Syd said.

Lucia exhaled in relief. "Nsayi is, like, seventeen, Syd."

"But we're so awesome. She would love it."

"Plus she plays guitar."

"I bet she could play anything."

"Good luck with that," Lucia said. To Sydney, no idea was too improbable. It was both her best and her most exasperating feature. "What do we still need for today?"

"There's a bunch of old stuff over here, but we need something blue."

Lucia pushed herself up off her knees. "I'll look down here." She hunch-crept down to the far corner and pulled out an opaque gray bin. As she knelt to pry it open, she noticed a pristine brown cardboard box hiding behind it, square and squat, and taped shut.

Lucia reached over to pick up this box, but it was unexpectedly heavy, as if it contained a block of stone. Instead she had to drag it into the light, leaving a sled trail across the dusty floor. She carefully peeled back the tape. It was dry and stiff—the box had never been opened.

Under the flaps lay a blank square of brown card-board. Lucia lifted it away to reveal a stack of ten-inch records, shrink-wrapped and glossy, all identical. The cover read THE COLD SHOULDER along the top and LOST EP at the bottom. In the center was a Polaroid photo of a wrecked blue guitar—a little blurry, the colors saturated. The guitar leaned against a black wall, broken-necked, splintered, strings limp. It was a blue Telecaster, like hers.

Lucia removed the top record and peeled away the glinting shrink wrap for a closer look. How could it be? There was a thumbprint-sized dent at the bottom curve of the guitar's body, rimmed by a crescent of bare wood. That was the dent she idly ran her fingers over while she was trying to think of lyrics or just spacing out. She knew it as intimately as the crosshatched skateboarding scar on her knee and the cowlick she twirled while she read.

"That's my guitar," she said.

"What?" said Sydney. "I think I found something blue. This ring. Or this could be the old thing. Or both! Come over here."

"Just a second," Lucia said. The frets looked different. But along with the dent, she could clearly identify the one long and two short scratches on the cream-colored pick guard—scratches she knew well. Even though her guitar was now downstairs in her bedroom, safe and intact, the image of it lying there with its neck broken unnerved her. Who would have mauled it so brutally? And when?

She flipped over the record. On the back was a photo of an empty practice room, and six song titles alongside grainy photo-booth head shots of three men. One had black hair and heavy lashes and scruff on his jaw. One had shiny hair falling in his eyes and a dimple in his cheek, a flannel shirt unbuttoned over a T-shirt, and was looking up and to the right. The third was pale-haired and -eyebrowed, gazing straight into the camera with an insincere scowl. THE COLD SHOULDER ⅠS WAS: MATEO GOLD / BASS, RYAN COATES / DRUMS, JESSE STRATTON / GUITAR. The small print at the bottom said © *1999 Broken Zipper Music.*

"Two blue things," Sydney announced loudly. "What's down there?"

"Nothing we can use." Lucia slid the record back inside the box. Why was her guitar on the cover? And what was her mom doing with a whole box of these records, unopened, in the attic? *Hidden* in the attic? All their other records were shelved in the living room in a case that stood taller than them both. The mystery was enticing, and yet that broken guitar—

Sydney started to sing in as low and booming a voice as she could muster: "*Girl, you're not a snail / Girl, you're not a tor-toise / Doesn't take an hour / To walk across an at-tic—*"

"I'm coming, I'm coming!"

"Hey, don't you think that could be our next song?" Sydney said, and began beatboxing.

In the bedroom below, Andrea stripped off her clothes and pulled out the dress she'd allowed herself to buy new, although deeply on sale, from a shop on Mississippi Avenue. She couldn't really afford to shop retail—thrift stores, clothing swaps with friends, and hand-me-downs had kept her and Lucia clothed for years—but last month she'd impulsively walked into this precious gentrifying boutique, flipped through the end-of-summer sale rack with a mix of scorn and longing, and landed on this dress that—oh shit—draped beautifully on her body and felt unbearably smooth against her skin. *For the wedding,* she justified. There would only be one.

The dress still smelled new, freshly manufactured and faintly sweet. It smelled like middle class. Like the clothes she used to receive for Christmas, and the clothes her parents would likely send to Lucia next month for her birthday—the grandparents her kid saw once a year, from whose weekend-long visits Andrea needed a month to recover, and whom she had very deliberately not informed about today's ceremony. The stakes were too high.

Footsteps thumped overhead as Andrea pulled on the dress. Lucia was exuberantly wound up about today, and for the child's sake, at least, she had to cut the wedding Grinch act. Why wouldn't the kids think it was fun? Lucia had seen weddings only in movies and on television. To them, this was a performance and a party. They weren't hung up on the history of heterosexual privilege, and by the time they were old enough to want it, gay marriage might even be legal here, all the panic bans of the aughts just a freaky historical phenomenon like Prohibition or McCarthyism.

So today, Beatriz, the love of Andrea's life, a citizen of Brazil whose student visa would soon expire, would marry their friend Topher.

The ceremony would be held in Topher's backyard two blocks away, where Beatriz's mail had been directed for the past five months. The staging had been elaborate and meticulous; Andrea had even borrowed her old post at the letterpress studio for a Sunday to produce a batch of convincingly twee invitations, mailed out with floral stamps. It was a citizenship marriage, a charade for immigration's sake, and the vows meant Beatriz could stay here. But still, the whole thing had gotten under Andrea's skin. She and Beatriz didn't even want to get married. They wanted to change the whole system. Why should citizenship depend on one exclusive form of a relationship? What about love between friends, community, love of work? Knowing Beatriz would be legally hitched to Topher, not her, and that they had to perform this relationship for the nation for the foreseeable months, maybe even years, with a closetful of Beatriz's clothes installed in Topher's bedroom, tampons stashed in his big gay bathroom, a joint checking account and tax returns, and a walk to collect her mail every few days—it rankled. For all her queer theory antinormativity, Andrea had come to understand that she was debilitatingly, uncoolly monogamous. When she wanted, she wanted fiercely and solely. When Beatriz had first moved in a year ago, each letter and bill that arrived for her had felt like a small victory, another claim staked. Once they diverted the evidence down the street, Andrea couldn't help but imagine what it would feel like if Beatriz—god help them—actually left.

"Luz! Syd!" she called up into the attic. "We've got to get over there."

She texted Beatriz. How's the bride?

Beatriz texted back, Full drag. U will either die laughing or crying.

Beatriz was being an enormously good sport about

this. She'd thrown herself into it as if it were community theater. Topher too had been a good player—he had a faggy crush anyway on Beatriz, who looked like a beautiful twink with her art mullet and muscle tees.

And here was Andrea, in a dress, preparing to sit in the audience and take photos she'd have to upload to Flickr, setting: Public.

Andrea replied: Can't wait to get you out of that dress.

Beatriz: Not so fast—u might like being fucked by a girl.

The backyard of Topher's tidy little gray ranch house was properly bedecked: a rented white tent over the food, grills lined up alongside it; a vintage bamboo bar covered in bottles; tiki torches everywhere, ready for dusk; a few dozen mismatched borrowed kitchen chairs on the lawn, split by an aisle of grass. Robin had hung sprays of wildflowers along the wooden fence. Sydney and Lucia broke into awed smiles. "Dust off your knees now, before people start taking pictures," Andrea told them.

All of it was for the photographs: authenticating detail. The beribboned gift boxes were in fact packed with household goods Andrea and Beatriz and Topher had harvested from their own homes. Just that morning, Andrea had looked high and low for the blender before remembering that she'd already wrapped it up.

Miracle of miracles, a clear sky on a mid-September Saturday afternoon. Their friends were already filling the yard. Andrea unclipped the leash and Bullet, now white muzzled and stiff in the hips, wandered about amiably sniffing people's hands before she sprawled under the cheese table and waited for luck to fall to the grass.

Flynn was walking around taking photographs with a camera lens the size of a dachshund. "Andy, kids, smile," he called out, and they posed obediently. Sydney turned out her foot like a red-carpet pro. "You guys look sharp," he said to Lucia and Sydney, and then to Andy, "Honey, it's a wedding, not a funeral."

"The bachelorette party took a toll," Andrea said. "Bow ties are a thing now?"

"They are." Flynn gave her a hug. "Don't worry, this will be over quick—and then we get to keep Beatriz."

When Lucia was born and Andrea's entire concept of love was abruptly and totally rewired, she had realized, with a nearly electric jolt, what a poor love match she and Flynn had actually been; what she'd pined for all that time was her idealized fantasy of the relationship. And when Lucia arrived, Flynn showed up. Flynn brought Andrea food and supplies and cleaned her house when she came home from Lucia's birth; for an entire academic quarter, Flynn and Flynn's girlfriend came and watched the baby on Wednesday evenings while Andrea attended night class to finish her BA. In 2005, when Flynn returned from top surgery in San Francisco, Andrea joined the rotation of friends who helped him drain the bags of blood and fluid, swapped out hot packs and cold packs as needed, cleaned house, brought him DVDs and sudoku puzzles. And as Flynn healed, he settled into his skin in a new way; he went from restless and perpetually uncertain to a person quick to joke, with a deep laugh and a new, sturdy broadness to not just his body but his presence.

"Thank you, buddy," Andrea said. "I'm really grateful you're in charge of the evidence. Seriously."

"Wouldn't miss it. It's the event of the season."

"Have you seen her yet?"

"The blushing bride?" Andrea hit his arm. "No," he said, "but I think you're not supposed to."

"I'm not the one who's marrying her," Andrea said.

"Oh yeah." Flynn nodded toward the house. "Living room sofa, last I saw."

Sydney perked up. "We have something to give her." She started toward the house.

"Ah-ah." Andrea caught her arm and gently tugged

her back. "I'll deliver it. You guys go ask Lawrence to help you set up the sound system." She gave the kids a little push toward Lawrence, over by the punch bowl with her doppel-banger girlfriend Carson, who looked like a younger, long-haired version of Lawrence. Within a month of dating they had adopted each other's speech mannerisms and merged their collections of band T-shirts. They didn't live together yet but there was already talk of a kitten.

Inside Topher's house, the kitchen was jammed with people. Summer was swiftly beheading pink and orange begonias and arranging the blooms around the base of the cake. No Beatriz in the kitchen. No Beatriz in the living room. Down the hall, Andrea knocked and pushed open each door, until behind the last one: Beatriz, in a simple long white dress hitched above her knees, sprawled on her back on the bed, eating cheese puffs from a bag. In her black hair, sleeked back femmeily, was an actual gardenia. Between her spread knees, a glimpse of her tighty-whities.

"Oh my god," Andrea said. "There you are. In a dress."

"Babe! I know, I haven't worn one since, like, confirmation." Beatriz propped herself up on her elbows. Her low voice had a sweet graininess and an emphatic way with consonants. "I was hoping you'd come find me. I left my phone somewhere out there and Topher won't let me out to find it."

She reached for Andrea, and Andrea hopped up onto the bed and straddled her waist. "I'm disturbed by how well this fits you," she said, tracing Beatriz's bared collarbone, which was still tanned from a summer spent in tank tops. "Are you not wearing a bra?"

Beatriz popped a cheese puff into Andrea's mouth. "Just two Band-Aids over my nipples." She slid a hand under Andrea's dress and then the bedroom door opened.

"Scandal!" Topher cried.

"I know, she's going to get orange powder all over her dress," Andrea said.

"Or your underwear," Beatriz said, wiping her thumbs on the waistband of Andrea's panties.

"My treacherous bride," Topher said. "It's enough to drive me into the arms of another man."

A knock at the door frame: Robin, hair piled into a minor beehive, smoky eyed and regal. Tattoos ran up her plump arms, ducked under her dress straps, and tunneled into her cleavage. "Well, hello," she said.

"You never saw this," Topher said.

"Don't tell immigration," Beatriz joked.

"What, femme-on-femme action, with a man watching? This is the straightest thing I've seen all day."

Topher brightened. "Oh! Someone text Flynn and get him back here with the camera."

"Actually, I came back to round you guys up. I think it's time to get moving."

"Hang on." Andrea dismounted Beatriz and the bed, dug into her bag, and pulled out a costume ring encrusted with fake diamonds encircling a blue stone. "Lucia and Sydney wanted me to make sure you got this. They found it in the attic. Old, borrowed, and blue. Three down."

Beatriz sat up and slipped it on her long, banged-up pointer finger. She'd been doing carpentry and house renovation for work and even a prenuptial manicure couldn't hide the damage. She laughed her throaty laugh. "You used to wear this?"

"I went through a vintage femme phase early in college."

"And you still have it! Such a hoarder."

"Oh lord, you should have been here when we helped her move into that house," Topher said.

Andrea cringed. "I'm sorry. I know. I keep everything."

"Even me," Beatriz said.

"Oh my god, especially you."

"Let's go make it official then," Topher said. "Time to get hitched."

"One more cheese puff before I go?" Andrea asked.

Beatriz gave her two at once. "Te amo."

"You really do. I love you too," Andrea said through the crumbs. "Wait, you need some lipstick."

Applying lipstick to a butch was like collaring a deer: unnatural, hopefully temporary, trust required. Andrea traced Beatriz's mouth with her own red lipstick. B's face was expectant, still, vulnerable. "There."

Beatriz carefully closed her lips, rubbed them together. "Good?"

"Perfect." Now the person marrying Topher no longer seemed like Beatriz, but a character Beatriz was playing: a dark-haired woman in a white dress and red lipstick.

Beatriz took Andrea's cheeks in her hands and kissed her carefully but firmly on the mouth. "Some for you too."

At the kitchen door, Beatriz stayed behind as Topher walked ahead to where the wedding party was assembled, and Andrea took her seat in the front row beside Sydney.

For veracity, they followed all the conventions. Flynn turned on a video camera. A cello started up with

STRAY CITY • 395

"Canon in D" ("we need to be as typical as possible"). Lucia came first, strewing flower petals; Robin had tucked some flowers behind her ears and the kid looked beautiful, her hazel eyes bright, a shy smile on her face. Then came three bridesmaids in their own blue dresses (Beatriz's friend Ana, Robin, and Topher's sister), and groomspeople dressed in black (Lawrence, Topher's boyfriend Mike, and his favorite ex, also named Mike). Then Topher took his place at the front with Meena, who was Internet-ordained by the Universal Life Church and had flown up from L.A. to officiate in a white suit. The cello switched to the *Lohengrin* wedding march and here came Beatriz, unescorted, walking herself down the aisle.

Despite herself, Andrea's eyes welled up at the sight of her beloved. Part of the reason she hated weddings so much was that despite her opposition to what they stood for—state sanction and control of personal relationships, property consolidation and transfer, etc.— they always stirred her to tears. The surreal indignity of her perfect, androgynous Beatriz in a dress, and yet this hopeless sentimentality. Beatriz, in marrying Topher, was binding herself to them all.

Lucia slipped into the seat beside her and took her hand. "Are you okay, Mom?" she whispered.

"Yes, baby," Andrea said, wiping her eyes.

"Sad cry or happy cry?"

"Happy," she said. Andrea slung her arm around her kid. If Lucia was anything like she had been, it might not be long, only a couple more years, before she pulled away from her mother's hugs instead of nestling into them. But now, Lucia leaned in, and her soft hair rested against Andrea's arm.

After the vows—brief and declarative—Sydney and Lucia went to their instruments.

Sydney turned on her keyboard, slipped on headphones, and pushed a few buttons importantly. Lucia tucked her hair behind her ears and slipped the Telecaster strap over her shoulder. She handled the guitar with extra care today—she pressed her thumb gently against the ding on its lower edge, inspected the neck. She ran her pick over each string to check the tuning. She tested the amp, adjusted a knob. She turned to the microphone and said, "Check, check." She and Sydney looked at each other, and Lucia nodded *one, two, three, four.*

Lucia could play. She was one of those people who picked up a guitar and just *could,* the way Andrea had always been able to draw whatever people set in front of her—it might take a couple run-throughs to nail it, but it was never a problem. Even on her full-sized guitar, Lucia's fingers stretched easily to form the barre chords, and she could sing in her clear, simple voice a tune that went one way while she plucked out a counterpoint on the strings. This musical ease, like the dimple in her cheek, must have been a gift from Ryan, not that Andrea wanted to point that out to Luz. Biology already took more credit than it was due. For ten years, she'd fielded people's questions and assumptions about Lucia's father or, at worst, "your husband." *Mrs. Morales.* Even during her brief desperate attempt to look as butch as possible—it was pointless, she let her hair grow back. Parenting immediately ungayed you in a stranger's eyes. But if there was any trace of Ryan in Lucia, Andrea was grateful that it was this. Lucia had an art, a lifeline she would always carry inside her. *Thank you, Ryan.*

Sydney kicked in with a sparse beat and a minimal yet stirring bass line on the keyboard. Two verses and two choruses about a fox and a squirrel sharing a den for the winter, a mutual survival plan that turns to love, and they ended the song on a bridge—an unexpectedly pleasing move—that Lucia sang in Portuguese. When they finished, the crowd burst into applause, and Beatriz ditched Topher to hug them both. She wrapped her arms extra tight around Lucia and whispered something in her ear that made her grin and nod. Beatriz kissed the top of her head. There, to Andrea, was the wedding's real kiss.

Back at Topher's side, Beatriz raised a sly eyebrow when Meena said, "Beatriz Ferreira and Topher Holt, I now declare you legally wed," and she and Topher pressed their lips together with laugh-suppressing smiles that a third-party watcher of the video footage could reasonably interpret as irrepressible joy.

They both wiped Beatriz's red lipstick off their mouths with the backs of their hands, and then thrust their fists into the air so the crowd could clap and cheer for the cameras.

All the living room furniture was pushed against the peacock-blue walls to clear a modest dance floor. Towering speakers brought over from the rock camp filled one end of the tiny dining room. Vintage lamps lit the corners, and a tangle of Christmas lights tucked in the fireplace sent a warm glow from behind the low orange couch that now barricaded it. Lucia stashed her heel-gnawing girly shoes under the coffee table and pulled on her turquoise Chuck Taylors. Sydney shed her suit jacket and loosened her tie. They were ready to hit the scuffed oak dance floor.

But no, Lucia's mom stepped up and held them

back: the first dance was for Beatriz and Topher. "Tradition," she said. "Sorry." And Lawrence played a very boring slow song about wise men and fools.

Uncle Flynn knelt between them. "Want to hold the video camera while I take stills?" he asked. "Just keep it aimed mostly on B and Topher." Lucia took the camera and held it as steady as she could while Beatriz and Topher looped arms around each other's waist and neck and swayed dramatically. On the tiny screen, they looked like TV. That person in the long white dress wasn't really Beatriz. Lucia looked up from the screen as the dance orbited Beatriz into her sightline. Beatriz gave her a wink and held up the hand with the vintage blue ring on it. There she was for real.

Lucia was the one who had found Beatriz. It was summer of 2008, the first time at rock camp for both of them. Beatriz arrived as the guitarist in an all-female five-piece punk band who had traveled from Brazil to volunteer and hang out in Portland for a month. Luz landed in her guitar class: three eight-year-old girls and this person with kind eyes and a ready laugh and infinite patience, who spent half her time on her knees or in a squat in order to meet them at their level. And she pronounced Lucia's name *Lu-see-a.* "You said it right," Lucia said when Beatriz first read it from her lanyard.

"Of course," Beatriz said. "How else would you say it?"

"Sometimes people say *Lucheea*. Or *Loocha*."

"That's not you," Beatriz said somberly.

"It certainly is not," Lucia said. Here was someone who understood her.

When her mother came to pick her up at the end of the first day, Lucia clutched Beatriz's hand and said, "Mom, this is my teacher."

"Lucky you," her mother said, and then blushed and focused on tightening the strap on Lucia's backpack.

"Lucky *me*," Beatriz had said. She added that Lucia was good at guitar. "She picks everything up like that." She snapped her fingers, and now it was Lucia whose face warmed with pleasure.

The way Lucia saw it, she'd brought Beatriz into their life, and then Beatriz and her mother fell in love. Which was weird at first, but it meant Beatriz wanted to stay. Life with Beatriz in it meant Lucia had another party to appeal to in family decisions (pro), but when the decision was unfavorable, this party stuck to her guns far harder than her mother (con). It meant she could spend more time unscrutinized, undetected, because she was no longer the only other person in the house (pro). It meant that Lucia now had an actual bedtime (con), and that her mom could usually sleep through the night (pro). Andrea almost never reached that point anymore where her voice grew tight and she'd say, *Lucia, if you keep stretching my patience I am going to break;* Lucia would ask, *How many pieces?* and her mom would say, *Seven,* or *One hundred,* or if it was a really hard day, a number like *Six hundred thousand and fifty-two.* Her mother almost never broke now, or if she did it was only into two or three pieces, easy for Lucia to mime picking up and patching back together to earn a smile. Now, when her mom stressed, Beatriz would cup the nape of her neck and her mom would lean into the hand and close her eyes and breathe. If that wasn't enough, Beatriz would say, "Okay, Luz, let's go on a mission," and they would head out for a grocery run or drive to the nickel arcade or take Bullet to the river. Beatriz said any errand could be fun if you had a buddy with you. "Want to go to Lowe's?" she'd say, and going to Lowe's suddenly sounded as good as Disneyland. They would walk down the lumber aisles inhaling the smell of fresh-cut pine boards and speculating about the tiny house on wheels Beatriz wanted to build in the backyard. "On wheels?" Lucia asked. "Does that mean you're going to leave in it?" Beatriz said hell no, it meant the three of them would have a house they could live in anywhere. Or a really luxurious chicken coop.

"Can I hold the camera?" Sydney asked.

Lucia clutched it tighter. "Not yet." She panned the crowd, taking in her mom and all their friends, her bonus aunts and uncles, leaning against the walls and perched on furniture, talking and pouring drinks; if they saw the camera moving over them, some made funny faces or flashed peace signs. The boring song came to an end and everyone applauded and Lucia shifted the camera back to the bride and groom as Beatriz gallantly dropped Topher into a deep theatrical dip. They stood and shook it off as Flynn reached over and turned off the camera. "Show's over," he said. "Let's party."

Meena and Lawrence were in the corner DJing with records and a laptop. Meena started with "Single Ladies"—Sydney knew the whole dance by heart and Lucia could follow along for most of it—and everyone put a ring on it. Then Lawrence took over and played the Delta 5, the B-52s, Gang of Four, jerky shouty bands Lucia's mother thought were *essential* and that Lucia liked because she'd grown up with them, but that Sydney could not abide. "Come on, Luz. This party needs help."

The two wove through the dancers to the DJ table.

"Can we play a couple songs?" Sydney asked. Meena

said, "Well . . ." and Lucia broke out her most anime-eyed smile: "Please?"

Lawrence relented.

Sydney plugged her iPod into the system and Lucia took the microphone triumphantly. "Ladies and gentlemen, are you ready to *dance?*"

The crowd clapped and whooped obligingly. With a flourish, Sydney pressed Play.

Staccato synths faded in, smeared with a telltale swoop of canned strings. Everyone on the dance floor paused a moment, ears cocked. Then eyes narrowed; groans went up. "Not this song!" someone said. "Please, god, no," someone else said.

"Please, goddess, *yes!*" Sydney thrust her fist in the air. Lucia leaned into the mic and said, "Let's *do it,*" and then the Auto-Tuned warble of Will.i.am shouldered in and sentenced everyone to "I Gotta Feeling" by the Black Eyed Peas.

Meena covered her face with her hands, laughing, and Lawrence moaned, "You guys, this is the worst," but Carson ran up and grabbed her hands and pulled her onto the floor. Lucia just rolled her eyes and she and Sydney high-fived. Lucia's mom and her friends had strong opinions about what songs were good and what songs were the worst, and as far as Lucia could tell it had nothing to do with the actual awesomeness of the song. The adults ardently praised songs that sounded crabbed and itchy, songs that were fuzzy and gnarled and droopy, songs that sounded like people shouting over garbage trucks crashing. But to Lucia and Sydney, if a song tasted like candy and made your body act of its own accord—foot tapping, fist pumping, a little extra swagger in your step—and it made the moment feel bigger, like a movie, like you were living *now* and *now* was huge and shimmering, it was the best kind of song. No matter what anyone else said.

And look: everyone was on the dance floor now, everyone was shouting *whoo-hooo,* everyone had goofy grins on their faces, they had all given themselves up to the silly greatness of a gigantic pop song that had played nonstop that whole summer—a song so vapid and so overplayed that by the end of the year, it might never be played again, and if it was, it would forever be cemented to this particular summer, a song that could invoke an involuntary twinge of nostalgia mere months after it fell from the charts. But now, the song was still number one. The moment dilated. Beatriz was married to them, and tonight *was* going to be a good night.

Lucia and Syd plunged into the crowd and flung themselves into the beat, and a circle opened up. Sydney moonwalked right into it and did the worm and cheers rose around them. Lucia's mother and Beatriz appeared at the edge of the circle, clapping and whooping, and when they saw Lucia they danced their way across the circle to reach her and Sydney. Beatriz looked more herself again, face washed clean and hair shaken down, handsome even in the incongruous white dress. Andrea's cheeks were flushed, her mascara smudged, and her eyes were so bright Lucia wondered if there were tears in them, though her smile was radiant.

"Show us your moves," Beatriz said. "We need some new ones."

Lucia grabbed her hand and said, "Just follow us." And they did.

[Immigration Questions Test]

As the final step to get a Green Card, either the immigrant or both halves of the couple will have an interview with a consular or USCIS officer. The immigrant's application will be reviewed, and both parties will be asked questions to test the validity of the marriage. It may be pragmatic to anticipate and practice common questions beforehand.

OFFICIAL ANSWERS   **THE REAL ANSWERS**

Where and how did you meet?

TOPHER: We met through my longtime friend Andrea. Beatriz was her daughter's teacher at this rock 'n' roll camp for girls, and one night we all went out for pizza. Something just clicked. I thought, *There's no woman I'd rather spend the rest of my life with.*
BEATRIZ: That's good.
T: Thanks.
B: For me, it was like . . . Topher was talking about this documentary class he was teaching at PCC, and he was very well dressed and smart, and I thought, *I* want to take that class. And I felt this jolt in my body. Like two magnets

ANDREA: That first time I laid eyes on her, I practically jumped. I was like, *Who* is *that?* Because after a while you've seen every queer in Portland a million times, even me, who doesn't get out a lot, and here was this beautiful person who was obviously from somewhere else—you could just tell by the way she dressed, it was a slightly different translation of queer andro punk whatever. And the way Lucia looked at her— that was new too. I also saw the way she never stopped moving. When the other counselors sprawled exhausted in the

(continued)

OFFICIAL ANSWERS

slamming together. I thought, *I could talk to this guy forever and never get bored.* So that's how it started.

THE REAL ANSWERS

metal folding chairs at the end of the day, she was still in the thick of the crowd, checking in with the kids, picking up stray cables and drumsticks. She had such purpose. This *energy.*

B: Andrea was, like, warm yet guarded at the same time, and it made me so curious. And I wanted to know who'd raised this kid who was so calm and fearless. Luz is only nine but she's so cool, how do you *do* that? What I said about Topher, that's actually what I felt about Andrea.

OFFICIAL ANSWERS

THE REAL ANSWERS

Where did you go on dates?

B: I took him to this Brazilian dance night at a place on Southeast MLK. I would not have guessed that a skinny white thing like him could shake his booty like that.

T: It's my thing.

B: You better not sound so gay when you say that.

T: Noted. Our other dates . . . we liked to go out for sushi? Especially the places with the conveyor belts and trains of sushi. And sometimes we went to Sassy's, where our friend Summer dances? But not when she was dancing, that's—for me—

B: —I might get jealous

A: The first time was at the rock camp showcase at the Bagdad Theater. Lucia's first band, Taco Night, played their glorious, arrhythmic debut/swan song performance, and I went backstage to find Beatriz and thank her. I was sure she'd be going out with all the other camp people afterward.

B: No way. After that week, all I wanted was a quiet drink in a dark place. I asked Andrea if she wanted to get one and she invited me over.

A: Lucia was in bed by eight. Beatriz was in mine by nine.

(continued)

OFFICIAL ANSWERS	THE REAL ANSWERS

OFFICIAL ANSWERS

if we were watching our friend.

T: Right. Beatriz gets jealous sometimes.

B: Now we just cuddle on the couch and watch movies.

T: So many movies.

THE REAL ANSWERS

B: Why delay the inevitable?

A: But we had real dates too. When Luz was staying over at Sydney's, we would go to shows or parties. Or out with our friends.

B: Karaoke at the Alibi or Chopsticks.

A: Once we drank a whole bottle of wine at that place on Alberta.

B: And when we got home we took those pictures with your phone—

A: Oh god. I deleted all of them the next morning. I can't even think about them.

B: Remember the one with the tie—

A: Hush now.

OFFICIAL ANSWERS	**THE REAL ANSWERS**

How many people attended your wedding?

T: About thirty? We kept it kind of small. Just close friends. And my mom.
B: My parents couldn't afford to come all the way from Brazil, so we're saving up to go there this winter. We sent them lots of pictures, though.

A: I never wanted a wedding, but I have to admit that once theirs was all under way I kind of wished it were mine.
B: Aw, baby.
A: Don't tell.

How do your parents feel about your choice of spouse?

T: My mom loves her.
B: His mom is super cool. My parents are very excited that I met Topher and that we are married. But they're a little sad that I am so far from home. They were like, Why not bring him to Brazil? Our recession just ended and

A: I would say they're dealing. They're a little awkward about it. They've only met her once. She killed them with kindness.
B: That's right.
A: Beatriz amps it up with them and comes across as so happy you can't be upset with her.

(continued)

OFFICIAL ANSWERS

THE REAL ANSWERS

up there it's so bad. But I love the USA.

T: Way to drive it home, B.

B: I am pretty sure my parents always knew I was gay, even though we never talked about any kind of dating ever for me. They know I'm living with Andrea and Lucia and that we do everything together. When I told them about Topher, they were stunned. But they warmed right up.

A: Ugh. Let's go on to the next question.

Do you use contraception? If so, what form?

T: Condoms?

B: No, let's say "nothing." It'll seem even more real, right?

T: Plus, it's true.

A: They asked me this at just about every prenatal checkup I had, and after Lucia was born. Finally I said "homosexuality."

B: I bet that shut them up.

A: It bought me a few seconds of silence.

OFFICIAL ANSWERS

How did he propose?

B: Actually, I proposed.
T: Ooh, I like that.

THE REAL ANSWERS

A: Wasn't it Topher's idea?
B: I thought it was Lawrence's idea.
A: Anyway, I'd slumped into a terrible depression at the thought of B leaving, and then someone brought it up, and Topher volunteered. Maybe it was a joke at first. But we all thought it was brilliant. None of us realized quite how complex it would be.
B: No, all you knew was what you remembered from the movie *Green Card.*
A: We didn't know it would take so *long.*
B: That's okay. I'm not going anywhere.

OFFICIAL ANSWERS **THE REAL ANSWERS**

What did you get each other for your last birthday?

B: Well, I got him a bottle
of good bourbon and
a book of Martin Parr
photography.

T: How did you know
that? She really knows me.

B: It's on the shelf there.

T: I got her . . . some
guitar stuff?

B: He got me a Big Muff.

T: A what?

B: It's a fuzzbox. A pedal.

T: Okay, yes. I gave her a
Big Muff. You are really
cracking yourself up with
this one, aren't you?

B: She got me a bike from
Citybikes, an eighties ten-
speed all fixed up. And
lights.

A: She built me this
beautiful simple dining
table with a reclaimed fir
top. It is the nicest piece
of furniture I've ever
owned. The kind of table
you keep for the rest of
your life.

OFFICIAL ANSWERS

THE REAL ANSWERS

Who sleeps on which side of the bed?

T: In real life, I sleep on the right.

B: I do too. One of us should switch so we don't have to worry about getting it wrong.

T: Good call. Oh my god, this could have sunk us.

B: I think I should move in with you for like a week.

T: We need to study.

B: You have no side. You take it all.

A: I thought I just stole all the covers.

B: No, you get the mattress too. I hover on the edge.

A: But I'm only, like, five-two. How much space could I really take?

B: That question is, like, your personal challenge to yourself every night.

LUCIA: What are you doing?

A: Luz! We thought you were asleep.

L: I couldn't. You guys are being loud.

B: Oh, it's not that you were secretly reading

(continued)

OFFICIAL ANSWERS   **THE REAL ANSWERS**

with your flashlight after bedtime?

L: Um . . .

A: She has a flashlight in there?

B: I saw it under the bed.

A: You are so busted, Luz.

B: Problem child.

A: Actually I used to do that too.

L: See? You should just let me read with the light on until I fall asleep.

B: You guys are sneaky.

L: What are you reading?

B: The questions that Topher and I were practicing earlier at his house. Now your mom and I are just answering them for fun.

L: Read one to me.

A: Okay.

OFFICIAL ANSWERS

THE REAL ANSWERS

How do you feel about having children?

T: Didn't we kind of answer that with the condom question?

B: Let's say we want to have two kids. No, four kids! Four new consumers to boost the American economy.

T: Let's go with two, honey.

B: Two boys and two girls!

T: I think we should wrap this up. You're getting punchy.

B: I am going to be the best resident alien they have ever interviewed.

B: I always wanted to have kids, you know.

L: You did?

B: Yeah. I just didn't know how it would happen.

L: Do you wish you had more of them?

A: Good question.

Do you?

B: There would be no point in trying to get more kids because you are my favorite kid ever, and you always will be. It wouldn't be fair.

A: Good answer.

L: I think so too.

The Beginnings

A ndrea had not been prepared for birth. She had stockpiled gifts and practical supplies and thrifted gender-neutral baby clothes for weeks, but none of it readied her for the night Lucia tore through her, opened her in a way that would never close. Birth turned her inside out, and when she saw Lucia's face for the first time, her wondrous touchable human face, and the faces of those around her (Meena's eyes streaming, Lawrence pale but smiling openmouthed with astonishment, her sister Annabel's blasphemous shout of joy), she went all out and all in. Exuberant pain, excruciating love—they were one and the same. A new ferocity roiled in her heart, shot through her entire body, pulsed through her blood. The industry that marketed motherhood in pastels and cursive was a joke. In reality it was dark red and animal and iron.

Every good and bad choice, every circumstance beyond and within her control, every little thing that had led her to this point, gazing into the dazed eyes of this tiny new creature, was worth it.

The birth certificate listed only Lucia and Andrea, the *father* line left blank by law. "Should I give you the father's name?" Andrea asked. The hospital attendant recording it asked if she was married, and when she said no, replied, "Then you can't." *All right then,* Andrea thought. *It's just us two.*

The early years were the hardest. Enrolling in night school as a condition of receiving welfare benefits. Desperately arranging babysitting swaps with the slightly-less-new mom who lived across the street, whom Andrea came to know now that they shared this common condition, and calling in friends, sick with gratitude for their willingness to help. The handful of humiliating times she had to call and ask her parents for money. The way time reshaped itself—a sleepless night would last forever and a workday was six hours shorter than she needed to get everything done. Blessed be WIC and CHIP and Head Start. Blessed be—no guilt—the television. Blessed be the Lego phase, which it turned out

Andrea had never outgrown either, and Lucia's learning to read. Blessed be the human safety net of friends. Blessed be well-employed Meena, who hooked her up with take-home proofreading assignments, pirated design software, and commercial illustration gigs. Blessed be Sydney, and Lucia's other friends along the way, Skyler and Raven and Montana and Miles, and their parents. Blessed be the older lesbian parents who emerged from quarters she hadn't known were there. Blessed be the library, the Goodwill on Killingsworth, five-for-five-dollars Annie's mac & cheese at Fred Meyer, and a landlord too elderly to realize she could raise the rent. Blessed be the fact that you can teach at a private school without certification. Blessed be the Rock 'n' Roll Camp for Girls.

For a long stretch in Lucia's life, Andrea couldn't imagine she would ever have the time or space to have sex again, much less fall in love. She was working her ass off: parenting, finishing her BA, teaching art to middle and high schoolers at a private school on the West Side. Lucia was her life partner, all-encompassing and ever-present. There was no time for art, except what she pulled together in demos for the students. The kid, the dog: her every waking moment was assigned to sheer survival, keeping them all alive and well, and no one she met was worth kicking either of them out of the bed at night.

When Lucia started preschool, Andrea thought it was time to break the longest sex drought of her adult life. But with whom? The dating pool to which her friends had free access was suddenly hard to get into. A lesbian with a toddler was saddled with a kind of adulthood from which the eternal youth of Portland shied violently away. Everyone loved Lucia, conceptually at least; she was a little mascot in her tiny Sonic Youth T-shirt and sneakers—but Andrea and kid were housebound for the night well before most people had even started getting ready to go out. The one who broke the drought was good for a couple of weeks until it became clear she was more taken with Lucia than Andrea. Then Andrea had to reassess: Lucia was off-limits to dates until Andrea was sure something would last, or at least seemed headed toward an enduring friendship. Some had little interest in hearing about Lucia; to them the kid was like a job or a pet, an element of life you left elsewhere when you wanted to enter the real world, be your true self. For most of them, there just wasn't time. There was more than enough lesbian baggage to go around; why pick someone with extra?

Then in 2008 came Beatriz, unlike any of the others. Beatriz liked kids so much she'd come from another continent to work at the camp; she knew how to talk to them, how to teach them and joke with them and keep them moving from one place to the next. The hurdle of introduction to Lucia was cleared from day one. Beatriz and Lucia were buddies. So Andrea could bring Beatriz over to the house from the start, and Beatriz taught Lucia more chords and tricks and beginner Portuguese. Brazil was not Mexico, of course, but even the fact of Beatriz's Latin American origins unlocked something unexpectedly deep in Andrea, a feeling of kinship and longing, a sense of rightness. Something that was new and familiar at once.

That first summer, Beatriz played shows around town and the Northwest with her band, and called and texted regularly from the road. Some nights she would sneak in after Lucia was in bed, and Andrea would be roused awake in the dark by a sheer want so strong it pushed through sleep.

Andrea couldn't tell if Lucia knew from the start and was just playing along, or if she figured it out along the way, but a few weeks in, Lucia said to Beatriz at dinner, "You should just stay here."

"Tonight?" Beatriz looked at Andrea, who nodded. "Okay."

Lucia looked satisfied. She added, "Don't go back to Brazil either."

"I have to. But maybe not yet."

The band went back to São Paulo at the end of July, but Beatriz postponed her ticket for another month and stayed with Andrea and Lucia, officially as a friend—until Lucia and Sydney crept into the kitchen, long past their bedtime, to sneak snacks and caught Andrea and Beatriz entwined up against the refrigerator. "Oh my gosh, they're *snogging!*" Sydney said, a word they'd picked up from *Harry Potter.* The kids ran out the door shrieking and giggling.

Andrea tried to have a careful conversation with Lucia the next morning while Beatriz showered. Now that the thrill of discovery had subsided, Lucia sat sullen and quiet. She kicked one foot slowly against the leg of the chair she sat on. Finally she said, "Beatriz was my friend first."

Andrea rubbed her back. "I know. And I'm so grateful for your friendship. I could never replace you in her eyes, Luz, I promise. I want a different kind of relationship with Beatriz. For one thing, I can't play guitar at all. That's for you guys to do. And you will always have that. You'll always be her friend."

Lucia didn't look up, but she stopped kicking.

"For another thing, honestly, what I want isn't the same as friendship. It's a different feeling."

"Do you *love* her?" Lucia asked.

"That's a strong word," Andrea said. Her heart thumped in her chest. "How would you feel about that?"

"Does she love you?"

Andrea said, "Jeez, I kind of hope so. What do you think?"

"Then she'd be here a lot?"

"That's true."

"Maybe she wouldn't go back to Brazil."

"Or at least she'd come back again soon."

Lucia thought about it. She hopped off the chair.

"Where are you going?" Andrea asked.

"To wake up Syd. I'm going to pour cold water in her ear."

"Oh no you don't." It was Beatriz, standing in the kitchen doorway, wet hair dripping down onto her black tank. She scooted after Lucia to scoop her up and Lucia squealed happily, which roused Sydney and foiled the plan.

What had Beatriz heard? It didn't matter. She and Andrea said *I love you* by week six. "Way too early," Beatriz said. "Definitely," Andrea agreed. "You should never say it before six months. Maybe it's easier for you to say it in English, because it's like toy language for you." Beatriz said, "Eu te amo." "Oh fuck," Andrea said, "now we really blew it." And they collapsed back onto the bed.

Then came the August day Beatriz had to fly back to São Paulo. They all kept hugging and kissing at the curb, going back for second and third good-byes, and when Lucia threw her arms around them both and clung with surprising force, Andrea thought, *We look like a family.* They watched the airport's wide revolving door swallow Beatriz and her guitar case and over-stuffed backpack and Andrea felt like some part of her own body was being physically pulled away.

When they walked in the front door, Lucia stopped and looked around the living room. Her mouth turned down, and her eyes filled with tears. "It doesn't feel the same," she said.

"It doesn't." Andrea rubbed at the bladelike sob in her throat. "We have to get her back, don't we?"

Andrea seldom thought of Ryan anymore, but that night, as she tried to fall asleep alone in a bed she'd grown used to sharing, she thought of the difference between Beatriz's departure and the quiet absence when Ryan had left ten years ago. When she had realized Ryan was gone, really gone, it was like all the windows had been smashed out: she felt vandalized, yet at the same time a barometric pressure had lifted. A spell had broken. Andrea didn't have to *try* so hard anymore, not in that way. The effort of attempting to feel: gone. She had breathed deep. The space was all hers. *She* was all hers. For only five more months, she got to belong solely to herself. Then Lucia would belong solely to her—or that's what she thought. It was more like she belonged solely to Lucia.

Beatriz's absence, though, was unbearable. A vacancy in the house. Andrea would do anything to get her back, and anything to keep her.

Beatriz figured out that she could stay longer on a student visa, so even though she already had a history degree from the University of São Paulo, she'd enrolled at Portland State for a second ostensible BA in environmental studies. She'd fallen in with a small crew of musicians and artists who renovated houses for a local real estate agent and were paid in cash. And so Andrea and Lucia now had Beatriz for over a year: Beatriz who could build shelves and desks and cabinets, who had rehoused all of Andrea and Lucia's books and records in elegant light wood. Beatriz who lay back on the couch reading nonfiction books about cultish religions and true crime, and regaled them with lurid anecdotes only lightly edited for Lucia's sake. Beatriz who made up funny songs on the spot, songs with Andrea's name in them, earworms that Andrea found herself singing under her breath as she prepped between classes. Beatriz who made dirty jokes that Andrea loved. Beatriz who, with the exception of fried bananas, couldn't cook for shit, comically unskilled in the kitchen, but who always took the cleanup. Beatriz who taught Lucia new fingerings on the guitar and let her use her effects pedals. Beatriz who was teaching them both Portuguese— Lucia was in a Spanish immersion program at school and caught on far more quickly. Beatriz who came to family dinner and slid right into place, refilling everyone's drinks and talking late into the evening until Andrea was yawning and Lucia had long since conked out on a couch. Family dinner was a larger, looser affair now, every two or three months, the most reliable chance busy friends had to see each other. All Lucia's life they'd made room for her at the table, and now they made room for Beatriz too.

Andrea wrote notes and drew tiny pictures and hid them in Beatriz's jacket pockets and wallet. The unwritten subtext of each: *Please keep us.* One afternoon in July, while Beatriz was volunteering at camp, Andrea opened the drawer of the other nightstand to hide a note, and found inside all the notes and drawings she'd ever made Beatriz. A nest of slips of paper. Some contained detailed mini-letters, some—from hurried mornings—just said *I love you, B* in superfine Sharpie on a bent Post-it. Some were dated, many were not. Days and months were shuffled together.

Andrea thought, *This is my money. On her, I would spend it all.*

Stethoscope

That box of records in the attic had been on Lucia's mind for over a week. Finally, she couldn't stand it. It was a Tuesday after school. Beatriz was working on a house in Southeast and her mom had called to say she had to stay an hour late at school for a meeting. Normally Lucia would have taken advantage of this by fixing herself a bowl of ice cream, three scoops, sprinkling it with anything that looked good—dry breakfast cereal, chocolate powder, maple syrup, cinnamon—and kicking back with an uninterrupted stretch of afternoon cartoons. But today she took the step stool from the closet and unfolded it in the hallway beneath the trapdoor.

The attic was strictly off-limits without adult supervision of the cantankerous ladder. But Lucia had watched her mother do this enough times that she had figured it out. With a toothy metal spaghetti ladle, she reached up and snagged the loop of rope that served as a handle. She tugged. Nothing happened. The door was heavier than she'd expected. She pulled harder and sank all her weight into it.

The door swung down with an indignant pop. Lucia fell back off the step stool and wiped out on the floor. Her right elbow burned and her ankle sent shooting pains through her leg when she stood, but she ignored it, righted the stool, and stepped back up to pull down the extendable ladder. She climbed into the cool dimness, heart thumping, and retrieved the top record from the box. Then she closed it up and pushed the box back to the deep corner it came from. The attic had to appear completely undisturbed.

Once she was back on the ground floor, though, Lucia realized there was no way she could push the ladder back into place, much less the entire dangling door. "I had to go back and find—no—I thought I forgot something up there," she murmured, practicing. "I thought I left my notebook with my lyrics in it. No, my notebook for school." All the way to her bedroom she rehearsed the line until it sounded forlorn and sincere. She shut the door behind her and pulled out her guitar.

Hers was unmistakably the same guitar as the broken-necked one on the album cover. It gave Lucia the most unsettling feeling. Most things in their home had come secondhand, and plenty of her clothes and books too, and she never knew the story of where they came from, they just showed up and settled in. Lucia had never thought about their history. But her guitar had known another life—another *death*, even.

Out to the living room she went, to listen for clues on the stereo.

The record's first song, "Stethoscope," was the best one. Lucia listened patiently to the other two on side one, and then played the first song again twice. She flipped the record and listened to side two. The fifth song was a slow one, she liked that, though she wished it were longer. The last one went on too long, like they didn't want to let go. A draggy jam. Lucia and Sydney hated jams. Except their own, which were awesome.

She picked up her guitar, checked the tuning, and turned the record back to side one, song one. Her fingers found the first chord. "You remember this one?" she asked the guitar. The strings hummed against her fingers. Learning a song was like climbing rocks, finding foothold after foothold until the path was easy to follow.

At first Lucia had thought she wanted to play the

drums. It felt good to hit something. But when she tried an electric guitar for the first time, she was hooked. She hit a single note and it rang out, crunchy and soaring at the same time. She pressed her fingers against the strings, which pressed back sharply, and strummed, and a wall of sound poured out. You could do anything with a guitar. You could make it sound watery and dark, or filigreed and delicate, or, with a quick stomp on the pedal, like a roar of dissatisfaction. You could make whole songs of your own. You could re-create almost all the songs on the radio or in your mom's record collection on a guitar, and most were surprisingly simple to break down into their parts. The mystery was not what they were made of, but what made them good. Lucia loved how her fingers tingled after playing, how her fingertips thickened, self-armoring.

When Beatriz pulled into the driveway half an hour later, Lucia jumped up to grab the record and slipped it back into its sleeve. She slid it under her bed as the back door creaked open and shut.

"E aí, chuchuzinha? Estou em casa!"

"Olá!" Lucia came into the kitchen, where Bullet was already wagging her tail and bumping her head against Beatriz's hand. She was getting better at Portuguese, even though sometimes she forgot and responded in Spanish. Portuguese sounded cushier, Spanish more percussive.

Beatriz gave Lucia a high five and both of them a quick affectionate scratch behind the neck. The guitar was slung across the couch, where Lucia had ditched it in a hurry. "You've been practicing," Beatriz said with approval. "New song?"

"Not really," Lucia said. "Just messing around."

"Good kid." Beatriz hung her messenger bag and jacket by the door and headed toward her room to change out of her work clothes. In the doorway to the hall, she took a startled step back. "*Merda.* Did the attic door fall down?"

Lucia wanted to say yes, but Beatriz sounded so concerned she couldn't. "I had to get something up there."

"You can't do that, Luz, that thing is heavy. You could get hurt."

What was her line? Lucia blanked. "I thought I left something up there." What was it? She added quickly, "It was a present for you."

Beatriz softened. "A present? Why would it be in the attic?"

"I didn't want you to find it."

"Was it up there? When do I get it?"

Lucia shook her head. "I didn't find it. I might have left it at Sydney's."

"You hid it too well." Beatriz laughed. "You're sweet, chuchu."

"Are you mad?"

"I should be, but . . . no." Beatriz gave her a sidelong look. "Are you worried your mom's gonna be?" Lucia strategically widened her eyes and nodded. "I'll take care of the door," Beatriz said. "Don't worry."

The question seemed so simple—*Mom, where did my guitar come from?*—but her mother looked stricken. She stopped chewing her spaghetti. "I'm not sure exactly," she said, but in a way that signaled she did know something and was stalling.

"What's up? Is that like asking where babies come from?" Lucia joked. She looked to Beatriz for a laugh and Beatriz obliged, but kept her eyes on Andrea.

"I think I got it at The 12th Fret," she said. "Yeah, it was from The 12th Fret."

"Did it cost a lot? Beatriz said it's a good guitar."

"Not too much. I did an art trade with them. I traded some design work."

"But you don't play guitar."

"I thought I might learn."

"Oh. Where did The 12th Fret get it?"

"Who knows where that guitar has been? It's older than all of us," her mother said. "Beatriz, do you want some wine? I think we need to finish that bottle on the counter."

Lucia understood she was not to ask any more questions about the guitar tonight. Which only made her curiosity leap from spark to blaze.

After dinner, she put on her pajamas as instructed, but she couldn't resist picking up the guitar, sitting down on her bed, and playing through the song again. When a song got in her head, it was all she wanted to do, work it out and play it over and over until she could close her eyes or look up from the frets and feel it move through and out of her body, part of her. Already this song was working its way in.

Andrea paused. Lucia's bedroom door was ajar, and through the gap she could see her sitting on the edge of her bed, head down, stretching her small fingers to form the chords on her guitar. The song she was playing—what was it? Something from a long time ago. From the radio? An old mixtape?

Luz shifted to the chorus and began to murmur under her breath, in that still-sweet small voice, *With you I need a stethoscope.*

A watery feeling rippled down Andrea's ribs. The Cold Shoulder. What was Lucia doing playing a Cold Shoulder song? After asking about her guitar?

It was all she could do not to push into the room and demand to know. Instead she closed the bathroom door behind her and sat down on the tile floor.

Luz's brown hair falling over her face like that, the blue Telecaster in her lap, the specter of Ryan inhabiting her small body.

Andrea tried not to ascribe too many of Lucia's talents and habits to anything other than the kid's own particular nature. After all, look how differently she had turned out from each of her parents. And to constantly seek evidence of herself in Lucia, though irresistible, seemed narcissistic. But whether by inheritance or coincidence, traces of Ryan sometimes surfaced. Maybe Andrea had only imagined that Lucia's early pots-and-pans banging was weirdly rhythmic. But there was also the time they were at the river with a few other parents and kids, and Andrea watched as Lucia picked up all their discarded towels and T-shirts and tried to fold them neatly. Lucia wasn't interested in hanging on to things either—not only did she easily let go of outgrown T-shirts and toys, sometimes she outright brought them to Andrea and said she didn't want them anymore. She liked everything to be put away in her room. She loved Sydney and had a few other friends, and other kids liked her, but Lucia wasn't interested in having large birthday parties or joining sleepovers. She just wanted to be with Andrea, Beatriz, and a couple of her rock camp buddies. Unlike Andrea, who loved being around people but hated standing in front of them, Lucia was an introvert yet an effortless performer.

And there was the model horse incident, at age seven. Andrea told Lucia that after she tucked her in for the night, Flynn and his girlfriend were coming to hang out at the house so she and Lawrence could see Quasi play at the Doug Fir. Lucia said she wanted to go to the Quasi show too. This was obviously out of the question—it was a twenty-one-plus show, and the headliner played at eleven. But Lucia's soft little face hardened right up. It wasn't a babyish tantrum—throwing a spoon, overturning a bowl, stomping, howling, going limp. There was no performance in it. No, Lucia went quiet, and then she went to her room. A minute later, there was a thud and two cracks.

Andrea found her on the floor, trying to gather the pieces of her favorite model horse, Bandit, a pinto yearling. Broken legs, a snapped tail.

She knelt beside Lucia. "Honey, what did you do?"

"I was mad." Luz looked down at the hooves in her hand and began to cry. "I was so mad, Mom. I'm sorry. I ruined Bandit."

It was better to hurt things than to hurt people or

animals, Andrea told her. But better yet, if you were mad, you should let it out with your words. Or your music. "Breaking something might feel good in the moment," she said, "but as often as not, you end up with something you can never fix."

She and Lucia put the yearling back together with superglue and clothespins, but it never stood steady again. Thin scars of glue ringed every mend.

It was a warning flare: coincidence or inheritance? How much *could* she raise Lucia, and how much of Lucia's becoming was not only cultural but cellular? Andrea had done everything she could to keep Lucia steady and safe, even as she parented against the wind. To be a single parent and a lesbian parent, with a Spanish last name no less, she felt she had to work three times as hard to be credible in the straight world. Among their chosen family and friends, they were deeply at home; after hours and on weekends, they had a luxurious, abundant, supportive community. But then there was school and work and the doctor and the dentist and the Internet. There she was not a parent but a *mom*, a species held in somber, near-spiritual regard while being for all practical purposes steadily crushed by the forces of public policy, like the American bison.

At least family court always favors the mother, Andrea reminded herself now. She pressed her hand to her chest. *But what if I've been a bad one? What if I've fucked up? What if she turns into Ryan and takes off one day, never to return?*

The music stopped.

Lucia's voice came through the door. "Mom? Are you crying?"

Andrea pulled herself up from the floor and wiped her eyes on the hand towel. "Oh, no, Luz, I'm just having allergies." She sniffed loudly for good measure. "Finish your song and then let's go to bed."

"Already?"

Andrea opened the door and there stood Lucia in her flannel polar bear pajamas and pink socks. Andrea fought the urge to scoop her into her arms like a little kid, which suddenly she wasn't anymore. "How about this, cub. You can leave the light on and read as long as you want."

Lucia looked surprised. "Is this because I'm almost ten?"

Andrea said, "Yes. Yes, it's because you're almost ten."

Practice

On Wednesdays, Lucia and Sydney went to the Girls Rock Institute, which was basically rock camp but after school. Rock camp and GRI were housed in a former machine shop between a trailer park and an industrial intersection; inside the warehouse, the warren of rooms were painted blue and purple and green or paneled in cheap fake wood, the industrial carpet was wrinkled and dirty, and the walls were covered with posters and printouts of women musicians. In the blue room, a wall of gear held shelves of pedals, picks, cables, and mics. The practice rooms were tiny former offices tricked out with seasonal fans or space heaters on the floor, amps, and drum kits. There were power strips everywhere.

Rock camp was the anti-school. In school, Lucia did

all her work and tried to keep a low profile as she ate lunch with her handful of friends. There were some unpleasant girls in the fifth grade this year who already fancied themselves mature and who'd taken their new seniority and precocious puberty as endowed power. Sydney had lucked out in the school lottery and attended Buckman, the arty elementary school in Southeast. But at rock camp, you were just whoever you were, or better. You didn't have to be cool to be cool. The counselors and band coaches and interns liked you. Campers argued sometimes but no one got to be the queen of anything.

The Tiny Spiny Hedgehogs set up in their preferred practice room, a closet-sized space at the end of the hall. It was cramped, but it had a hefty amp Lucia liked, plus a window that overlooked the warehouse's narrow parking strip and the thick wall of blackberry bushes looming behind it. The bushes were off-limits now because a camper had found used syringes there during the outdoor silk-screening workshop.

While Sydney set up her keyboard and their band coach, Shannon, turned on the amps, Lucia played "Stethoscope" on her unplugged guitar.

"Is that new?" Sydney said. "I like it. It's fast."

"It's not mine. It's by some band called the Cold Shoulder."

"I remember that band," said Shannon, digging a patch cord out from the back cavern of an amp. "God, I haven't heard that name in forever."

"Did you know them?" Lucia asked.

Shannon sat back on her haunches. "Not really. They were a guy band that played around town for a while. There were a lot of those. That must have been the mid-, late nineties."

"Were they good?"

Shannon shrugged. "I don't even remember. They were one of those bands where for a minute it seemed they were going to break out and be really big. Then they broke up. I don't know that song you were playing but it sounded good, coming from you." She held up the purple cable. "You guys need to put these away on the gear wall when you're done, by the way. Don't just stuff it in the amp."

"Sorry," Lucia said. "Do you know Jesse Stratton?"

Shannon laughed. "Nope. Just stories." She stood and brushed off her knees.

"What stories?"

Sydney gave Lucia a skeptical look. "Why are you obsessed with this old band? Can we practice now?"

"A girl I knew went on a date with him once, and he was playing his own album on the tape deck when he picked her up."

Sydney stamped her foot. "Let's go, Luz."

One hour, two minor arguments, and half a new song later, the Tiny Spiny Hedgehogs packed up their gear. Sydney's mom was always late to pick them up, and they secretly liked it. They'd sprawl on the donated couches by the entryway, reading battered copies of *Bitch* and *Bust* and *Rolling Stone* and eavesdropping on the teenage interns, their idols.

Today while they waited, Lucia told Sydney about the record with the picture of her guitar on it. Yes, she was totally sure it was her guitar. No, she hadn't asked her mom about it. "I started to at dinner but she got all awkward and changed the subject. It makes me think there's something going on."

Sydney started to fidget with excitement. "We have to find out ourselves. Let's research." Sydney seized any excuse to get on a computer.

They begged Ariel to let them use the iMac in the recording studio, claiming they had to look up the lyrics to a song they wanted to cover. Ariel was eighteen, with a lip piercing, dark shaggy hair, and a denim vest stenciled with the name of her band on the back. Though she was a monster on the drums, she was gentle as a bunny and always danced with the kids during lunchtime shows at camp. They loved her.

"As long as you promise not to touch anything but

the computer," Ariel warned as she unlocked the door. "Or it's my ass in trouble."

They promised.

The studio had carpet and fake-wood paneling, microphones with round mesh screens hovering in front of them, PAs and mixing boards and hundreds of levers and knobs that they didn't know how to use yet—you had to be fourteen. Lucia inhaled deeply. The air was thick and smelled like gear and something quiet but alive.

They squeezed into a broad rolling office chair together and wheeled up to the desk. Sydney commandeered the computer and swiftly verified that the Cold Shoulder *Lost EP* cover did indeed depict Luz's guitar. "Holy buckets of rats."

"I told you!"

They turned up a handful of photos of the Cold Shoulder, three guys posed in various configurations. But they could find no evidence anywhere of Jesse Stratton playing the blue Telecaster.

"Maybe 1999 was before the Internet," Lucia said.

"People still took *pictures*."

Lucia wrenched the keyboard away from Sydney and typed *jesse stratton*.

They learned that after the Cold Shoulder, Stratton had released one record under his own name, then moved to Brooklyn and continued to make music as a solo project called Deep Dark Woods. He seemed to mostly play a Rickenbacker or an acoustic. His website turned up a 404 error page.

"This is weird." Sydney drummed her fingers on the desktop. "Wait, did you read the inside thingie of the record? Who took the picture?"

Lucia realized she had only glanced at the insert long enough to see that it didn't have any lyrics printed on it.

Back home, she took the record from behind her bed and pulled out the insert. The single square sheet had a collage of black-and-white photos of the band playing. A brief list of thank-yous. And at the very bottom, photo credits—first for the live shots and head shots, and then there it was: *Cover photo and design by Andrea Morales.*

Questions

Andrea was on her hands and knees under the kitchen sink, unscrewing the U-pipe section of the drain. Lucia appeared behind her; she could see the kid's denim knees and Converse, one turquoise and one purple. "Mom, I have a question."

"Fire away."

"Do you know what really happened to my guitar?"

"What do you mean, love?" She emerged into the light and sat up. "Is it missing? Did something happen to it?"

"I mean a long time ago, before it was mine."

Andrea set down the wrench. "Tell me what you're talking about."

"I saw a picture of it with the neck all broken. Like really broken."

Fucked. That was the word. Andrea pressed her lips together. If Lucia had been going through her box of old Polaroids, Andrea would have to explain some drunken hijinks and far too many cigarettes. And that time in college when she and Vivian had wrapped themselves, nude, in clear plastic cling wrap. And— who knows what else. "Where'd you see that?"

"On the cover of a record. It said you took the picture."

"Oh. The record." Andrea frowned. Surely that EP was long out of print. "Where did you see *that?*"

"I think it was at Sydney's house," Lucia said vaguely. "I just wanted to know if that was my guitar. I'm pretty sure it is."

"Yeah. Someone had smashed it up, so I took a picture of it before I got it repaired, and the band liked the picture. They thought it would make a good image for their last record, since they were breaking up."

"So it was your guitar, and someone broke it?"

"No, it wasn't mine then. It was given to me as sort of . . . a gift."

"I thought you got it from The 12th Fret."

"I got it *fixed* at The 12th Fret." Andrea wiped her brow. Lucia should be the one to role-play the immigration officer from now on.

"Did Jesse Stratton give it to you?"

"Jesse?" She laughed at the thought of Jesse Stratton giving her anything but a practiced suave grin. "No."

"Then who?"

Forward, Andy, she thought. How to say as little as possible as truthfully as possible? "It belonged to a guy named Ryan. He played drums in that band. That was his guitar."

"Did you buy it from him?"

"He gave it to me. Well—you could say I gave it to *him,* too. I mean, originally, it was his. He broke it. I took it to the shop and got it fixed. Like it is now. All better. And all yours." Andrea picked up the wrench again, ready to return to the fixable problem under the sink.

"Wait, if you gave it to him, why do I have it?"

She stopped. "He left it here, Luz. When he left Portland. For good."

"He didn't want the guitar?"

"Well . . . no, I guess he didn't. Or he didn't want it enough to come back for it."

"Why didn't someone mail it to him?"

"Luz," Andrea said sharply, "I have to finish clearing out this pipe, and it smells like wet death down here."

"Sorry. I was just curious." That forlorn voice.

Andrea hated herself when she snapped at Lucia. "I

know." She exhaled heavily and pulled off her rubber gloves, one finger at a time. "Honey, would you mind getting me a glass of water? My hands are all gross from these gloves."

Lucia filled a pint glass with water and handed it over. She sat down on the floor in front of Andrea and looked at her expectantly.

"Actually," Andrea said, "I did offer to send it to him. And he said no, and that I should just keep it."

Lucia waited for more, then said, "That's it?"

"That's it. And now it's yours."

"But that's crazy. It's a really good guitar. Beatriz even said so the first time she saw it."

"It's an awesome guitar."

"Why wouldn't he want it back?"

"I never knew him well enough to understand how his mind worked, babe. Just count yourself lucky. That guitar was meant for you."

Andrea could feel the flush rise in her cheeks, and she took two more fast drinks from the water glass. Lucia was studying her face. "You know what? I need plumber's tape. When Beatriz comes in from the garage, tell her I had to run to Lowe's, would you?"

"Can I come?"

"No, you should stay put. I'll be right back."

————————

This was the story Andrea and her friends had hashed out together, the one they agreed was the smartest, honest yet vague, life-affirming: Lucia's bio-dad was a friend who had helped out Andrea. He gave her a seed so that Lucia could join her in the world, and he left Portland before Lucia was born. He didn't really want to be a father, Andrea explained. But he was a good friend in the end, because he gave Andrea the best gift she ever received.

The first time Lucia asked about him was at age three, when they unwittingly went to Oaks Park on Father's Day. "Do I have a father?" Andrea froze but Meena stepped in like a champ and said all families were different: some had fathers and some had mothers and some had both.

As Lucia grew older, more questions arose:

What was his name? (John, Andrea said. Which was legally Ryan's first name.)

Do I look like him? (Not really. You sort of have his eyes, and your hair color is halfway between his and mine.)

Do you have a picture? (I don't. We didn't take as many pictures in those days. It was expensive to develop.)

What was his job? (He cut hair, mostly.)

Why did he leave? (He was the restless kind. He never stayed anywhere long. One day he just took off. But I wasn't surprised.)

Did he not want me? (It was not like that. He didn't want to be a dad, not to anyone, but he did want me to have you, and you to have a good life. He knew that I would love you double.)

Can I meet him? (Honestly I don't know what became of him, baby. If he ever gets in touch with me again, I'll let you know.)

Andrea pulled into the lot at Lowe's, turned off the car, and called Beatriz's cell phone.

"You went to get plumbing tape? I have some in the basement, dummy."

"Is Lucia in the same room as you? Can you go somewhere she's not?"

Andrea waited while the falling rain thickened on the windshield, blurring the world. "Okay, I'm in the bedroom," Beatriz said. "What's up? Are you okay?"

Andrea's breath was tight and shallow in her chest, each inhalation a gasp. "I think she's going to figure it out. She's going to figure out who her—who the man who is her father is. I don't know what to tell her, Beatriz, I don't know what to tell her. I'm not ready." The air in the car thickened, humid as breath; it seemed as beige and dingy as the upholstery. She rolled the window down an inch and tried to drink the cool gray air outside. She pressed her hand against her pounding heart, as if she could hold it quiet. Such a cliché, the heart, until fear or love struck and it got literal, became the muscle of the feeling.

Beatriz told her the first thing to do was leave the parking lot. "We'll figure it out, Andy. Go stand in the lumber aisle and smell the wood. Then get back in the car and come home." *Come home.* It was all Andrea had ever wanted to hear.

Andrea wouldn't discuss it until Lucia's light had been safely out for a full hour. Then she closed the bedroom door behind them and explained in a hushed voice. The song Lucia was playing. The odd questions about the guitar. Somehow she'd seen the album cover. "She's onto something. Fucking Internet! I don't know how to stop it."

"She's smart, Andy. If you don't tell her who he is, she's gonna figure it out anyway. Better she hears it from you than from one of your friends. Or the fucking Internet."

"I don't know if she's ready."

"I think she's more ready than you. What are you afraid will happen?"

"Worst-case scenario? That he'll want her." It had always been there, usually latent, sometimes not, the fear that Ryan would somehow find Lucia and stake his claim. Andrea knew it was irrational, that he was hardly the kidnapping type (but who ever took up with someone they thought was a kidnapping type?), and there were abandonment clauses that probably stripped him of his legal rights, but still. She had forbidden everyone she knew from posting pictures of Lucia on Facebook or MySpace or wherever people were now posting their antic evidence and self-portraits, where they gazed coyly into a webcam, looking at themselves looking at themselves in arm's-length images that somehow managed to be both vain and insecure.

Beatriz set her hands on Andrea's shoulders and held her steady. "He's the one who left and never came back."

"But do you know why he didn't come back?" Andrea sat heavily on the edge of the bed. "I told him not to. I told him I didn't need him. It's my fault."

"What do you mean you told him?"

"He'd been gone a week. I finally tracked him down with caller ID. He was in some random town in Minnesota. I told him not to bother coming back. And he didn't. What if Luz learns that? What if she hates me? I can't have her hate me. Not already. Not until she's a teenager, at least." Andrea dropped her gaze as Beatriz studied her face. What did she see now?

Beatriz said, "If he had really wanted to be in her life, he would have found a way." Andrea looked up. "You were still here, right? Did you change your name? Did you go into hiding?"

"No. Never."

Beatriz shrugged and released Andrea's shoulders. "See? Not your fault."

"Okay. True." Andrea wiped her eyes. Beatriz went to the dresser and dropped her work pants. Then Andrea had a terrible thought. "But what about this? What if Lucia finds him, and he doesn't want anything to do with her?" Andrea pulled off her shirt, balled it up, and threw it hard at the hamper. "All this time I've been able to protect her from the fact that he ditched us. I didn't want her to feel abandoned. I wanted her to feel fully wanted. He can't just fuck that all up."

"Who is this guy?" Beatriz said. "Is he that big an asshole?"

"No, he's not an asshole. He wasn't. I mean, I liked the guy. I *slept* with him, multiple times, which is saying a lot."

"Did you love him?" There was a smile on Beatriz's face, a loaded one. Part skepticism, part suspicion.

"No."

The smile fell. "That sounded more like a question than an answer."

"We said *I love you* at some point, but the feeling was not—for me, it was not that kind of love." Andrea tried to summon it, to replay the feeling so she could clarify. But all that emerged was a faint nauseous tingle of wrongness. "I honestly can't even recall what I felt for him," she said. "It was ten years ago."

Ten years ago! Her brain had barely finished forming at that point. And time had seemed endless. She and her friends had joked back then about their quarter-life crisis—which was no crisis at all, and they tacitly knew it, they said the words *quarter-life crisis* with a capricious false dismay, fully aware they were only halfway to midlife, and twenty-five years on this earth had already seemed forever, eternal, the abundance of time to come unfathomable. Then, they could still remember the details of elementary school, high school intrigue, and every college course they had taken, each house they had lived in and the rent they had paid there. They still remembered every weekend escapade, every teenage prank, the name and face of every person they had kissed. They had not known how much there was to forget, what could be forgotten that you wanted to hold on to, and what you desperately wanted to shed but could never let go.

Beatriz carefully removed the tiny black hoops she wore in her ears and dropped them on the dresser top. "Do you think that will ever happen with me?"

"What do you mean?"

"You say you love me now, but in ten years maybe you'll say you don't even remember what you felt for me." Beatriz pulled her sports bra up and over her head and Andrea's breath caught. She still felt unbelievably lucky every time she caught sight of Beatriz in her tight boy-short underwear, a glimpse of her breasts before she turned her smooth tan back toward the dresser.

"Oh my god, you? In ten years, I won't remember what it felt like *not* to love you."

"Yeah?"

"In ten years, Lucia will be nineteen. Nineteen! She'll be away at school, or on tour or something, and it'll just be you and me here."

"We'll miss her." Beatriz came to bed in her boxers and tank top. "But not all her drinking and running around."

"We'll stay up late and play our music as loud as we want," Andrea said.

Beatriz lay down and pulled Andrea to straddle her body. She gripped Andrea's hips. "We'll fuck on all the furniture."

Andrea tipped her head down and whispered, "I won't have to be so quiet when I come."

Beatriz slid her thumb inside the edge of Andrea's underwear. "You still need practice on that."

Andrea's eyes went hazy. "I do."

"You won't forget this? Not even in ten years?" Beatriz said.

"Not if you keep teaching me."

"Good girl."

Search

Sydney's mom made these things she called cookies: cold damp lumps of oats and raisins, flavored with cinnamon and the barest amount of brown rice syrup, tenuously held together by bananas. Having grown up with them, Sydney was immune and ate them as automatically as kibble. Lucia took one every time, and was disappointed every time. But she loved Sydney's mom, Mariel, who was tall and fat with long silver-streaked hair and a sparkling nose stud, and who seldom kept track of how much Sydney used the computer. Lucia was only allowed thirty minutes, and it had to be in the living room where Andrea could see.

They took their plate of cookies to the family room in the basement, where the kid computer was. Sydney lived in a big foursquare house with two floors plus a basement, and a cedar-fenced yard full of garden beds and rain barrels. There were three bathrooms. Lucia tried to use all three on each visit, at first for the novelty, and then because it became a *thing*.

As they settled in at the iMac, Sydney said, "It's kind of cool that the *drummer* is your *dad*."

That was weird to hear.

When her mother and Beatriz had told her the evening before, they never called him her *dad*. Beatriz slipped and said *father* once, and her mom amended it to *bio-father*.

The three of them were seated around the dining table, assembling their own tacos while the new Os Mutantes album played in the background. Lucia loaded her tortillas with black beans, white cheddar shredded so fine and airy it was like poodle fur, and a stripe of pineapple salsa—tacos so fat she could barely fold them. Beatriz kept getting up and going to the kitchen to get another crucial ingredient they'd forgotten. Her mom had only one spindly taco on her plate, and she was eating three beans at a time with her fork.

"Luz," she said. "I know you've had a lot of questions lately about your guitar. Sorry I've been a little flustered about them."

"Yeah," Lucia said through a mouthful. "You've been kind of weird."

"I know. I've been a real freak." Her mom didn't even tell her not to talk with her mouth full. "It's just, well. It sounds like something you've been researching a little? Maybe online? I won't be mad, it's okay."

Lucia said yes, but she'd only been on the Internet with permission. She hadn't been sneaking.

"I believe you, baby, it's okay. It's that—so it seems you're getting to an age when you're curious about things, and you're old enough to find information on your own."

Her mother was speaking to her very seriously now. She was talking to Lucia the way she talked to Beatriz about the immigration application, focused and intent. "So we want to make sure you have all the information you want about—your own history. If you want to know? Maybe you know all you need to know."

Lucia suddenly knew what her mom was talking about. "Like who's my . . ."

"Your biological father," Andrea said.

"It's John," Lucia said. Her mother's friend who moved away and disappeared. Of whom she had no pictures. Lucia had had the occasional bout of curiosity over the years but there wasn't much to tell of him.

Her mom shot Beatriz a worried glance. Beatriz set a hand on her wrist and gave it a gentle squeeze. Her mom said, "John is his legal first name. But he actually went by his middle name." She took a deep breath. "Which is Ryan."

Lucia set down her taco. "Ryan."

The guitar. Her guitar belonged to Ryan.

"Ryan Coates?" she said.

Her mother nodded.

Until now her father had been an idea, a biological reality as invisible as an atom. Suddenly, he had a face. Lucia's head went all tingly. "May I be excused for a minute?"

Bullet followed her into her room. Lucia shut the door behind them and patted the bed to invite her up, but the dog eyed the leap and instead settled with a heavy thump onto the rug. Lucia went to her guitar. Its weight was solid and familiar in her hands. She sat down on her narrow bed and held the guitar. She thought of his hands on it. Maybe his fingerprints still clung to it somewhere. Or maybe she'd smudged them all away with her own.

She tilted the guitar forward, bent her head, rested her cheek on its smooth back. She pressed her ear to the wood and listened. As if the guitar could tell her something. As if it could contain an ocean, like a shell. All she heard, of course, was solid silence. If you wanted a guitar to speak, you had to pluck the strings yourself.

———

Lucia had told Sydney only the basic facts. The feelings were under wraps—she needed more time with them. And Sydney calling him her *dad* sounded wrong. Lucia had a mom, and a Beatriz. It was strange enough that he now had a face. That she played his *guitar.* That *he* was the one who had broken it in the first place. She hadn't told Sydney that part either.

"He's not exactly my *dad*," she said. "He's my male biological contributor."

"He's your paternal unit."

"He gave my mom one tiny microscopic sperm, and she built the rest of me completely by herself."

"Whoa, dude."

"That part's the same for you too." Lucia dropped her remaining so-called cookie on Sydney's plate and wrested the keyboard away from her friend. "I get to type this time."

ryan coates cold shoulder

A brief Wikipedia entry about the band: 1996–1999, Portland, Oregon. Jesse Stratton and Mateo Gold linked to pages all their own but the name Ryan Coates appeared in ordinary black type, unclickable. The Cold Shoulder had an earlier record whose back cover photo was harder to parse than the *Lost EP* photo—he was grainy and blurry, with his hair falling into his eyes while he played.

They tried an image search and the page came up tiled with a handful of pictures, many repeated multiple times. Live shots, a few publicity shots of the band, a handful of magazine articles. Lucia clicked on a photo of the three men standing on the Broadway Bridge beneath a cloudy sky. Ryan wore a knit beanie that pushed his hair down in waves around his ears, a dark jacket, hands jammed in his jeans pockets. He was looking at the camera here, an easy smile on his face, lips closed but relaxed, a dimple curved in his left cheek.

"Save that one," Lucia said.

Jesse was usually in the center of the photos, and the live shots seldom showed much of Ryan—a face in the background lit red or blue, or a blur of motion. But they found three more worth keeping. One of the three band members chest-deep in a California swimming pool, clothed, dripping wet and looking up at the photographer; one that showed Ryan in profile, laughing, while a grinning Mateo rubbed his eyes and Jesse, front and center as usual, raised a can of beer to the camera; one posed in a posh hotel hallway, all three with silk ties slung loosely around their necks over their regular

T-shirts and jeans, with the text, cut off from the other page of the spread:

THE COLD SHOULDER HEAT UP:
The Northwest's Next Great Post-grunge, and Touring with

There were two videos on YouTube, songs from the first album Lucia didn't know, and they watched them each twice. There was no MySpace or Facebook or Bandcamp or anything that existed in this century.

Sydney printed out the photos for Lucia, inkjet-spotty and streaked, and asked if they could now watch YouTube videos of a dance called jerking.

Lucia said sure and excused herself to the bathroom.

Whenever people told one of her friends that he or she looked just like whatever parent, Lucia seldom saw it. Like, Sydney was sometimes told she looked like her dad. They were both skinny with slightly weak chins, but Sydney's dad was over six feet tall and had shaggy salt-and-pepper hair and a stubbly face. And he was a man. People used to call Lucia Andrea's "mini-me," which was a little creepy, but when Lucia looked into her mother's face she saw her mother, not herself. The face Lucia saw in the mirror was entirely different. Yet adults were always looking for these traces—like how they couldn't listen to new bands without identifying all the parts that sounded like the bands *their* age. Syd looked like Syd. Luz looked like Luz.

Now she studied her face in the bathroom mirror and tried to isolate any feature that wasn't at all like her mom's. Her medium-brown hair. Her hazel eyes, brown at the center and blue-green at the rims, not as round as Andrea's but slightly longer and narrower. She pressed her mouth into a closed smile like Ryan's in the bridge photo, and the dimple appeared in her right cheek. But her kid face showed none of the angles of his adult man face—his cheekbones, his strong straight nose. She had her mother's small, soft nose and full cheeks.

Back in the family room, she said, "Do you think I look like him?"

Sydney had already pushed the chairs aside and was bouncing on the balls of her feet, warming up to dance. The iMac screen was cued to a video of teenagers in tight jeans and bright sneakers.

"Maybe in the eyes?" Sydney said. "Otherwise, I can't tell."

"We both have a dimple, but mine's in the other cheek."

Sydney bent her knees deep and wiggled her skinny rear. "I think you look like a tiny spiny balled-up hedgehog who needs to dance."

Lucia slid the printed photos into her school note-book and zipped her backpack shut before she joined Sydney on the carpet. Sydney hit the space bar, and the music blared from the tinny computer speakers. In a minute they were both breathless and laughing. "Is this right?" Lucia said, twisting her feet around in a spiral, and Sydney said, "I don't know, but it looks good to me," as she dipped into a deep knee bend and fell to the floor.

Later, Lucia sat on her bedroom rug and examined the pixelated printouts. She looked longest at the band photo on the Broadway Bridge, the one where his gaze was most direct. She held it up to face her at eye level. She said, "Hi."

Videotape

That weekend, no one felt like cooking family dinner, so they all biked over to the new gentrified pizza place in Woodlawn where Lawrence's girlfriend, Carson, worked. She'd offered up her employee discount, which was a good thing: "Twenty-three dollars for a pizza?" Andrea said, scanning the menu. "North of Alberta, no less." Her stomach turned.

"What recession?" Lawrence said darkly.

Even with the economy's recent yearlong plummet, none of them could afford to live anymore in the neighborhoods where they'd come of age. Even Failing Street had shot up far beyond their means. All over town, new earth-toned paint sleeked over old wooden siding—conspicuously and deceptively neutral. Bright cedar privacy fences sprang up where chain-link and open space had left the view clear. Unruly front yards and tangled rosebushes were shamed out by tidy mulched beds, every plant mapped and spaced. Black neighborhoods were becoming white neighborhoods and white neighborhoods were becoming rich neighborhoods. They couldn't even afford to live in Meena's Belmont duplex, which she was able to rent out for three times the late-1990s mortgage she was paying, partially funding her new life in L.A. Hatchbacks and hoopties gave way to strollers and Outbacks. One corner of the Pearl warehouse where they'd mounted their queer art show now housed a coffee shop with a $10,000 espresso machine, and the rest contained a store that sold hand-tanned leather couches that cost five figures and decor gathered—no, "curated"—from around the globe: draped hides, $40 candles in somber boxes, carvings by uncredited artists. Even the bands had changed. Less earsplitting, seditious noise and gleeful defiance; more midtempo beats, soaring harmonies, introspection, and uplift. Songs you could play in restaurants and television commercials. Bands that changed other people's lives.

And yet. It was still home. Most of them had moved farther north, into North Portland and north-er Northeast, and there it still felt familiar: cheap burritos, karaoke seven nights a week at Chopsticks III How Can Be Lounge, video rental stores with the business-sustaining porn corner behind a curtain in the back, strip clubs, dive bars that were not yet Dive Bars™, disheveled houses and cars from the 1970s and 1980s. Restaurants with daily-changing menus cropped up here and there, and baby boutiques now populated Mississippi Avenue, but everything had slowed way down. And though work was hard to come by again, and houses were foreclosing around them, at least there was a sense that the tide of wealth that threatened to drown them all had receded. The bubble had burst. But they were never in the bubble.

While they waited at a reclaimed-wood table for what had better be the best pizza of their lives, Andrea gave Lucia a pocketful of quarters and sent her to play the vintage pinball machine in the corner. As soon as the kid was fully absorbed, her shoulders twitching like she was being electrocuted, Andrea laid out what had happened for her friends.

"She hasn't brought it up again," Andrea said. "I don't know what to do. Should I try to talk to her about it?"

"She's probably just absorbing it," Lawrence said.

Robin rested her elbows on the table and, winding a long lock of black hair around her hand, asked, "How does it make you feel?"

Andrea cracked open a beer. "Like, I dealt ten years ago with Ryan's leaving and thought I was done with it. But no, it's back. Even in his absence, here he is all over again."

Topher's boyfriend, Mike, shook his head. "Always under the straight man's thumb."

"And I don't want to tell her that he just bailed like that."

"Oh, you can't," Robin said.

"I won't."

Lawrence turned to Beatriz. "How does it make *you* feel?"

Beatriz said, "I just want Lucia to be okay. That's the most important thing." She took a deep swig of her beer. "I mean, I don't know the guy. But he seems like an asshole."

"He wasn't *terrible*," Lawrence said. Andrea kicked her under the table. "I mean for a straight man." Another kick. "I mean except for that he evaporated at dawn like a vampire and left you to deal with everything by yourself. Yeah, that was terrible. But at least you got to—" A final kick. "Ow. Yes. Bad."

"I keep wanting to explain myself without explaining why I did what I did. But I think I'll only dig a deeper hole if I try to do that."

"Give her space," Beatriz said. "That's all we can do." Andrea suspected Beatriz needed the same. She'd

chin back into her neck. Sydney dissolved. It always worked.

"You little monkey." Beatriz dove a hand toward Lucia's ribs and both kids shrieked and leaped back. "Okay, okay, let's go home."

In her room, Lucia flipped over her shoe and recited the phone number over and over. She made it into a little song to commit it to memory. Then she grabbed a black Magic Marker from the kitchen drawer and crossed the number out. An inky black rectangle that her steps on the pavement would rub right off.

Lucia lay down on her bed. She stretched out her arms and legs, and wrapped her hands and hooked her feet around the edges. This was her bed. This was her body reaching to all corners of her bed. This was her life. This was where she was born and where she lived, Portland, with her mom and her dog and her aunts and uncles and her friends and her bandmate; this was the whole world she knew. This was her planet. But here was this new moon in orbit, exerting strange gravity. Lucia held on tightly to the covers. She loved her life. She didn't want to leave it. But what was on the moon? How could she not wonder?

The Voice

Fuck, it was cold for October. Twenty degrees colder than usual, all month, the coldest fall he'd ever known here. Leaves already weeks gone, and frost on the windshield this morning. Ryan turned down the dirt driveway—the cold made for a harder, tighter crunch beneath the tires—and pulled over to the turnout. Kelly's pickup rolled in after him and pulled into the garage. He always let her have the garage, a gesture she pretended to refuse only the first time.

The day had been a good one. Even with a cancellation at the barbershop, three walk-ins had shown up and his chair stayed full: Bemidji State students back from fall break; his favorite old guy, Stan the ex-logger; and just before closing, Everett, one of his first friends in Bemidji. You never knew who would stick—people

Ryan had once thought he'd know forever were long gone, and the scrappy teens from the carnival concession stand who'd offered Edith Head a hot dog were now friends he'd known for a quarter of his life. Since they'd met, Everett had grown from a bashful boy who requested spikes and streaks to a drily funny, heavy-set twenty-six-year-old who kept his thick black hair tidy and lived his punk aspirations through his work. He'd found his purpose working at the juvenile residential treatment center, trying to be a role model for fellow Native kids and a gentle man to all the youth, who mostly knew masculinity as a brittle and brutal condition. And he was formidable at air hockey. Ryan had trimmed him up clean, swept the shop, and then he and Everett walked to Brigid's Pub for burgers and a game of air hockey before Everett headed to his evening shift. Donita was bartending and gave them a cup of quarters from the till to load up the jukebox with something decent: "Gonna die if I hear Nickelback one more time." Then Kelly had shown up, and they had a couple of drinks, and she was the one who suggested coming to his place. "Don't you teach a nine o'clock on Thursdays?" he'd asked, and she'd said she was giving a test tomorrow: "No prep! I can just roll in there and administer."

Now inside the door, they shared a tipsy kiss—she

always kissed better when she'd had a drink, more relaxed and insistent at the same time—and then she set about getting the planned bourbon and ice cream.

Edith Head wound around Ryan's legs, croaking, while he scooped a pungent lump of wet food into her dish. She couldn't swing kibble anymore. Kelly found the bourbon in its cabinet over the sink. "Your time machine is blinking," she said.

"Ha ha," he said. The telephone base was flashing *1, 1, 1.* Kelly had almost given up on persuading him to get a cell phone. ("I don't want to be found all the time," he said. "What if I want to find you?" she asked. "You will," he said. "I always come home eventually.")

Ryan cradled the phone to his ear and clicked the voice mail button as he opened the freezer. The light had been out for weeks, he made a mental note to fix it—

The voice was a child's. A young girl's. Polite. Formal. A faint tremor in it.

The cold air of the freezer ran up his arm and into his chest.

Lucia. That was the name Andrea liked.

Kelly grabbed his shoulder. "Dude. Are you having a seizure or something?"

The voice mail ended and he stood in front of the open freezer, staring into the dim foodscape.

"No, sorry." He shut the door and turned to her. He clicked off the phone.

"The ice cream?"

"Oh yeah." He opened it again and took out the pint.

Kelly gave him that look—Sociology Eyes, he called it, when she peered at him as if he were one of her study subjects. "What's up?"

Ryan tried to push the voice mail into a mental drawer, shut it and go on with this night. But it wouldn't leave. That small clear voice. *I think you might be my— never mind.* "Just a kind of odd message."

"Odd how?"

"I couldn't quite understand it."

Kelly offered to listen and reached for the phone, but Ryan demurred, said he'd listen again later. He dropped the phone on the counter and swept an arm around her waist. "You're all I want to listen to right now, Professor. Where's that bourbon?"

This is Lucia.

That night Ryan lay awake while Kelly slept soundly beside him, nude except for her wool socks. Edith snored in her bed on top of the dresser.

He had a life now—a life in which Lucia did not exist. His mother didn't even know about her. No one knew about her.

In the first year or two he'd written her several letters he'd never sent. What would be the point? To mythologize himself? Set up some kind of unfulfillable longing? Creep out Andrea? The last thing the kid needed was to think she had a father out there somewhere who'd ditched her. Whatever story Andrea had told her would be one she could live with. For once he'd done the thing that would be better for someone else, or so he'd told himself at the time. He'd let it go.

The way he had trained himself to think about the kid was as if he had given it up for adoption, to Andrea. Women weren't expected to talk about the pregnancies they'd terminated or babies they'd given up, so why should he? From the stories Everett told from the juvenile center, well, it was clear that no dad at all was better than a bad one.

Would he have been a bad one? He'd have cheated on Andrea, most likely. He usually did cheat on women back then. And he'd never had much interest in preverbal humans. Though he did like how psychedelic and freaky they were in that little-kid stage, he wanted nothing to do with meltdowns and high volumes and excretory fixations and mollifying snacks. Teenagers were all right. If anything interesting in them survived the sausage factory of public schooling and consumer culture, that's when it revealed itself. For some reason he had pictured the kid finding him at eighteen. A near-grown girl. He pictured her with black hair pulled back messily, or maybe cut short and bold. Inexplicably, his imagination sometimes put fingerless gloves on her.

This version of her was tough and cool. Impervious to doubt and hurt. Didn't need or miss or want something as conventional as a heterosexual white biological father. She would just be . . . curious. She'd pull out a cigarette and offer him one. He'd say no thanks, and then remember to scold her. Except at eighteen, it would be her right to smoke, and not his to parent her; she'd be her own adult person then. They could see eye to eye.

But ten years old? Too soon for him. He needed at least eight more years to be ready for this.

He padded out to the cold kitchen and listened again to the message.

I'm looking for Ryan Coates.

Fuck.

Underground

A gray Saturday morning. Her mom and Beatriz had gone to get groceries at Fred Meyer, leaving Lucia on the couch with a blanket and her book. Lucia waited until the house was entirely hers for ten minutes—no emergency returns.

On the second try, the call went through. Lucia stood at the sound of his *Hello?* on the other end. A man's voice. Medium deep.

"Hi, it's me. Lucia. I left a message?"

"Yeah, I heard it."

"Is this . . . Are you . . ."

"Have you talked to your mom about this?"

"A little."

"Does she know you're calling me?"

Lucia headed toward the basement door. Even though no one else was home, it seemed safer to go underground. "Yes?"

"Be honest."

"Not really." She descended the wooden steps. The basement smelled dark and cool. The dehumidifier hummed busily in the corner. Bullet stopped in the doorway at the top—the stairs were hard on her joints now—and lay down at the threshold, watching Lucia.

"Okay, we probably shouldn't be talking until I've had a conversation with her."

Lucia pulled the chain on the ceiling light. "I have your guitar."

"You do?"

"Yeah. The one that was on the record cover."

A little laugh of disbelief. "Do you play it?"

"Uh-huh. I'm in a band."

"No way. You're in a band."

"With my friend Sydney. We met at rock camp. We're called the Tiny Spiny Hedgehogs."

"Wow. Do you, like, play shows?"

Lucia sat on a storage trunk next to the clothes dryer and toyed with the latch. "We played at the rock camp showcase, at our friend's birthday, and at a pizza place," she said. It didn't seem right to mention Beatriz and

Uncle Topher's wedding—her mom had stressed that she had to be very careful about that until the green card was issued. "We have, like, eight songs now."

"That's impressive. Maybe you should make a record."

"Really?"

"Sure." He seemed to think better of it. "Actually—you don't want to become a novelty band. You don't want too much too soon or you'll never want to play music again. Those kids with stage moms—speaking of which, I really shouldn't—"

Lucia said quickly, "Are you in a band? I saw a video of you playing on TV."

"Not anymore."

"Why not?"

"I don't know. My band broke up, the one I cared about. And then I didn't want to be in a band I didn't care about. It's easier when you're young, you'll play with anyone just to try it out."

"I like playing with Sydney, but we have some creative differences."

"Oh really?" He laughed. Lucia flushed with pleasure. Usually Sydney was the funny one.

"That's what my mom calls it. But at least we have fun. My first year at rock camp I was in a band with four other girls and we fought every day. One of them hit another one over the head with the mic."

He did it again, laughed. "Ouch."

"Some people should *not* be allowed to have microphones."

"You could say that about half the people I played with."

At the top of the stairs, Bullet scrambled to her feet, ears up. Lucia heard the back door creak open, and the dog whined and started to wag. "I gotta go," Lucia said. "They're home. Bye."

She hung up.

"Luz?"

"I'm in the basement," she hollered back. She stuffed her phone into her hoodie pocket and took the stairs two at a time. It came to her as she rounded the corner: "I was looking for my horse T-shirt." She knew the T-shirt was in Beatriz's drawer—Beatriz loved that shirt and had borrowed it from her. It was the first time she felt a lie come so easily. If you thought ahead for a few seconds, and grafted it to a truth, you could slide right through.

Beatriz unwrapped her scarf and said, "Desculpa. I have that one."

"Thief!" her mother said to Beatriz.

"It's okay," Lucia said with an angelic smile. "I like when Beatriz wears it." Her mother's eyes went soft and she kissed Lucia's head. Lucia felt guilty and pleased at once.

Her pulse beat hard and she felt heat around the edges of her vision. She had a secret—a huge one. And she'd made Ryan Coates laugh. His number was now a song in her head.

The Bill Comes In

Andrea never looked at the cell phone bill, but this month, she'd gone over her daytime minutes and Verizon had charged a ridiculous fee. The table held stacks of bills. For almost all her adult life, she had barely squeaked by at best; she'd had to declare personal bankruptcy when Luz was eighteen months just to clear the credit card debts. Then she landed the teaching job—which was at a private school, so the pay was low, but for the first time she had a salary and benefits. Half the kids blew off art class, treated it like a joke, plaster penises and crappy drawings of cartoon characters, but they were easily outweighed by those who realized art class was a refuge: the ones who had real talent and the misfits who took their lunches to her classroom to eat. Every cent of her money had gone toward absolute necessities and Lucia's day care, but she had learned how to survive.

Now, with Beatriz's part-time income and share of the rent and utilities, the weight had lessened—they squeaked by more easily—but Andrea still tracked every dollar, and forty cents a minute for going over was a stab in the gut. How could they have been so careless? Had Beatriz called Brazil? Or was it Beatriz's work? They would have to increase the minutes on their family plan.

She pored over Beatriz's call log. There were a few ten- and fifteen-minute day calls that added up. Nothing international. She glanced at the log of Lucia's— usually it was only a few numbers, hers and Beatriz's and Sydney's.

But what was this? A 411 charge, and two calls to a 218 number.

Where the hell was 218?

Lucia crossed her arms in front of her chest. "I didn't know 411 calls cost money."

"Luz, you should have asked me first. *Us* first."

"Would you have let me?"

"Probably not!"

"See?"

"What did he say to you?"

Lucia's voice got small. "He said . . . Sydney and I should make a record. Then he changed his mind and said we had to be careful not to be a novelty."

Beatriz nodded, but Andrea said, "*Career* advice? That's rich. Did he say anything about me?"

Lucia shook her head.

"What are you looking for, Luz?" Andrea dropped to her knees in front of her daughter. "What do you want to know? I'll tell you whatever you want to know."

Lucia said, "I want to meet him."

Andrea sat back on her heels. "What?"

"For my birthday. It's the only thing I want. The *only* thing."

Andrea couldn't speak.

Beatriz stepped in. "You've thought about this, Luz? Or are you just saying this now?"

"I've thought about it a lot. All week. I wouldn't ask for it if I didn't mean it."

Andrea found her voice. "We're not enough?"

Beatriz touched her shoulder. "I don't think it's about that, Andy."

"I mean, what do you think he's going to give you? He *left*. He left before you were even—"

Beatriz gripped her shoulder harder. "Babe! Stop." Andrea covered her mouth. She'd almost said the unforgivable, the thing she never wanted Lucia to know. Bad mother.

Lucia's eyes filled with tears. "I don't know why! I just want to. I just want to see him in real life."

Beatriz let go of Andy and wrapped her arms around Lucia. "We'll talk about it, Luz, okay? It's a lot to think about. Give us a little time. Okay?"

Lucia began to cry openly. "He was really nice."

"Oh Jesus," Andrea said.

Beatriz shot her a look that was part compassion, part warning. "We'll figure something out."

Still on her knees, Andrea fought the urge to beg Lucia to—to what, feel differently? To not want what she already wanted? To not wonder what she of course wondered? For the first time in years Andrea was angry at him, she realized, furious that what he'd given— what he'd *left behind*—he could also take away. He couldn't take custody, not that, but something nearly as frightening: he could seize Lucia's imagination, her heart. She could come to believe in him. He could leave her now too.

Don't be your mother, she thought. *Don't push her away.* She breathed deeply, in, out. "It's your life and your decision to make," she said. "Beatriz is right. We'll work it out for you."

On the Road

For two weeks Andrea begged the sky for a snow-storm, prayed for impassable Rockies, hoped the car might break down irreparably on the way home from school, or the immigration office would schedule an interview for the day before Thanksgiving. She checked the weather in Spokane, Missoula, Bozeman, Dickinson, and Bismarck every day, eager for a meteorological disaster that would foreclose on the imminent possibility of their own. But no. The weather moved on, the roads remained open. Andrea took the Monday and Tuesday of Thanksgiving week off from school. Since flights to Bemidji, Minnesota, inexplicably cost more than flights to Paris, they would make a road trip.

Beatriz and Lucia planned the route on Google. They sat on the living room couch with the laptop while

Andrea wrote lesson plans for the substitute teacher. Neither Beatriz nor Lucia had ever been to the mountains or the Midwest. They wanted to visit a concrete dinosaur park, they wanted to go skiing, they wanted to see bighorn sheep and mountain goats.

"How can you be so excited about this trip?" Andrea asked Beatriz.

"What's my other option? Dread and fear?"

"That's where I am."

"I know. And Luz is gonna pick up on that and then how's she going to feel? If you make it weird, it'll be weird. Do I want to go meet the guy whose sperms hatched in your egg or whatever?" Beatriz flapped her hand like a cat swatting at a bug. "Not really. Does Lucia? Yes. Do I want to take a crazy long road trip with the girl I love and the other girl I love and see a lot of weird shit and different lands? Yes."

Early on a Saturday morning they packed the Corolla wagon. As she shut the trunk, Andrea felt like they were leaving for good, like they would never return to this: this little shingled bungalow, this life, this perfect three of her, Beatriz, Lucia.

How briefly she had gotten to have everything she wanted and loved. Her mopery about the wedding now seemed so petty. She would have married herself off to anyone necessary to keep this unbearably sweet life intact. Playing gin rummy around the coffee table. The mornings when Andrea would get up to make coffee and return to the bedroom to find Lucia in her place, chatting with bedheaded Beatriz. Camping out in the Mount Hood National Forest—okay, they'd only done it once, but they were planning to go again next summer and this time they'd rig a bear hang for their food like they were supposed to. Making pancakes. Beatriz teaching Lucia a Nirvana song in the living room, Lucia concentrating on the plaintive guitar riff as Beatriz sang the verses, until the chorus, where they both laid into the chords, and Lucia howled, "*In the sun, in the sun I feel as one*," in her fearless clear voice, and all three of them hollered, "*Maaa-rried!*"—and then Andrea would thump out the drum fill on the table or counter—"*Buuuu-ried!*" Yeah, yeah, yeah, yeah.

Thunk. Click. Their duffels and backpacks and a booklet of CDs and a Harry Potter audiobook from the library. That's what they had now. And a road atlas in which Andrea had traced their route in highlighter so Lucia could follow along, a sheer blue line like a vein, pumping them from home to wherever the fuck they were headed.

Andrea took a moment to swallow and breathe and compose her face before heading to the driver's seat.

If Lucia detected dread or fear or resistance, she'd go underground. *In that way*, Andrea thought, *she's just like me.*

They spent the first night in Wallace, Idaho, an old silver-mining town. ("What's a brothel?" Lucia asked. "Well, now it's a coffee shop," Andrea answered. "I'll tell you in the car.") At the Stardust Motel, Lucia hopped into the spaceship parked by the sign, posed for pictures, and then they went to their room and ordered bad cheese pizza that still tasted good. Lucia sprawled on a double bed all her own, gorging herself on pizza and cable television. Andrea muted the commercials. Family vacation. If only.

As they rose higher into the Rockies, snow appeared and thickened. Cellular service went out for long stretches. The temperature dropped. Beatriz blasted the heat and muttered, "*Caralho!*"

"I know what that means," Lucia warned triumphantly.

"Is it too cold?" Andrea asked. "Should we turn back?" Beatriz shot her a look. "Kidding," she muttered.

A river ran alongside the highway for a long while, dark water coursing beneath marshmallowy snow-capped rocks and banks.

Was this the way he'd driven? Andrea wondered. What the fuck was he thinking?

Those had been strange days. When she woke up alone that morning, she had known in her gut. That note—Ryan never left notes like that. "Love you"? No way. He was a person who came and went and sent a postcard later. Always already gone. She'd sat with the note for a minute. She reflexively made a full French-press pot of coffee, and drank her half while the rest grew cold and bitter and overextracted. She poured the remains over the porch railing and watched the grounds hit the dirt, looking like dirt. Then she went about her day: fed the animals, walked the dog, went to work. Kept resting a hand on her abdomen so she could feel the baby's movements inside and out. At Artifacts, Ted noticed this and asked if the critter was kicking yet, and she said no because she did not want to be touched. She called the house once, no one answered, she left a message. Before she went home, she stopped for groceries to give him extra time to get back, just in case; when she arrived, the house was as she'd left it, the note still on the table, Bullet frantic with relief. The answering machine was blinking. She sat and listened to the messages—one her own voice, checking for him; three from Ryan, sounding wired and impatient and apologetic at once. Eastern Washington? There was no reason for him to be out there. The baby turned inside her and she remembered last night: the kick, his hand on her abdomen, his withdrawal. "Oh, please don't be a cliché," she said aloud. She made half a box of spaghetti and ate the entire thing out of the saucepan. She changed into pajamas and watched an *X-Files* rerun with Bullet on the couch. Meena called and she let the machine answer. She got into bed early and read for five minutes before her eyes began to blur and she turned off the light.

Andrea had been half-asleep when the fourth call came. She recognized that she was now supposed to run to the phone and grab it, out of her mind with worry, or livid; the script of such a thing dictated that she scold, or beg, or jubilate. But she had no desire to scold or beg or jubilate. Fuck the script. Eyes closed, she turned her head to better hear his voice coming through the tiny speaker in the living room, scratchy and plaintive as a four-track recording. Soon Ryan stopped talking and with a click, the house went quiet again. Just the gentle hum of the refrigerator, Bullet's fluttery dream whimpers, the sound of her own breath. A peace came over her. The only thing she had to do was take care of herself and the baby. Let the rest happen. *I will just wait,* she thought. *I will wait and let him reveal himself.*

And now, to think this was where he had been. How did he pull off such a drive in that decrepit old van?

"Mom." Lucia tapped her shoulder. "Can I see your phone?"

Andrea said no, they had to save the battery. Instead, they played Twenty Questions. Lucia went first. She thought for a minute. "Okay. Ready."

"Who are you?" Beatriz said.

"You can't just ask that!" Andrea said.

Lucia giggled. "That's for me to know and you to find out."

Eastern Montana. The horses stood close together in their corrals and fields, thick-furred and plush. In Billings, oil refinery smokestacks shot flames. They dutifully visited the dinosaurs in Glendale and crossed into the Badlands, its corrugated buttes the color of blood and flesh and bone. They pulled off at a scenic overlook and got out of the car, zipping their coats to their chins against the wind. "Oh my god, look behind us," Beatriz said. An idling semitruck pulled away to reveal a bull bison standing at the edge of the parking area nibbling the brown grass. He was horned and mountainous, shaggy flanks like a landscape. Lucia asked for Beatriz's phone so she could take a picture. She moved toward the bison as if magnetically pulled, and when Andrea realized she wasn't stopping, she had to run over and grab her arm. "But he's eating. He's not scared," Lucia protested. "I just wanted to get a little closer."

The kid had no sense of danger yet. That was the problem.

A night in Belfield at the Trapper's Inn. In nearby pastures and backyards, small derricks swung back and forth like strange little toys. "What are those?" Lucia asked. "They're funny."

"They look like oil things," Beatriz said.

"In North Dakota?" Andrea scoffed. "That would be weird."

The land settled into snow-dusted fields flecked with beige stubble and a flatness that outdid even Nebraska. The occasional boulder heap in a field was the only topography. The view was one-eighth land and seven-eighths sky.

The light was different here on the plains, clear and thin where Oregon in late autumn was gray and muted. November had always made Andrea a little sad, dimmed her. But this was a particular winter light she recognized from childhood.

Forests filled in around them when they crossed into Minnesota. They finally drove into Bemidji in a cobalt-blue twilight, the land white, the trees black, the scattered houses' windows incandescent gold.

Andrea clutched the wheel tighter. Beatriz read the directions aloud. Otherwise, they were all three silent.

"Left here." A dark bait shop, a motel with vacancy, a gas station in a cold pool of light. The trees a black torn edge along the sky. The road darkened as they left the town behind.

"Right at the stop sign."

Lucia sat forward in the back, seat belt taut against her chest. In the rearview mirror Andrea saw how she looked out the window, eyes wide and scanning, as if she'd see him emerge from the woods. Was Lucia nervous? She looked a little nervous, her lips tight enough to draw in the shadow of her dimple.

"Do you want to check in at the hotel first, Luz?" Andrea asked the mirror.

Luz's eyes darted to meet hers. "No," she said decisively.

Oh. She was *excited.*

Beatriz set her hand on Andrea's neck and rubbed the nape. Andrea leaned into it. *Hold me up,* she thought, and she did. But what about Beatriz?

"Are *you* okay?" she asked.

"I'm okay," Beatriz said. "We're almost there. Left."

The road they turned onto was packed snow over

gravel, narrow, barely two cars wide, a pale stripe through woods and modest fields, marshes with frosted cattails. Andrea flicked on the brights. Living in a city, she had almost forgotten about brights.

"Here," Beatriz said. "On the left."

Click-click, click-click, the needless blinker. A black mailbox with stick-on numbers, mounted on a wooden post. The driveway, narrow and flat, curved through trees and then opened on a clearing with a little cabin. The shades were down, but a glow filtered around them. He was home.

Andrea killed the ignition. The heat died but the car was still warm. "Well," she said, not moving to unbuckle her seat belt. "Here we are."

The light came on over the front door.

The Wait

Ryan tried to look around his house as if he'd never seen it before. If this were the first time he'd crossed the doorway, what would he think about the man who lived here?

It would take them three days. He'd done it in just over one. *I'll text you as we get near,* Andrea had said on the phone.

I don't text. I don't have a cell phone, he'd said.

Of course you don't, she'd said. *And I thought I was a Luddite for not joining Facebook. Well, we leave Saturday so we'll be there Monday evening. Should I, like, call when we're close?*

Just call if something goes awry, he said. *I'll be here.*

Very nineties.

I guess that's fitting.

———

"This might have been worth mentioning sooner," Kelly said grimly. "What else are you not telling me?"

"You have a whole life that precedes me," he countered. "I don't need to know everything."

"Come on, Ryan. You know where I stand on the important stuff." Kelly was thirty-four and didn't want kids, which was a pleasant distinction between her and most of the available female stock up here. She had a doctorate from Arizona State but she'd grown up in Fargo and was tough as nails. She never wore makeup or sunscreen, so she had a few extra lines that crinkled around her eyes, and even in October the faint pale outline of her tank-top tan dipped across her collarbone and shoulders.

Ryan had thought the two of them might be onto something. But when Kelly's pickup coughed to life and growled out of the driveway this time, he knew that was the last he'd see of her for a while. Possibly ever. Possibly just a while. It was impossible to avoid someone here, the options were limited, and after a long enough cooling-off period he'd probably start to look good to her again.

It was Sunday night. They'd be here tomorrow. He vacuumed and swept again. He sat at the table and wrote Kelly a short, sweet letter to drop in the mail tomorrow or the next day. It had never failed him, the letter, especially if he put a little drawing on the envelope. By the time she received it and thought about it, they'd probably have come and gone. Who would these people be, anyway? Who was this kid? His sole input had been genetic—she'd known only Andrea, and Portland, her whole life, and that's what would determine her. What kind of kid came out of there? Portland was a place he barely thought of anymore, and spoke of even less. He'd been in Bemidji long enough that no one asked, and besides, *Where did you come from?* wasn't a question people asked much. In Portland people always asked because the answer was never "Here."

Every now and then he'd come across some rapturous piece online about the fantastical wonderland of Portland—it seemed the *New York Times* discovered it anew every three months. They cited Powell's Books, Forest Park, the obvious, but also a million restaurants and cafés he'd never heard of that were now established staples. And the neighborhoods they cited as shopping and dining meccas, arts districts—Alberta Street? North Mississippi Avenue? It was another city they described. He wondered about his old haunts, his old apartment. The Portland in his head was sticky dark bars, cafés that were really diners, damp junkies, the big old craftsman houses he and his friends could never afford to live in now, the stretch of gray months where you had to turn on the lights at noon. He'd appreciated it most upon leaving and returning—descending toward hills nearly black with evergreens, or crossing the Columbia River, or driving in at night when the neon and streetlights seeped color into the mist. It had been a great place to escape and a great place to come home to, but a hard place to *stay.* Anyone not in a band seemed to go nowhere else. Andrea practically had moss growing on her back.

Yet everything in Portland, no matter how fixed it appeared, seemed to split apart so effortlessly. A high erosion rate. The roots ran shallow. Even Andrea and her beloved queer community were as bad as or worse than anyone—they clung so fiercely to each other, and yet they'd cheat or fall out and entire friend networks would break into pieces. The band had felt like home; Andrea had briefly felt like home; he had lost, or given up, both of them.

Now he had a real one. Ryan's house had been used as a hunting cabin for several years before he moved in as a renter, and a year later he'd persuaded the absentee owner to sell it to him. It was one story, built in the 1940s, with split-log siding painted dark brown and forest-green trim. It came with dirty rust-colored carpet and bunks in the lone bedroom and a harvest-gold refrigerator with yellowing shelves. The garage floor had been piebald with auburn deer bloodstains. Friends came over to help him clean and fix it up. People here knew how to fix and build the way his Northwest friends knew their way around a guitar. A different DIY culture, a different basic knowledge.

To his surprise, living out in the woods suited him. He learned all the trees' names and developed allegiances with and animosities toward various birds. Noticed tracks and where the deer bedded down. Winter was the best—it was the longest, hardest season, but also the most clean and beautiful, and no mosquitoes. He had come to love how when snow fell it absorbed all sound, the air cottony with it; how in the morning, the trees cast blue zebra-stripes of shadows across the white; how the hard-packed snow squeaked underfoot. Ryan hadn't intended to settle down in Bemidji so long, but he had grown deeply attached to this patch of land. And his friends were loyal and smart. They got each other through rough patches. The long-term small-town weirdos were a different species from the urban kind he'd known; each lived against the grain in their own way, with little expectation of reward for their idiosyncrasies, grateful to find like-minded people of any stripe.

Bemidji was a place people were *from*. Most had grown up here or nearby; they had stayed, or they had left briefly and then returned. With twelve thousand people and a small state university, this was the biggest town in the region. It had a dogged little food co-op and an old woolen mill and a new tattoo parlor. The stores in town hung signage in Ojibwe and English. Ryan's friends ranged from their twenties to their seventies. For his fortieth birthday last December, they'd thrown a big party out at Bud's place, merging it with the winter solstice party Bud usually held. There was a bonfire six feet tall and mountains of hot food in the house. Crossing that line into forty had been a relief. His twenties and thirties solidly behind him, *done with,* forty was like an absolution. So he'd thought.

At the barbershop on Monday, Ryan was so distracted he nearly shaved a stripe into the side of a client's head. He closed early, at three, and went home. There was nothing more to clean. He had a cup of coffee. He had a shot of bourbon. He brushed his teeth. He forced himself to eat a banana. The house grew dim and he turned on the lights. He walked out to the end of the driveway and then back in to see what it looked like from the approach. If he was in there, you could see whatever dumb thing he was doing. Normally he never dropped the blinds, since no one could see his place from the road, but he went back inside and let them all down.

Finally, a car slowed on the road.

Headlights in the driveway.

A momentary urge to shut off all the lights, like his mom had done on Halloween when they had no candy to give. He wanted to head out the back door, to the open space of the yard and the dark sky and the waxing moon overhead.

But no. The motor went quiet. A few seconds later, he heard car doors thunk shut.

The most peculiar feeling. He imagined he was in a movie, playing the improbable role of a man meeting his . . . daughter for the first time. What kind of movie would that be? A war movie?

He flicked on the outside lights.

He pulled on his sneakers and coat and opened the front door.

Everyone

Lucia could hardly breathe. It was like magic, a little cabin back in the dark woods, with a gold glow seeping out from the edges of the windows and snow that gleamed a soft blue-white. This was where he *lived*.

She unbuckled her seat belt and got out of the car. The cold was sharp and bright. She inhaled deep to feel the shock of it all the way in her lungs. Her body tingled. Her mother and Beatriz emerged from the car now too; they told her to zip up her coat and put on her hat, but she shook her head, she didn't feel cold at all, and now the front door was opening.

He was tall and stood in the light. Then he pulled the door shut behind him, and now he was walking toward where they stood in the shadows of the driveway. He moved into their space and the light fell behind him. She could hardly look at him and yet could not look away.

"You made it," he said in the voice she knew from the phone. It was really him. "Hello."

"We made it," her mother said. "Here's someone for you to meet."

Lucia felt Beatriz's hand steady on her back. "I'm Lucia," she said.

"My god," he said. "You really are." He extended a hand to her and she took it. His fingers were long and rough and warm. She looked at his hand and then at his face. He looked older than the pictures on the Internet, like a real adult man now; his hair was shorter. But then he smiled. There was the dimple. "Wow," he said.

Lucia just nodded, unable to even blink, much less talk. She had summoned him from the ether and now here he was. She had touched his hand. He had spoken to her. It was impossible and yet it was true.

"And this is Beatriz," her mother said.

Beatriz kept her hand on Lucia's back and extended the other to him. She flashed a quick, professional smile as he shook it.

"I'm Ryan."

"I figured." Beatriz stamped a foot. "It's really cold here, isn't it."

"Come in," Ryan said. "I bet you could use a drink."

"I bet *you* could," her mother said. He glanced at her uncertainly, and then she laughed and he did too.

"No comment," he said.

In the doorway, Ryan knelt to scoop up a cat, orange and bony with X-ray eyes. Andrea couldn't believe it. "Is that Edith Head?"

"Still alive and well," he said. "And eager to sneak outside."

They filed in after him and stood in the warm living room. Logs burned in a small stone fireplace. A tidy little house. The minimum furniture necessary. The kitchen had pine cabinets aged to a deep honey color and the counter was dark orange Formica. But the wood floors looked refinished. A beat-up acoustic guitar leaned against the wall in the corner.

Edith, still in Ryan's arms, let out a scraped yowl. Ryan released her and she took a few stiff steps. Andrea knelt to pet her. Edith took one look at her and then, with miraculous speed, bolted under the couch.

"Oh, come on," Andrea said. "Is she mad at me? The nerve. Edith! I didn't abandon you."

"How do you know her?" Lucia managed to say.

Her mother looked up at Ryan for a moment. "She was a stray who moved into my house."

"She ended up coming with me when I left Portland," Ryan said carefully.

Lucia knelt beside Andrea and peered under the couch. Edith was a hunched mound, her back turned to them. "Why would she be mad at you?" she asked her mother.

"Because I didn't say good-bye." Andrea gazed at her knees. Then she stood with a brusque laugh. "No, I doubt she even remembers me anyway."

"Well, she doesn't run from strangers," Ryan said.

"Okay, so it's personal," Andrea said.

"Cats." Beatriz smiled tensely. "They're deep."

Ryan said, "Who's hungry?"

While she poured four glasses of water from the tap, Andrea tried to swiftly process the literal reappearance of Ryan Coates in her life. He was nervous tonight, she could tell, but at the core he seemed steadier, more grounded, than when she'd seen him last. His dimple still showed through the gold and silver scruff of his short beard. His hairline had barely receded. His neck was lean. She saw Lucia-like elements where she'd expected them, like in the color and shape of his eyes, and where she didn't, like the look he sometimes got before he answered a question, as if he were peering through an invisible window. She eyed him with a reverse heredity—to her he looked like Lucia, not the other way around. Did Lucia see it too? She wasn't saying much but Andrea could tell her entire body was an antenna right now.

And Andrea couldn't help but wonder what Beatriz, she of many strong opinions, thought of all this. If she looked at him and thought, *That guy?*, if she judged Andrea for sleeping with him, if she were the kind of jealous person who would *picture* Andrea sleeping with him; oh, the thought made Andrea squirm now—what had that even been like? Out of flummoxed curiosity she tried to recall it for a moment, but all she could remember was a patch of fur on his stomach. On the one hand, she wanted Beatriz to see Ryan as no threat at all, and on the other she hoped Beatriz wasn't repulsed to the point where she questioned Andrea's judgment. A touch of nonthreatening gentle mockery, later when they were alone, would strike the balance. It might be more than she could hope for tonight.

Andrea took a seat next to Lucia at the table, where Ryan set out snacks. Beatriz stood behind Lucia like a bodyguard, leaning on the counter. There was a jar of peanut butter, a bowl of crackers, a block of cheese, a bag of baby carrots, corn chips, and a jar of salsa. "What is this, a backstage rider?" Andrea said.

"Old habits," Ryan said. He handed Beatriz a small juice glass of bourbon, neat.

Andrea sawed off a slab of cheese for Lucia, offered

another to Beatriz, who refused, and kept it for herself. She was starving. The cracker level was scant. "You have a beard now," she remarked.

"Just like everyone in Portland." Beatriz took a swig of her bourbon.

"This isn't fashion," Ryan said. "Keeps my face warm."

"I forgot what it's like to live with real winter." Andrea shuddered pleasantly. "How do you like all the snow?"

"I love it. But shoveling it's a bitch."

"Why is it a bitch?" Lucia asked.

"*Ryan*," Andrea said.

He said, "It looks all light and easy, but it's super heavy to lift."

"Like records," Lucia said, and Ryan nodded with approval.

Andrea gave her a surprised look. "Yeah."

Beatriz asked for a refill of bourbon. Andrea said, "You should eat something."

"No appetite," Beatriz said. "I'll eat later." Ryan poured more bourbon into the glass.

"So, Beatriz, how long have you . . ." Ryan waved a cracker in the air.

"Been in this country? On and off since last summer. Don't worry, I'm legal."

"I was going to say 'known Andrea.'"

"We've been together a year and a half," Andrea said. "Beatriz is amazing. She's great with Luz."

"I am," Beatriz said.

"I'm great with *her*," Lucia said. That made Beatriz laugh. Beatriz held out her palm for a low five under the table and Lucia smacked it. Andrea watched Ryan watch them. His smile was impossible to read.

"So how's your band doing?" Ryan asked Lucia.

Lucia shrugged. "Fine."

"That guitar working out for you? Not too heavy?"

"Would you ask her that if she were a boy?" Beatriz said with a cool smile.

"I don't know," Ryan admitted. "She's just . . . small. There's a lot of hardware on that one."

"I like playing it," Lucia said, worried. "It's not too heavy."

"She's good," Beatriz said. "She can really play."

"Beatriz just taught her 'All Apologies,'" Andrea said.

Lucia rolled her eyes at Andrea. "I can play lots of things."

"Want to play something? I have a guitar out in the living room. It's acoustic, though."

Beatriz said, "She can handle an acoustic too." She took a deep gulp.

Ryan raised his hands. "I don't doubt it. It just feels different when you're used to an electric."

Lucia looked nervous. "I have to go to the restroom."

"Down the hall," Ryan said.

Beatriz said, "Make sure the seat's down."

Lucia didn't really have to go. She stood at the sink and looked in the mirror to try to see what he saw. It was weird to look at him. Lucia wished that he would lie down and go to sleep, or that she could shoot him with a tranquilizer dart like a cougar or bear, so she could stare at him, study everything. Hold her hands up to his. Look at his face. Study the shape of his ears. But he was moving and upright and tall and live, and so she kept averting her eyes instead.

She wondered if he thought the same about her. Every once in a while they would make eye contact and both almost seemed to blush. Like each wanted to stare at the other. But they couldn't. It was too much to be in the room with him, especially with Beatriz and her mother there.

In the medicine cabinet there was nothing interesting. In the drawers of the sink, an electric trimmer, a deodorant that smelled like pine candy, some stray Band-Aids and ointments.

When she came out, he and her mother were the only ones at the table. She didn't want to sit there between them. The air was too thick. "Where's Beatriz?" Lucia asked.

"She stepped outside," Andrea said.

This fucking *cold dead corner of Earth,* Beatriz thought as she fetched her secret cigarette from its deep corner of the glove compartment. Her hands shivered so much she could hardly even light it. Andrea's dread, she realized now, had been a source of comfort all this time. Beatriz had been the buffer; she got to be Lucia's good guy and Andrea's rock. But now, here, what was she? An extra. As soon as she saw that *hello* smile crack Andy's face, she'd felt an ice cube in her chest. And Lucia, staring at Ryan like that, eyes wide with wonder. In an instant, with zero work, he got to be the *real* parent. She was the latecomer, the immigrant, the speaker of English as a second language—third, for her, but no one was counting. The person she'd married to stay with Andy wasn't even Andy.

She hated him, hated him, hated him, and especially hated the little glimpses of Lucia she saw in his face. She was glad he had a beard that covered half of it up. She was glad the cat had run away from Andrea, either didn't recognize her or rejected her, a sign of how long and how deep the rupture had been, and she hoped Lucia took note. Why had Andrea been so worried all this time? No matter what happened, Lucia was indisputably *her* kid.

For the first time Beatriz felt truly homesick. Not just *I miss the food, I miss the slang, I miss the music,* but that feeling of home as a place where you currently are not. She dragged slowly on the cigarette and tried to locate the source. She wasn't homesick for São Paulo, or for Portland, or for any particular place. She was homesick for Lucia and Andrea. They were her home now. Suppose the worst happened and Lucia and Andrea pulled away from her, and reconfigured around this biological triangle. Where would Beatriz go?

Smoking as a form of deep breathing. It steadied the breath, kept the tears at bay. If Beatriz let herself cry out here, she was certain icicles would form on her face. Plan: to get through tonight without fucking it up for Lucia. That might mean: stay outside until they're ready to go. She wrapped her scarf more tightly around her neck.

Lucia pulled on her coat and mittens and picked up Ryan's buffalo plaid hat with earflaps. Her mom had one like this too. No one was looking—she couldn't resist. His hat was huge on her head; it wobbled there like a large lid on a small jar. She took it off and put on her own snug knit cap.

Beatriz stood by the garage, lit like an animation, a crisp black figure in a pool of light on the packed snow, a ghost of smoke ribboning from her mouth. She turned at the sound of the door closing and looked startled to see Lucia. "Luz." She dropped the hand holding the cigarette to her farther side.

"Hi, B." Lucia jammed her hands in her puffy pockets and walked to her. "You shouldn't smoke."

"I don't. Only when I'm really—" She looked down at Luz. "I'll put it out." The cigarette fell to the ground and she crushed it into the snowy gravel with one precise stamp of her boot.

"Promise you won't do it again?"

Beatriz thought for a moment. "No. I won't make a promise I can't keep. But I promise I won't do it much."

Lucia shivered and pressed herself against Beatriz's warm side. Beatriz wrapped an arm around her and said, "How are you doing?"

Lucia shrugged and kept her eyes on the ground. "Good."

"I bet it's kind of weird for you?"

"I don't want it to be weird."

"Oh, meu amor. Me neither." Beatriz rubbed a hand up and down Lucia's arm, then stopped and held her tight for a moment. Lucia sank into Beatriz's coat, detected her familiar warm smell under the less-familiar scent of the cold wool. It anchored her. "Hey," Beatriz said. "I want to take a little walk to the end of the driveway. Join me?"

They walked down the long curve of the drive and the trees slid a screen over the house. They were in darkness. No streetlights. But the moon was nearly full and reflected off the thin snow enough so they could see. The air was acutely clear. They breathed deep, cold, brain-cleaning breaths. The trees opened up and they came to where the driveway met the long road. They stopped, mittened hand in mittened hand.

"Hey, look up," Lucia said.

The sky was black, crazy with stars so thick they smeared in white streaks. "Holy hell," Beatriz said. "That's a lot of stars."

"Isn't it weird that they're all dead and we're just seeing their light now?"

Beatriz shot her an amused glance. "That's awfully goth."

"I read it in *National Geographic*."

"Well, you know, in Brazil, they're seeing the same stars, but they're reversed."

"What?"

"Yeah. And it's summer there right now."

"Brazil is upside down."

"Maybe *this* place is upside down," Beatriz said.

"I want to go to Brazil," Lucia said. "Can I go with you?"

"Really?"

"*Yeah,* obviously," Lucia said. "Would you ever take me with you?"

Beatriz's eyes were tender. "Of course. I would love to take you to Brazil."

Lucia couldn't help herself, she hopped up and down. "When?"

"We have to save up. It might be a while. Practice your Portuguese."

Lucia breathed a long sigh, pursing her lips so her breath poured out in a faint narrow cloud. "How about this," she said. "Estou com frio."

"Sim! Tão frio." Beatriz shuddered deeply.

"Can we go in now?"

"Yes. I'm ready. Vamos, Luz."

Ryan had thought that seeing Andrea might nudge awake all the old hard stuff, the resentment and longing and sick feeling, the love. But here she sat at his table, a familiar face—if etched a little deeper, the shape of her features more defined—and the feeling was more like a small old room lit low inside him. Storage. No need for the contents anymore, but here they were, a lantern passing over them. For the first year or two after Andrea, he'd thought, at times with resolve and at times with remorse, that he'd never fall in love again. But he'd found that there were different ways to be in love. Never again was it as hot, as consuming; gone was the scorched-earth feeling; the thrill of new discovery was now a gently tempered one. But he knew the terrain better and never again got lost in it. It was a relief that she could show up like this, walk into his house and pour herself a glass of water with one ice cube in it, and the feeling it stirred up in him was simply recognition.

"Beatriz okay? She seems a little on edge," he said.

"She does," Andrea said. "But she wanted to come. She urged us to, once Lucia asked for it. She's big on transparency."

"She good to you?"

"Crazy good. The best. I didn't expect to find anyone like her. I got lucky. How about you? Anyone in your life?"

"Yes," he said hesitantly. Why? He didn't want her to think he was all alone. Foolish. But he wasn't much of the time, so why not just round it up to yes.

Andrea sat up straighter, almost too enthusiastic. "That's great. What's her name?"

"Kelly?"

"Is it serious?"

"Fairly."

Andrea looked around the place. "Like, move-in serious?"

"Nah," he said. Whenever the time came and a girlfriend started talking about moving in together, he got skittish and it fell apart. He'd worked hard to have his own place, his own space, and he couldn't stand the possibility of *that* falling apart. He'd rather lose the relationship. Maybe with Kelly he would do it. Maybe. But probably not. "She's great, but I've found I really prefer to live alone."

"I'm not the last woman you lived with."

"Actually, you are," he said. Andrea's hand hit the table. "Am I the last guy?"

"Uh, *yeah*. To my mother's dismay." (That conversation had nearly shut down their shaky truce for good. Mom: *If you did it once, would it kill you to try it again? I don't understand you. I don't understand you people.* Andrea: *I just don't feel it.* Mom: *Don't tell me it was only* him. Andrea: *It was only him, Mom. And barely him.* Mom: *That child needs a father.* Andrea had hung up the phone and did not pick up another Mom call for six months.)

"I never did meet her."

"Lucky. She might have tracked you down and been

here on your doorstep years ago." Andrea laughed grimly. "She came out after Luz was born and started plotting to sneak her out for a guerrilla baptism. My sister busted her."

"So your child is a godless heathen?"

"Happily, yes."

"What's she like?"

"She's fantastic. She's a little weirdo. I have no idea where she's headed, but I think it's in a good direction."

"How so?"

"She's quite practical and levelheaded most of the time, and then she'll get together with her friend Sydney—"

"The Tiny Spiny Hedgehogs friend?"

"How do you know that?"

"She told me on the phone."

"Oh. Yes, that one. And they set each other off. They get incredibly silly. For a while it's funny, and then it's like trying to wrangle drunk monkeys." She sighed. "But I'd rather that than whatever comes with puberty. She's starting to get secretive. I want her to have a rich inner life, I don't want to pry. But Ryan, I'm so worried she's going to start to hide things from me and hate me."

"Why would she do that?"

"Because I'm her mom. And that's what *I* did."

"But you're not *your* mom."

"I hope not." Andrea picked up her bourbon glass and poured the last watered-down drops into her mouth. "I had no idea what I was doing. God, we knew nothing back then." Oh, those years. She didn't resent Ryan, hadn't thought, *You should be here,* but she did think, many times, *This would be a lot easier if I could hand her over to another parent.* Then, in those sweet exhausted moments when the baby slept in her arms and there was nowhere to go, nowhere else she could be, she murmured, *Look at what he missed.* She kissed Lucia's tiny perfect ear, relished the warm weight of her on her chest. *Stupid motherfucker.* The love was enormous, painfully large, larger than her own body. Ryan could have been in on that. But he'd bolted. He'd missed it all.

"Oh, Ryan. Did I do the wrong thing?" She folded her arms on the table.

"What? Coming here?"

"No." She shook her head. "Telling you not to come back."

He sighed. "Why are you worrying about this? No point in thinking like that now. Here we are."

"But did I fuck you up? Would you have wanted . . .

I thought I was giving you permission to leave. That you wanted permission."

Ryan prickled. Here was an old familiar feeling from the Andrea days. "I never needed permission from you. For anything."

"Of course," she said apologetically. "I guess what I'm saying is, do you wish you'd stayed?"

Look at her tormenting herself all over again. Andrea would forever tie herself in knots, and probably had been for the past ten years. How completely herself she still was. He said, "I don't think it would have worked between us."

"No, it definitely wouldn't have. I mean for Lucia."

"Oh. It would have been a mess."

"I suppose we spared her that."

"I have plenty to answer for myself, Andy."

"No." Andrea reached out a hand and touched his arm, a quick, urgent press. "I didn't want you to. I wanted her to be all mine. And I got what I wanted, for better or worse. Better, I hope, for her sake."

"Look at that girl. You did really well."

"I did, didn't I." She sat back and let out a long shuddering breath. "Sometimes I can't believe I did. Especially when it was just me."

"Hard, huh."

"Oh my god. So fucking hard."

"I'm sorry."

"When you look at her, do you think, *That's my kid?*"

"Honestly, I don't know what to think. It's a lot, Andy. It's a lot to take in."

"I know."

"What I think is . . . I think we have the same color eyes."

"She has long hands too, like you."

"And I think, I'm not into kids, but this one, I can tell she's good."

Lucia and Beatriz shut the door quietly behind them. Beatriz tucked Lucia's mittens into her hat and set them on the chair by the door. Her mom wiped her eyes quickly, but she was also smiling.

"Hey, kid," Andrea said. "Hey, love."

Beatriz took a seat at the table, sat back in her chair, and crossed her ankle over her knee. "I don't know if I've ever seen stars like that," she said. "And it's so quiet."

"You see why I never want to live in a city again."

"It's cold enough to kill me," Beatriz said. "But it is beautiful."

Ryan lifted the bottle. "Want to finish this?"

"No, I'm good," she said reluctantly.

"Go ahead," Andrea said. "I'm driving."

Beatriz slid her glass forward. "Just, like, a centimeter then."

Lucia didn't want to sit at the table and talk. All adults did was sit and talk. It made her legs twitchy. "Can I put on a record?" she asked.

"Sure," Ryan said. "Do you—" He caught himself. "You probably know how to do that."

"Yes," Lucia said decisively. Beatriz shot her a triumphant smile.

The records stood in a small vintage cabinet, maybe fifty of them. Lucia knelt and flipped through. Most were old and weathered, thrift-store records. Classic country, old soul, the Kinks, a Norwegian punk compilation, several eighties bands she'd never heard of. Then she landed on a Cold Shoulder record—not the ten-inch EP she had at home, but a full-sized twelve-inch called simply *The Cold Shoulder*, from 1997. Eleven songs.

Lucia figured out the stereo, which had silver levers and knobs instead of buttons, and gently set the needle down on the record. She loved the sound of those first few rotations, the hush and faint crackle. Then the song started. The guitars were coarser than they were on the EP, the singer's voice rawer, but the drums were still taut and precise.

"Is this what I think it is?" her mother asked.

"Your band?" Beatriz pointed a baby carrot at Ryan.

"So long ago." Ryan looked a little embarrassed. "I honestly haven't heard this in years. It's just in the stash. I don't know if I can listen to it again."

"I can't even remember the last time I heard this," Andrea said. "It's one of those records that just became part of that era."

"I've never heard it. It sounds pretty good," Beatriz said.

"I can ask her to change it," Andrea said, looking to Beatriz and Ryan.

"No, don't," said Beatriz. "It's her choice. We have to let her play it."

Lucia leaned back on her heels to address them. "I wouldn't have changed it anyway," she said.

"Okay, then next time I get to hear your band," Ryan said.

"The Tiny Spiny Hedgehogs?" Lucia said.

"Yes. Fair's fair."

"Oh, if you want to be extra fair, it would be Taco Night," Beatriz said. "That's her first band."

"Taco Night sucked," Lucia said, which got the

laugh she was hoping for out of Beatriz. "You have to hear Tiny Spiny Hedgehogs."

"Got it," Ryan said.

"They are really really good," Beatriz said.

"We've recorded two songs with GarageBand. But Mom won't let us have a MySpace."

"Good. I think the Internet is creepy, and I'm an adult man."

Andrea said, "You can send him a tape through the mail."

"Why don't I just send it by owl?" Lucia said.

"Close enough."

The adults started talking about obsolete technology, a boring subject they always found entertaining. Lucia moved closer to the speakers and got down on her hands and knees.

The cat was still under the couch, back legs sprawled, eyes dilated to nearly black. Tufts of dust and fur floated around her.

"Hey, cat," she said. What name had her mom called it? She couldn't remember.

The cat remained impassive. Lucia reached a hand under the couch and the cat raised the corners of her lips in a silent *eh* and scooted farther away.

Lucia lay down on her back. The rug was soft and plush underneath her. At home the few throw rugs lay directly on the scratched-up wood floor, but this one had a cushiony padding underneath it. She imagined a forest floor of thick moss would feel like this. The first song ended and a new one started; she could feel the kick drum, a soft steady thud, along her back.

"Come here," she said gently. She reached toward the cat and let her hand lie limp on the floor. After a moment, the tips of whiskers brushed her palm. She lifted her hand slightly and the cat pressed her head into it. Lucia stroked her cheeks and ears and the cat stretched out her neck, eyes closed, rolling her face around.

"Good cat. Come on." Lucia withdrew her hand and patted her chest.

The cat emerged from under the couch. Her bony hips sagged, and her orange fur looked damp and sort of clumpy, even though it was dry to the touch. Her pupils contracted, her eyes the light green of new leaves.

Lucia patted her chest again. Edith climbed up and stiffly settled in.

Her body weighed almost nothing. Lucia ran her hand over the cat's small insistent skull, along the corrugated line of her neck and back, down to the points of her hips, where her tail rose in a satisfied question mark and subsided again. Her fur was thin and soft. Her paws opened and closed and she began to purr.

The purr rattled her whole body, a living thing itself, a vibration like life.

There was laughter in the kitchen. Lucia closed her eyes and soaked in the warmth of this old animal, this elder who had lived longer than she had, who knew her parents before she herself came into the world, who was near the end of her own long life. Her father's cat. Or was it her mother's cat? Or, Lucia decided, she was no one's cat at all. She was her own. Her own self, her own life. Her own secrets and favorites and sorrows and preferences. Her own millions of memories that none of them would ever know.

"I wish I had known you," Lucia murmured. "I could have had a cat."

The cat settled in deeper and flexed her toes. The thin, sharp claws pierced through Lucia's sweatshirt and T-shirt and into the skin of her breastbone—a delicate, bearable pain.

Acknowledgments

Thank you to my creative, curious, and infinitely supportive parents, Deane and Jill Johnson, who inundated me with love and books, and my brothers, Nate and Daniel.

Thank you to PJ Mark, my brilliant fierce agent.

Thank you to Jessica Williams, my visionary editor, whose talent, insight, and intelligence proved transformative.

Thank you to all of the superb Custom House crew, especially Geoff Shandler, Liate Stehlik, Laura Cherkas, Aja Pollock, Kelly Welch Rudolph, Katherine Turro, Eliza Rosenberry, and Mary Ann Petyak. Thank you to Michael Taeckens for your expert navigation. Thank you to R. Kikuo Johnson, Mumtaz Mustafa, and William Ruoto for your art and design.

Thank you to readers and advisers Brian Perez, Sean Martinez, Carrie Brownstein, Amanda Paulk, Donal Mosher, Torrence Stratton, Frances de Ponte Peebles, and Andrea Ferreira Schumacher. Extra effusive thanks to Nicole J. Georges, Peyton Marshall, Amy Thielen, and Kara Thompson for essential early reads.

Thank you to all my Portland and ex-Portland friends and families and rock camp comrades. This book is a homesick love letter to you.

Thank you to all the queer writers and fighters and artists.

Thank you to all my students over the years, for all you have taught me.

Thank you to the Iowa Writers' Workshop for getting me going, and to the Wallace Stegner Fellowship for lighting the spark that became this book. Thank you to all my teachers, especially Tove Dahl, Bruce Burkman, Helen Bonner, David Walker, Ellen Douglas, Frank Conroy, Marilynne Robinson, James Alan McPherson, John L'Heureux, Elizabeth Tallent, and Tobias Wolff, and my fellow Fellows and workshop-mates.

Thank you to the MacDowell Colony, the Virginia Center for Creative Arts, and Signal Fire Arts for transformative writing residencies. Thank you to the *Willamette Week* for access to the archives. Thank you to Oberlin College and the College of William & Mary for crucial support.

Thank you to Emmett and Sylvan for long clarifying walks and lying at my feet while I write, and to Seven for being Edith.

Thank you forever to Kara, for giving me new ways of knowing.

Chelsey Johnson received an MFA from the Iowa Writers' Workshop and a Wallace Stegner Fellowship from Stanford University. Her stories and essays have appeared in *Ploughshares, One Story, Ninth Letter, The Rumpus,* and NPR's *Selected Shorts,* among others. She has received fellowships to the MacDowell Colony, the Virginia Center for the Creative Arts, and Signal Fire Arts. Born and raised in northern Minnesota, she currently lives in Richmond, Virginia, and is an assistant professor at the College of William & Mary. This is her first novel.

HARPER LUXE

THE NEW LUXURY IN READING

We hope you enjoyed reading
our new, comfortable print size and found it
an experience you would like to repeat.

Well — you're in luck!

HarperLuxe offers the finest in fiction and
nonfiction books in this same larger print size and
paperback format. Light and easy to read, HarperLuxe
paperbacks are for book lovers who want to see
what they are reading without the strain.

For a full listing of titles and
new releases to come, please visit our website:

www.HarperLuxe.com

NE
APR   2018